Ulives

SUN COAST CHRONICLES 3&4

Presumption
of Guilt

Books by Terri Blackstock

Soul Restoration
Emerald Windows

Restoration Series
1 | *Last Light*
2 | *Night Light*

Cape Refuge Series
1 | *Cape Refuge*
2 | *Southern Storm*
3 | *River's Edge*
4 | *Breaker's Reef*

Newpointe 911
1 | *Private Justice*
2 | *Shadow of Doubt*
3 | *Word of Honor*
4 | *Trial by Fire*
5 | *Line of Duty*

Sun Coast Chronicles
1 | *Evidence of Mercy*
2 | *Justifiable Means*
3 | *Ulterior Motives*
4 | *Presumption of Guilt*

Second Chances
1 | *Never Again Good-bye*
2 | *When Dreams Cross*
3 | *Blind Trust*
4 | *Broken Wings*

With Beverly LaHaye
1 | *Seasons Under Heaven*
2 | *Showers in Season*
3 | *Times and Seasons*
4 | *Season of Blessing*

Novellas
Seaside

TERRI BLACKSTOCK

#1 bestselling suspense author

Ulterior Motives

SUN COAST CHRONICLES 3&4

Presumption of Guilt

ZONDERVAN®

ZONDERVAN.com/
AUTHORTRACKER
follow your favorite authors

ZONDERVAN®

Ulterior Motives
Copyright © 1996 by Terri Blackstock

Presumption of Guilt
Copyright © 1997 by Terri Blackstock

Requests for information should be addressed to:
Zondervan, *Grand Rapids, Michigan* 49530

ISBN-10: 0-310-60955-0
ISBN-13: 978-0-310-60955-1

Published in association with the literary agency of Alive Communications, Inc., 7680 Goddard Street, Suite 200, Colorado Springs, CO 80920.

Interior design by Sue Vandenberg Koppenol

Printed in the United States of America

07 08 09 10 11 12 • 18 17 16 15 14 13 12 11 10 9 8 7 6 5 4 3 2 1

Ulterior Motives

*This book and all those to follow it
are lovingly dedicated to
The Nazarene*

ACKNOWLEDGMENTS

I could not have written this book if I had not known what it is to be a mother or a stepmother. So I'd like to thank my children for the invaluable material they've given me.

My thanks to Michelle, my firstborn, who is so much like me that it makes her angry sometimes. But unlike me, Michelle has extraordinary gifts. She can sing like an angel, and write like a poet, and think like a philosopher. She feels things deeply, has compassion and encouragement for those who hurt, and is never afraid to share the good news with those who are lost. I can't wait to see what God does with her!

My thanks to Marie, my baby who's not a baby anymore, who has probably been used of God more than anyone else to teach me about gentleness and patience. Her sensitive side sometimes requires more care than the average child, but I suspect that that is one of God's special gifts that he intends to use in his time. She has other gifts, as well. She is an organizer and planner, and rarely forgets anything, and her fertile imagination is as well-developed as her sense of humor. She is a friend to many, even at her young age. I know God has special plans for her, too.

My thanks to Lindsey, my stepson, who is both peacemaker and jester. He has the special gift of bringing harmony wherever he goes, making people laugh, putting them at ease. He sees people through special eyes, not as others see them, but as God sees them. I see God working in him already, preparing him for something big!

None of these children has had the privilege of sailing through life without jostles or bruises. No child of divorce has that privilege. But I firmly believe that God will use each jostle, each bruise, for good in these children. He's making them into precious instruments already.

Thanks, guys, for giving me all of the emotions I needed to write this book!

CHAPTER ONE

He had never killed before, but it hadn't been as difficult as he'd imagined. It was a simple thing, really. The element of surprise, along with the right weapon and the adrenaline pumping through him in amazing jolts, had made it all happen rather quickly. There had been no noise, no hopeless pleading for mercy. He hadn't even had to look in his friend's eyes as he'd pulled the trigger.

With one foot on either side of the body, he bent down and probed his victim's pockets with his gloved hands. Loose change spilled out onto the floor, along with a set of keys. He took the keys and stepped away from the body, leaving it where it had dropped.

Hurrying up the stairs of the elegant art gallery—the walls accented with paintings from known and unknown artists—he reached the office. The door was locked, and he fumbled for the right key and opened it. The pungent scent of paint dominated the small studio, along with the smell of mineral oil. Canvases lay propped against the wall in varying stages of progress; in the back corner sat several framed paintings waiting to be exhibited downstairs and possibly sold. Some old, cracked, and damaged paintings by well-known artists sat in stretchers awaiting restoration so that they could be sold at European auctions for thousands of dollars.

But none of these things were what interested him.

On the other side of the studio was another door, and he unlocked it and went in. It was the office from which Dubose, who now lay dead on the floor of the gallery, had conducted his business with important clients, and as always, it was immaculate and tasteful, with antique Chippendale chairs in the corners and a Louis XIV desk at the center of the room, a throne-like leather chair behind it. On the polished desk sat a small banker's lamp, a desk diary, a Rolodex, and a calculator. Behind it, on the lavish credenza, was an eight-volume set of the *Dictionary of Painters and Sculptors*, widely known in art circles as the definitive resource on lost and stolen art across the world.

He pulled the chain on the lamp, lighting a circle beneath it, then opened the desk diary and turned to this week. There it was, written beneath tomorrow's date—the name and number of the man Dubose had kept so secret. The man Dubose was to have met with tomorrow. He tore off the page, folded it neatly, and slid it into his coat pocket. Tomorrow he would contact the man and take over the deal himself. He needed only one thing more, and he knew exactly where to find it.

He unlocked the small doorway at the rear of Dubose's office that led up to the attic. He turned on the yellow lights that lit the top floor of the building. Slowly, carefully, he made his way up the stairs.

The attic smelled of dust, and the floor creaked beneath his feet as he stepped between boxes, over stacked antique frames, past discarded sculptures and paintings. What he wanted was in a corner of the attic—in a long wooden box built into the top corner, in which Dubose had stored what they'd worked together to hide for so many years. He opened the panel and reached inside.

It was gone.

Shock and fear made his heart race, his skin turn cold. He pulled a box over to step up and look inside. The compartment was empty.

Rage exploded like lava inside him, and he whirled around, scanning the contents of the attic. Where could it be?

He sank to the dusty planks beneath him and slid his gloved hands through his hair. Someone had taken it. But who? Had Dubose realized that he was going to be double-crossed by his partner? Surely not; he'd played it too carefully. Dubose hadn't known what was coming.

He felt himself growing dizzy with fury as he rose. He steadied himself on the rail as he made his way back down the stairs, through the office and studio and back down to the gallery. The body still lay facedown in a pool of blood. He had acted too quickly, he thought. He should have made sure he had what he wanted before he pulled the trigger. Now it was too late for Dubose to tell him where it was.

He would have to figure it out for himself.

Already, he had a good idea, and he would find it no matter what it required. It was his, and he had earned it. No one else was going to reap the profits of his labor.

He didn't care who else had to die.

CHAPTER TWO

Christy Robinson stretched as tall as her six-year-old body would allow and reached for the bottom branch of her favorite backyard tree. She could touch it with the tips of her fingers, but that wasn't good enough to pull her up.

"Use the ladder," her mother called from the screened porch of their home. "That's why I had it built."

Christy backed up from the tree and eyed the ladder that went up the tree's trunk to the tree house nestled in the branches. "No, ladders are for wimps," she called back to her mother. "Watch this, Mommy! Are you watching?"

Sharon came outside onto the patio and leaned back against the apricot stucco of her huge Florida home. She was dressed in a blue business suit and high heels, and her short auburn hair rustled in the wind that was a little too cool even for February in St. Clair, Florida.

Satisfied that she had her mother's full attention, the little girl got a running start and leaped high to grab onto the branch.

She swung for a moment, then flipped until her feet came up between her arms. She wrapped her legs over the branch and hung upside-down, looking at her mother as her face slowly turned crimson and her foot-long cotton-colored hair flopped beneath her. "See? Told you I could reach."

"If you hurt yourself I'll kill you!" Sharon said, moving closer as if to catch her as the child righted herself and began climbing farther up. "I knew Jake was putting the tree house too high."

"No, Mommy," Christy said as she made her careful way higher. "It's perfect. Just right. Mr. Jake said I had to get used to heights if I'm gonna jump out of airplanes when I grow up."

"Over my dead body!" Sharon returned. "I need to have a little talk with Jake about putting these ideas into your head."

"They're my ideas!" Christy said. "I put them into *his* head."

Sharon tried not to be nervous as her daughter—who looked tiny so high up—reached the tree house and took the last step to the top of the ladder that went into the entrance hole at the center of the tree house's floor. Christy had insisted on the hatch in the floor, rather than a front door, and Jake had built it exactly to her specifications.

"The kid knows what she wants," he'd told Sharon. "Might as well do it her way, if she's the one who's going to use it."

When she was satisfied that Christy was safely inside, Sharon called up, "I have to go in and finish some paperwork, honey! Don't climb down until I get back here. I'll leave the window open so I can hear you."

Christy stuck her face in the square doorway. "Okay, Mommy. I'll call you when I get through making my guitar."

A guitar? Sharon thought with a smile. There was no telling what the child was making it out of. She had spent the past week collecting tissue boxes, drink cans, milk cartons, paper towel rolls, rubber bands, and heaven knew what else. All of them had been carried up in a backpack and stored like little treasures inside the tree house.

Still smiling, Sharon went back inside the huge house and looked through the front windows for any sign of her sixteen-year-old, Jenny. Sharon had told her to come straight home from school to baby-sit Christy so that Sharon could make it to the closing of the house on Lewis Street. She was only a few minutes late, but it worried Sharon nonetheless.

She went into her study and made some necessary revisions on her paperwork, frequently glancing out her open window to keep an eye on Christy. Then she loaded the papers into her brief case, took it into the den, and set it in a chair next to a small Queen Anne table covered with framed pictures in a variety of sizes and shapes. The pictures told part of the story of their family. Sharon and her two daughters graced the table in elegant antique frames, their faces representing different ages and eras of their lives. The girls' father was conspicuously absent in the pictures on this table. But upstairs, in the children's private domain, one could find the whole story. Sharon and the two girls—Jenny and Christy—and their father and his new wife, Anne, and the two young children that new family had produced, half-sisters to Jenny and Christy.

It was a tangled web, this modern family with all its branches and extensions, and she would have moved heaven and earth to stop it from becoming this way. But that decision had been taken out of her hands. Marriage was sacred to her, and divorce had never been an option. But her husband had not held the same sentiments.

She heard a car pull into the driveway, and rushed to the kitchen to look out the window.

Sixteen-year-old Jenny, who wore her prettiness with uncertainty, got out of her little car and headed for the door. Though her blonde hair was recently brushed and her make-up was flawlessly applied—no doubt she'd touched it up in the bathroom during her study hall—Sharon could see by the look on Jenny's face that something was wrong.

Sharon opened the door. "Hi, honey."

"Hi."

Sharon noted the despondence in Jenny's voice—and remembered that her moods were sometimes sincere, sometimes practiced. One never knew if Jenny's crises were really crises or just part of the daily drama that was the life of a teenager.

"Sorry I'm late," she said. "I had a note on my windshield from a friend in trouble, and I had to go help."

"That's okay. I'm not late—yet." Sharon rushed back into the den and grabbed her briefcase, then returned to the kitchen. Her daughter had not yet kicked off her shoes and gone to the refrigerator, her usual routine upon arriving home, which meant that something was on her mind. "Something wrong, honey?"

Jenny plopped into a chair, her long blonde hair falling into her face as she covered it dramatically with her hands. "Oh, Mom, it's just awful! This friend of mine—someone I care a lot about—is in trouble, and I've been trying to help. I really need to get back there. I can take Christy with me. It's just—I have to go. Mom, they're in such a mess!"

These were real tears, Sharon noted with surprise. She set her briefcase down and stood next to Jenny, pulling her close. "Honey, tell me. Who needs you?"

The words burst out: "Mom, these friends of mine, they're married and have these precious little kids, and yesterday he got fired from his job for no reason at all. And to make matters worse, they got evicted from their house and last night they spent the night in their car—their *whole family*. They didn't have any money, so they ate food that people had thrown away behind a fast-food restaurant."

"That's awful," Sharon said. "Who are they? Someone you know from church?"

"No. Not from church. They're friends from Westhaven."

Westhaven was an artsy area on the west side of St. Clair. It was the area where Ben lived—Sharon's ex-husband and Jenny and Christy's father. Since her children had an entire life in Westhaven on alternate weekends that she knew little about, the explanation didn't surprise her.

"Mom, can you picture those little kids sleeping in the back-seat of their car?" Jenny cried. "It's not fair."

Sharon's own eyes began to well. "No, it's not. Where are they now? Can you get in touch with them?"

Jenny sniffed and looked up at her. "Yes, I know where they are."

"Then go get them and bring them back here. At least we can give them a place to sleep and some food until they get on their feet. We have plenty of room."

Jenny hesitated, but her wet eyes were hopeful. "Mom, are you sure?"

"Of course. When I bought this house, I promised myself that I'd never turn away anyone in need. I would never deliberately let some poor family sleep out on the street when we have five bedrooms. Besides, it wouldn't be the first time we've taken somebody in."

"But you don't even know who they are."

"It doesn't matter who they are. They're welcome here."

A tentative smile broke through Jenny's tears.

"What are you waiting for?" Sharon asked, getting up and heading for the refrigerator to see if she needed to make a trip to the store before their guests arrived. "Go get them. My closing won't take long. I'll hurry home, change the sheets in the guest rooms, and cook something nice for supper. Don't worry about Christy. I'll take her with me."

But Jenny kept sitting there, staring, as if she had something else to say but didn't quite know how to say it. "Mom?"

Sharon checked the pantry, distracted. "Hmm?"

"There's one more thing you should know."

"All right," Sharon said. "Shoot."

"This family . . . it's Dad and Anne and the kids."

Sharon felt the blood draining from her face. Slowly, she turned to face her daughter. "Is this a joke, Jenny?"

Jenny didn't look amused. Tears filled her eyes again, and she wiped her face as it reddened. "It's no joke, Mom. Mr. Dubose fired Daddy yesterday, just out of the blue, and took all his credit cards that the gallery had given him. Daddy was living in the apartment provided by the gallery, and Mr. Dubose told him to get out last night. They had no place to go, and Mr. Dubose refused to give Daddy his last paycheck or the paintings he still had in the studio."

"And your father didn't have any savings? Any money in his wallet?"

Jenny closed her eyes. "Mom, you know Daddy's never been good with money. He's an artist, not a banker. The gallery took care of things for him so he could paint."

"Well, what did he do to get fired?" Sharon spouted.

"Nothing!" Jenny shouted back. "He has no idea what happened."

"Right," Sharon bit out. "Just like he had no idea how Anne got pregnant while he was still married to me. Life is a big mystery to your father."

"Mom!" Jenny cried.

Sharon leaned over the kitchen counter, angry at herself for breaking her cardinal rule not to put Ben down in front of his children. She let out a ragged sigh. "I'm sorry. I shouldn't have said that."

Jenny sank down into a chair. "Mom, you offered to let them stay here. You said it didn't matter who it was."

Sharon swung around. "That was before I knew it was them! You lied to me, Jenny! You set me up!"

"I did not lie!" Jenny cried. "I just didn't tell you who they were! I knew you would refuse to help if you knew, and I wanted you to see how hypocritical that is!"

"Your father lost his job and his home, and now *I'm* a hypocrite? How do you figure that?"

"Because you'd help anyone else! The Golden Rule applies to everybody but Daddy, doesn't it, Mom? 'Doing unto the least of these' is great—unless the least of these is Daddy."

"Jenny, you can't be serious! It's crazy to think that I, of all people, would take him in, with that woman who destroyed my family, and those children that she loves to flaunt in my face!"

"Mom, I've seen you spend entire weekends working at shelters with winos and runaways. I've seen you go to prisons and teach Bible classes to inmates. If you'd do it for them, why not for my father?"

"One very good reason," Sharon said coldly. "Because he brought every bit of this on himself. He's irresponsible, and it's catching up with him!"

"But Emily and Bobby are my sister and brother! They don't deserve to eat out of a garbage dump or sleep in a car."

"They're your *half*-sister and brother. There's a big difference."

"They're my *sister* and *brother*, Mom, whether you like it or not. And if they were in the same predicament and didn't belong to Daddy, you'd be one of the first people I know to help them." She tilted her head pleadingly. "Please, Mom. Won't you let them stay here just for a few days? We have all this room—five bedrooms—and they have nothing!"

The thought of inviting the man who had cheated on her and betrayed her, not to mention the woman who had wrecked their marriage, to sleep in her home was repulsive. It had taken Sharon five years to lose the pain, to learn not to grieve each time the kids went to spend their alternate weekends with their father. When she saw Anne, Sharon no longer seethed with hatred for this woman who had seduced her husband, then delightfully announced that she was having his child. Yes, she had grown beyond the misery. But this . . .

"They *cannot* stay here," Sharon said, setting her hands on her hips. "You can put a guilt trip on me for this if you want to, and blame me for everything, and convince yourself that this is all my fault, but I can't take that man and that woman into my home. I can't do it! It's too much to ask."

The crushing disappointment on Jenny's face made Sharon feel about an inch tall, and she found herself getting angry about her daughter's grief.

"Mom, what are they gonna do? This is my father, and my family, and I love them! Little Bobby's getting sick, and there they are out in their car. And it's cold—"

"Bobby's sick? Whatsa matter with him?" Christy stood in the doorway holding a makeshift guitar made of a tissue box with rubber bands for strings and a paper towel roll for the neck. The whole thing glistened with transparent tape.

"Christy, I told you not to come down without me!"

Christy looked apologetic. "I wanted to surprise you with my guitar." She strummed it, making a discordant sound, and danced a little. Ordinarily, Sharon and Jenny would both have laughed, but neither was able to at the moment.

Christy stopped dancing and looked up at her sister's red, wet face. "What's wrong, Jenny? What did you say about Bobby being sick?"

Jenny seized the moment to get her clout-carrying little sister involved. "He doesn't have a place to live! Neither do Daddy or Anne or Emily," she blurted. "And we have this huge house, but Mom won't let them stay here."

"Oh, for heaven's sake . . ."

The little blonde girl came farther into the kitchen, her huge eyes full of distress. "Why can't they stay here, Mommy?"

"Because!" Sharon glared at Jenny for dragging the child into this. "Jenny, you're not playing fair."

"Neither are you!" Jenny's face was growing redder as the tears came faster, and though Sharon knew she was, indeed, being manipulated, she also knew that it wasn't an act. Jenny was seriously tormented by her father's plight. "Mom, how would you feel if your father were out on the street? I know you hate Daddy and Anne, but think about the kids. Christy and Emily are close, Mom, really close—and right now Emily hasn't had a bath in two days, she hasn't slept in a bed, she hasn't eaten a full meal. Mom, she's only five years old! She shouldn't have to face this. And the baby just cries all the time. They need to take him to the doctor, but they don't have any money! Mom, just forget how you feel about him, and do this for *me*. Please!"

Sharon looked from Jenny's pleading eyes to those big blue eyes of her younger child, staring up at her with disbelief that she couldn't help her father when he was so obviously in need. She grabbed her purse and yanked out her wallet. "I'll give them some money for a hotel and food. That's all I can do."

"Really, Mom?" Jenny asked. "You'd do that? Because that would help. He'd probably even like it better."

Sharon breathed a laugh. "I'll bet he would." She jerked the money out of her billfold and began to count it. When she looked up again, she saw the hurt looks on her daughters' faces.

She took a deep breath, trying to calm down, hating herself for the feelings coursing through her. "No matter what you think, Jenny, I don't hate your father. I never wanted to see him destitute. I'll give him as much as I can." She handed her the stack of bills. "I have $150. I just went to the bank today. Give it all to him."

A smile broke through Jenny's tears. "Thank you, Mom. This means so much."

Sharon decided not to reply to that, so she leaned over and kissed Christy on the cheek. "Go get your shoes on. You and Jenny are going to take the money to Daddy while I go to my appointment."

Christy hugged her fiercely. "Bye, Mommy."

Deep love rose inside her for the small child she had raised virtually alone. "You be good, okay? And when you get back, no tree climbing. That tree is off-limits unless I'm home."

"Okay. Can I take my guitar to show Daddy?"

"Of course. Maybe you can play it for him and cheer him up."

She hugged Jenny and felt the extra squeeze her daughter gave her.

"We'll see you tonight, Mom."

"Yeah," Sharon said. She got her briefcase and headed for her car.

CHAPTER THREE

Tony Danks stooped near the body. It had been found by a cleaning woman who had called the police, frightened out of her wits. Her 911 call had been almost incoherent. From the looks of things, the man had probably been dead since yesterday. Tony studied the change lying on the floor, as if it had fallen out of the victim's pocket. Something didn't ring true. Change didn't just jump out of pockets like that. He pulled out his notepad and jotted down the possibility that this had been a robbery, even though his wallet looked undisturbed in his back pocket.

Squatting beside the body, he reached into the pockets himself and found only a pair of keys. Probably the keys to the gallery, he thought. He took them out and dropped them into an evidence bag in case they were needed later.

He looked up at the photographer. "Did you get a shot of this change lying here?"

"Yeah," the cop said. "You can go ahead and tag it."

With rubber-gloved hands, Tony began to pick up the bloody change and drop it into a bag of its own. He came to a gold money clip with the initials BLR. "Hey, Jack? What did you say the victim's name is?" he asked the cop who'd been the first to arrive on the scene.

"Louis Dubose."

"Hmm," he said, and dropped the money clip into another bag. "The initials on this say BLR."

"Maybe he's our killer," the photographer said. "Maybe it fell out of his pocket."

Tony was skeptical. "If so, there were an awful lot of things falling out of pockets."

He got another bag and pulled the hairs from the victim's fingers. "On the other hand, there was probably a struggle before the killer shot him in the back. Who knows?" He carefully tagged the hairs. They would be sent to the lab today and would probably go far in helping them to identify the killer.

He stood up. "So what's the story on that apartment at the back?"

Jack checked his notes. "According to the cleaning woman, some artist named Ben Robinson lived back there until yesterday. Looks like he moved out in a rush. Left all the furniture behind, but no clothes or personal items."

"Ben Robinson," Tony repeated. "BLR. I'd say he's the first person we need to question."

"If we can find him."

"We'll find him," Tony assured him.

The front door opened and Larry Millsaps, Tony's partner, came in brandishing a bag. "You'll never guess what I found in the dumpster out behind the gallery."

"What?" Tony asked.

"The murder weapon. A .22."

"Did you run a check on it?"

"Yeah. It's registered to a Ben Robinson. At this address."

Tony looked back around the gallery, where other cops were videotaping, fingerprinting, photographing. "What do you bet that our Ben Robinson has long blonde hair?"

"Did you find some?"

"Yep. That and a money clip with his initials. Looks like he was in a hurry to leave, too. Didn't stick around long enough to clean up."

"I'd say it's time to make an arrest," Larry said.

"I'm right behind you," Tony told him.

CHAPTER FOUR

B obby was sound asleep when Ben Robinson checked his family into the inexpensive motel room, carrying the bags of food they had picked up at the nearby fast-food restaurant. Ben laid the six-month-old baby down on one of the double beds, covered him with the blanket he was wrapped in, and felt his head. "I think his fever has gone down," he told Anne, who was ushering Christy and Emily in. "The Tylenol helped."

Jenny sat down next to him, careful not to disturb the sleeping baby. "The least Mr. Dubose could have done was give you his crib."

Anne set the bag of two-liter drinks on the table. "He said all the furniture belonged to the gallery," she said in a weary monotone.

"It did belong to the gallery," Ben said, his tone reflecting hers.

"Yeah, well, we should have seen this coming," Anne went on. "When you depend on other people, you wind up out in the street, sleeping in your car."

"Mommy, can I eat now?" Emily asked.

"Sure, sweetheart." Anne's tone softened as she looked down at the five-year-old, a couple of inches shorter than Christy, and with shorter hair, although in color it was identical to Christy's. It was obvious to anyone that they were sisters, even though they did have different mothers. She dug into the bag for Emily's burger. "Christy, here's one for you."

Christy looked questioningly at Jenny.

"I told you we don't need anything," Jenny said. "Christy and I can eat at home. You need to save your money."

"I could tell she was hungry," Anne said with a half-smile. "Besides, it wouldn't be fair for her to sit there and watch us eat and not have anything herself. Here, Chris. Your drink is in the box."

Christy smiled and went to get it.

Jenny got up from the bed and went to her father, who stood leaning against the wall, his pale eyes distant and dismal. His usually clean blonde hair was oily because he hadn't had the chance to shower since yesterday, and he had it pulled back in a pony tail, a look that her mother found disgusting, but all her friends considered cool. He was unshaven, and she noticed the tired lines under his eyes. Without those lines, he could have passed for her older brother, rather than her forty-year-old father.

She slid her arms around him from behind and laid her head against his back. At six feet, he was almost a head taller than she. "Daddy, are you okay?"

He pretended to snap out of it, and smiled. "Yeah. I was just thinking. Somehow I've got to get all my paintings out of the gallery. They're my livelihood. If I could sell them, or at least take them to another gallery . . ."

"Have you tried calling Mr. Dubose again?" Jenny asked. "Maybe he's cooled off by now, and he'll talk."

"I tried," Ben said. "There's still no answer. Besides, he had nothing to cool off from. I didn't do anything to prompt it."

"Are you *sure?*" Anne asked again, as she'd asked a thousand times since yesterday. "Ben, *think.* A man doesn't fire you from your job and evict you from your home the same afternoon, if you haven't done anything. If you could apologize, maybe—"

He stiffened. "Anne, how many times do I have to tell you? There's nothing to apologize for! When are you gonna believe me?"

She held up a hand to stem the argument, and breathing a deep sigh, turned back to the children.

"This is awful," Jenny whispered.

Ben nodded and raked his hand through his long disheveled hair. "I never would have dreamed I'd have to take money from your mother to keep my family off the street."

"Mom didn't mind. She was happy to do it."

"Yeah, I'll bet." Catching himself, he muttered, "It really was nice of her. She didn't have to do it."

Jenny sighed and looked helplessly around the room. Little Emily was so tired that she could hardly eat, so Jenny went over and pulled the cotton-topped five-year-old into her lap. "Come on, Emily. Let me help you with this."

She began to feed the child one french fry at a time.

"She needs a nap," Anne said. "She didn't sleep very well last night. Bobby kept coughing, and the car wasn't all that comfortable."

"Anne, if Bobby gets worse, you'll take him to the emergency room, won't you?" Jenny asked.

Anne shot Ben a look that said they couldn't do even that without money. "Yeah. Somehow, we'd convince them to treat him. There's always the health department. They treat indigents."

Ben stiffened, knowing that her remark had been intended to sting. "We are not indigent."

"Right," Anne said sarcastically. "We're just homeless, penniless, and jobless. At least we're not sleeping under a bridge somewhere. I guess I should brace myself. That could be coming."

Ben went into the bathroom, the only place to which he could escape, and slammed the door behind him.

The sound woke Bobby, and he began to cry, making Ben feel even worse. He sat on the lid of the commode, rubbing his stubbled face, fighting feelings of terror and despair.

So he had come to this.

As always in times of stress, old tapes of Sharon's voice played in his mind.

You're irresponsible, Ben. When are you going to grow up and start acting like an adult?

You're selfish! You don't care about anyone but yourself. You think you've got it all figured out, with your artsy friends and your own set of rules. But this charade of a marriage is going to show everyone just how much of a loser you are.

She had been in pain when she'd said those words, reacting to his own cruelties. But knowing that didn't take away the sting of her accusations—and now he wondered whether he hadn't just proven that they were all true.

He only wished he hadn't spent every penny he made, always counting on the gallery to keep handing over monthly paychecks for his restoration work and the rights to show his work exclusively. He should have been smarter with finances, like his ex-wife was. In five short years, she'd gone from being a struggling real-estate agent to a six-figure wage earner. When she'd bought that house last year, he had convinced himself that it was intended as a slap in the face to him—a way of showing him what he could have had if he hadn't left her for greener pastures. But then he'd felt ashamed of those thoughts when he'd heard how she'd taken in a couple of unmarried pregnant women who'd needed a place to stay while they carried their babies, and then a family whose house had burned down. Her success, he'd finally realized, didn't have anything to do with him at all, one way or the other. She'd simply worked hard for herself and her daughters. His feelings that she was rubbing his nose in her wealth was his problem, not hers. He was the one who made comparisons. She had just gone on with her own life.

And he had his life with Anne. Although it had grown increasingly difficult as the infatuation had worn off and reality had set in, he had tried to make it work. He wasn't going to hurt two more children through a needless divorce. It's not as if he was a victim here. He had the power to turn this around.

But right now, he hated the feeling of Anne's disgust with him, so much like Sharon's. In fact, he realized, she had started reciting Sharon's tapes. Without using the same words, her very tone suggested that he was stupid, selfish, irresponsible, a loser . . .

But he'd prove to them that he wasn't a loser. He had to pull himself together, had to be rational. There was much to be done in the next few days.

Jenny was walking Bobby around the room, trying to make him stop crying so that Anne could eat, when a hard knock sounded on the door.

Anne, who was sitting with food balanced on her lap, sent a pleading look to Jenny. "Would you get that?"

"Sure." Still carrying the crying baby, Jenny stepped over Christy, who was sitting in front of the television, and opened the door.

Two men stood outside, one, a brunette dressed in jeans and a windbreaker and the other, a tall blonde, in khakis and a sport coat.

Bobby still cried, so the man in the sport coat had to raise his voice to be heard. "We're with the St. Clair Police Department," he said, flashing a badge. "I'm Detective Tony Danks, and this is my partner Larry Millsaps. We're looking for Ben Robinson. Is he here?"

"Sure ... uh ... just a minute." Anne began to put her food down, and Jenny stepped back over Christy and went to the bathroom, bouncing the crying baby on her hip. She knocked on the door. "Daddy, someone's here to see you."

Ben came out, looking more drawn and weary than she'd ever seen him.

"Someone's here," she repeated, then gave a worried glance back at the cops. "Policemen," she whispered.

Bobby's crying grew louder, and the baby reached for his mother. Anne took him, then followed Ben to the door.

"Officers," Ben said with a nod as he reached the door. "What can I do for you?"

"Ben Robinson?" one of the men confirmed.

"Yes," he said.

The one with the windbreaker pulled a pair of handcuffs out of his pocket. "I have a warrant for your arrest for the murder of Louis Dubose. You have the right to remain silent—"

"No!" Anne screamed, and Jenny rushed forward.

"Daddy!"

"Murder?" Ben asked as they got the cuffs on his hands. "What do you mean, murder?"

"He was found dead an hour ago," Tony Danks said. "You have the right to an attorney. If you can't afford an attorney—"

"There must be some mistake!" Anne cried. "My husband didn't kill anybody."

The baby was screaming louder, and now Emily and Christy abandoned their food and stood holding hands, fearfully watching the scene.

Jenny grabbed her father's arm as they tried to pull him toward their car. "Daddy, tell them you didn't do it! Tell them!"

"It's okay," Ben said hoarsely. "We'll straighten it all out."

But his family, stunned and terrified, watched as he was guided into the back seat of the squad car—and he looked anything but confident, trembling, his eyes wide. They watched wordlessly as the car pulled out of sight.

CHAPTER FIVE

The phone was ringing when Sharon walked into her house. She had just closed the deal on the house on Lewis Street, then had shown three houses to Mrs. Milford, a client who she suspected would never settle on anything. Dropping her purse and briefcase, she picked up the phone.

"Hello?"

"Oh, Mom, thank goodness you're finally home. I've been trying to reach you, but you never answered your car phone."

"I was showing houses. I must have been inside when you called. What's wrong?"

Jenny was crying, and her pain came right through the phone. "Oh, Mom!" She sobbed, caught her breath, and tried to go on. "Daddy's been arrested! They think he killed somebody!"

"What?"

"Mr. Dubose, the gallery manager, was murdered, and they think Daddy did it. Mom, he couldn't have! He was with us! But they won't listen—they don't believe us, and they say he was killed yesterday. Daddy was the last one to see him alive, so they're blaming him. Mom, I don't know what to do! My father is not a murderer!"

"I know he's not," Sharon said. "Jenny, where are you?"

"At the police station. We're all here. Anne's a basket case, and the kids are all upset . . . Christy and Emily don't understand, but they're smart enough to know that their daddy's going to jail! Mom, we've got to get him out!"

Sharon held the phone between her ear and shoulder and grabbed her purse. "Jenny, I'm coming down to the station. I'll be there in ten minutes. Does your father have a lawyer?"

"No. They can't afford one."

"I'll call Lynda," Sharon said. "She's one of the best lawyers in St. Clair."

"Yeah, I forgot she was a lawyer. Mom, ask her to hurry," Jenny said. "They're in there with him right now. Oh, and Mom? Could you stop by the store and get some cough syrup for Bobby? He's coughing his head off."

Sharon didn't like the thought of detouring on her way, but she muttered, "Sure. I'll bring it."

She hung up the phone and quickly dialed Lynda Barrett's number. They were good friends from church, and she knew the number by rote.

"Hello?"

"Oh, Lynda, I'm so glad you're home. I didn't have time to look up your office number."

"Sharon, what's wrong?"

"Ben ... my ex-husband ... he needs a lawyer. He's been arrested for murder."

"Murder?" Lynda repeated.

"Lynda, the man's one of my least favorite people, and he's capable of a lot. But he's not a killer. You've got to help him. I'll pay you, if he can't. He's at the police station, and they're interviewing him as we speak."

"I'll be there in five minutes," Lynda said.

Sharon hung up and breathed a sigh of relief. Then she rushed out, more concerned about the state of mind of her children than that her ex-husband was being accused of something he couldn't possibly have done.

CHAPTER SIX

Ben hadn't had a shower since yesterday, and as he sat in the over-heated interrogation room—no doubt kept that way by design—sweating and trying to answer all of their questions, he wished he'd at least had time to take a quick bath before the police had come. With his oily ponytail, a two-day growth of stubble, and clothes he'd had on for two days now, he must look like a biker who wouldn't think twice about killing his boss. Now he wished he'd never let his hair grow this long. But he liked the bohemian look that said he didn't have time to worry about his appearance because he was too busy cultivating his imagination. Part of the look was for effect, he admitted, but part of it was reality. Often he got so lost in his work that he *didn't* remember to shower, shave, or eat. That was why he still didn't have the mid-life paunch that most of his contemporaries had after crossing the forty-year mark. He had crossed it last October, and still prided himself on looking ten years younger.

"Look, I told you," he said, keeping his voice even so he wouldn't appear to be losing his temper. "The last time I saw Louis he was locking himself in his office."

"But you were angry at him, weren't you?"

"Yeah, of course I was angry. You'd be angry, too, if your boss threw you and your family out into the street, and wouldn't even give you your last paycheck!"

Lynda Barrett, who had burst in just moments before and announced that the family had retained her to be his lawyer, touched his arm to shut him up.

Ben had almost told her no-thank-you when he'd realized that the aggressive brunette was Sharon's friend. But when he'd seen that she knew the two cops well, he decided to accept her services. Maybe she'd have some pull with them.

"Larry, Tony, my client has already told you everything he knows."

"He hasn't told us why we found the murder weapon in a dumpster behind the gallery—a pistol that was registered to him. And his fingerprints were all over the glass," Tony said.

"No way," Ben argued again. "I've never owned a gun in my life. I don't even know how to use one."

"Were his fingerprints on the gun?" Lynda asked, taking notes.

"No. The killer obviously wore gloves."

Lynda looked up, smiling wryly. "Larry, you said his fingerprints were all over the glass. If he was wearing gloves, how could that be? Make up your mind."

"I *did* put those fingerprints on the glass," Ben said. "We live in back of the gallery, and the day before I was fired, my little girl, Emily, was playing peek-a-boo with me outside the glass. We both got our fingerprints all over it. I meant to clean it off."

Tony pretended to be making a note. "Fingerprints due to peek-a-boo."

"I'm serious!" Ben said.

"There was obviously a struggle," Larry went on. "There was some overturned furniture."

"That doesn't mean I was there," Ben said.

"There was also a money clip next to the body. It obviously fell out of the killer's pocket. It had the initials BLR, and your fingerprints."

Ben sat straighter. "My money clip? I don't even know where that was. I haven't carried that in a couple of years."

"And there were strands of hair in Dubose's hands, like he'd gotten in a struggle and pulled it out of the killer's head. Blonde hair about your length. At first we thought it was a woman's, but now that we see you . . ."

"So I'm a killer because my hair is long?" Ben asked.

Lynda was still taking notes. She flipped her shoulder-length hair behind an ear. "Where was the entry wound, guys?"

"His back," Tony said, shooting Ben a look. "That ought to make you proud. Courage that matches the hair."

"I would never shoot someone in the back! I would never shoot anyone period!"

Lynda shot Ben a stern look, telling him to shut up. "So if he was shot in the back, then you must have figured out the range by now. How far away was the gun when it went off?"

"We're guessing a few feet."

"All right, then, how did he get a handful of Ben's hair if his back was to him and he was a few feet away?"

"They obviously fought before he turned his back."

"That's ridiculous!" Ben shouted. "I've never fought with him in my life! I don't fight with anybody! That's not my style!"

"Ben, let's go back," Larry said, playing the good guy in the good guy/bad guy routine. "Think about what you two talked about in your last few conversations. Was there anybody else there? Anyone you talked about?"

"No. He was kind of preoccupied."

"With what?" Larry asked.

"I wish I knew. Probably with his plans to throw me out. Then yesterday, out of the blue, he told me I was terminated and that my family and I had to be out of the apartment within the hour. I was stunned. I couldn't believe it."

"Angry, too, huh?" Tony asked.

"Of course I was angry. I was furious."

Lynda nudged his arm again. "That's enough, Ben."

"Not angry enough to kill him! But it was crazy. I tried to go up to my studio and get my paintings, but he said the gallery owned them—that they had paid me to paint them— and that I couldn't take them. I lost my temper when he refused to give me my last paycheck—"

"Ben, as your lawyer, I'm telling you that you've given them enough," Lynda insisted.

"But I have nothing to hide!" Ben said. "All we did was argue, and then he went up to that office of his and locked himself in. He said if I didn't leave within the hour, with my children and my wife and everything we owned, he'd have the sheriff escort me out. So I went to the apartment and started packing. We were gone an hour later. I tried calling him several times from pay phones to reason with him, but the line was busy."

"We can get the records from the phone company," Lynda told Larry and Tony.

"That'll only prove that a call was made to the gallery. It doesn't prove that Dubose was alive when he left him."

"Right," Ben snarled, slapping his hands on the table. "I got into a knock-down, drag-out fight with Dubose and shot him, then left my gun exactly where I knew you'd look for it, then called him afterward just to see if he was really dead."

The detectives both stared at him without amusement, and Lynda closed her eyes and began to massage her temples.

"I'm being sarcastic!" Ben shouted. "Why did I call the guy if I thought he was dead? And about that gun, you need to check out that registration, because I'm telling you, I have never owned one! Ask anybody. You won't find a registration with my name on it."

"We already have, pal."

Ben looked flustered. "You can't. It's impossible. I don't believe in owning guns. I have small children."

"Tell it to the judge," Larry said, jotting another note on his pad.

"People have been known to use other people's names and credentials to get guns," Lynda pointed out. "He has an alibi, Larry."

"Yeah, his wife. Big surprise."

"My children, too," Ben said. "One of them is sixteen years old. She's old enough to remember where I was when."

"Daughters are usually loyal to their fathers," Tony said.

"Then ask my ex-wife! She hates my guts and would probably love to see me rot in jail, but she'll tell you that Jenny was with me part of yesterday and this afternoon."

"We will," Larry said, getting to his feet. "But even if she corroborates what you've said, we've got enough to book you."

Ben covered his face with his hands, unable to believe what was happening. When both detectives had left the room, he turned to Lynda. "I'm gonna have to stay in jail?"

"Until morning, at least," Lynda said. "It'll be okay. You won't spend the most comfortable night of your life, but tomorrow morning I can probably convince the judge to let you out on bond. You have no prior arrests?"

"Not even a traffic ticket," Ben said wearily.

"That should play in your favor. Show up in court with your whole family in tow—all four kids—and maybe he'll show mercy and let you out pending the Grand Jury investigation."

Ben closed his eyes. "My children are all going to know I'm in jail. What kind of image is that for a father?"

"They'll also know you're innocent," she said.

"How do *you* know I'm innocent?" Ben asked angrily. "You don't even know me. If all you know of me is what my ex-wife has told you, then you probably think I'm the scum of the earth."

"Wrong. Sharon's an intelligent woman, and she was married to you for a long time. She wouldn't have married a maniac."

Ben breathed a laugh. "You haven't talked to her lately, have you?"

Actually, she had. "She says you're a good father, Ben. That tells me a lot. She just thinks you were a lousy husband."

Ben shook his head. "That's why I hate this town. You make one mistake, and everybody in town knows about it."

Lynda wore a half-smile as she got up. "Look, I believe your story, and I think I can get you out tomorrow. Then we can start working hard on your case."

"There's a killer out there," Ben said. "Nobody's even looking for him. He got away with it."

"Well, maybe we can put our heads together and figure out who it is." She stuck her notebook into her briefcase and shut it. "Ben, they're going to put you into a holding cell for the night. Just be patient. You'll probably be in a cell alone, so you'll be safe. I'll see if I can pull some strings to get them to put you in the new wing. The old one is kind of creepy. Oh, and the hearing is early tomorrow." She reached for the doorknob.

"Hey," he said before she could leave. "Tell my wife it's going to be all right. Try to make her feel better about this. She's a good person, regardless of what Sharon may have told you."

"Sharon hasn't said anything to me about her," Lynda said honestly.

"Right. Then you heard it from the famous St. Clair grapevine. All those church ladies who spend all their time exchanging gossip disguised as prayer requests."

Lynda couldn't help chuckling. "Don't worry. I'll forget whatever I've heard. See you tomorrow at the arraignment."

CHAPTER SEVEN

The small St. Clair Police Department was teeming with cops, people filing complaints, criminals waiting to be booked, and friends and family members waiting to bail them out. Sharon, who was able to fit in almost anywhere from soup kitchens to inaugural balls, felt as though she stood out ridiculously in her business suit and heels. She stood uncomfortably at the door and looked around for her children. She spotted Christy sitting with Emily in the middle of a crowd of seething gang members. Jenny sat a little farther down, between two women who could have been hookers. Anne was pacing and bouncing Bobby as he screamed at the top of his lungs.

Sharon rushed across the room and grabbed Christy's hand to pull her out of the midst of the street gang. Five-year-old Emily followed as they found vacant seats at the other end of the waiting area. Jenny got up and followed as they passed her.

"Mom, thank goodness you're here," she whispered. "Anne doesn't handle a crisis very well. She's really losing it."

Sharon shot Anne a look. The woman saw her and quickly turned her head.

Sharon dug into her purse and pulled out the bag with the cough syrup. "Here, Jenny. Give her this. I also got one of those little measuring spoons I used when Christy was younger, so she can give it to him now."

"Thanks, Mom," Jenny said, then dashed to her stepmother.

Anne took the medicine reluctantly, looking more chagrined than grateful. Without acknowledging that Sharon had brought it, she headed for the bathroom to give it to the baby.

Sharon was glad she was gone. "Where's your father?"

"In that room over there. He's been there since I called you. Anne and I both signed statements saying that he couldn't have killed Mr. Dubose, because he's been with one or both of us since yesterday. But they're saying he did it when Mr. Dubose fired him. He's the only one they can prove was there yesterday, even though Anne saw him alive through the window when they were leaving their apartment."

Sharon looked toward the room. "How does your father get himself into these things?"

"Mom!" Jenny's tears had a hair trigger, and they filled her eyes now. "Daddy didn't have anything to do with this. You know that!"

She was instantly ashamed. "You're right; I'm sorry. Your father picks bugs up in his hand and takes them outside to keep from killing them."

"That's right!" Jenny said victoriously, as if that would be just the evidence she needed to clear her father. "Mom, tell them. They'll listen to you."

"I will, when I get the chance."

The door to the interrogation room opened, and Lynda Barrett came out. "Wait here with the girls," Sharon told Jenny, and hurried across the floor to meet Lynda, her heels clicking a staccato beat on the dirty tiles.

"Lynda, what's going on?" Sharon asked.

"Well, it doesn't look good," Lynda admitted. "He's going to have to spend the night in jail. His arraignment is tomorrow morning, and maybe then we can get him out on bond."

"Bond? They're not really charging him with murder, are they?"

"I'm afraid so."

Flustered, Sharon leaned toward her friend, intent on making her understand. "Lynda, I was married to the man for twelve years! He's not capable of murder! He's never even been able to bring himself to spank the kids. He's a lot of things, but he is *not* a killer."

"Sharon, the murder weapon was registered to him."

"Well, what did he say about that?"

"He said that it couldn't have been, that he's never owned a gun in his life."

"That's probably true. He wouldn't even know how to use one."

"Everybody knows how to pull a trigger. That's all the court cares about. He probably will be arraigned, Lynda, but if things go well, we can at least get him out pending an indictment."

"Excuse me!" The voice behind Sharon was Anne's, and Sharon swung around and saw the seething woman, still holding her crying baby. "This is none of her business," Anne said to Lynda. "If you're my husband's lawyer, you should be discussing my husband with me, not her! She doesn't even have the right to be here."

Sharon's teeth came together. "I'm here because I didn't want my children unattended in a police station, Anne."

"They're not unattended. They're with me."

"Forgive me if I thought you might be a little preoccupied, seeing how your husband has just been arrested for murder and all." People were starting to watch them. Sharon lowered her voice. "Look, I'll just go talk to my daughter, and you two can have a private conversation."

Her face was burning by the time she reached Jenny.

"What did she say?" Jenny asked anxiously.

"That this was none of my business. She's got so much nerve. It never fails to amaze me."

"She said that? Really? But I thought—"

"After I gave her that money, and brought the cough medicine, and hired a lawyer . . ."

Jenny's face changed. "Mom, I was talking about Lynda! What did *she* say about Daddy?"

"Oh." Sharon felt stupid and mentally kicked herself. Why was it that her dignity began slipping away bit by bit whenever she was near Anne and Ben? She tried to shift her thoughts. "Lynda said that he would have to spend the night here."

"No!" Jenny cried. "Mom, he can't! There are criminals in jail! He didn't *do* anything."

"Tomorrow is the arraignment, honey."

"What's that?"

"That's when they ask his plea and decide whether to set bond."

"Well, then he'll get out, won't he? There's not any evidence. He can tell them he wasn't there and prove it!"

"Honey, the arraignment is not really for presenting evidence. But Lynda feels sure he can get out tomorrow."

Jenny wiped her eyes. "This is like a nightmare."

"It sure is," Sharon whispered.

Anne turned away from Lynda, mascara-muddled tears staining her face, and she called Emily. Both Christy and Emily came to her, holding hands. "Come on, honey," she told the five-year-old. "We're going back to the motel."

"What about Daddy?"

"He's going to stay here tonight. We'll see him in the morning."

Sharon stood back as Jenny went to kiss Emily and Bobby good-bye. "Anne," Jenny said, "do you want me to come and help you take care of the kids?"

Anne glanced stoically at Sharon and lifted her chin, as if to hide any evidence of vulnerability. "No, thanks. We'll be fine."

"Okay," Jenny said weakly.

"You'll be here in the morning?" Anne asked.

"I sure will," she said. "Try to get some sleep, okay?"

Anne nodded and gave her a hug, then leaned down and kissed Christy on the cheek. Christy returned it easily, a gesture that bothered Sharon more than she ever would have admitted. Christy didn't follow as Anne led Emily out of the building. "Poor Anne," Jenny said, watching her go. "It's like her life is falling apart."

"I remember that feeling," Sharon muttered.

"Mom!"

Sharon took Christy's hand and started to the door. "Come on, girls. Let's get out of here."

Later that night, as Christy was changing into her pajamas, she found in her pocket the little army men that Emily had gotten in her Burger King bag. Emily had no pockets in her own pants, so she had asked Christy to hold them for her.

Christy set the little men up on her dresser and wondered if Emily had missed them. She had been so excited about them when she'd gotten them, even though Christy had found them a disappointment. Emily didn't have many toys, though, and the ones she did have were packed in a box in the back of their car. Carefully, she picked the little army men back up and held them securely in her fist. She would call Emily, she thought, and tell her she had them, so at least she'd know they weren't lost. And maybe she could offer her something else, just to make her feel better about Daddy.

Christy looked around her room for something Emily would like.

Her collection of porcelain dolls lay carefully arranged on the French provincial canopy bed, but she knew that Emily wouldn't really like those, because they broke so easily. On her shelves was a menagerie of stuffed animals. Though Emily had never been in her room before, Christy knew that she would like Simba, the little stuffed lion, better than any of the others. She climbed up on her chair and reached for it.

It was soft and good to sleep with, she thought. Maybe it would keep Emily company, and keep her mind off her troubles.

Clutching the stuffed animal in one hand and the army men in the other, Christy ran down the hall to Jenny's room. Jenny was on the phone, as usual.

"Jenny," she whispered, as if keeping her voice low would not disturb her. "Do you have the number of the motel?"

Jenny put her hand over the receiver. "Why do you need it?"

"I want to call Emily," she said. "She left her army men. They're real important."

Jenny frowned. "Christy, those aren't important. It can wait."

"She'll cry if she thinks she lost them," Christy said. "She doesn't have anything to play with. I want to tell her that she can have my Simba, too."

Jenny stared at her for a moment, then smiled. "That's sweet of you. Okay, just a minute, and I'll look up the number."

Christy waited as Jenny continued her phone conversation while simultaneously searching the phone book. "Here it is," she said. "I'll circle it for you."

Christy looked hard at the circled phone number. Then, stuffing Simba under one arm, she took the book and headed down the stairs to the study, where her mother had a separate phone line. She climbed into her mother's big chair behind the desk, laid the book open on the desktop, and set the toys down. Picking up the phone, she punched in the number slowly, checking and rechecking each digit against the phone book.

"Holiday Inn," a woman's voice said.

"Can I speak to Emily, please?" she asked.

"There's no one named Emily who works here," the woman said. "Can someone else help you?"

Christy hesitated. "No, I need Emily."

"Emily who?" the woman asked, irritated.

"Emily Robinson. She's my sister."

The woman's voice softened. "Honey, you have the wrong number."

Tears of frustration filled Christy's eyes, and she hung up the phone. Had they gone back home? she wondered. Had they forgotten to tell her where they were?

She dialed their old number and waited through three rings. Finally, an operator's voice cut in. "I'm sorry. The number you've called has been disconnected . . ."

"I want to speak to Emily!" she cried over the voice. When she realized it was a recording, she slammed the phone down and looked helplessly at the phone book again. How could she get in touch with her?

She sat at her mother's big desk, looking at Simba staring expectantly at her, and those three army men poised to strike. What if they had put Emily in jail, too? she thought. What if they had put Bobby and Anne there?

Helpless about her father's plight and about all the other things she didn't understand, she began to cry into her small hands.

Her mother came to the door. "Oh, Christy . . ."

Sharon crossed the room and pulled Christy up into a tight hug, then sat back down with the small girl in her lap.

"I miss Daddy," she squeaked. "And Emily forgot her army guys."

"We'll take Emily her army guys tomorrow when we see her, okay?"

"But she'll cry when she thinks they're lost, and I wanted to call and tell her, but she's not there."

"Honey, it'll be okay. She's probably so tired after everything that's happened that she won't even think about them. Tomorrow will be soon enough. You're going to see her first thing in the morning. And your daddy, too."

"I am?" Christy asked hopefully.

"Yes. You and Jenny are going to court, and they'll both be there."

She wiped her eyes. "Will you be there?"

Sharon thought about that for a moment. "Yes. I think I will go. I'm worried about your daddy, too. But Daddy needs for you and Jenny to sit with Anne and Emily and Bobby, so the judge can see what a beautiful family your daddy has."

The words, though delivered softly, had a little bit of a bite to them, and Christy recognized it. Wiping her eyes, she sat up on her mother's lap. "I want to sit with you. Will you sit by us, too?"

"No, honey," she said. "Anne wouldn't appreciate that. But I'll be there if you need me."

Christy suddenly felt very tired, and she began to cry again. Her mother hugged her tighter as she laid her head on Sharon's shoulder. "Mommy, can I call and talk to Daddy?"

"No, sweetheart. They don't let him have phone calls where he is."

"I know where he is," Christy said. "He's in jail. You don't have to act like I don't know."

"It's all just a mistake, honey. He'll be out soon."

"You promise?" Christy asked.

Sharon hesitated, and Christy knew that she wasn't going to promise. Sliding off her mother's lap, she grabbed up her Simba and the army men, and started for the door.

"Where are you going, honey?"

"To bed," Christy muttered.

"But it's still early, and you don't have to go to school tomorrow since we have to go to court."

"I'm tired," Christy pouted, rubbing the tears on her face. "I need my rest."

Ordinarily, Sharon would have smiled, but the words were spoken with such dejection that she didn't find them funny.

"All right. Come on, and I'll tuck you in. And we'll pray for your daddy."

Christy slept with Simba and the army men that night, eager for morning to make sure her father was all right.

CHAPTER EIGHT

T he cell was cold and dimly lit. Ben lay on his two-inch-thick mattress stretched across sagging steel springs and tried to sleep. A few cells down, a man sang out a painful dirge in a voice that could have made him millions. How had he wound up here?

Same way I did, he thought. He watched a roach crawl across the ceiling and closed his eyes as it got directly overhead. Jail. He couldn't believe it.

He rolled onto his side and pulled the threadbare blanket up to cover him. Two voices exchanged curses down the way, and a third screamed for them to shut up. Someone closer to his cell banged out a rap beat with a spoon on the edge of his bars, a sound so annoying that he too longed to scream "Shut up!"

Anne was probably scared to death. Anne, who had once made him feel like such an important man; Anne, who had believed in his work and his dream to become a renowned painter; Anne, who had vowed that she would follow him to the ends of the earth, regardless of the consequences, if he would just make her his wife. Over the past five years, after two children and a lot of ups and downs, that deep passion had faded into a more practical (and even cynical) kind of relationship, the kind that he had fled from with Sharon. Did Anne have even an ounce of love for him left? He doubted it. Instead, she was probably wondering what she'd ever seen in him in the first place. He was wondering that himself.

Anne deserved a husband who was strong, resourceful, able to provide. Up to now he'd been none of those things. It was long past time to change that. No matter how many paintings he'd sold, no matter how many important showings he'd had, no matter how many art critics were writing positive assessments of his work, it didn't amount to anything when he was broke, homeless, and lying in a jail cell.

The roach dropped onto his chest, and he jumped up and brushed it off. He kicked it under the bars, out into the corridor, then leaned against the cold iron and looked up the darkened hall.

Would they let him out tomorrow? They had to. He couldn't bear the thought of being in jail until his Grand Jury hearing, separated from his children and his wife.

Somehow, he had to get out tomorrow. And Lynda Barrett was the only one who could get him out. She was Sharon's friend, and one of those superstitious Christians. Still, he did trust her.

After all, he had little choice. There were ways to change his family's luck. But he had to be free to pursue them.

CHAPTER NINE

I t was after midnight when the telephone rang in Anne's motel room. She hurried to answer it before it woke her children. "Hello?"

"Anne, is that you?"

The voice sounded distant, and the static over the line made it difficult to hear. "Yes. Who is this?"

"Nelson," the voice said. "Nelson Chamberlain. I'm in London, but I've just heard about Louis's murder."

Chamberlain, who lived in St. Clair even though he traveled most of the time, was one of Ben's biggest supporters. He'd bought at least four of his paintings and sold several more for him in just the past year. He had also been one of Louis Dubose's closest friends. "It was a shock to all of us," she said, shoving her hair back from her face. "Did they tell you who's been charged with the murder?"

"I heard they'd arrested Ben. Is that true? Anne, what's going on?"

"Nelson, it's a long story, but Louis fired Ben yesterday for some unknown reason and told us to move out. The police think that Ben killed him for revenge or something. He's in jail right now." Her voice cracked, and she looked up at the ceiling, trying to fight the tears. "The arraignment is tomorrow. I don't know what we're going to do. I'm worried sick that they'll hold him until the Grand Jury investigation. Longer, if he's indicted. He's been framed, Nelson. All the evidence points to him, but I swear he didn't do it."

"This is incomprehensible," Nelson said. "I can't believe it's happening."

"Me either. And if they do set bond, I have no idea how to come up with it. A bail bondsman might not give it to us—we're not even employed."

"Don't worry about the bond, Anne," Nelson said. "I'll post it. I'm not at a number where I can be reached tomorrow, since I'm hoping to fly home to St. Clair for the funeral, but I'll phone the courthouse in the morning and have the money wired to them."

She caught her breath. "You'd do that?"

"Of course I would. I know Ben didn't kill anyone. We've got to get him out of jail."

"You're saving our lives," Anne cried. "I don't know how to thank you."

"Thanks aren't necessary. Just tell Ben to keep his chin up. I'll call you when I get back."

When she had hung up, Anne sat back against the headboard of the bed and savored the relief that she would at least be able to post bond. Nelson hadn't set a cap on the amount he was willing to pay, and she knew that he'd get his money back when Ben was acquitted. It was the one bright spot in an otherwise horrible day.

She slid back under the covers and tried to sleep. But sleep didn't come. She lay on her back, staring at the ceiling, until morning intruded on the room.

CHAPTER TEN

T he day was unusually cold for Florida, but that was no surprise. Everything else seemed out of kilter, too. Sharon walked into the courtroom and glanced around at the faces of other family members, lawyers, and accusers who had come to face the judge today. On one side of the courtroom sat the row of inmates awaiting arraignment. Ben was among them in his orange jumpsuit, looking as haggard and disheveled as she had ever seen him.

Jenny had brought Christy earlier; they were sitting with Anne. Jenny was holding little Bobby in her lap, bouncing him to keep him content, while Emily squirmed restlessly in her mother's lap—holding the army men that Christy had insisted on bringing her this morning. Christy sat beside Anne, dark circles under her eyes, dressed in her Sunday best with a big white bow in her long hair.

Lynda Barrett was the only one among them who looked confident and unafraid, as if she knew what she was doing here. Risking Anne's wrath, Sharon approached Lynda and quietly leaned over her shoulder.

"How's it looking?" she asked.

Lynda looked up at her hopefully. "Things are moving pretty fast this morning," she said. "The judge must have a golf game this afternoon."

The judge hammered his gavel, marking the decision in the previous case, and Sharon found a seat a couple of rows back.

"St. Clair versus Robinson," the bailiff called out.

Ben got to his feet, and Lynda went to stand beside him. After hearing the charge, the judge asked, "What is your plea?"

"Not guilty," Ben said loudly.

Lynda requested that Ben be released on his own recognizance pending the Grand Jury investigation, but the prosecutor pressed to keep him in jail, citing the violent nature of the crime Ben was accused of and suggesting that the streets of St. Clair weren't safe with Ben free. Lynda refuted his points one by one, making special note of Ben's alibi.

"Your honor, since my client has no criminal record, not even a traffic violation, it would be senseless to keep him in jail. He has a wife and four children who depend on him." She gestured toward them.

The judge regarded the family. Then, taking off his glasses, he read back over the forms on his table. "Miss Barrett," he said, looking up at Lynda and shoving his glasses back on. "I see here that Mr. Robinson was evicted from his home just two days ago."

"That's right, your honor."

The judge braced his elbows on the table and leaned forward, peering at her with impatient eyes. "Explain to me how I can release him if he doesn't have an address."

Lynda didn't hesitate. "Your honor, he's going to get an address very soon, but he has to be out of jail to do so. He was just evicted the day before yesterday. Yesterday he was arrested. He hasn't had time to find a place for his family to live."

The judge shook his head. "I'm sorry, but in light of the fact that this is a murder charge, and he is homeless, I can't in good conscience release him. It's hard enough to keep up with people until a trial when they do have an address. When they don't have one, it's just impossible."

"But your honor, it's not his fault he was evicted!"

"Your honor," the prosecutor interrupted. "The fact is, the murder followed the eviction. The murdered party was his landlord. It seems obvious to me that his homelessness and the murder that took place shortly thereafter are related, so I strongly advise you not to let this man back onto the streets."

The judge nodded as he looked back over the papers. "I'm sorry, Miss Barrett, but unless a man has an address, there's no way that I can release him. I'm afraid you're going to have to stay in jail pending the Grand Jury investigation, Mr. Robinson."

"No!" Anne cried, springing up. Jenny began to wail, covering her face and shaking her head.

Suddenly, Sharon rose. "Your honor."

The outburst surprised the judge, and he looked back into the crowd, trying to figure out who had had the audacity to interrupt his court proceedings.

"Your honor," she said again, drawing his attention to her. "I am Ben Robinson's ex-wife. My name is Sharon Robinson. And he does have an address."

The judge looked back at his papers. "Well, it says here—"

"Your information is out-of-date," she said, slipping out of the row she was sitting in and heading toward the bench. "Your honor, Ben and his family are going to stay with me until he's acquitted."

Jenny caught her breath.

Ben looked at her as if she had just turned into a chicken and begun to cluck.

Sharon couldn't believe what she had just done. She looked back at her older daughter, saw the gratitude in her eyes, and hoped that, alone, would be enough to see her through this.

"Your honor, I'm absolutely certain that my ex-husband did not commit this crime. And to prove that, I'm willing to have him and his family live in my home until the hearing. They will have an address, your honor."

The judge looked dumbfounded.

"Well, uh, Mrs. Robinson—it is Robinson, isn't it?"

"Yes," she said.

"This is highly unusual, and it's against my better judgment. The man doesn't have a criminal record, though, and looking out here at his family, I don't relish the thought of locking him up for an extended period of time. In my courtroom, I prefer to think that a man is innocent until proven guilty. Therefore, if I could have Miss Barrett's word that this is not some kind of farce, and that this man will not take this opportunity to skip the country, then I suppose I could grant you your request. I'll release him on $100,000 bond."

There was no relief in the breath Sharon took. In fact, it was full of dread.

Turning, she caught the full impact of Anne's reaction. Anne's eyes were narrowed, glaring with shock and anger, as if she had no intention of doing what Sharon had suggested.

"Thank you, your honor," Lynda said.

The gavel hammered again. The next case was called. And Ben was taken back out until his bond was posted.

Lynda hurried across the floor to Anne and Jenny to explain the procedure for posting bond. Sharon stood back, watching her teenager weep with a mixture of despair and relief.

Lynda ushered them from the courtroom, and Sharon followed them to the hall, keeping her distance as if she would be flogged if she were caught hanging too close. Christy spotted her and ran toward her, her bow bouncing as it slipped lower on her hair. "Mommy! Daddy got out of jail!"

"I know, honey," she said.

She looked toward them again, and saw Lynda starting back toward her. Her friend's eyes were sympathetic and grateful. Lynda hugged her. "That was a really great thing you did," she whispered.

Sharon's eyes were filling with tears already. "You can call for the men in the white coats now. I'm ready for them."

Lynda smiled. "It was the only way he could have gotten out," Lynda said.

"But how am I going to stand this?" she whispered. "I don't get along with his wife, and I barely get along with him."

"Then why did you do it?" Lynda asked.

Sharon glanced at Jenny, still weeping openly with joy. Christy wasn't sure what was going on, but she had gone back to Emily and was holding her hands and jumping up and down. "I did it for my children," she said. "It would kill them to think of their father in jail for any length of time. I'm not going to make them go through that."

"So instead you would put yourself through this?"

Sharon breathed a deep breath and wilted. "Don't overpraise it, Lynda. I wish I could say I'm doing this out of the goodness of my heart, but I'm afraid I'm going to spend the next few weeks seething. But I know that Ben is not a murderer. And the sooner we prove it, the sooner this nightmare will be over."

CHAPTER ELEVEN

A n hour later, Sharon watched out the window as Ben's station wagon pulled into her driveway. She could just imagine what had taken place when Ben had encountered Anne. He'd probably been lambasted. By now, the whole idea of moving in with her husband's ex-wife had probably sunk in, and Anne must be livid.

Ben got out of the car with the baby on his hip and grabbed one of the suitcases he had stuffed in the back. Anne lingered behind as if to busy herself with something—anything—to delay her entrance into the home.

Ben came tentatively to the open door and peered inside. "Hi," he said.

"Hi," Sharon returned, all business. "Come on in. I'm putting you and Anne in the bedroom at the back, third door on the left down the hall. Emily can sleep with Christy upstairs in Christy's room, and I got our old crib out of the attic for Bobby. He'll be in the room next to you."

Ben whistled under his breath. "I guess I've never been farther in than the den. I didn't realize you have two extra bedrooms."

"It's a big house," Sharon admitted.

He stood there staring at her for a moment, holding that baby on his hip. If he'd been anyone else, she would have been reaching to hold the baby by now. She had always wanted another one of her own. But now she tried not to even look his way as he came in.

"This was really nice of you, Sharon," he said. "You didn't have to do it. It was the last thing I expected."

She turned away and began chopping carrots on the big island at the center of her kitchen. "I *did* have to do it," she said. "I saw the look on my daughters' faces. And last night, Christy was so upset—I'd do anything to spare the children from the pain of seeing their father stay in jail."

"Well, whatever the motive, I appreciate it."

A moment of loud silence passed between them as Sharon continued chopping the carrots.

"I didn't kill him, Sharon."

Sharon turned back to him and looked down at the floor, studying the big square parquet tiles. "I know you didn't, Ben."

"I'm gonna get out of this," he said. "I know it looks pretty hopeless, but I've got to fight it."

"I know."

She heard Emily and Christy giggling and chattering as they walked up to the house.

Anne, on the other hand, was still bitterly angry. She marched into the house carrying a box and wearing a sour look on her otherwise pretty face. Sharon had trouble looking at her. She always had. "Hello, Anne."

Anne's face was red as she lifted her chin and faced Sharon. "I want you to know that I'm against this," she said. "I don't like it a bit."

Sharon nodded. "That's fair."

"I don't really know why you did it," she went on, tears filling her pale blue eyes. "But I don't trust you. I don't want any favors from you."

Sharon fought the urge to rail back at her that the last thing on earth she wanted was to do Anne Robinson any favors, but instead, she turned back to the carrots. "It doesn't look like you have a choice," she bit out.

"Maybe not for now," Anne told her. "But the minute I can get into my own place, we'll be out of here."

"Come on, Anne," Ben said cautiously. "We need to be thanking her instead of badgering her."

Anne turned on him then. "Don't you dare defend your ex-wife to me!"

"I'm not defending her," he said. "I'm just trying to point out that you're being a little irrational. We don't have a place to live, so she offered us her home."

Thick silence stretched out over agonizing seconds as Anne struggled with the emotions battling on her face . . . anger, humiliation, pride, distress. Finally, Ben handed the baby to her. "We're at the back room on the left. Why don't you take Bobby and go get settled in?"

"I've got a roast in the oven," Sharon said to Anne's back as she left the room. "It's for dinner tonight."

Anne shot her a scathing look, as if about to tell her that that dinner would go uneaten, but then she looked down at Emily and her face softened. The child would have to eat, as would the baby and her husband. Anne herself might fast for as long as she was here, but not her family.

Sharon almost felt sorry for Anne as she left the room, carrying her box of meager belongings in one arm and the baby in the other.

Jenny, who must have pulled into the driveway behind Anne and Ben, came to the door, her eyes lit up like a little girl in a doll shop at Christmas. Christy and Emily were on her heels. "Oh, Mom, you are so awesome! This is gonna be so great!" She threw her arms around her mother again, almost knocking her down.

Christy took Emily's hands and began dancing with her, her long blonde hair bouncing. "Emily gets to live with us! Emily gets to live with us! Mommy, it's gonna be so much fun! And Daddy'll be here right where we live, and we can see him all the time."

Bitterness welled back up in Sharon. If it hadn't been for Ben's recklessness with their marriage, Christy would never have had to know what it was like not to have her father living with them.

She turned back to the carrots, all her compassion for Ben slipping away. "Well, you guys have a lot of work to do," she said quickly. "Christy and Emily, why don't you go unpack? Give her some of your drawers, Christy. You two will be sharing a room."

The little girls squealed with delight, and ran up the stairs to Christy's bedroom. Ben followed them, knowing not to push Sharon any further.

When Jenny and Sharon were the only two in the kitchen, Jenny asked, "Mom, are you all right?"

"I'm fine. But Jenny, this isn't gonna be easy."

"I know," Jenny said softly. "But it'll work out. You'll see."

Sharon checked the stove, as if something might have changed in the last half hour since she'd put the roast in. If it hadn't been an electric oven, she might have considered sticking her head in it.

"Mom, I know you and Anne don't like each other."

Sharon breathed a laugh and closed the oven. "Now, there's an understatement."

"But don't you see?" Jenny asked. "That just makes it all so much greater. I mean, what you did. Letting her come live here, and Dad, and the kids. I mean, it's easy to do nice things for people you like, but when you do it for people you don't like . . ."

Sharon stiffened and turned around. "I did it, okay, Jenny? You don't have to keep on with this."

"But Mom, I mean it."

Sharon sighed and went to the medicine cabinet to look for aspirin. "I'm getting a headache."

"Maybe you and Anne will become friends," Jenny suggested. "She's really nice, most of the time. We've gotten to be kind of close, and—"

"I think the best we can hope is that we'll learn to tolerate each other," Sharon interrupted, hating the bitterness rising inside her. "And we've got a long way to go."

Jenny put her arms around Sharon's neck and forced her to look at her. She was as tall as her mother already, and it amazed Sharon that she had been as small as Christy not so long ago. Time was flying. Finding it hard to hold onto her bitterness with that sweet face smiling at her, she returned the hug.

"I love you, Mom. And you really are living your faith. I'm sorry about what I said yesterday."

"Oh, that's okay," Sharon said, letting her go. "I knew it was just manipulation."

"Hey, that's my job," Jenny said. She stepped back and gave her mother a serious look. "I'll help while they're here. It'll be good for me, too. I'll learn responsibility. I can help with Bobby and the kids. It'll be nice to have them around the house, won't it, Mom? To have the house full of kids?"

Sharon sighed. "Jenny, I know this is going to be fun for you. But I hope you'll be sensitive to the fact that some of us won't take very well to it. Not only that, but your father could still wind up in prison."

"He won't, Mom," Jenny said. "We're gonna find out who really killed Mr. Dubose. We're gonna prove he's innocent."

The determined tone in Jenny's voice alarmed her. An image flashed through Sharon's mind: Jenny out scavenging the streets in search of the real murderer. She took Jenny by the shoulders and looked straight into her eyes. "You are going to stay out of it. You are not going to pry around to find Mr. Dubose's murderer. Do you understand me? We're talking *murder* here. This is dangerous."

Jenny hesitated. "Mom, somebody's got to do something."

"I'll do everything I can," Sharon promised her. "I have as much at stake now as you do."

"What do you mean by that?"

"The sooner we clear your father, the sooner they can go back to their own lives."

Jenny's face fell so hard that Sharon thought she heard it crash. "Yeah, I guess it's not forever, is it?"

Sharon almost laughed, but she stopped herself. "No, honey, it's not forever. Now why don't you go help the girls get Emily's things put away?"

Jenny's mood changed quickly, and as she whirled to jog up the stairs, Sharon noticed the bounce in her step and the joy in her eyes that her family had finally been grafted back together again.

Anne had managed to get Bobby to sleep by the time Ben made it back to the bedroom. As he entered, she was sitting on the window seat, gazing out over the backyard. There were plenty of trees, and a swing set for Christy, and that tree house that Sharon had hired someone to build. It was clear from the way she gazed out the window that Anne envied Sharon's home.

He stood behind her and began to massage her shoulders. "You okay?"

When she looked up at him, he saw the tension on her face. "This is hard, Ben. Really hard."

"It doesn't have to be. The kids are thrilled."

"The kids don't have a clue." She jerked away from his massaging hands, got up, and went across the room to the suitcase. As she began to unpack, tears came to her eyes. "How did all this happen?"

"It'll be okay," he said. "Just trust me."

"I *have* trusted you," she snapped. "When I told you I was worried about our being so dependent on the gallery, you said to trust you. When I told you that we needed our own home for security, you said to trust you."

"Owning our own home wouldn't have helped us today, Anne. I still would have been set up for murder charges."

"Yes, but we could have gone back to our own house, instead of living off of your ex-wife." She stopped and looked up at him, her eyes tormented. "It's humiliating, Ben. It's my worst nightmare."

"You're being melodramatic," he said.

"No, I'm not!"

"Look, if you're worried about something going on between Sharon and me, it won't. I'm married to you now."

"Being married didn't stop you before, did it?"

It was a low blow, and he took a step back. "If I recall, you played a part in that, too."

She didn't like being reminded of that, so she turned back to the suitcase and jerked out a stack of his shirts.

"Anne, look at the bright side. I get to be with my kids. Emily and Christy get to be together."

"That's right," she said, swinging around again. "One big happy family, huh? Just like it was before I came into the picture. Daddy and Mommy back in the same house. The only thing wrong with this picture is me!"

He turned to the window. "Anne, it may not have occurred to you, but I'm the one who spent the night in jail. To have to come crawling to my ex-wife for help, to let my kids see me destitute and in trouble—you think I wanted it this way?"

"I don't *know* what you wanted," she said, flinging more clothes into the drawer. "I have no idea. All I know is that your name is being smeared all over the papers as a common murderer, and you've got me living in my archenemy's house. From where I stand, life with you isn't looking too good right now."

Ben looked back at her. "Anne, I need you to pull yourself together. You're my only alibi. If you start falling apart—"

"Alibi?" she almost shouted, then quickly lowered her voice. "That's another thing, Ben. I told them I was with you the whole time yesterday, but the truth is, I wasn't. When you went for that walk, you were gone over an hour."

"We needed some distance, Anne—because we were fighting, just like we are now," he said. "What do you think? That I jogged over to the gallery and killed Louis in that hour?"

"No!" she cried. "I don't think that. But *they* might if they knew!"

"Then don't tell them!"

She turned away and jerked another stack of clothes out of the suitcase. "This is a nightmare, Ben. I hate it."

"So do you want out? Is that it?"

"Out of what?"

"The marriage. The commitment to stand behind me no matter how tough things get."

"Where would I go, Ben?" she asked through compressed lips. "Whatever money I came into this marriage with is gone now. I can't even afford to take my child to the doctor. And I'm not really up to taking more money from your beloved ex!"

"Then get a job! If you're so dead set on getting away from me, then make some money and leave!"

"I'm not leaving without my kids, Ben."

"And I'm not letting you take them."

"Fine." Her face was reddening, and she crumpled over and dropped on the bed, breathing out a heavy sigh. "I'm stuck with you, then."

Ben had never been one to keep the tough-guy act going when a woman started to cry, so he sat down on the bed next to her and let out a ragged breath. Putting his arms around her, he pulled her against him. "Look, I've messed up once before, and my kids had to pay for it. I don't want another family to break up. Please, just relax and try to get through this. We can do it. We've had tough times before."

"Not like these," she cried.

"No, and neither have the kids. We have to be strong for them."

She tried to pull herself together. Wiping her face, she said, "I'm tired, Ben. I haven't slept since we left our apartment. How many days ago was that?"

"We've only been gone two nights. But I know how you feel. I haven't slept much, either. Can we just write this fight off to fatigue? Can we just forget the stuff about leaving each other for now?"

Again, she pulled away. "I don't know, Ben. I just don't know how much more of this I can take."

"You need rest," he said. "Why don't you take a nap while Bobby's asleep? It may not last long. If he wakes up, I'll take care of him."

"And what will you be doing?" she asked suspiciously. "Puttering around in the kitchen with your first wife?"

He sighed. "No, Anne. You don't have to fear Sharon. I'm the last man on earth she'd be interested in now."

"Oh, great," she said. "But if she were interested, it wouldn't be a problem for you, right?"

"Wrong. You're putting words in my mouth."

"No. I'm just interpreting them." She got up and started out of the room. "I don't think I can sleep right now. I'll go help Emily get unpacked."

Sharon decided to set the table alone, dreading the moment when everyone came to the table. When she'd finally gotten all the food into serving bowls and put them on the breakfast counter so that everyone could serve themselves, smorgasbord-style, she went to round everyone up.

Ben was on the telephone in her study talking to Lynda about the possibility of hiring a private investigator to try to find the real killer. Sharon knew that she would have to foot the bill for that, and the fact that he hadn't even asked her made her angry. On the other hand, it was worth whatever it cost to get Ben off the hook and out of her home. Jenny, who seemed not to know the purpose of chairs, sat on the floor in front of him, listening intently.

She told them both to come to the table. "Where's Anne?" she asked Jenny before she left the room.

"I think she's watching TV with the girls. I'll tell her."

"That's all right," Sharon said, determined not to let her feelings inhibit her. "I'll tell her myself."

She walked up the hall and went into the den. Christy sat on the floor next to Emily, both of them engrossed in some sleazy tabloid show that she normally didn't allow Christy to watch. Since it was just going off and a preview of the news was flashing on, she let it go. Anne sat in a recliner staring at the screen, but Sharon suspected that she didn't see any of it. Her mind seemed a million miles away.

"It's time for dinner, everybody," Sharon said in a light, upbeat voice. "Wash your hands, girls."

"Okay, Mommy." Christy got up to reach for the remote control. But just before she could turn the television off, the news came on—and a picture of her father flashed across the screen as the headline story. "A local man is the primary suspect in . . ."

"Mommy, look! It's Daddy!" Christy shouted.

Sharon froze, and Anne slowly leaned forward. "Ben Robinson, local artist, was arraigned today on murder charges. The gallery owner where he worked was found dead—" As the anchor spoke, footage showed the body covered with a sheet being wheeled out on a gurney. "And evidence points to the disgruntled artist who lived in the studio and had been fired the day of the shooting. We'll have this and other stories when we return in a moment."

Sharon rushed forward to turn off the television as Christy and Emily gaped up at her, their eyes round with horror over the image of the dead man in their father's gallery. The man the newscaster said their father had killed.

"Go wash your hands, girls," Sharon snapped.

Christy couldn't move. "Mommy, is that the man they said Daddy—"

"Your father didn't kill anyone," Sharon said quickly. She turned to Anne angrily. "I would think you'd be a little more careful about what the children watched, especially today."

Anne bristled. "I had no idea that was about to come on. You were standing there, too."

"But I never would have allowed them to watch that stupid tabloid show. Whatever happened to Barney?"

Anne's tired face reddened. "This isn't about Barney or a tabloid show, Sharon. At least have the decency to say what you mean."

The girls left the room quickly, and Sharon watched them go, flustered. "You're right," she said through her teeth. "It isn't about the tabloid show. It's about them seeing their father called a murderer on television. We're going to have to be careful and monitor what they watch. Any fool would know that today of all days—"

"Oh, that does it!" Anne said, springing out of her chair and heading for the door. Sharon watched her, furious, and saw the girls still hovering together in the hall. "Girls, I said to go wash your hands!" she yelled.

Anne spun around. "Hey—you can order your kids around, but leave mine alone!"

"Fine," Sharon grated through her teeth. "Dinner's ready." She stormed out of the room, but Anne was right behind her.

"Hey, you know, this wasn't my idea. I don't like it. Like you said, I'm here because I have no choice."

"I know that," Sharon said. "But I did have a choice. I invited you to come here of my own free will."

"Why?" Anne shouted. "What's in it for you?"

Sharon stopped midstride and spun around to face Anne. "My children love their father, and it killed them to know he was in jail. I did it for them, not for either one of you!" she returned. "But that doesn't change the fact that I have rules in this house about television, and I don't want my children watching graphic images on the news about how their father murdered some guy—"

Ben walked in and Sharon stopped in midsentence.

"What are you guys talking about?" he asked.

"The news!" Sharon blurted.

"Yeah," Anne said, turning on him and beginning to cry again. "You're already all over it. Everybody we know is going to think you're a killer. You're a disgruntled employee, after all!"

"The news?" he asked.

Sharon knew she shouldn't add fuel to this fire, but she felt the need to enlist Ben's help. "Ben, your wife just let your children see Dubose's dead body being taken out of the gallery."

"Give me a break!" Anne shouted. "I had no more idea that was coming on than you did!"

"You should be more careful!" Sharon yelled.

Jenny walked into the room, carrying Bobby. "You woke him," she said quietly.

The censure in her voice stopped them both, and Sharon felt like a child being reprimanded by a teacher. Gritting her teeth, she went into the kitchen and began sticking serving spoons into the bowls. "Someone's gonna have to start eating," she said through gritted teeth. "Come on, Jenny. Eat!"

Jenny put the baby into the high chair that hooked onto the edge of the table and began to fix herself a plate. Sharon heard Anne whispering behind her to Ben, and she wanted to scream. Instead she just decided to leave the room.

"Where are you going, Mom?" Jenny asked when she was almost out of the kitchen.

"To find Christy and Emily," she said. "They ran out of the room upset."

Jenny shot a glance to her father and Anne, then silently took her plate to the table.

In her room, Sharon closed the door of her bedroom and struggled with the emotions coursing through her. She wanted to tell Anne to get herself and her family out of her house, and not to expect any more help from her. But the truth, Sharon admitted, was that she hadn't done what she'd done for Anne's sake at all— she'd done it for Jenny, and she'd done it for Christy. And she had

65

even done it for Ben, though he was the last person she ever wanted to feel compassion for.

Her only choice now was to quickly get this murder resolved so that they could get out of her house.

She picked up the phone and dialed Lynda's number.

"Hello?"

"Lynda, it's me," Sharon said.

"How's it going?" Lynda asked knowingly.

Sharon couldn't even speak for a moment. "Lynda, you've got to help me."

"I'm doing everything I can."

"I know," Sharon said. "But I mean, *really* help me. I'll pay for the private detective you were talking to Ben about, no matter what it costs. We've got to find out who really killed Dubose and get Ben off the hook so we can get them out of my house."

Lynda was quiet for a moment. "What happened?"

"Let's just say that Anne and I rub each other the wrong way. There's so much friction that I'm afraid I'll catch fire."

Sharon could hear the smile in Lynda's voice. "Well, I had a feeling that might be a problem."

"He's being set up, Lynda. Someone's framing him. And it couldn't be that hard to figure out who."

"That's my thinking exactly," Lynda said. "Look, relax and try to get through this. I know this is hard for you, but as soon as I find out anything I'll be in touch. I know Ben's life hangs in the balance. Trust me, I'm not taking this lightly."

"I know you're not," Sharon said, falling back on her bed. "But you've been a little distracted lately with Jake and falling in love and all that kind of stuff—"

"You act like I'm a boy-crazy teenager."

"Call it jealousy," Sharon said, her tone serious. "I just can't remember what it's like."

Lynda chuckled. "Well, having Ben around might remind you a little bit."

Sharon quickly shook her head. "I'm wondering what I ever saw in the man in the first place."

"See how far you've come since the divorce? There was a time when you thought your life was over, and that you'd never get over Ben. Now you can't even remember feeling that way."

"I guess God has a way of anesthetizing us against those painful memories," she said. "And time heals. As far as I'm concerned, I wish Anne and him the utmost happiness—far, far away from here. Meanwhile, I just have to keep reminding myself that this is the right thing to do."

"It is," Lynda said. "There didn't seem to be an alternative— at least not one that would be fair to the kids. But you'll be all right. You're a sweet lady, and God can use you in this."

"You're a good friend, Lynda," Sharon said. "And a pathetic optimist."

"Let's hope I'm a good lawyer. Ben's gonna need one."

CHAPTER TWELVE

E ric Boudreaux sat in his opulent suite at the Tampa Biltmore, studying the stock quotes in the newspaper that had been delivered to his suite that morning. His appointment was in less than two hours, but he still hadn't heard from Louis Dubose.

The television news droned in the corner. Occasionally, he glanced up to see if anything interested him.

"... art gallery owner Louis Dubose ..."

Startled, Boudreaux looked up at the screen to see the face of the man he had never met before, except by phone. Leaning forward, he grabbed the remote and turned the volume up.

"... was found dead after being shot in the back. Police sources say the gun, which was found in a dumpster near the gallery, was registered to Benjamin L. Robinson, a local artist who was residing in the gallery. According to sources, Robinson was fired and evicted the day of the murder ..."

Eric listened, stunned, trying to follow the words, but all he was certain of was that Dubose was dead. How could that be?

He had flown from France for this very appointment, anxious to get his hands on the prize that would make him even richer than he already was. If Dubose was dead—

The phone rang, and he snatched it up. "Boudreaux," he said in his heavy French accent.

"Yes, Mr. Boudreaux," a voice said cheerily. "So nice to hear your voice. I trust your flight was a good one?"

Boudreaux frowned. "Who is this?"

"My name is John Lieber, and I'm a close friend and colleague of Louis Dubose. I'm afraid I have bad news."

Boudreaux looked back at the screen, but a commercial was playing now. "Yes. The murder."

"The murder," the man said sadly. "You've heard the news, then. Our friend was murdered brutally. A terrible thing. So unexpected."

Boudreaux was quiet. Dubose had not mentioned another contact, although Boudreaux had suspected that he wasn't involved in this business alone. He would act cautiously, he thought. It was difficult to trust Americans, and he did not like doing business with them.

"I was Dubose's partner in our little enterprise," the man said. "And I see no reason that it can't go on as planned. I'd still like to meet with you and make the exchange."

"You have it?" Boudreaux asked hopefully, his thick eyebrows arching.

"It's in a safe place," Lieber said. "It may take me a short while to secure it."

"How long?" Boudreaux asked. "I must return to France."

"Just another day or two. I give you my word it will be worth your time. After all, you didn't come all this way just to return home empty-handed."

Boudreaux considered that for a moment. He couldn't take the chance of walking into a trap. He had an impeccable reputation, and no one had ever suspected him of being involved in anything that wasn't legal. What if somehow he had come under suspicion, and international art detectives were setting him up? Things weren't going smoothly enough. Yet he wanted what he had come here for . . .

"How . . ." He tried to put the words together correctly. "How may I trust you?"

"You *have* to trust me," Lieber said, "because I have the greatest find in the art world this century. If you don't trust me, you'll lose out."

Boudreaux nodded slightly, but didn't say a word.

"Please. Just stay where you are for another day or, at the most, two. I'll be back in touch as soon as we can make the exchange. Dubose would have wanted it this way. He wouldn't have wanted this sale to be jeopardized because of some unfortunate circumstances."

Boudreaux wasn't convinced. His instincts all screamed for him to get on the plane and head back out of the country. But Lieber was right. This was the find of the century.

"I will stay until I hear from you," he said grudgingly. "If I do not hear within two days, I will leave."

"Fair enough," the man said. "I'll be in touch. And Mr. Boudreaux? You won't regret this."

CHAPTER THIRTEEN

The children were missing.

While the others were looking inside, Ben went out back to see if they were in the yard. The little tree house nestled in the oak in the backyard was a new development since he'd last been here. Sharon had hired someone to build it for Christy because she loved to climb.

But building a tree house was the father's job. He should have been the one to design and execute it, and that bothered Ben as he peered up the ladder. It looked sound enough, though. The truth is, he probably couldn't have done a better job. But it was the principle of the thing. If Sharon had asked him, he'd have built the little house.

On the other hand, Anne would have probably had a fit about his being over here at all, and it would have gotten too complicated . . .

Sharon had probably done the right thing. Christy deserved a tree house. She shouldn't have to deal with the divorce fallout every time she wanted something. Besides, her mother could afford it. Despite the financial pit Ben had left her in, Sharon had thrived since the divorce. She had a way of always bouncing back. No matter how bad things looked, good things came out of it for her. She was lucky that way.

His luck hadn't been so good.

He heard crying in the tree house. Gripping the rungs, he slowly started up the ladder. He got to the hatch at the bottom and knocked lightly on the floor of the house. "Anybody home?"

The hatch opened and Christy's wet, red face greeted him. "Come in, Daddy. We're crying."

The announcement almost amused him, but when he pulled himself in, the sight broke his heart. Christy moved back to sit by Emily. They both sat Indian style, holding hands as they wept.

"What's wrong, girls?" he asked softly.

They looked at each other. "Nothing."

Ben climbed farther up into the tree house and tested the boards to see if it would hold him. It had been well built, he admitted. But these days Sharon did everything first-class. She had the money to.

He sat down on the floor next to Christy, and Emily climbed into his lap. He pulled Christy up onto his other leg and held both of his children tight. "Now, tell Daddy what's wrong."

"It was the news, Daddy," Christy said. "They said you killed Mr. Dubose."

"You know I didn't. You do know that, don't you?"

"But we're scared."

"You know Daddy didn't kill anybody, don't you?" he asked again.

Both of the girls nodded, and fresh tears rolled down their faces. Ben buried his face in Christy's hair.

"Girls, this is the worst time in Daddy's life. Sometimes things just don't go like you plan. But I didn't kill Mr. Dubose, and I'm gonna find out who did, and it's gonna be okay. Let's look at the good side," he said, trying to cheer his daughters up. "We're all here in the same house together."

"But Mommy hates Miss Sharon," Emily said, rubbing her eyes.

Ben shook his head, saddened by the complications adults, in their weakness, throw at the children who depend on them. He kissed his youngest daughter's cheek. "Honey, it's just real hard for them. They were both married to me, and it's kind of weird, all of us living here together."

"Are they gonna fight all the time?" Emily asked.

"Let's hope not."

Christy touched Ben's face, rubbing the rough growth of stubble. He hadn't shaved since they'd been evicted. "I've been praying for you, Daddy."

"I know, sweetheart," Ben said. "You just keep right on doing that."

He looked around at the little building they sat in. "I haven't been up here before, Christy. Nice place you've got here."

"Thank you," she said, wiping her face.

"But it needs a little paint, doesn't it?"

She looked around as if she'd never noticed it before.

"I tell you what," he said. "Since I'm gonna be here with nothing to do for a little while, maybe we can start a project."

"What kind of project?" Emily asked, her face brightening. "You mean a painting project?"

Emily loved to paint, but his studio had always been off-limits to her. The idea of being involved in one of his projects now had enough appeal to distract her from her sorrow.

"Yeah," he said. "How about if we come up here tomorrow and start painting? We could paint the walls, and the floor, and the ceiling, and—"

"We could paint pictures on it," Christy piped in.

"Sure, we could paint a mural. It would be gorgeous."

"Nobody can paint a mural like you can," Emily said.

"All right, then, we have some plans to make. I want you two to go inside and eat supper, and then after supper, get some paper and draw pictures just like what you want on the walls of the house."

"Can we paint on the outside, too, Daddy?" Christy asked.

"Sure we can. We'll paint anything you want, as long as we clear it with your mom."

Christy and Emily forgot their grief as their minds reeled with possibilities. Ben wiped both their faces and kissed them on the cheeks.

"I love you guys."

"I love you, too, Daddy," they each said.

"Now, go in and eat supper. Your moms are worried about you. Then you can get started on the designs. I'm just gonna sit up here for a minute by myself."

He watched as they scurried down the ladder, and for a moment he hesitated, thinking about what had just taken place. Here he sat in the little tree house built by someone that his ex-wife had hired because Ben himself was no longer a factor in their family. And here were his two children, one from each marriage, best friends and loving each other as sisters. Now, arrested for murder, he was back in the home, but with his new wife and children . . .

Nothing about this was natural. It was as bizarre a set of circumstances as he could have imagined.

How in the world had he come to this? No job, no income, facing the possibility of going to prison . . .

The depression and anger that had been pulling him like quicksand since Dubose had fired him pulled him further under. Miserably, he slipped out of the hatch and climbed back down the ladder.

Sharon didn't have an appetite for the meal she'd cooked, so she stayed away until everyone had left the table. Then she ventured back into the kitchen to clean up. Anne was already loading the dishwasher, and when she looked up, Sharon saw that she was crying.

Sharon pretended not to notice.

"I'm cleaning up," Anne said.

"That's all right," Sharon told her. "I can do it. Why don't you go take care of the kids?"

As if Sharon's words had been an indictment, Anne dropped the pot on the counter and wiped her eyes. "Look, Sharon, the kids are being taken care of. They're playing upstairs, and Jenny's with them. Don't act like I'm neglecting them."

"I didn't say that," Sharon said. "Did I say that?"

"I know what you were thinking."

"All right," Sharon said, crossing her arms and squaring off with the woman. "What was I thinking, exactly?"

"You were thinking that you've waited six years to see us in this position," Anne said, tossing down the hand towel she was holding. "You were thinking that we deserve all this, and you're secretly delighted that we're in all this trouble."

"That's not true," Sharon said. "And I resent it."

"I can see right through all your generosity, Sharon!"

"That's enough, Anne." The words were Ben's, and both women swung around.

Anne's tears came harder now. "Don't you dare defend her!"

"I'm not defending her," Ben said. "She doesn't need defending. Now calm down." He crossed the room and cupped his wife's chin. "Anne, look at me," he said.

She looked up at him with her red, furious eyes.

"You're really stressed out, honey, and I understand that. So am I. But lashing out at Sharon is not going to help. It'll just make things worse, and we need to concentrate and keep our heads clear right now, okay? We don't have time for all this bickering."

She fell against him, and he held her for a moment, letting her cry. Sharon turned away, suddenly feeling like an intruder in her own home.

"Look, you go lie down," he whispered to Anne. "You need a break. Just go take a nap, and let Jenny look after the kids. She loves it."

"But Bobby's sick. It's almost time for his cough medicine."

"I'll give it to him," Ben said. "Go on now. I need you to be rested. There are going to be a lot of sleepless nights between now and the Grand Jury hearing."

Sharon watched her leave the room. Ben turned back to Sharon and shot her an apologetic look. "Sharon, I'm sorry. She's not herself. She's usually a sweet, warm person. Once you get to know her—"

"Spare me." Sharon turned away and started wiping the counters.

Ben's voice trailed off, as though he knew his mouth was leading him down the wrong path. "Okay, never mind. Listen, if you don't mind, I need to make some calls. Do you mind if I use your study?"

"Fine," Sharon said. "Oh, and if you need to paint, we could probably find some place around here for you to do it."

He shrugged. "Thanks a lot. I'm just not feeling real creative right now. I did promise the girls we'd do some painting in the tree house, though. You don't mind, do you?"

"No, I think it's a good idea. It's about time Christy's father got involved in her life." She turned back to the dishes and began scrubbing them with a vengeance.

Ben couldn't think of a response that wouldn't just make things worse, so he started out of the room. The phone rang, and he turned back. "I'll get it. It might be Lynda."

He picked it up. "Hello?"

He hesitated, then in an agitated voice, asked, "Who is this?"

Sharon turned around. "Who?" she whispered. He only shook his head, indicating that he didn't know.

"What are you talking about?" His face began to redden. "I have no idea what you're talking about!"

"What is it?" Sharon asked in an urgent whisper.

Ben put his hand over the phone. "Call the police," he mouthed. "Trace the call."

"It's him?" she asked in disbelief. "The killer?"

He nodded frantically and gestured for her to hurry.

As Sharon rushed to the car where she could call from her cellular phone, Ben continued the conversation. "You've got to tell me what you're looking for," she heard him say. "I can't read your mind."

She reached the garage and threw open her car door, and frantically dialed 911 on her cellular phone. After hearing what she had to say, the dispatcher transferred her. She waited, on hold, wishing someone would pick up.

After a moment, Ben burst through the door with Anne on his heels. "Do you have the police department?"

"Yes," she said. "But it takes an act of Congress to speak to the right person. I'm on hold—"

"He's looking for something," Ben cut in, raking his hand through his long hair. "I don't know what it is. He wants me to leave it at the airport at 10:30 tonight, but I have no idea what he's talking about. He threatened me. Said he'd go into the next phase of this nightmare if I didn't bring him what he wants."

"Well, what could it be?" Anne asked. "Didn't he give you a clue? Are you supposed to guess?"

"He thinks I already know," Ben said. "That's what's so bizarre."

Giving up, Sharon slammed the phone down. "Come on, Ben, we've got to go to the police station."

Anne looked stunned. "He doesn't need you to go with him."

Sharon felt reprimanded and quickly got out of the car. "You're right. Go! Somebody needs to tell somebody. Here. Take my car so you can call Lynda on the way. She probably needs to know about this."

Ben looked back toward the house. "What about the kids?"

"We'll take care of them," Sharon said. "Between Jenny and me they'll be okay."

Anne started running back into the house. "I'm not leaving Bobby. I'll take him with us."

Sharon looked as if she'd been slapped down, but she said nothing.

As they waited, Ben tried to work back through the conversation. "He said to get a black Travel-Lite garment bag from Walmart. That's what I'm supposed to deliver it in. He was very specific that it had to be that brand."

Sharon frowned, wondering why. "Well . . . all right. I'll leave Jenny with the girls and I'll run to Walmart and get one while you're gone. Who knows? Maybe it'll come to you. Maybe you'll figure out what he's looking for."

He nodded. "If the police believe me, this could clear me, Sharon. If they could catch him tonight . . . I could be off the hook."

New hope brightened her eyes. "That's right!"

Anne came back out, carrying Bobby with one arm and the diaper bag and her purse on the other. "Okay, let's go. I'm ready."

"Good luck," Sharon told him. "And don't forget to call Lynda. She probably needs to meet you at the station."

CHAPTER FIFTEEN

ony Danks scribbled on a legal pad as Ben related the phone conversation, every nuance of his body suggesting that he didn't believe a word of it. Larry Millsaps looked doubtful, too, though his eyes remained focused on Ben's as he spoke. Lynda sat beside Ben, occasionally prodding him with more questions that she thought might strengthen his story. Anne stood in the corner of the room, quietly swaying to keep Bobby from waking up.

"So ... did you record this phone conversation?" Tony asked without looking up from his scribblings when Ben finished the story.

"No," Ben said. "Of course not. I didn't know he was going to call."

"He already told you that Sharon tried to get a trace started, Tony. She got put on hold," Lynda pointed out.

"Did anyone pick up on another line and hear any part of the conversation?" Tony asked.

"No, I don't think so," Ben said. "Why?"

"I just wondered if there were any witnesses."

"Sharon saw me talking to him."

"Oh, that should hold up in court," Tony said sarcastically. "'Your honor, my wife saw me on the phone.' Case closed."

"She's not his wife," Anne clipped. "I am."

"Oh, that's right," Tony said. "He lives with both of you."

The statement only further inflamed Ben, and he stood up, knocking his chair back with a clatter. Leaning over the table, he asked, "What do I have to do to prove that he called?"

Tony glanced at Larry, who seemed to be deep in thought with his hands clasped in front of his face. "Well, we checked the phone records," Tony said. "There is a record of a call that came to that house at about that time, but it was from a pay phone. It really doesn't prove anything."

"Why not?" Ben asked. "The guy obviously didn't want the call traced."

"Because it could have been anyone," Tony said. "How do we know it wasn't a salesman or something? You could have played this out to throw us off your scent."

"Then come with me tonight," Ben said. "I'll deliver a black garment bag just like he said. Someone will pick it up, and you can get him. Then you'll see."

"What will you put in the garment bag?" Tony asked. "Your story is that you don't know what he wants, remember?"

Ben wanted to break something. "It's not a story, man! This is all so crazy, why would I make it up?"

"Why?" Tony laughed and glanced at his partner, who didn't join in his amusement. "Well, let's see. You've been accused of murder. All the evidence points to you. You're probably going to spend the rest of your life in prison—I don't know, Larry, can you think of any reason he'd want to make this up?"

"It's a pretty common ploy," Larry said matter-of-factly. "Cast suspicion on someone else. Try to get the magnifying glass off you."

Ben threw up his hands. "I don't *have* to make it up! I didn't do this! And I can't believe you morons are sitting on your duffs while some murderer is walking free out there. It hasn't even occurred to you that you could be wrong—that *if* I'm telling the truth, the trail of the real killer is getting cold while you just sit there. That's what's wrong with our criminal justice system. It depends on idiots like you!"

Lynda had stood up halfway through his outburst, and now touched Ben's arm to calm him down. "Come on, Ben. This won't get you anywhere." She looked back at the two cops, who looked more stubborn and determined than ever. "Gentlemen, if we have to tell a Grand Jury that we gave you the opportunity to catch the real criminal, and you declined, it isn't going to look good. And the fact that my client just called you idiots shouldn't change the way you investigate this crime at all. His temper may be on edge right now, but I'd say ours would be, too, if we'd been accused of a murder we didn't commit." She sat back down and leaned on the table to face Larry. "What do you say, Larry? Tony? Can't you at least escort him to the airport tonight? See what happens?"

Larry glanced at Tony and shook his head. "Lynda, if we jumped every time a suspect pointed us to someone else, we'd never get any sleep. I left before dawn this morning to investigate a shooting in a bar, and I'm tired. Besides, I have a wife at home who's expecting me for dinner."

"She understands what you do for a living," Lynda said. "If I know her as well as I think I do, she wouldn't want you to pin a murder on the wrong guy just so you could be on time for dinner. And we both know that you've gone without sleep to get the job done before this. What about you, Tony?"

Tony laughed under his breath. "So let me get this straight. After working fourteen hours today, I'm supposed to go with this guy to the Tampa Airport—which is roughly an hour from here—so that he can respond to a phone call he can't prove, by leaving an empty bag by a window so that an imaginary person can pick it up?"

"Forget it!" Ben said, shoving the chair again. "Just forget it. I'll go myself."

"No, you won't, pal," Larry said. "You're not allowed to leave town until you're cleared."

"What if he's telling the truth?" Lynda shouted, making them all look at her. "What if—just what *if*—he's telling you exactly like it happened? Whoever was on that phone *threatened* him if he didn't deliver that bag! Larry, put yourself in his shoes. What if it happened to you? What if you tried to tell the police everything that had happened, but they wouldn't listen?"

Something about those words softened Larry's face. He looked up at Ben, his eyes lingering pensively on him. Tony kept scribbling.

Anne stepped forward, her eyes full of tears. "I'll go."

Everyone looked up. "What?" Lynda asked.

She cleared her throat. "Somebody has to go. I'll do it. I'll take the bag and leave it where he said, if Ben can't leave town. Maybe that would be okay. And we can stick something in the bag. Even if it's not the right thing—what he's looking for—maybe it would be enough time for the security cameras to get a picture of him as he takes it. Or maybe I could take a camera and get his picture somehow . . ."

Ben slammed his fist against the wall. "No way! This guy's a murderer! I'm not letting my wife do this."

Larry shook his head.

"I can get permission from the judge to let Ben go," Lynda said. "But to do that, I'll have to explain how the police force refuses to cooperate."

Larry looked up, rubbing his fingers down his face, leaving it red. "Forget it, Lynda. I'll go with him."

"You will?" she asked.

"Yeah. And there'd better be something to see." He looked wearily at Tony, who rolled his eyes as if he couldn't believe his partner had caved in. "Are you in, Tony?"

Tony blew out a breath heavy enough to puff his cheeks. "I guess so."

"All right," Lynda said, getting down to business. "Now, I want you two to start thinking like cops. Think you're up to that?"

Neither of them appreciated the question, and neither answered.

"What should he put inside the bag? How does the man intend to get it without being seen? And why would he want such a specific brand of garment bag?"

"It's obvious," Tony said with a sigh. "It's the most common garment bag sold. This alleged criminal is probably going to bring one just like it and make a quick exchange. If he doesn't, we'll know that our friend here was pulling our strings all along."

Ben disregarded that. "What should I put in it? He didn't give me a clue about what he's looking for. It could be anything."

"It's obviously something that would look natural in a garment bag," Lynda said. "Maybe you should just pad it with pillows or something. You're just going to have to wing it."

Ben sighed. "All right. He said to set it beside the window next to Gate C–23 just after the last flight from Atlanta lands at 10:30."

"You'd better mark the bag, so that you can prove that he took yours. And guys—" She turned back to the two cops, who looked less than enthusiastic. "At the airport, shouldn't you be watching for anyone who has a bag like this? Maybe searching them?"

"Lynda," Tony said impatiently, "if there's a guy waiting to make an exchange, the last thing we'd want to do is alert him to the fact that we're there. Besides, if we catch him before the exchange, there won't be any clues that he's the guy. We'll call Tampa PD and Airport Security and let them know what's going on, and make sure a security camera is taping in that spot. If he makes the exchange, we'll be there, and we'll see him." But he didn't sound as if he expected to see anything.

"You'll have to get him immediately after the exchange," Ben said. "Otherwise, he'll see that he's been had, and he'll retaliate."

"Retaliate how?" Larry asked grudgingly.

"I don't know," Ben said. "But frankly, I'm not real anxious to find out. He's messed my life up enough as it is."

As Ben and Anne drove back to Sharon's house, Anne was quiet, brooding, and he knew what she was thinking. She was blaming him for all of this, and he supposed she had every right to.

Christy and Emily were sound asleep when they got in, and Jenny was upstairs working on something in her room. Sharon was closed into her bedroom as if she'd had enough of them all.

Quietly, they made their way through the house and put Bobby down into the crib.

They went to their bedroom, but the tension in the room was too stiff for either of them to relax. It was like the tension before he'd left Sharon, when she'd known he was having an affair: so thick you could slice it open.

"Why don't you go on to bed?" he asked. "I'll wake you when I get home."

She shook her head and sat down on the bed with her feet beneath her, looking like a little girl. "I won't be able to sleep until I know what happened."

He sat and put his arms around her. "It's gonna be okay. Tonight we'll catch the guy who's doing this to us, and by tomorrow they'll drop all charges against me."

"Then can we move out of this place?" she asked.

"Yes. I'll get Lynda to get a court order to get my paintings out of the gallery, and I'll find another gallery to display them. We'll be back on our feet in no time, and we won't depend on anyone else."

She seemed to relax.

The doorbell rang. Ben kissed her gently and got up. "Time to go," he said.

She looked so pale and tired that he hated to leave her. "Good luck," she said. "And be careful. *Please* be careful."

"I promise." He hurried out into the hall and saw Sharon on her way to answer the door. She was wearing a long robe, and her feet were bare beneath it.

"It's for me," he said in a low voice. "Tony Danks and Larry Millsaps. We're going to make the delivery. Did you get the bag?"

"Yes," she said. "It's on the couch." She followed him to the living room and answered the door as Ben examined the garment bag.

"Hi," she said to the two men as she let them in.

Tony Danks smiled at her. "Did we get you up?"

"No," she said. "I was waiting to see what came of this. You guys have a long drive to Tampa. Are you gonna make it?"

"If we leave now," Larry said, checking his watch. "It's 9:00. We should be there by ten." They stepped into the living room and saw Ben stuffing the garment bag with some wadded paper grocery sacks.

"What are you doing?" Tony asked.

"Filling the bag up. It has to at least look like it's holding something."

The two cops just stood back, hands in pockets, looking as if they couldn't care less whether the bag looked convincing or not.

"I'll drive in my car, in case he's watching for me," Ben said. "You guys can follow me."

"You try to get on a plane, Ben, my boy, and we'll drag you off before it's even off the ground," Tony said. "Got it?"

Ben's face hardened, and he shot Sharon a look. "They don't believe me," he said. "They think this is all a hoax."

Sharon caught her breath. "Then why are you going?" she asked the cops.

"Just doing our jobs," Larry said.

She moaned. "I can promise you that it's not a hoax. Please— don't drop the ball on this."

Tony smiled reassuringly. "We'll do the right thing, Ms. Robinson. You don't have to worry."

She looked at him uneasily. "All right. I guess you'll just have to see for yourself."

Ben lifted the bag. "I marked the bag with this yellow thread on the shoulder strap, so that if we don't see him take it, we can catch him with it afterward. It shouldn't be noticeable."

"Good thinking," Larry said, obviously humoring him.

Trying not to let their obstinacy distract him, Ben headed out the door and got into his car.

The two cops started to follow, but Sharon grabbed Tony's arm and stopped him before they were out the door. He towered over her, but she looked up at him with determination in her eyes. "I'm his *ex*-wife. I haven't been a fan of his in six years. But I can promise you that he's not lying. Please take this seriously."

His blue eyes softened, and he smiled slightly as he patted her hand where it still held his arm. "Don't worry," he said.

She stood at the door and watched as both cars pulled away.

At the airport, they parked in the short-term parking area. After watching to see that Larry and Tony were behind him, Ben got out and took the garment bag from his backseat. Carrying it by the hook at the top and slung over his shoulder, he headed into the airport.

He paused at the flight schedule monitor and scanned it for the last flight coming in from Atlanta. It was ten minutes late, he saw, and coming in at Gate C–23.

Tony followed him up the stairs, then watched him stop at the security gate to lay his bag on the belt. As it made its way through the X-ray, he glanced around.

He grabbed the bag when it reached the end, headed to the C terminal, and counted off the gates.

Tony slowed his step as Ben reached the gate where a couple of dozen people milled around, waiting for the plane from Atlanta to arrive. Ben went to the window where the caller had told him to leave the bag, and keeping it hanging over his shoulder, looked out into the night for the plane.

Tony could see no sign of it yet. In the window, he saw the reflections of people behind Ben. No one looked suspicious. No one carried a bag like Ben's. Milling by, Tony went into the terminal, looking like anyone else about to catch a flight. His eyes scanned the faces there: those of women walking by with strollers, couples holding hands, tired, rumpled businessmen waiting to catch their flights home. Was one of them really a killer, or was this all some grand hoax?

He spotted lights to the north as a plane began to land. It touched down, slowed, and turned. As it taxied toward their terminal, he heard the announcement that Flight 438 from Atlanta had landed.

He could see Ben's hands trembling as he set the garment bag, doubled over, down beside the window. He looked around, then crossed the corridor and headed for the men's room. Neither Tony nor Larry followed. Tony ambled closer to the bag to peer out the window, waiting for something to happen. He knew Larry kept his eye on Ben as he came back out of the rest room.

The ramp door opened and passengers began filing off. A crowd quickly formed in the hall outside the gate, blocking Tony's view of the garment bag.

Concerned that the bag may have been switched while view was blocked, he pushed through the crowd and headed back toward the security gate, looking for anyone who carried a bag like

Ben's with a yellow thread tied to the shoulder strap. He saw several similar bags, but none with the yellow thread.

He looked back up the corridor, wondering if Larry had seen anything. Slowly, the crowd by gate C–23 began to thin out, and he saw the bag still lying there, the yellow string still tied to it.

He saw Larry on the other side of the gate, still looking casual in his windbreaker and jeans. The perfect time to switch the bags would have been when the crowd was crushing in. The fact that it hadn't happened might mean that something was wrong.

Frustrated, Tony started toward the men's room, caught Ben's eye, and nodded for him to follow. Tony didn't acknowledge him as he came in. He went into a stall, pulled a notepad out of his pocket, and wrote, *No one's made the switch yet. Go home and we'll keep watch. There's another cop parked beside you in the garage. He'll follow you home. Don't try anything stupid.*

He shoved the paper into his pocket.

Ben was washing his hands when Tony took the sink next to him. He reached into his pocket, pulled out the note, and set it on Ben's sink without looking at him. Then he dried his hands as Ben read it, watching as the artist closed his eyes in frustration.

Tony found a seat next to Larry at one of the nearby gates, in perfect view of the garment bag, which lay there by itself, waiting for anyone to pick it up. It would probably be taken, all right, Tony thought, but not by the killer.

He watched as Ben came out of the rest room and trudged back down the corridor toward the main terminal.

Sharon was asleep on the couch in the living room when Ben got home. The door woke her, and she sat up. "What happened?"

"Nothing," he said. "He didn't come. At least, not while I was there. Have you heard from Larry and Tony?"

"They weren't with you?"

He shook his head and dropped into a chair. "I left them there. They had another cop follow me home. They could still be waiting, for all I know. If this guy doesn't show, they'll be convinced that I made it all up. They're pretty much convinced, already."

"Did they jeopardize anything?"

He rubbed his face. "No. Actually, they did a pretty good job. No one would have known they were cops or that they were with me." He dropped his hands and shook his head as he leaned it back on the chair. "I just can't figure out what happened."

The phone rang, and they both jumped. "I'll get it," Ben said, snatching up the extension on the table next to him.

"Hello?" His face reddened as he listened to the response, and Sharon got up and stepped toward him.

"I took the bag like you said," he insisted. "I put it exactly where you told me."

She held her breath, certain he was talking to the killer. Ben sighed heavily. "Okay, so I faked it. But you have to believe me. I have no idea what you're looking for, or I would have given it to you. There's nothing I know of that's worth a murder rap."

Sharon covered her face with her hands. The killer knew he'd been set up. Now what were they going to do?

Ben's breath was coming faster. "What do you mean, something worse?" He paused, and his face drained of color. "If you'd just tell me, straight out, what you want, I know I could get it. Why won't you just say it? Just tell me, and—" He looked up at her, his eyes dismal. "He hung up."

Sharon's eyes were as defeated as his as she watched him hang up. "What did he say?"

Ben closed his eyes. "He could tell when he saw the bag that it wasn't what he wanted. I folded it over when I laid it down, and that clued him. It must be bigger. Longer. I don't know. Maybe it's a painting. But which one? There's nothing of mine that's valuable enough for murder. Even the pieces I was restoring weren't that important. And there were some reproductions in the gallery, but who would kill over a reproduction?" In frustration, he threw a pillow across the room. "I just don't know what he wants!"

She tried to sort it all out, but she was too tired. "Well, there's no point in hashing this out right now. I'd go to bed if I were you. There's nothing more you can do tonight."

"You go ahead," he said. "I'll call the police station and report this call. At least they can pull Larry and Tony out of there. No use having them stay there any longer for nothing." He blew out another frustrated breath. "If only I'd had time to hook up a recorder before that call. The cops still don't believe the first call ever came, and they're sure not willing to use their own resources to prove it."

Wearily, Sharon got up and padded to the doorway, then turned back. "Anne said to wake her up when you got home. She wanted to hear."

He nodded. "I'm glad she slept. It's been a while. I think I'll just let her keep sleeping."

"Whatever." She paused awkwardly for a moment, then finally whispered, "Good night."

"Good night," he said, then picked up the phone and started to dial.

CHAPTER SIXTEEN

T he crying baby woke Sharon in the middle of the night, and she lay in her bed staring at the ceiling and waiting for someone to quiet him. The crying went on for fifteen minutes, and finally she got up and pulled on her robe. Someone was going to have to attend to him. His parents were so tired that they might not wake up.

Quietly, she padded up the hall toward the room where she had put his crib, stepped in—and jumped when she saw Anne rocking the screaming baby in a rocking chair.

"Oh! I didn't know you were up."

Anne shot her a contemptuous look. "You thought I was just letting my baby scream?"

Sharon sighed. She really wasn't in the mood for this. "I'll just go back to bed, then."

"I'm sorry he woke you up," Anne said. "He's sick. He's got a fever."

Sharon hesitated at the door, then turned back and bent over the baby. She touched his forehead; he was burning up. "Do you need a thermometer?"

"Yes," Anne said quietly. "If you have one."

Sharon went to the kitchen and found the thermometer, the pediatric Tylenol syrup, and an infant measuring spoon. She brought the thermometer to Anne and watched as she stuck the digital thermometer under the baby's arm. "Can you give him this?"

"What is it?"

"Tylenol," she said.

"It might help." Anne took it, and under her breath, added, "Thank you."

Sharon stood there a moment, waiting to see what the temperature was. The little thermometer beeped, and Anne took it out from under his arm. "A hundred one," she said.

"He's pretty congested," Sharon said, "so he may have an ear infection. Mine used to get them all the time."

"I've already thought of that," Anne said wearily. "I just don't know what I can do about it."

"Well, do you want to take him to the doctor?"

"I can't afford it," she said through clenched teeth, shifting the baby to hush him. "We have no money. Don't you understand?"

Sharon felt slapped down again. "Look, I'll be happy to pay the doctor bill."

"I don't want any more favors from you."

"Your child is sick!" Sharon blurted. "Besides that, no one in the house can get any sleep until he's well. Will you please take him to the doctor and let me pay the bill?"

Tears came to Anne's eyes as she stared off into the darkness. "All right," she said. "I guess I have no choice. I'll take him in the morning."

Sharon stormed back to her room and flopped onto the bed, her blood boiling. What had she done to deserve this woman's wrath? After all, it was Anne who had broken up their family, who had come between Sharon and her husband. How dare she come in here and act like Sharon was her enemy? And while Sharon was trying to help her, for pete's sake.

She tried to pray but the words wouldn't come, and as the baby continued to cry late into the night, she lay sleepless and exhausted, desperate to figure out a solution to this problem that seemed to have no end.

CHAPTER SEVENTEEN

The police station was less chaotic than last time, Sharon thought. She stood just inside the door scanning the desks for Larry or Tony. Dark circles ringed her eyes, and she felt as though she had been beaten during the night.

As she spotted Tony slumped over his computer, looking just as tired as she felt, she resolved to do something about that situation right now. She headed for his desk, but he didn't look up from his computer as she approached. He had the weary, distracted look, yet his face reminded her of a younger version of Robert Redford.

Since the first time she'd met him, she'd been wary of him, for his good looks were like a big red warning sign to be careful. Ben had been too handsome for his own good, too, before he'd grown his hair so long and cultivated that bohemian, too-creative-to-care image. Good-looking men needed constant affirmation and consistent hero worship—if they didn't get it, they strayed, and told themselves they were right to do so.

But Tony didn't look as if he'd spent a lot of time in front of the mirror this morning. He had shaven, but his hair looked more rumpled than usual. His eyes were bloodshot, and she suspected he'd gotten about as much sleep as she had.

She cleared her throat to get his attention, but still, he didn't look up. She stepped closer and tried again.

"Excuse me," she said. He looked up unappreciatively, but when he saw her, his face changed instantly.

"Mrs. Robinson," he said, standing up and reaching to shake her hand.

"Sharon," she corrected. "I do still use Robinson, but I dropped the 'Mrs.' six years ago. I was hoping you'd be in this morning. I was a little doubtful, since it's Saturday and you worked so late last night."

He gestured for her to sit down and sat back in his own chair. "Yeah, nothing like wasted time."

She sat down and leaned forward, trying to keep her voice low enough that others wouldn't overhear, but loud enough that he could hear her over the din in the station. "That's why I wanted to talk to you. I was worried that what happened last night might have led you to believe that . . ." Her voice trailed off, and she struggled to find the right words.

"That Ben might have been leading us on a wild-goose chase to get himself out from under the glass?"

She shrugged. "Something like that. I was afraid that you'd come back here and stop investigating—just write the murder off to an angry employee, and quit looking for the real murderer."

He leaned his elbows on his desk and took a deep breath. "Sharon, you're very loyal. That's admirable. But has it ever occurred to you that your ex-husband may really have done this?"

"No," she said with certainty. "Not for a second. It goes completely against everything I know about him. And I've known him for twenty years. Two before we were married, twelve years during, and six after."

He clasped his hands in front of his face and studied her as she spoke. When he didn't answer, she leaned back hard in her chair. "Why would I be so intent on proving him innocent if I didn't believe that?"

"Because you're the mother of his children," Tony said. "Most mothers don't want their children growing up with the stigma of having a father in prison."

"Oh, for heaven's sake," she said, leaning forward again. "It goes completely against his character, in every way. He's a make-love-not-war kind of guy. If you knew him like I did, you'd know how absurd this all is."

"I've seen his temper, Sharon. He's even admitted to losing it with Dubose." Tony's gaze didn't leave her face as he asked, "When he cheated on you, did you feel you knew him then?"

She sat slowly back and held Tony's gaze. "How do you know that's what happened?"

He nodded toward his computer screen, and she saw Ben's name in a block at the top. He had been looking into his background.

"When I count back from the birth of his next child, I don't have to be a genius to see that wife number two was pregnant already when the divorce papers were filed."

Sharon was getting angry. Was he making *her* out to be a liar now? "So you know what led to my divorce. I don't see your point."

"Point is, you don't always know people as well as you think you do."

"Okay. And?"

"And, if he lied and cheated once, maybe he could do it again. Maybe he *could* have had some motive strong enough to make him want to kill his boss. Maybe it was anger, or maybe it was something else."

"Why would he do it?" she asked him. "He'd lose his job, his home, his credit cards, his income—why would he do something so stupid?"

"He'd already lost those earlier that day." He turned back to his computer and scrolled down. "I've been looking over his history here, Sharon. He looks like a man who doesn't do a lot of planning. His financial state is a good indication that he flies by the seat of his pants. He doesn't always think things out."

"All right," she conceded. "He's definitely guilty of that. But that doesn't happen to be against the law."

"No, but it could be a clue that the man isn't always going to be predictable. That maybe sometimes he could act in a fit of passion. Artistic temperament can be very bizarre sometimes. Remember Van Gogh?"

"Van Gogh was insane," she said. "Ben is not. He's a little irresponsible, a little self-absorbed, a little scatterbrained, but he is not insane. And he's not a killer. How could I let him and his family move into my house if I thought for a second that he was?"

"Instead of proving the probability of his innocence, Sharon, that could just prove the probability of your state of denial."

"Denial?" She got to her feet and leaned over his desk, putting her face close to his. "You think I'd take in the man who cheated on me and the woman who wrecked my marriage and the children she rubs in my face—all because I was in denial? Trust me, Tony, there's no denial here. Neither Ben nor Anne are my favorite people, and frankly, my first instinct is to let them sink or swim. Last night was close to the worst night of my life. This woman hates my guts for existing, and instead of being grateful that I put a roof over her head, she's spitting nails and acting like I've locked her in there by force. If I were in denial, Tony, there might be a lot more harmony around my house right now. But my only thought is to get them out of there as soon as humanly possible. The only way I see to do that is to help Ben prove his innocence. And it looks like I'm going to have to depend a lot on you to do that."

Her eyes seared into his, and he sat motionless as she unloaded.

"Now you can take the easy way out and stamp this case solved, or you can consider some other probabilities. For starters, the probability that I am an intelligent woman who wouldn't be in the position I'm in unless I had complete faith in Ben Robinson's innocence. If for no other reason than that, you should at least keep looking. Consider the probability that someone really did call him last night. That I wasn't hearing things when the phone rang. That someone threatened him and told him to make a delivery at the airport. That he doesn't have a clue what they want. Could you do that, Detective? Could you just consider it? Just in case you really don't have all this figured out, and there's some killer still out there who's laughing his head off at the St. Clair police for falling so easily for this frame-up?"

Tony took a deep breath and rubbed his eyes, then leaned back and crossed his arms over his chest. "For your information, that's why I came in today, even though it's my day off and I didn't get much sleep last night. I've already started working on locating other people who may have had vendettas against Dubose. We've been in touch with some of his other colleagues, some of his friends, some of the art dealers who frequented the gallery. We're looking for other motives, Sharon. That hasn't stopped just because Ben has been charged. But that doesn't mean that I'm optimistic about finding anything. Ben is the most obvious suspect. Those phone calls—frankly, Sharon, they prove nothing. So he has an accomplice. I'd have guessed that anyway. Probably a woman, based on his history. Sharon, everything points to Ben."

"Yeah, like a neon sign. Like big red arrows. What kind of fool would leave that much evidence behind? It's so obvious that it was a setup. And now this maniac is calling my house, making threats, and I'm afraid of what might happen next!"

"But you're not frightened of Ben?"

"No!" she said too loudly, then realized others were looking her way. Trying to calm herself, she lowered back into her chair. "How many times do I have to tell you? He can't even spank his children. He barely raised his voice to me in twelve years of marriage."

"That is some feat, considering your temper," he said with a half-grin. "Did you ever get in his face like you did in mine just now?"

She lowered her face into her hands and gently massaged her tired eyes. "Look, I'm sorry. I'm a little on edge. This may be just another case to you, but it's altering my whole life. It's serious."

He softened then and looked down at his hands. "I realize that. I didn't mean to make it seem like I was taking it lightly. I'm really not. I'm working hard on this case because I don't want to make any mistakes. Whatever you may think about the St. Clair PD, we're very thorough. Ask Lynda. She knows firsthand."

"Well, you can ask Lynda about Ben, too. We've been friends a long time, and she's heard it all." She was getting very tired, and she felt that her body showed it. She studied him for a moment. "Have you ever been married, Tony?"

He shook his head and grinned slightly. "Can't say I've had the pressure."

She lifted her eyebrows at the play on words. "Then it's no wonder that you can't understand how sure I can be that Ben is innocent."

Tony stared at her quietly for a moment. "I guess you're right. I can't understand it. But I'll respect it. And I'll keep it in mind. Fair enough?"

She nodded and got to her feet again. "It's fair as long as you find the killer. Do you think whoever did this will come after Ben? Or that he's a threat to any of us in the house?"

Tony shook his head. "Sharon, *if* Ben was set up, then he's the last one the murderer would want to touch. He wouldn't want to give himself away. And he sure wouldn't want to do away with his scapegoat."

She considered that. "I guess you're right." She reached out to shake his hand again. "I appreciate your time, Detective."

"Anytime," he said, getting to his feet and holding her hand a little longer than necessary. "In fact, if you ever feel like you need to escape the pressure for a while, just give me a call and we'll go get a cup of coffee or something."

She smiled. "I will."

"And if you think of anything else I need to know, don't hesitate to call."

"All right. Thanks."

She said good-bye and headed back across the precinct, feeling a little better than she had when she'd come in. She wasn't sure whether the visit had been merely therapeutic, or actually helpful. She got to the door and waited as several people came in, then looked quickly back over her shoulder.

Tony was still watching her.

Her heart jolted, and she told herself that she'd have to take him up on that cup of coffee soon. As she hurried out the door and back to her car, she had the gentle beginning of a smile on her face.

B en unlocked the door with Jenny's key, and opened it for the girls. They had gone to the art store to buy supplies for their mural on the tree house, which Ben was determined to paint in spite of the mess he was in. The children were chattering nonstop as they bounced into the house. Then suddenly they fell silent.

Over their heads, Ben saw the open pantry, the cans that had fallen on the floor, the cabinet doors. The two little girls gasped. "What happened?"

Jenny grabbed his arm. "Dad, somebody's been in here."

Ben motioned for her to stay back and went into the den. The cushions were on the floor, and books had been pulled off the shelves. He saw that the girls had not obeyed his silent order, and had followed close behind him. He hurried into the living room, and they stood gaping at the scattered cushions and the open closet, its contents spilled out onto the floor.

"Dad, who could have done this?"

"Get the girls and go next door," he said quickly. "Then call the police. Wait there until I come for you."

"Why?" Jenny asked. "Do you think whoever did this is still here?"

"I don't know," he said. "Just do it."

She grabbed the girls' hands. "Come on, kids. We have to go."

"But who made this mess?" Christy asked. "Mommy's gonna die."

"I don't know. Just come on."

"What about Daddy?"

Jenny didn't answer as she pulled them out the door.

The police were there in ten minutes, and while Ben followed them around the house, making sure that no one was hidden there, Larry and Tony came in.

Ben looked at them with resignation as they came up the stairs.

"What's going on now?" Tony asked wearily.

"Somebody broke in," Ben said. "We were all gone, and this is what we came back to."

"Anything missing?" Larry asked, looking into the rooms he passed.

"Nothing that I can see. Sharon would know better, though. She's showing some houses this morning."

"I saw her earlier," Tony said. "She didn't mention where she was heading."

Ben raked a hand through his hair. "I think they may have been looking for something."

"Looking for what?" Tony asked skeptically.

"I don't know. Whatever I was supposed to have delivered last night, probably."

"Oh. Right." Tony blew out a heavy breath. "Ben, was there anyone with you when you discovered this?"

Ben looked insulted, but not surprised. "Yes. My kids."

"Where are they? I want to talk to them."

"They're next door. I sent them over there as soon as we saw all this. I was afraid whoever it was was still in the house."

"All right," Tony said. "Larry, I'm going over there to talk to them. You can handle it from here."

Larry nodded. "No sweat."

Tony trotted back down the stairs. Just as he reached the kitchen door, it flew open, and Sharon burst in. "I saw the police cars!" she said in a panic. "What's going on?"

"Everyone's fine," he said to calm her. "We got a burglary call. According to your ex-husband, someone broke into your house."

She looked around at the contents of the pantry on the floor, the cabinet doors—through the arched doors, she saw the mess in the den. "I'd say he's right. Is anything missing?"

"Televisions, computers, stereos are all still here. You might check your jewelry, and anything else you had that was valuable."

"Where are the kids?" she asked quickly.

"Next door. Ben sent them over when they got home."

"Good," she said, turning and rushing back for the door. "I want to go make sure they're all right."

"I'll come with you," he said. "I need to ask them some questions."

Christy watched out the window of her elderly neighbor's living room, fascinated with the police cars in her driveway and in front of her house. She saw her mother's car, which had not been there before, and she jumped up and down and yelled to her sisters. "Mommy's home! Can I go tell her what happened?"

Jenny came into the room, accompanied by Mrs. Milton, the retired schoolteacher who had gotten the girls a plate of cookies to distract them. "No, Christy. You stay here until Mom or Dad tells us to come home."

"But why? We're missing all the excitement."

Jenny pulled back the curtain and looked out the window. "I know, but—I can't believe all this. Somebody's really out to get Daddy."

"Mommy's coming!" Christy said as she saw her mother hurrying across the lawn with the cop who'd arrested her father trailing behind her. She jumped up and ran to the front door to fling it open. "Mommy, somebody robbed our house!"

Sharon bent down and hugged her younger child. "I know, honey. But it's okay." She looked up at Jenny, then at Emily hunkering in the corner, looking a little frightened. "Are you all okay?"

"Sure, Mom. We're fine," Jenny said. "Is he still in there? Did he take my computer or my stereo?"

"I don't think so," Sharon said. She looked at the widow still holding the plate of cookies. "Thanks for taking them in, Grace. I appreciate it."

"No problem," the older woman said. "Come in and relax for a minute. You look so tired."

"It's been a tough couple of days," Sharon admitted. "Grace, girls, this is Detective Tony Danks from the St. Clair Police Department. He needs to ask you a few questions."

"Me, too, Mommy?" Christy asked hopefully.

"You, too," Tony said, sitting down so he'd be eye level with the child. "Tell me how you found out the house had been broken into."

Christy's eyebrows shot up with excitement. "We came back from the art store, and there was stuff all over the place. Mommy, it's a mess!"

"I know, honey. I saw it."

"How long were you gone?" Tony asked Jenny, and she sat down across from him, much more serious than Christy.

"About an hour, I guess," she answered. "Daddy is going to help the girls paint a mural on Christy's tree house, and we went to get some art supplies. Most of his paints are still at the studio."

"All right," Tony said, pulling out the pad he kept in his pocket and making a note. "Jenny, Christy, Emily, I want you guys to think real hard when I ask you this question. When you left, who was the first one in the car?"

"I was!" Christy shouted, shooting her hand in the air.

Emily raised her hand, too. "No, it was me. We tied!"

"If we tied, then how could you be there first?" Christy asked. "I was first."

"No, I was."

"Okay, so you both got out there first," Tony said, chuckling. "Who was next?"

"I was," Jenny said, frowning. "Why?"

"So your dad was the last one out of the house?"

"Yes," Jenny said. "He locked up."

"How long was he in there before he got to the car?"

She looked disturbed at the question, and looked questioningly up at her mother. Sharon shrugged and nodded for her to answer. "Well, I don't know. A few minutes. He said he couldn't find his wallet."

"Did he find it?"

"Yes, and he came on out."

"I see." He made a note of that, then glanced up at Sharon. She was getting that look on her face that said he had a lot of nerve, but he pressed on. "Now, you went to the art store, and bought supplies, right? Did you stop anywhere else?"

"No," Christy volunteered. "We went right there and right back."

"All right. Who was the first one back in the house?"

"We all went at the same time," Jenny said. "The girls went in first, then Dad and I were right behind them."

"And which rooms did you see?"

Jenny looked confused. "Well, uh . . . I saw the kitchen, and the den, and then I went into the living room. That's when Dad sent us over here."

"So you didn't see the rest of the house?"

"No."

"Did any of you?"

"No," Jenny said. "Dad wanted us out in case he was still there."

Sharon was getting impatient. "What are you getting at, Detective?"

"I'm just asking questions," he said. "Now, your dad's wife. Emily's mom. Where is she?"

"She took Bobby to the doctor," Jenny said. "He's sick."

"And how long has she been gone?"

"Hours," Jenny said. "They had to work her in, because she didn't have an appointment."

He made another note, then looked up at Mrs. Milton. "Grace, did you see any cars over there earlier? Anybody who didn't belong there?"

"No, I'm afraid not," the woman said. "I didn't know anything was wrong until the girls came running over."

"Okay. We'll question some of the other neighbors to see if anyone saw anything."

"Good," Sharon said.

He got up and held out a hand for Christy, and she shook proudly. "Thanks for your help," he said.

"Sure. Can we go home now?"

"Stay here until the police get finished. Sharon, can I speak to you outside?"

"All right." She thanked Mrs. Milton again, then followed him out into the yard. "What is it?"

He saw Larry on his way across the yard to speak to him.

"Sharon, in light of our conversation this morning, I know you're not going to like what I have to say," Tony said as Larry approached.

"Oh, no. You're not going to blow this off like it didn't happen, are you? You're not going to ignore this! This is *my house!*"

"I'm not convinced anything happened," he said. "Ben was the last one to leave the house. He hung around in there long enough to have pulled the cushions off, opened some doors, upset some shelves. Jenny only saw the front rooms when she came back. Between the time they got home and the time the police showed up, he had plenty of time to go through the rest of the house, making it look like someone had been there. There was no sign of forced entry, no one has seen anyone who didn't belong here—"

"You haven't questioned everyone yet! You don't know!"

"And it doesn't look like anything was taken," Larry added. "It doesn't look like a robbery."

"You people are nuts. Why would Ben do this?"

"The same reason he staged that little drama last night. To throw us off. Make us think we've got the wrong guy. He's desperate, Sharon, and frankly, I'm beginning to wonder if it isn't dangerous having him in the house at all."

"So what are you saying?" she asked, keeping her voice low so her neighbors and kids wouldn't hear. "That I should send him back to jail? Just because you refuse to believe that someone actually could have broken into my house to look for whatever it is he thinks Ben has?"

"It just looks too suspicious, Sharon."

"And it may not have been Ben who did it," Larry conceded. "It could have been his wife, trying to help him out."

"No way," Sharon said. "There's a killer out there, and he's framed Ben, and he's called and threatened him, and now he's broken into my house, and you aren't going to do one thing about catching him, are you?"

"Sharon . . ."

"I had more respect for you when I left the station this morning, Tony. I thought you might really have a conscience, that you'd do a good job no matter what it cost you. That you were a good cop. But I was wrong."

He looked as if he'd been slapped across the face. "Sharon, I'm doing my job."

"No, you're not! You're passing the buck because you're too lazy to consider any other possibilities."

"We are considering them, Sharon," Larry said. "We just have to tell you what our gut instinct is. It's not unusual for someone accused of a crime to try to throw us off the track. We have to tell you if we think the man living in your house is putting your family in danger."

"We're in danger, all right," she bit out. "But I obviously can't turn to St. Clair's finest for help. The danger isn't coming from my ex-husband, detectives. It's coming from your apathy!"

She turned and fled into the house, leaving them both standing in the driveway. Tony stood there for a moment, watching her go. Finally, he turned and started walking away from the house.

"Where are you going?" Larry asked.

"To question the neighbors," he said irritably. "Might as well get started. We have a lot of ground to cover."

The police were finishing their report and clearing out as Sharon came back into the house. She found Ben sitting alone at the dining-room table, his hands covering his face.

"What was he looking for, Ben?" she asked, leaning in the doorway, suddenly feeling too weak to stand straight. "What does he want?"

"If I knew . . ." He rubbed his eyes and looked up at her. "Do you at least believe he was here? That I didn't do this?"

"Of course I do. I wish it *had* been you. I wouldn't be so scared."

"I ought to just let them take me back to jail."

"Right," Sharon said. "That should solve everything."

"Well, look at your house. He ransacked it."

She shook her head. "Actually, it doesn't look so bad. We can put it all back together. It just feels so creepy, knowing he was here."

He rubbed his temples, trying to think. "I was just going back over everything with the cops. In the second phone call, he said it was too long to fold the garment bag. That's how he knew it wasn't what he wanted. It's got to be a painting . . . something really valuable . . . maybe rolled up. I've been trying to think of all the things I was working on in the studio. There were a couple of things Dubose bought recently that I was restoring. They had some value, but not this much."

"Maybe if you could get back into the gallery and look around, you could find it."

"If that's where it is, why didn't he find it when he killed Dubose?" He looked up at her with helpless eyes. "Sharon, I know how this looks."

She heard a car pulling into the garage, and glanced out the window. "Anne's home."

"I don't know how much more she can take," he said.

Sharon knew the feeling, but she didn't voice it. "Guess I'll get busy putting Humpty Dumpty back together again."

He got up wearily. "I'll help. We'll all help."

Sharon left the room before she had to confront Anne again.

CHAPTER NINETEEN

T he telephone in Eric Boudreaux's elegant hotel room rang, and he picked it up quickly.

"Yes?" he said in his French-accented voice.

"Mr. Boudreaux! How are you?"

Boudreaux was quiet for a long moment. "Impatient. As a matter of fact, I was just planning to ring the airport and book a flight back tomorrow. That is, unless you have something for me."

"I, uh . . . I need another day or two. Please. I'm trying to be very careful so as not to call too much attention to us. One can't be cavalier about an exchange of this sort."

"You do not have it, do you, Monsieur Lieber?"

A pause. "Of course I have it. And you want it. Dubose showed you the snapshot of it, didn't he?"

"He did. But I have yet to touch the picture."

"You'll touch it, my friend," the voice said with a chuckle. "Very, very soon. Don't return home just yet. I want you to have it, but if you return home, I'll have to offer it to another buyer."

"This was not in the agreement," Boudreaux said. "I was to stay for two days, then return with the picture."

"No one counted on Dubose's untimely death."

"No, you are right," the Frenchman said. "And I must tell you that I am growing quite suspicious, myself. I don't relish the idea of being a—how you say—accomplice to murder."

"I had nothing to do with his death. Nothing at all. It was an unfortunate coincidence that it happened the very week you were to meet with him."

"But if his death was motivated by greed because of this picture," Boudreaux said, "I would hesitate to do business with anyone involved. My reputation is flawless, and I intend to keep it that way. My crimes have always been harmless."

"And they will continue to be, sir. Trust me."

"Then when will you deliver?" Boudreaux asked.

"Soon."

"Tomorrow," he insisted. "If I do not hear from you tomorrow, I will leave."

There was a sigh. "You'll hear from me. Please, wait until you do. I anticipate having the painting by tonight. You will have it immediately after that."

"If I do not, you will have to bring it to me in LeMans," Boudreaux said. "Smuggling it through customs will be your problem, not mine."

"I'll be in touch tomorrow, Mr. Boudreaux. You won't be sorry you waited."

"I sincerely hope not," Boudreaux said, and hung up the phone.

CHAPTER TWENTY

Sharon took the easy way out and ordered pizzas that night, so that they wouldn't have to subject themselves to a sit-down dinner all together. She worked into the night putting things back where they belonged. When they were finished, everyone went to their bedrooms early, and Sharon went up to tuck in Christy and Emily.

"I'm glad Bobby's better," Christy said as her mother covered her with the Laura Ashley comforter. "He had a bad ear infection."

"And an earache, too," Emily added.

Sharon smiled. "Well, he should sleep better tonight."

"Mommy, are you scared?"

Sharon's smile faltered. "Why do you ask that?"

"Because that man was in our house. What if he comes back?"

"He won't," Sharon said. "Everything's locked up tight, and we're all home now. He won't come while we're home."

"Are you sure?"

"Positive," she lied. "Emily, are you comfortable? I could get you a softer pillow if you need it."

"I like this one," Emily said, snuggling up next to Christy. "I wish I could live here all the time."

Sharon smiled in spite of herself. She took a deep breath and asked, "How about if we say prayers together?"

"Okay," Christy said, "but you lie down between us."

Sharon crawled between them on the bed and got under the covers. She put her arm around Christy, and Emily snuggled up to her as well, expecting the same affection. Sharon grinned and slid her arm around her. The children didn't understand the politics of their family, she thought. And that was good.

She prayed aloud for their father, and for the man who was out there causing so much trouble, and for Bobby's ears and his cold, and for the safety of everyone in their home. When she finished, she lay there a moment, holding both girls.

"Tell us a story, Mommy," Christy said. "Please."

"I'll tell you part of one," Sharon said. "And then you tell me part."

Christy giggled. "Okay. You start."

Sharon sighed and thought for a moment. "Once upon a time, there was a little girl named . . ."

"Named Beth," Christy said. "Can that be her name, Mommy?"

"Okay, Beth. And she lived in a beautiful little cottage with flowers all around."

"And it had this cool climbing tree in the front yard, didn't it, Mommy?"

"That's right."

"No, that's wrong!" Christy changed her mind and sat up in bed. "The cottage was *in* the tree!"

"Okay," Sharon said. "And Emily, what color do you think the flowers were?"

"Purple!" Emily cried.

"That's right," Sharon said. "How did you know?"

Emily shrugged and giggled.

"But one day, something terrible happened."

"What, Mommy?" Christy asked, her eyes growing big. "Did somebody break into her house and rob her?"

Sharon thought for a moment. "No. One day, she went ice-skating on the pond near her house, because she didn't live in Florida, she lived in . . ."

"Alaska!" Christy provided.

"That's right. And she went ice skating, and while she was gone, some mean man came and . . ."

"Picked all her flowers!" Christy said. "And he sold them at the flea market, because they had fleas!"

They all laughed and lay back down, and Sharon went on with the story.

Anne climbed the stairs and walked up the hall to say good night to Emily. As she neared the door, she could hear laughter. It was good to hear Emily giggle again, she thought, and she paused and listened. Then she heard Sharon's voice, embroidering a story that had them both enthralled.

She went to the door and looked in. Sharon lay between the two girls on the big canopy bed, an arm around each of them, giggling right along with them.

Anne stepped back, suddenly jealous again. Not only were they beholden to Sharon because of their dependence on her for shelter and money, but she feared that Emily was getting too attached to this home and this family. She was losing Ben, she was losing Emily, and she'd already lost control of her life . . .

Slowly, she went back down the stairs to Bobby's room. He was sleeping soundly now that he'd been given the medication he needed. She sat down in the rocking chair in the darkened room, trying to figure out where to turn with the anxious, dangerous emotions holding her in their vicious grip.

CHAPTER TWENTY-ONE

The phone rang once, and as usual, Jenny quickly answered it. After a moment, she yelled down the stairs, "Daddy! It's for you!"

Ben took the call in the study, hoping it was Lynda. "Hello?"

"Ben, it's good to hear your voice."

"Nelson?" he asked.

"Yes. I'm still in London. I had hoped to get home to attend Louis's funeral, but there was too much fog on the ground, so the planes weren't taking off."

"How did you know where I was?"

"When I had the money wired to the courthouse, the secretary there told me you had moved in with your ex. I have to admit it was a little surprising. If I'd known you really didn't have a place to live, I could have offered you the use of my house."

"Yeah, well, I appreciate it, but it's a done deal now. We have to stay until this whole thing is cleared up. Listen, thanks for the bond money. I promise you'll get it back. I'll be acquitted."

"Of course you will. Have they got any leads?"

"I seem to be the only one. Despite the fact that this guy even broke in here today."

"Broke in? Are you serious?"

"The police don't seem to think so. They think I did it."

Nelson paused a moment, as if thinking. "Look, the moment I arrive, I'll go straight to the police and vouch for you, for what it's worth. This is ludicrous. Ben, do you think Louis was involved in something we don't know about?"

"Who knows?" Ben asked dejectedly. "When do you think you'll be here, anyway?"

"Probably in the next couple of days, if the weather clears. Have you thought about what you're going to do for money?"

"Yeah, a lot," Ben said. "I didn't get my last paycheck, and my paintings are all still locked in the gallery."

"Well, I've picked up a few things here that need some restoration work. Do you feel like doing them?"

"Of course," he said. "I need the work."

"Fine. Well, just cross your fingers that I'll arrive there soon. It's all going to work out, Ben. You'll see."

CHAPTER TWENTY-TWO

ome was a word that Tony only had a passing acquaintance with, especially these days when he spent so much time working. As he came in now, he shrugged wearily out of his sport coat and unfastened his shoulder holster. Dropping it on the counter, he carried the sport coat through the immaculate living room and into the bedroom. He hadn't slept much in the last few days, but the bed was made, anyway. Everything was in its place, perfectly in order. Normally, he found some degree of comfort in the small house he had built for himself, once he realized that he would probably never be married.

He walked across the white carpet and into the walk-in closet, where he hung his coat. Then, stepping out of his shoes, he padded back into the living room. Slumping down into his favorite chair, he pulled up his feet and stared at the vaulted ceiling.

It had been a horrendous, grueling afternoon, grilling neighbors who had seen nothing but wanted to waste his and Larry's time talking, trying to find out what was going on in the interesting and complex family that occupied the Robinson house. He'd learned more details than he'd ever intended to gather today—that Sharon Robinson rarely dated, that she was very successful on the real-estate scene, that her children were the best behaved on the street. He'd heard stories of how she'd helped elderly neighbors during the power outage last summer when the temperatures had soared to over 100 degrees. One single mother had shared how Sharon had kept her kids for an entire week while their mother was hospitalized for a ruptured appendix, then took care of her for a couple of weeks more until she had recovered.

She was too good for her own good, some of the neighbors agreed. And they all lamented the fact that she had been bamboozled into taking in her no-account ex this way, especially when everyone knew he'd killed that Dubose fellow. He suspected there would have been neighborhood complaints about his even being in the neighborhood, if it weren't for their great respect for Sharon herself.

But it wasn't those conversations that kept playing through his mind, but the one he'd last had with her. She'd said his apathy was dangerous. He worried that her generosity was.

He glanced at the phone and thought of calling her, just to let her know that he had taken it all seriously, that he had interviewed neighbors and had spent much of the early evening running down a list of people found in Dubose's Rolodex, matching them with his desk diary, and trying to determine who they needed to talk to next. But none of that mattered, he thought. He had done all that work mostly to humor Sharon. In his mind, Ben was the murderer, and all the work he did would only prove that. He just couldn't understand why it was so hard for her to see.

Maybe it was because she'd been married to the guy, he thought. She couldn't admit that she had been blind all those years. That he was ruthless and cold-blooded. That she'd had children with a man who could kill.

No one liked facing up to facts like that.

But he worried about her, and about the undying loyalty and unwavering faith that could get her into trouble. He wondered if she'd cooled down, or if, in the dark quiet of her night, she was wondering if, just maybe, Tony could be right. If Ben might have done all this, after all.

His eyes strayed to the telephone, and he started to pick it up. Then he thought better of it. He didn't need to entertain these lingering thoughts about Sharon Robinson. She had too many problems. He needed to do his job and stay away from her. Wasn't that what he'd told Larry so many times? His cardinal rule—not getting personally involved in his cases—had always stuck, even when his partner disregarded it.

But he wasn't sure why he couldn't shake her from his mind. He could pick up the phone right now and call any number of women to have dinner with him and go have a drink at the Steppin' Out across town. Or he could just show up there, and meet new ones. It was his common MO for Saturday night.

Tonight, however, his heart just wasn't in it. And he wasn't interested in meeting any other women. Tonight, only Sharon Robinson occupied his thoughts.

He tried to rationalize. He told himself that this case wasn't about her. She was only involved by virtue of her former marriage to the defendant. If he called her, it wouldn't be a conflict of interest, would it?

He looked at the phone again, and finally picked it up. Quickly, he dialed information, asked for her number, then punched it out. He waited as it rang once, twice . . .

"Hello?"

It was her older daughter's voice, and he cleared his throat and said, "May I speak to Sharon, please?"

"Yes, just a moment."

She was polite, he thought, just as the neighbors had said. He waited for a moment, then heard another extension being picked up, as the first one cut off.

"Hello?"

"Sharon? It's Tony."

"Yes?" she said coldly, obviously still perturbed at him.

He smiled. "I just wanted to see how you're doing."

"Fine, thank you."

He could see that this wasn't going to be easy, so he softened his voice and gave a stab at being contrite. "Look, I'm really sorry I made you mad today. But I spent the rest of the day interviewing neighbors. None of them saw anything, so now I'm working on friends and colleagues of Dubose who might have had a vendetta against him."

She let that sink in for a moment, then asked, "What about the fingerprints?"

"They all belonged to those of you living in the house. No one new."

She was quiet again. "Well, at least you're trying. I appreciate that."

His smile returned, then faded again. "Are you sure you're okay?"

He imagined her sinking into a chair, letting down her guard. "Yeah, I'm okay. Just tired. I don't know how well I'll sleep tonight. Tony?"

"Yeah?"

"I'm sorry about all the things I said to you today. I was under a lot of stress, but I had no right to lash out at you like that. You were just doing your job."

"You didn't think I was doing it well. You have the right to that opinion."

"Yeah, but I didn't have the right to beat you up with it. I'm sorry."

He couldn't believe he had called her to apologize, and had wound up getting one from her.

"You work really hard, don't you?" she asked. "Day and night, weekends . . ."

"It depends on what I'm working on. It's not usually so bad."

"But you and Larry are the only two detectives in the whole force, aren't you?"

"That's right," he said.

"Then you get all the junk. How do you ever have any time to yourself?"

He smiled. "I take time. I could say the same thing about you. From talking to your neighbors, I'd say that between being the best real-estate agent in town and the best neighbor on your block, not to mention the best mother and the best ex-wife, I can't imagine how you ever get time to yourself."

She laughed softly, a sound that lightened his heart.

"For instance, what were you doing when I called? I'll bet you were cleaning up the mess from the break-in."

"Wrong," she said. "I finished that earlier."

"What then?"

He could hear the smile in her voice. "If you must know, I was under the fig tree."

"Under the fig tree?" he asked. "Is that a fig tree in your backyard?"

She laughed louder now, and he couldn't help grinning. "No. That's an oak. 'Under the fig tree' is just an expression."

He let his feet down and sat up. "What does it mean?"

"Have you ever read the Bible, Tony?"

He frowned. "No. I can't say I have."

She didn't seem surprised. "Well, there's a passage in the first chapter of John, where Jesus is calling his first few disciples. He finds Philip and tells him, 'Follow me,' and then Philip goes and tells Nathaniel that he's found the Messiah. Nathaniel doesn't believe him, so Philip tells him to just come and see. Nathaniel goes with Philip to meet Jesus, and when Jesus sees him, he says, 'Here is a true Israelite, in whom there is nothing false.' And Nathaniel asks him how he knew him."

"Yeah?" Tony asked, a little surprised that a Bible story could hold his interest for this long.

"Jesus says, 'I saw you while you were still under the fig tree before Philip called you.'"

"So? He saw him under a tree. What's the big deal?"

"In those days, 'under the fig tree' meant 'seeking God.' When a man wanted to pray, often the coolest place was under a fig tree, so he'd go there to be alone and to pray. It became a common expression. Instead of saying you were praying and seeking God, you'd say you were 'under the fig tree.'"

"Oh," Tony said. "So you meant that you were praying?" The thought made him a little uncomfortable. As long as they were talking about some story in the Bible that had nothing to do with him, he was fine. But he hated it when these spiritual subjects cropped into his own comfort zone.

"Right," she said. "So you see? I do get some time to myself now and then. Sometimes I just have to take it."

"But I didn't mean praying time. I meant time that's good for you. Recreation. Something that's not an obligation, but a pleasure."

"I don't pray to fulfill an obligation, Tony. And it's pure pleasure. Even when I'm on my knees begging him for answers."

"Yeah, I know," he said, though he didn't have a clue. "But I just mean . . . well, you know, people like you . . . like us . . . they're prone to burnout. It's a big danger, you know. You have to take time out. Do things for yourself. Go to a movie. Out to dinner. Whatever."

He didn't know why he was getting so tongue-tied and nervous. He asked women out all the time, and he was smooth. Very smooth. Tonight he felt like an awkward kid asking the homecoming queen for a date.

"Well, yes," she agreed. "Those things are nice. If you have someone to do them with."

"Well, of course. I mean, not by yourself. Maybe with someone. Like me." He grinned then and winced, covering his face and kicking himself for sounding like a jerk. He leaned forward, holding the phone close to his ear. "Sharon, I'm trying to ask you for a date, but I'm doing an incredibly poor job of it."

There was a stunned silence for a moment. Finally, she said, "Well, yes. I mean, if it's okay. Not a conflict of interest or anything. I mean, you are working on Ben's case."

"It should be okay," he said.

She drew in a deep breath and let it out quickly. "Well, okay. When?"

"Well, we could wait until the case is over . . . but that could be a while. And frankly, I don't want to wait that long. How about tomorrow?"

"Tomorrow's Sunday," she said. "I go to church twice on Sundays. But you're welcome to join me."

He had walked into that one, he thought, but he could walk right back out. "Church and I don't really get along," he said. "How about after church tomorrow night? What time do you get home?"

"About seven-thirty," she said. "I guess dinner would be all right."

"Are you sure?"

"Yeah, why not?"

He smiled. "Okay. Great. I'll make reservations someplace nice. And I'll call you tomorrow afternoon and let you know what time."

"All right," she said. "I'll look forward to it."

Again, he felt like that awkward kid as he leaned back in his chair and mouthed "yes!" to the ceiling. Then trying to temper his voice, he said, "Well, I'll talk to you tomorrow then. Good night, Sharon."

"Good night."

He hung onto the phone as she hung up, then dropped it into its cradle and stared back at the ceiling again. What had he done?

He was going out with a woman who was tied up in a case he was working on, and she was a Christian, and she had kids, and she had her ex-husband who was quite possibly a killer living with her . . .

Great going, Tony, he thought. *You know how to pick 'em. The more complicated, the better. Like you don't have enough problems already.*

But it didn't matter to him as he sprang out of his chair, fully renewed, and headed for the kitchen to find something to eat.

Across town, Sharon smiled and stared at the telephone for a long moment. She had consented to going out with the cop who was trying to prove Ben's guilt. She had consented to going out with a guy who had never read word one of the Bible, a guy who was obviously uncomfortable talking about spiritual things, a guy who would never darken the doors of a church unless a crime had been committed there.

Was she crazy?

Probably, but it had been so long since she'd been attracted to any of the men who had asked her out. Maybe just one date wouldn't hurt. She could use the distraction—and the boost—after all the tension around here.

And there was no shortage of baby-sitters.

The truth was, she looked forward to it, but that anticipation only scared her. Tony was certain that Ben was a killer. Tony, who saw criminals every day, heard all their excuses, their alibis, their lies. Could it be that he saw something in Ben that she couldn't see?

She got up and pulled on her robe and padded up the dark hallway. What was Ben doing now? Where was he?

She saw a light on in her study, and went to the door. Standing back, she listened. Was he in there?

Slowly, she peered around the doorway.

Ben was there, reclining back in her leather chair, his feet propped on her desk. On his chest slept Bobby, his breathing much better now that he'd been medicated. Memories flooded through her of the same man lying on an orange bean bag with newborn Jenny on his chest. She had a snapshot of it somewhere. Could that same man have turned into a killer?

Confused by her disturbing thoughts, she turned and headed back to her room. She turned the light out and curled up on her bed. Wondering whether she'd done the right thing by agreeing to go out with the detective, she went back under the fig tree again.

CHAPTER TWENTY-THREE

It didn't feel like Sunday. To Jenny, the fact that her dad and Anne didn't care to go to church depressed her. It had felt weird, getting ready and trying not to wake them, and then there had been all the wailing when Emily had wanted to go with Christy, but her mother had awakened and tried to talk her out of it. Sharon had finally shamed Ben and Anne into letting the child go, and they had angrily gotten her dressed. The truth was, Jenny hadn't been so keen on going herself, since everyone there knew that her father had been arrested for murder. It was embarrassing, humiliating. But she needed their prayers, she thought, and she supposed that the gossip she would have to endure was worth it.

She had felt bad for her mother when she'd had to come home from church and cook a huge meal that would feed seven, since neither Ben nor Anne had shown enough initiative to start lunch before they'd gotten home. Then she had helped her mother clean up, since Anne stayed in the same room with Sharon as little as possible.

When Anne had asked Jenny to go to the store to get some more formula and diapers for Bobby, Jenny had welcomed the opportunity to get out of the tense house. She had volunteered to take Emily and Christy with her, hoping to give her mother a little reprieve from all her responsibility. Since she was going anyway, Sharon had given her a list of other things they needed.

Now, as she pulled into the parking lot of the Kroger and saw how crowded it was, Jenny almost regretted agreeing to come. She cut off the car and looked into the backseat at the two blonde girls seat-belted in and holding hands. "Now, girls, I have a list," she said. "Don't beg me for candy and stuff. It'll drive me crazy."

Christy looked crestfallen. "Not even gum? Not even Popsicles?"

"Not even Reeses?" Emily asked.

"No! Nothing! Now, come on."

In the store entryway, Jenny spotted a video game. Perfect. She pulled out some quarters and handed them to the girls. "Here. Stay and play the game for a while. When you finish, come find me."

"Will you get Popsicles?" Christy asked.

"And String Things? And Reeses?" Emily added.

"No junk. Mom said."

"That's not junk. Popsicles are not junk!"

"Okay, but just Popsicles."

"But I need String Things," Emily whined. "Mommy always puts String Things in my lunches for school. I need String Things for tomorrow."

"All right," Jenny gave in. "I'll get some. Just go play. Please!"

The two girls headed for the game. Breathing a sigh of relief, Jenny went into the store, determined to fill her mother's list as quickly as she could.

Emily was not as good at video games as Christy was, and she quickly "died." Because they had both spent their fifty cents, they began to look around for something else to do.

Spotting the bubble gum machines outside, they headed through the electric doors. Christy checked each slot to see if anyone had forgotten their candy, while Emily wound each handle to see if it would miraculously release some.

They had almost given up when a man came by and, chuckling, reached into his pocket for a quarter for each of them. "Here you go, girls. It's on me."

Christy looked up at the man who wore a straw Panama hat and dark glasses. "No, thanks, Mister. I'm not allowed to take things from strangers."

"I'm no stranger," he said with a kindly smile. "Not to Emily." He pulled his glasses off briefly and winked at the child.

Her eyes rounded. "You're Daddy's friend."

"You know my daddy?" Christy asked.

"I certainly do." The man smiled and put his glasses back on, then inserted the money into a machine, turned the knob, and caught the candy as it came out. Giving a piece to each of them, he nodded toward his car. "As a matter of fact, I have something in the car that your father needs. Would you girls mind coming with me to get it? You could take it to him." He squeezed Emily's nose. "I also have some jelly beans in the car. If you like them—"

"We do!" Emily cried. "Come on, Christy!"

The two girls bounced out behind him as he led them to his car.

Jenny pushed her loaded cart to the long line at the cash register. Thankful that her sisters had not hounded her while she was shopping, she glanced over at the play area. She didn't see them.

Sighing, she got out of line and went to the candy aisle, expecting to find them there. There were children admiring the colorful bags of treats for the Valentine season, but Christy and Emily weren't among them.

Frustrated, she decided to start at one end of the store and look down each aisle until she found them. She should have told them to stay where they were. And she should have known that they wouldn't.

She looked up every aisle in the huge store, to no avail. Again, she checked the play area, but they weren't there.

Then she remembered that Christy loved the candy machines, so she abandoned her cart and looked through the glass doors. No one was there.

She was beginning to get worried, but her anger at them overpowered it. She went to the manager's booth at the front of the store, and waited in line until it was her turn. "Could you please page my sisters over the intercom? They're somewhere in the store, but I can't find them."

They took down the little girls' names and sent out a page. When five minutes had passed with no answer, Jenny began to worry. Abandoning her cart, she went back to the first aisle; then her speed picked up as she turned a corner and ran into a stock boy, causing him to drop a box of cans. "I'm sorry!" she said, helping him pick them up. "Have you seen two little girls with blonde hair?"

"No," he said, annoyed. "I haven't."

She looked back at the front desk. The children still hadn't answered the page. Quickly, she ran back to the front. "Look," she said, breathless, "they've got to be here."

"I'll try again," the manager said. "Just hold on."

The page went out again, but there was still no answer. She headed outside, thinking they may have broken the cardinal rule of leaving the store, and she searched up and down the sidewalk for them. Beginning to get frantic, she ran out to her car and looked inside. They weren't there.

Where could they be?

Perspiring and breathless, she ran back inside and headed to the back of the store where the swinging doors led into the warehouse. She burst through and found two workers. "Have you seen two little blonde-haired girls? Five and six years old? One was wearing . . . a little red outfit with hearts on it, and the other was . . . Oh, I don't know what Emily was wearing!"

"No, they haven't been back here," one of them said.

By now her breath was coming in gasps, and she pushed out of the doors and ran up each aisle and down the next, calling out for them at the top of her voice. Store patrons were staring, and a few started to join her in the hunt.

Realizing the problem was serious, the manager got on the intercom. "If anyone has seen two little blonde girls, ages five and six, who answer to the names Emily and Christy, would you please come to the front desk?"

Jenny was in tears by the time she had searched the whole store a second time. Frantic, she made her way to the desk. A customer was standing there talking to the manager.

"Miss?" the manager said, now visibly shaken. "This woman says she saw the children getting into a car with someone. We've called the police."

"A car?" Jenny asked, breathing in a sob. "They couldn't have. They were with me. They know better than that!"

"One of the little girls had on a red tunic with hearts and some red leggings, and the other one was wearing something purple, I think," the woman said.

Jenny felt dizzy, and her heart sank. "That was them. Who were they with?"

"A man," the woman said. "He had on a straw hat and sunglasses. I think his hair was brown, but I'm not sure. He was maybe 5'9" or 5'10", average weight. They looked like they knew him and got into the car willingly. They were smiling and laughing, so I didn't think anything of it."

"They *couldn't* have!" She began to tremble, then asked, "Can I use your phone? I have to call my parents."

Her hand trembled as she tried to dial the number. The phone rang, and she closed her eyes. After a moment, her father answered. "Hello?"

"Daddy?" she said, trying to control her voice. "You didn't come and pick up Christy and Emily, did you?"

"What do you mean, did I pick them up?"

"Did you or Mom pick them up?" she shouted.

"No. No one's gone anywhere."

She sobbed again, and dropped her head on the counter. "Daddy, someone's taken them! They're gone!"

CHAPTER TWENTY-FOUR

"Where are you taking us?" Christy asked tearfully as the man drove much too fast down Highway 19 leading out of St. Clair.

He didn't answer.

"He lied," Emily whispered. "He didn't have any jelly beans."

"We're gonna get in so much trouble," Christy whispered. "Jenny's gonna kill us. And Mommy will punish me for my whole life."

"Quiet back there," the man barked. "You're getting on my nerves."

They stopped talking, but continued to cry.

"Did you hear me? I told you to shut up!"

The girls put their arms around each other, trembling with fear and trying hard not to make noise.

He pulled off of the highway and turned onto a long dirt road.

"Maybe he's taking us home," Emily whispered.

"I don't think so."

"Then where is he taking us? What is he gonna do with us?"

"I don't know," Christy said. "Maybe he's not really mean. Maybe he just likes little girls."

"He doesn't act like he likes us," Emily whispered. "Maybe he's gonna hurt us."

They clung to each other as he turned down a dirt road and took them far into a patch of woods. Finally, they came to a small structure that looked like a toolshed. The car stopped.

The back door opened, and the man reached for Christy's arm. "Come on. Get out."

She slid across the seat and got out, then with a burst of adrenaline, kicked the man with all her might. "Run, Emily!"

Emily took off running, but the man grabbed Christy around the waist and bolted after the other child. He caught her before she could get far, and grabbing a fistful of hair to guide her, he pointed them toward the shack.

"See that?" he asked through his teeth. "That's where we're going."

Christy's crying grew louder, and Emily screamed and struggled to make him let go of her hair. He dragged them, writhing and trying to break free, to the door of the shed, opened it, and threw them in. They each hit the dirt floor, and Christy bumped her head on the edge of a shelf. She screamed out, but the man only slammed the door behind them.

Christy curled into a ball, holding her cut head as warm blood seeped around her fingers.

They heard him locking the door, and then going back to his car. The car door slammed, the motor roared to life, and he drove off.

Emily was sobbing and groping around, trying to find Christy. "Christy, where are you?"

"Here," she cried.

Emily's hand reached out to touch her, and they clung to each other. "I want Daddy," Emily cried.

"Me too," Christy sobbed. Blood dripped into her eyes, burning them, and she wiped it on her sleeve. On her hands and knees, she groped until she found the wall, then the door. Emily followed close behind her, her little fist clutching the back of her shirt. Christy slid her hand up the door until she found the doorknob. She jiggled it, but it had been locked from the outside.

She tried to stand up, but Emily cried, "Don't leave me! I can't see!"

"I'm right here. I'm just standing up."

Emily stood with her, still clinging to her. She pushed on the door as hard as she could, then rammed her small shoulder against the wood, like she'd seen people do on TV. It was no use.

She kicked it with all her might, then began to bang on it. "Help, somebody! Let us out!" she screamed, pounding it with her fists. Emily joined her, pounding and screaming at the top of her lungs.

"Let us out! Help! Let us *out!*"

But they could hear the car driving away on the long gravel road.

As he drove away, Nelson Chamberlain smiled with satisfaction. Ben was probably squirming by now and preparing to make the exchange. Nelson had just provided Ben with an irresistible incentive.

He'd definitely gotten lucky. He had expected to have to take the teenager, too, which would have made the whole situation much more difficult to manage. But when she'd left the girls to fend for themselves, he'd had the perfect opportunity.

His smile faded, as he realized how deep he had gotten. Normally, he didn't like to get his hands dirty. It had been unpleasant enough working with the thug who'd had the fake IDs and credit cards made for him—one set under Ben Robinson's name so he could purchase the gun, and another set under the name of John Lieber. The murder had been even more distasteful. He had been lucky enough to find the money clip with Ben's initials; Ben had left it behind in the medicine cabinet of the gallery's apartment—along with a hairbrush, which had provided the strands of Ben's hair that Nelson had planted in Dubose's hands. Yes, all of this had been distasteful, but he'd had no choice.

He had come this far and didn't intend to stop now. Too much was invested. Too much was at stake. It wasn't easy maintaining the lifestyle he loved. A few bad investments had seriously depleted his funds. The financial injection he'd get from this transaction was essential. Things had to work out before his creditors and generous friends abroad realized he wasn't what they thought he was.

The hundred thousand dollars he'd donated for Ben's bond money had been well worth it. Ben couldn't deliver anything if he was behind bars. It would have been useful to frame Ben for

Dubose's murder—that had been his original plan, and a good one. But now there was something he needed more than a fall guy, and only Ben knew where it was. This kidnapping, of course, would transfer suspicion away from Ben, even for the murder. But it couldn't be helped. Nelson was desperate to make the delivery to Boudreaux quickly. Besides, everyone thought he was still out of the country, so even if they did look earnestly for another culprit, they would never suspect him.

If things went the way he expected, he should have what he wanted and truly be out of the country, and out from under any chance of suspicion, before the sun came up tomorrow.

CHAPTER TWENTY-FIVE

T he sound of Sharon's wailing when she heard the news cut through the walls of her house and could be heard all over the neighborhood. She ran out to her car and screeched out of the driveway. Ben, Anne, and Bobby were right behind her in the station wagon.

They were at the grocery store parking lot in record time, and saw the fleet of police cars with their blue lights flashing. Sharon pulled her car up to where she saw Larry and Tony with Jenny, slammed it into park, and jumped out. Ben's car screeched to a halt behind her.

"Jenny, where are they?" she shouted. "Weren't you watching them?"

Jenny was sobbing, and Tony set his arm around the teen to steady her as she looked up at her mother. "I'm so sorry, Mom. I lost them. I let them play at the video game, and the next thing I knew they were gone!"

"What are you doing to find them?" she asked Tony. "They're so little. They must be scared to death. You've got to find them!" Her voice was rising in pitch with each word, and Larry tried to calm her. Ben was standing behind her now, and Larry faced them both.

"We have an eyewitness who saw a brown-haired man with a straw hat and sunglasses, average weight, 5'9" or 5'10". Does that sound familiar to you?"

Sharon looked helpless. "It sounds like a hundred people I know."

"We also have a description of the car. It was a blue Taurus, a rental car, but our witness didn't notice the agency. We also have an all points bulletin out on it. We've got cars at checkpoints all over St. Clair, and we've notified the state police to watch for him if he leaves town with them. But right now we need your help. I know you're upset, but we need to keep our heads clear so that we can move as fast as we can."

"What do you need?" Ben asked.

"We need pictures so we can distribute them all over the area. And we need to set up some phone lines in your house so that we can trace any ransom call you might get."

"He said he would take something of mine," Ben said. "He threatened me, the night he realized I didn't deliver what he wanted."

Furiously, Sharon stood up to face Ben. "It's him, isn't it? He took our children!" She shoved Ben back against another police car. "Give him what he wants, Ben!" she shouted. "Give him what he wants so I can get my baby back!"

"I . . . don't . . . know . . . what he wants," Ben said through his teeth. "If I knew, I'd take it in two seconds flat. I have *two* kidnapped children, Sharon. Don't you think I would do whatever I could to—"

"Stop it!" Anne commanded as she stepped between them. "We don't have time for this. We have to find them!"

Sharon swung around to Tony and grabbed the lapels of his sport coat. "If you'd listened when Ben told you! If you'd looked for the killer instead of pinning it on him—this maniac wouldn't have my child!"

She saw that television crews were beginning to gather, and one camera was aimed at her. Shaking her head, she pushed through the crowd and back to her car. "I'm going after them. I'll find them!"

Tony stopped her. "Sharon, you can't! We have people looking for them, but we need your help here."

"All right!" she screamed, shaking his hands off of her. "Tell me what to do! But don't make me just sit here while he gets farther away with the girls!"

Hours later, as it began to grow dark, there was still no word. Two cops stayed at their house, waiting for the ransom call, while Larry and Tony beat the streets trying to find any leads on who could have the children. This case took precedence over every other. There hadn't been a kidnapping in St. Clair in almost twenty years, and that one had been a parental abduction. Now the whole town of St. Clair was searching for the children. Posters were hung on every pole, every wall, every window. Church friends came to the house in a steady stream, bringing food—the only thing they knew to do—and leaving with stacks of posters with the faces of the two children.

Jenny had been sedated, and slept in her room. Bobby also slept peacefully now that he'd been medicated and was on his way to recovery. But Anne, Sharon, and Ben paced the living room waiting frantically for the phone to ring.

It was nearing dark when Tony and Larry returned to the house. Their expressions were grave, and Sharon began to feel nauseous at the thought of what they might say.

"Sharon, Anne, Ben—would you all please sit down?"

"You found them," Anne said, her face turning white with fear.

"No, no," Tony said quickly. "We haven't found any trace of them. Not yet. But we need to ask you a few questions."

"Sure," Sharon said. "Anything. What?"

Larry looked uncomfortably at Tony. "We need to know every place any of you went today, starting with the time you got up until right after the abductions."

"Oh, here it comes," Ben said. "I should have anticipated it."

Puzzled, Sharon and Anne looked at him.

"Don't you see?" he asked. "It's the parallel investigation. While they're looking for the guy who took our kids, they start to consider that we might have done it ourselves."

"What?" Anne asked, astounded.

Sharon got to her feet. "Why would we do that?"

"We're not saying you did, Sharon," Tony said. "It's a matter of protocol. Really. Just routine. For our reports."

"Now I remember," Sharon said. "A couple of years ago, that kidnapping in Virginia or somewhere. They discovered that the mother had killed them. But you don't think . . ."

"Sharon, we're not accusing anyone," Tony said. "We just have to ask a few questions."

"It's me, Sharon," Ben said. "Since I'm an alleged murderer and a pathological liar, I had to have done this, right? Another ploy to throw them off my scent!" He swung an arm and knocked a vase off the table, sending it crashing to the floor. He turned and stormed out of the room.

"Where are you going?" Larry asked loudly.

"To call my lawyer," Ben said. "I'm not saying another word until she's here."

Sharon and Anne gaped at the two detectives as Ben rushed out. "He didn't do this!" Sharon shouted. "He's their father! He was here with us the whole time! You had a witness who saw them get into the car with a man! You need to expend your energy trying to find that man, instead of wasting your time on this!"

Tony sat down, looking weary.

"Sharon, we have to ask the questions," Larry said. "You need to help us by answering them. We haven't stopped the investigation. It's still going on. But it's department policy that we cover every possibility. And with the extenuating circumstances—"

"I don't care about extenuating circumstances," Sharon cried. "This whole nightmare has been extenuating from the beginning!" She wiped her face and paced across the floor. "What about me? Am I suspect?"

"No one is suspect," Tony said.

"Why not? Maybe I had some stupid ulterior motive. Maybe I had some deep hatred against Emily, so I hired someone to kidnap both of them."

"I guess being the stepmother," Anne said, "I'm a prime suspect, too, huh?"

"We told you! We're not accusing anyone."

"You're accusing Ben!" Sharon shouted. "Admit it. You think he did it, and that would be just as absurd as either of us. They're both his kids!"

"They're just questions, Sharon! Just questions!" Tony shouted.

Ben came back into the room. "Lynda's on her way over. She said that none of us should say another word until she gets here."

"Fine," Larry said, sitting back in his chair and crossing his arms. "We'll wait."

Tony nodded. "Fair enough."

Seconds ticked by, as everyone found some spot in the room to focus on. Finally, Anne cried, "Why doesn't that phone ring?"

"He wants us to sweat," Ben said quietly.

"But what about the children? It's getting dark, and they'll be so afraid. Emily doesn't have her blankie or her little doll that she sleeps with. What if he doesn't feed them? What if they're hurt?"

"They can't be," Sharon whispered. "We just have to pray that they'll be all right. We just have to have faith."

But her faith seemed as flimsy as Anne's and Ben's as they waited for Lynda to arrive.

They waited, Tony and Larry sitting on the couch, Sharon leaning stiffly against the piano with her arms crossed, Ben pacing, and Anne in a chair watching out the window, as if the kidnapper would suddenly drive up and let the children out.

The doorbell rang. It was Lynda and Jake.

"What's going on, Tony?" Lynda asked. "Why are you badgering these people?"

"We're not badgering them, Lynda. We just want to ask some questions."

"All right," she said. "Everybody sit down."

They all took places around the room, except for Jake, who hung back in the doorway. "I'm gonna go hang some posters, guys," he said. "Lynda, are you sure you can get a ride home?"

"No problem," she said. "I think I'll be here for a while."

He touched Sharon's shoulder and squeezed hard. "Sharon, I'm praying for them. We're gonna find them. We've got hundreds of people out looking. You know that, don't you?"

Sharon touched his hand and squeezed back. "Yeah. I have more faith in you guys than I do in these so-called detectives."

Tony looked up at her, stung.

"At least somebody's doing something," she added.

Jake nodded soberly. "I'll see you later then," he said, heading out the door.

After the sound of his car died away, Lynda spoke up. "All right," she said to Larry and Tony, "ask anything you want. I know that my clients want to give you any answers that can help you find the children. But I'm not going to let you bully or badger them, and you're not going to get away with hanging this on them."

"So now they're *all* your clients?" Larry asked.

"That's right," she said defiantly.

Ben leaned forward, looking ragged and haunted. "Look, before you ask anything, can I just ask you something?"

Larry shrugged. "Go ahead."

"Think of the logic here, guys. If I really killed Dubose, why would I leave all the evidence—the gun registered to me, the money clip, the fingerprints. And it's even more illogical that I would add to that by doing something with my own children—" His voice broke off. "But think about it. If I'm being set up, and Dubose was killed because of whatever it is this maniac is looking for, then wouldn't it make sense that he'd kidnap my children to have leverage over me? He thinks I have whatever it is, so he wants to force me into handing it over."

"Sure, that would be logical," Larry said. "Logical enough for you to count on."

"What's that supposed to mean?" Lynda asked.

"It's the conspiracy theory," Sharon snapped. "Oswald didn't kill Kennedy—it was the Republicans. And this kidnapper didn't take our kids—Ben did, only he staged it so carefully that it would look like someone else did it. He was actually in two places at once, and he didn't look anything like himself, and it wasn't his car, but he was behind it, because the other way seems too blasted logical!"

Lynda touched Sharon's hand and gestured for her to be quiet.

"Just find my baby!" Sharon shouted, standing up and knocking over her chair. "Stop sitting here and find them before it's too late!"

CHAPTER TWENTY-SIX

Their eyes had adjusted to the dark. Above them, too far to reach, hung shelves cluttered with gardening tools. A bag of feed leaned against the corner, and a lawn mower was parked near the back. The whole space was no larger than Christy's walk-in closet at home, and the floor was made of dirt and getting colder the later it got.

"I'm hungry," Emily said, her voice hoarse from screaming.

Christy's head still throbbed, and the cut stung. Her bangs were bloody and matted to her forehead. "Me, too. But Daddy will come get us real soon. I know he will."

"What if he can't find us?"

"He will. He's real smart."

"But I want to go home *now*," Emily whimpered.

"Me, too," Christy said.

They listened hard to the wind whistling around the corner of the building, and the raindrops pattering on the roof. Thunder cracked, and both girls screamed.

"It's just thunder," Christy said, trying to sound brave.

"I hate thunder," Emily cried.

"But it can't hurt us," Christy said, remembering what her mother had told her so many times. "We're safe in here."

Emily began to wail as thunder cracked again.

"We could pray," Christy tried.

"I don't know how."

Christy put her arm around Emily. "Just close your eyes," she whispered, "and I'll do it."

"What if God can't hear us through the thunder?"

"He will," Christy assured her. "Thunder is no big deal to God. He always hears children's prayers. Mommy told me so. Now bow your head."

"I don't want to."

"Just do it!" Christy shouted. "Bow your head now or I'll quit trying to make you feel better!"

"You're *not* making me feel better!" Emily cried. "You're making me feel worse."

"I'm the one with the hurt head!" Christy snapped. "And I'm not acting like some whiny little baby!" She started to cry even as the words came out of her mouth, and finally Emily reached over and hugged her.

"I'm sorry."

Christy sucked in a sob and wiped her eyes. "It's okay. Will you bow your stupid head now?"

Emily stuck her thumb in her mouth and bowed her head. They clung together as Christy started to pray.

"Dear God, we're really scared . . ."

The thunder and rain raged around them as Christy prayed, but before she even got to "Amen," Emily had drifted off to sleep.

Christy held her for a long time before she too finally surrendered to sleep.

CHAPTER TWENTY-SEVEN

The storm was getting more violent, as if the universe were conspiring against them. Sharon paced outside in her screened porch, while they continued questioning Ben inside. Desperately, she clutched Christy's Simba doll against her and railed mentally at God, bargaining with him, pleading with him to bring her child back. She was angry, she was frightened, she was confused.

When Tony stepped through the back door, she squelched the urge to throw something at him. "What do you want? I thought you were finished interrogating me."

"We are, for now," he said. "Sharon, are you all right?"

She breathed a despairing laugh. "Funny how things work out, isn't it? We were supposed to have had dinner tonight. Who knew that instead I'd be out of my mind with terror?"

"We'll find them. I know we will."

"Dead or alive?" she screamed at him. "Before or after it's too late?"

He looked down at his feet, and she clutched the Simba doll tighter. "I just want Christy back. I can't stand the thought of her being out there somewhere." She pressed her hands against the brick wall, staring out at the night. Lightning struck, brightening the night sky, then blackening it again. A sharp clap of thunder followed.

"That's it," she said, shoving past Tony into the house. He followed behind her as she grabbed her purse and started digging for her keys. "I'm going out there," she said through clenched teeth. "St. Clair isn't that big. I'll find them. I'll drive down the streets with my windows rolled down, and listen for their voices. I won't come back until I've gotten them."

She bolted through the kitchen and out the side door, Tony at her heels.

"You can't do this, Sharon," he argued.

"Yes, I can!" she screamed. "You can't stop me. I'm not under arrest! I can go anywhere I want to."

"You're not in any condition to drive, Sharon. And the weather's bad. If I have to, I *will* arrest you just to keep you from doing something stupid."

"But somebody has to look for the children!" she screamed. "We can't leave them out there. Do you know what it's like for a little girl in a storm? Even at home, she's terrified. She sleeps with a night-light on every night. And the hall light. And if it's damp and cold, she catches cold real easily. I've got to get to her . . ."

Feeling helpless, Tony reached for her. "You've got to leave it to the professionals, Sharon. Trust them."

"I *can't* trust them," she cried, shaking free of him. "I can't. Christy trusts me. I'm the only one. She knows I'm always there for her. I've never let her down. Never. When she's scared or tired or hungry or sick, I've always been there." Her voice broke. She was getting hoarse from crying, but she kept on. "I'll find them. I know I can. I know St. Clair better than anyone. I've sold property in every section of the town. I'll think of hiding places."

Tony glanced back toward the door. "All right, listen. I'll go with you. You're too upset to drive, so I'll drive and you can tell me where to go. Fair enough?"

She nodded and breathed another sob. "Yes, all right."

"Okay. Just let me tell Larry."

He went back to the door and saw Larry standing with Ben and Anne in the doorway. "Larry, I'm gonna take her for a ride just to make her feel better. She has a car phone, so give us a buzz if anything comes up."

Larry looked concerned. To keep Ben and Anne from over-hearing, he stepped outside. "Are you sure this is a good idea? You're a cop, not a social worker. It's not your job to make her feel better."

"Larry, it's either ride with her or arrest her," Tony said in a low voice. "She's losing it, just sitting here like this. I can't blame her."

"I want to go, too," Anne said from behind Larry. "Take me with you."

Sharon heard, and swung around. "No! You and Ben have to stay here in case they call!"

"You can't go," Larry added. "I still have some questions. We aren't finished."

"But we've told you everything!" Anne cried.

"Look," Tony said, "if we find one child, we'll find both. Your husband needs you. So does your baby."

Larry coaxed Anne back into the house before she could protest further.

Feeling as if he'd been caught on the front lines of a major war, Tony hurried out to her car before Sharon could leave without him.

Sharon insisted on Tony's driving twenty miles per hour with both windows down. His left side was getting drenched as they went, and her car's interior was beginning to soak up the rain like a sponge. They had been all through the rural parts of St. Clair, up one street and down another, searching for places where a deranged kidnapper might have hidden two little girls. One time, she had been positive that an old, condemned house was where the children were, and he had been forced to follow her through the muddy yard and the pouring rain, up the broken steps of the porch, and into the rat-infested house. The children hadn't been there, though there was evidence that someone had been using it for a crack house, and he made a mental note to follow up on that later.

Now, after driving for two hours, he wondered how to broach the subject of going back to her house.

"We'll never find them, will we?" she asked.

"Not like this," he said.

She shivered as the cold rain soaked through her. "I should have dressed Christy warmer today. I should have made her wear a jacket."

"It was in the seventies earlier, Sharon. You couldn't have known."

"Yes, I could have," she said. "We knew there was a killer out there already turning our family upside-down. I should have realized the kids were in danger."

He didn't know what to say. It seemed that everything he attempted only made things worse.

"You try to teach them things, you know?" she railed. "Like, never talk to strangers. Look both ways before crossing the street. Eat your vegetables. Brush your teeth. But you never really think about teaching them how to survive in an emergency . . . how to get help . . . how to get home . . ."

Tony reached for her hand and squeezed it. It was as cold as ice. "Don't underestimate their instincts. Even children have good ones."

"But I've sheltered her so. I didn't want her to know that evil like this existed."

"You were supposed to shelter her. That's your job. Don't beat yourself up because you didn't prepare her to be kidnapped."

Quiet settled over them for a moment. Rainwater soaked her hair and trickled down her face as she gazed at him. "I almost lost it with Anne before we left. I just couldn't take any more."

"That's normal," Tony said. "And you have a lot of anger in you. For good reason. It's natural that you'd want to lash out at them."

"I thought I was different," she whispered.

He looked at her. "Different how?"

"Better," she said. "I thought I had all the biblical principles down, that I knew how to behave in any circumstance, that I could stand up to any tragedy, that trials would only make me stronger."

"And?"

"And I think I've just been fooling myself."

Tony frowned and moved his eyes back to the wet road. "You think those principles don't work, after all?"

She shook her head. "No, that's not it. I know they work. I think I've been fooling myself about what I was capable of. Christianity isn't about becoming a better actress. Hiding your feelings. *Doing* all the right things. It's about changing your heart. And I think mine has a long way to go."

Tony let those words sink in. They were foreign to him, for he couldn't fathom anyone being more self-sacrificing than this woman who had taken in her ex-husband and the woman he left her for. "You have a pretty good heart, from where I sit."

"I have a *petty* heart," she said. "Petty and angry and vindictive."

"Vindictive? How do you figure that?"

She began to cry again and shook her head with disgust. "Vindictive because I wish Emily had been taken alone. That it was just their child who'd been kidnapped. That mine was at home, safe and sound . . . because some part of me feels that they deserve that." She looked at Tony, her eyes glistening. "Isn't that terrible?"

He came to a red light and sat still for a moment, looking at her, wishing he could touch her and offer some comfort. But he knew better. He was a professional and had to maintain some detachment. Still, her tears reached straight into his heart, and he found himself doubting the logic of his own strict rules. "Sharon, there's not a mother out there who has a child kidnapped, who doesn't wish it was someone else's child. You're not horrible. And you're not vindictive. You're just distraught because something has happened to your child that you can't control. I don't have any kids, but if I did, and this happened, I'd probably have snapped and killed twenty people by now. I think you're a very special lady for analyzing your own heart at a time like this."

She dropped her forehead into her palm and wept quietly for a long moment. No other traffic was on the road as the storm raged around them, so he ignored the green light and watched her cry.

He reached across the seat and took her hand, almost tentatively. She accepted his touch, so he squeezed gently. "I want to find Christy for you," he whispered. "I'd kind of like the chance to get to know her. She's a pretty cool kid, from what I've seen. Any little girl with such a special mom is someone I'd like to make friends with."

She looked up then, and he saw the torment on her face and wished from the deepest places in his heart that he could take it from her and carry the burden for her.

"I'm gonna find her for you, Sharon."

She sucked in a sob and nodded as if she believed him. When he moved the car forward through the intersection, she leaned her head back on the wet seat. "Let's go home," she said. "Jenny might be awake by now. She's going to need me."

"Okay," he whispered. But he kept holding her hand as he drove her back to her house, where those who loved the two little girls still kept vigil through the night.

Back at Sharon's house, Ben, Anne, and Lynda still sat at the kitchen table with Larry, who had asked them a zillion questions a dozen times each. Ben had answered as patiently as he could, knowing how it looked to the police who had seen more bizarre cases than his, if not on their own turf, then in other precincts across the country. People did murder their bosses. Parents did sometimes do harm to their kids. He just didn't know how to convince them that he wasn't among them.

"All right, now, for a minute, let's assume that you're telling the truth, and that someone else killed Dubose, and wants something you have, and kidnapped your kids to force you into giving it to them. So let's go back over it all. Try to think of everyone who came into the studio to see Dubose the week leading to his death."

"I have," Ben said. "I've given you the names of everyone I could think of. None of them seemed angry at him or agitated in any way."

"Then can you think of a time in the days leading to his death when *he* was agitated or angry? Maybe after a phone call?"

Ben stared at the table, retracing the last few days. Dubose had been moody, quiet, and Ben had the feeling he was aggravated with him.

"There was something about his mood," he said, finally. "He was distant. Preoccupied. Like I had made him mad or something."

"Had you?"

"No. We usually got along real well. He was happy with my work ... and was real generous to us. I thought he might have some personal problems."

"Then you hadn't had any blow-ups with him?"

"None."

"Wait," Anne said, her eyes widening. "There was a blow-up, Ben. Remember a few days before we were thrown out, when you found that hidden painting? You said he bit your head off about that."

Ben frowned. "Yeah, but it was so silly. I thought he was just in a bad mood."

Larry leaned forward and gazed intently at him. "Why didn't you mention this before?"

Ben threw up his hands. "I didn't think it was related. It happened days before the murder. And it was such a little thing. I had gone up to the attic looking for an old-fashioned frame for one of my paintings. I thought I might find something up there, since he stored a lot of stuff there. But I bumped my head on something, and a rolled-up canvas fell out. I unrolled it, and it looked just like the famous painting *The Multitude,* by the sixteenth-century Italian painter Marazzio. I got excited—I'd heard that that painting had been stolen several years ago. So I took it downstairs and stretched it out on a table. It looked so authentic, I could have sworn—"

"Was it the real thing?" Larry prompted.

"Well, no. Louis walked in and saw what I had, and he blew a fuse. Started yelling at me that the attic was off-limits. Which was pretty strange, because that just didn't seem like him. I apologized and told him to calm down, and I asked him if he knew that *The Multitude* had been hidden up there in a specially built compartment. Someone else owned the gallery before Louis, and I figured *they* might have hidden it there—although, when you think about it, they wouldn't have left it there. Anyway, he finally did calm down, and he looked at the painting, and quickly discovered some mistakes. They were tough to see, because the picture has a crowd of hundreds of people, supposedly at the Sermon on the Mount. But Louis said he was very familiar with all of Marazzio's work, and this wasn't real. He knew his stuff better than anyone I know, and he had a keen eye because he saw a lot of fakes that people tried to pass off as originals. Of course, he admitted his main clue that it was a fake was that the original had been recovered a couple of years ago."

"What did he do with it?"

"I don't know. I told him we should frame the picture, reproduction or not, and display it in the gallery, but he refused. He took the painting and rolled it back up, and I never saw it again."

Larry stared down at his notes now, thinking. "Why would anyone have hidden a reproduction?"

"I have no idea. It really didn't make sense, but I figure someone might have mistakenly thought it was the real thing. Who knows?"

Larry's eyes were riveted on Ben's when he asked, "Do you think there's any possibility that this Marazzio reproduction could be the painting our kidnapper wants?"

Ben frowned and considered that for a moment. "No. Why would anyone kill over a reproduction? It's practically worthless."

"What if Dubose lied, or was just wrong about that stolen painting being recovered?" Lynda asked. "What if it was the real thing? Do you think a real Marazzio could cause all this trouble?"

"A genuine Marazzio, particularly *The Multitude*, would be worth millions. Yeah, somebody might kill over it."

"But wouldn't they realize that when they sold it, they'd be sitting ducks with a murder and kidnapping attached to it?"

Ben shrugged. "It depends. The statute of limitations in Italy for stolen art is ten years. Paintings like that one disappear for a decade or more, then suddenly turn up at an auction one day, supposedly found by accident." He shook his head. "It doesn't matter, though. It was a reproduction. The real one was found a couple of years ago."

"Are you absolutely sure?" Lynda asked him.

"Yes. Louis knew his stuff. He traveled a lot, buying and selling important pieces of art, and he knew. For someone to go to all this trouble over a reproduction, they'd have to be fooled into thinking it was real. But I don't see that happening here. Anyone willing to pay what a real Marazzio is worth would check it out and find out that the real thing has been found."

"Then explain why Dubose fired you just a few days later, when you say it was completely out of his character. There must have been something else going on."

He turned his palms up and shook his head. "I don't know. I have no idea. Maybe the painting had nothing to do with it. Anyway, even if it did, I don't know where the reproduction is. I went back up there the next day to see it again, just out of curiosity, but it was gone. I don't know what he did with it."

Larry sighed. "We've got to find it. It might be what he wants."

"If I had it, and knew that was what he wanted, I'd have given it to him by now, and have my girls back in their own bed tonight."

Lynda touched Ben's hand, as if to offer some small bit of comfort, and looked beseechingly at Larry. "Larry, the man's been through enough. Leave him alone. Go look for the children."

Larry stared at them both over steepled fingers, then nodded reluctantly. "All right, Ben," he said. "That's all for now. But I may have more questions later."

CHAPTER TWENTY-EIGHT

A light rain pattered against the window as Lynda Barrett sat at the desk in the corner of her den, hunched over the books she had picked up from the library on her way home from Sharon's. There had to be something here. Something that might give her an idea about what to do next. She felt helpless. It had been bad enough trying to defend a man for murder when all the clues pointed to him, but the kidnapping gave it a terrible urgency. She felt sure that Ben wouldn't be a suspect much longer, since they had confirmed that he was home with Lynda and Anne when the kidnapping occurred.

Desperate to get to the bottom of this complex case, she flipped through pages and pages of art books, trying to learn more about Marazzio and the painting that Ben had discovered. If it wasn't the original, then it probably had nothing to do with the case at all. But if there was even a chance that it was, it might be the key both to clearing Ben of the murder charges and to finding the kidnapper.

Coming to a chapter on famous lost paintings, she scanned the pages for Marazzio. She found him listed halfway through and quickly began to read.

She heard a knock at the kitchen door, and before she could call "come in," the door opened. Jake, who had lived in her garage apartment since the plane crash that had changed his life, came in and peered around the doorway to the den. "Hi," he said. "I couldn't sleep and I saw your light on. Are you all right?"

She smiled up at him. He looked good, standing so tall without his cane, though he still had a slight limp. He was handsome—even more now than he'd been before the crash, because now she knew his true character. In her mind, his looks weren't marred by the scar that slashed one side of his face. That scar had special attraction for her, because it had special meaning. It was because of that scar that they had both bonded as human beings rather than adversaries. She cherished it now.

"I'm fine," she said, sitting back in her chair and holding out a hand to him. He came over to her and bent to kiss her. She reached up and touched that scar that felt so familiar beneath her fingertips.

"You sure? You were so shaken about the kidnapping."

"So were you."

"Yeah, well. That Christy's a character. I just hate the thought that . . ." His voice trailed off, and he slumped into a chair and looked at the floor.

"Yeah, me, too," she whispered. "I went to the library a while ago and got everything I could find on Marazzio—you know, the painter? I thought maybe that reproduction Ben found had something to do with all this. The police searched the gallery tonight and didn't find it. I can't help wondering—if it was just a worthless fake, where is it? Who took it?"

"Find anything?"

"No," she said, rubbing her eyes. "Well, a couple of things, but I don't know if they're important. I feel like I'm barking up the wrong tree with those kids out there somewhere. . . ." She dropped her forehead into her hand. "But then I tell myself that I have to leave the kidnapping to the police. My job is to help Ben. I have to somehow help him figure out who could be setting him up. *That* will tell us who the kidnapper is, and who the killer is."

"Not a very comforting thought, is it?" Jake asked. "That the kidnapper is the killer."

"No," she said. "It isn't."

"Well, I've been trying to think what I could do," he said. "And it came to me. As soon as it's daylight, I'm gonna head out to the airport, and Mike and I are gonna take one of the planes up and scan the landscape. See if we can spot the Taurus they were taken in. Who knows? Maybe it's parked somewhere and we can see it. It's a long shot, but it's something."

She smiled slightly. Flying was Jake's passion, but he'd lost his license after the crash due to his temporary paralysis and his blindness in one eye. He was waiting for the opportunity to get his medical release and try to get his license back, but until now, he hadn't been ready. "You gonna do the flying?" she asked.

"I might," he said. "Mike's a certified instructor. As long as he's with me, it's not a problem."

"It's been a long time. Are you sure you're ready?"

"I've never been more ready," he said. "Maybe I'll see something. You never know."

She thought about that as her smile sobered. "Even if you don't see the car, make a note of any hiding places on the outskirts of town. We could try them."

"There's not much to go on, is there?"

"No, there's not." She closed the book she was reading and stood up. "I just hope Larry and Tony will let up on the parents now that it's so obvious that they weren't involved."

"Sharon obviously couldn't have done anything like that. She's got a heart as soft as marshmallows. But what about Ben or Anne? Do you think they could have—"

"No," she said without question. "I think Ben was telling it straight from the beginning. He was framed. Somebody killed Dubose and left a trail that pointed to Ben."

"But why the kidnapping?"

"I don't know. There are still too many questions. It seems strange. If the killer wanted us to think Ben did it . . . then why would he kidnap Ben's kids? It would obviously indicate that someone else is the culprit, after all. The minute the police realize someone else is involved, Ben is out of the hot seat."

"Maybe the killer's desperate. Or maybe he's just sure he won't get caught. Maybe he's trying to manipulate Ben in some way. Needed the kids so he could work a deal."

"Yeah, but why? What does he want?"

"I'm with you. That reproduction keeps coming to mind."

Lynda looked back at the book she'd been flipping through. "But a reproduction isn't worth much. Certainly not all this."

They heard a car in the driveway, and Jake went to the kitchen and glanced out into the night. His mother sat there in the red Porsche that was once his—the toy he had cherished more than any other possession. It looked more ridiculous each time he saw her driving it. But he had given it to her free and clear. He had expected her to sell it and buy a condo or something. But she was having the time of her life driving it all over town.

"It's Mama," he said to Lynda over his shoulder. "She probably came to get some of the posters of the girls. She's working the late shift at the diner tonight and said she'd put some up and hand them out to her customers."

"Great."

Jake went to the door as his mother got out of the car, dressed in tight knit black pants, an over-frilly pink blouse, and four-inch heels. She had gotten her hair done, Lynda noted as Doris bopped in. Her roots weren't quite as black as they'd been the last time she'd seen her. Though the woman had been hard to swallow when she'd first come to St. Clair, Lynda was growing fond of her now. She was a lost soul, desperately trying to find herself. That it had taken the woman fifty-something years to do it was not her fault.

"Hey there, boys and girls!" Doris said, clicking into the kitchen and reaching up to pat her son's cheek. She took one look at Lynda and gasped. "Heavens to Betsy, girl, you look like something the cat dragged in."

Lynda's smile crashed. "I do?"

"You look like you haven't slept in a month of Sundays."

"Well, this kidnapping's got me really worried . . ."

"Of course it has!" Doris said in her Texas twang. "Those poor little sweet boys . . ."

"Girls, Mama," Jake said. "They're girls."

"Well, just imagine them out there with some awful person. It just makes my skin crawl. But honey, when this is all over, let me give you a make-over, won't you? If you're gonna keep my boy happy, you're gonna have to take better care of yourself. He's the type has to fight the ladies off with a stick, ain't you, Jake?"

Jake grinned and winked at Lynda. "No, Mama. Not really. And I think Lynda's beautiful. We're both tired, that's all."

"Well, we've got to get out there and find these kids," Doris said. "Now where are those posters you were gonna give me?"

He handed her a stack, and her face twisted as she looked at the sweet faces. "Bless their hearts. They're so little. Oh, maybe some of the truckers who come through the diner will know something. I'll give these out to everybody who comes in tonight."

"Good," Lynda said. "I've set up a television interview this morning for the parents. Maybe a personal plea from them will get people's attention."

"Television?" Doris asked, her hand immediately straying to the blonde mop piled on her head. "Why, you know, if you needed some help with that, I'll be off work at seven. I've had a little experience with this sort of thing. When my friend Spud McKinley ran for mayor of Slapout, I fixed his wife's makeup before they did their campaign ad. You remember Spud, don't you, Jake? The kid who used to shoplift cigarettes from the corner store? Lived in the trailer park across from us? Anyway, he didn't win, but his wife had the prettiest makeup job you've ever seen. If that mother looks anything like you do right now, she's gonna need a makeup job."

"That's okay, Doris," Lynda said with a smile. "We're not really concerned with makeup. Besides, there are two mothers. The children have the same father, but they're half-sisters."

"Is that so?" Doris asked, leaning back against the counter as if settling in for some juicy gossip. "Well, that's interesting. Are they all gonna go on TV together?"

"Probably."

"Hmmm. They'll probably sell that story to Hollywood and make one of them miniseries out of it."

Lynda didn't quite know how to respond to that. "Thanks for passing out the posters, Doris." She gave the woman a hug, and Jake followed his mother out the door. "You be careful now, Lynda. Messing around with murder ain't no picnic."

She smiled. "Jake's the one you should worry about. He's going to fly tomorrow for the first time since the crash."

"You're what?" Doris asked, spinning around to face Jake. "Son, are you out of your mind? After what happened to you, you would want to fly again? Lynda, you're not gonna let him do this, are you?"

Lynda laughed. "Since when have I had control over anything Jake did?"

"Honey, you've got more control than you know. You just don't use it right."

"Come on, Mama," Jake said, rolling his eyes. "I'll walk you to your car."

Lynda could hear Doris chastising Jake all the way out to her car.

CHAPTER TWENTY-NINE

It was raining outside when the doorbell rang and Larry let Lynda in. Since most of the police force was looking for the girls, Larry and Tony had decided to stay at the home all night in hopes that a ransom call would come. Jenny still slept, sedated, upstairs, and Sharon paced the house, clutching Christy's Simba doll and praying. Anne stayed busy with Bobby, who was still fussy because of his cold, though the tormented, distracted expression she wore and the swelling of her eyes testified to the fact that Emily was never off her mind.

"I couldn't sleep, so I thought I might as well come on over," Lynda said as she followed Larry into the dining room of the house, where all of their tracing equipment was set up in anticipation of the phone call. "I've been doing a little homework, trying to find a motive. I got some books on Marazzio's work. I thought maybe the reproduction was a clue, somehow, and that if we could just get to the bottom of the motive, we might have some lead on who the killer and kidnapper are."

"Good. I was thinking about doing the same thing."

"Then you'll finally admit that Ben was set up?"

"I'm not admitting anything," he said wearily. "It's too soon. But while we're sitting here waiting with no leads, we can at least get a little culture."

Tony came into the room and said hello to Lynda, then picked up a Marazzio book and began flipping through. "This about that artist guy?"

"He's not just any artist," Lynda said. "According to what I've read, Marazzio's paintings have a high price tag."

"How high?"

"Millions. Three of his paintings have been stolen over the past fifteen years. Two have been recovered, and sold for millions. But this book must be outdated. At the time of its printing—three years ago—*The Multitude* still hadn't been found. The book said it was worth a whopping twenty million."

"Get outta here," Tony said. "You can't be serious."

"It's true."

Tony looked more seriously at the book in his hand, and flipped through, looking at the shots of his paintings. "Do you think the painting Ben found could have been the real thing?"

"It's possible," Lynda said. "Though I doubt it. Dubose was probably right. It probably has been recovered since this book was printed. Shouldn't be too hard to find out."

"This is ridiculous, anyway," Tony said. "People don't kill and kidnap over a picture slapped on canvas, do they? This has got to be about something else." He lowered his voice and said, "There's more here than Ben Robinson is telling. Mark my word."

"Maybe, maybe not," Larry said.

Sharon came to the doorway and looked in. It was clear that she had been crying, and she wore a fragile, haunted look. "Oh, Lynda, it's you. I thought maybe it was someone with news."

Lynda went around the table and hugged her friend. "We're working on it, Sharon."

Sharon looked down at the books on the table. "Marazzio?" She looked frustrated that they were wasting time on that. "You don't honestly think my child was kidnapped over that picture, do you?"

"No, I don't," Larry admitted. "But it's the only unusual thing that happened before Ben was fired and Dubose was killed. I don't know if there's a connection, but if there is, it might help us with the kidnapping, too."

"Instead of reading books and waiting for the phone to ring, you should be out combing the county for the girls. It's storming outside, and the whole night has passed without a phone call!" Her voice broke off, and she covered her face. "What if this maniac has hurt them?"

Tony got up and urged her to sit. Pulling his chair up close beside her, he said, "We've got people out there looking, Sharon. No one's going to get past our checkpoints with two little girls in the car. We're searching every boat and every plane that leaves St. Clair, and every man driving alone is going to have his trunk searched. We're also compiling a list of every rental car in the county with the description the witness gave. We'll find out who rented them, and that might give us some ideas."

Sharon whispered, "You think he put them in the trunk? That's horrible. Christy will be terrified. And it's thundering. She always sleeps with me when there's thunder."

"Maybe we'll find them soon. It'll be morning in a couple of hours, and we'll have the advantage of daylight."

Lynda bent over her and stroked her hair. "Sharon, as soon as the sun comes out, Jake and Mike are going up in a plane to see if they can spot the car anywhere, or get some idea where they may be. So that means all the bases are being covered. They'll be searching on the ground, in the water, and in the air."

"It's not enough!" she cried. "It won't be enough until they find them!"

The telephone rang, and they all jumped.

Ben bolted for the telephone in the kitchen, but waited and looked through the dining-room door to Tony—as he'd been instructed. Tony, who held his hand over his own phone, nodded that he was ready to begin tracing, and Ben picked it up.

"Hello?"

"Are you ready to give me what I want now?" the muffled, disguised voice asked.

"Where are my children?" Ben asked, the blood draining from his face. "Where are they?"

"I asked you a question."

Sharon rushed toward Ben. Anne already stood next to him, hanging on every word. "I don't even know what you're looking for!" he shouted.

"The painting, you con artist. You know I'm looking for the painting!"

"*What* painting?" Ben asked. "Is it . . . is it one of *my* paintings? Because Dubose didn't let me leave with any of them. But if you'll tell me which one, maybe I can get back into the gallery and get it. Please!"

"What do you want, Ben?" the voice asked. "For me to spell it out for those cops sitting there with their tape equipment, waiting for me to state it for the record?"

Ben was silent.

"I'm getting tired of these games," the voice said. "Your girls are getting tired of them, too."

"Where are they, you scumbag? Where are my children?"

"They're in a damp, dark place. Picture it, Robinson. Those two beautiful little girls screaming for their daddy. And you're the only one who can help them. All you have to do is give me what I want."

"I don't *have* what you want!" Ben said, breaking into tears and leaning his forehead against the wall. "I don't *know* what you want!"

The phone went dead in his ear.

Sharon swung back to Tony and Larry, who were each on another telephone, and were now barking orders.

"Did you trace it?" she asked, her eyes wide with hope.

"Yeah," Tony said, putting his hand over the receiver. "He was at a pay phone on the east side of town. A unit should be there by now."

"He's gone," Larry said, shaking his head and dropping his own phone. "The booth was empty when our guy got there."

"Oh, no!" Sharon cried. "I don't believe this!"

"They're combing the area. It's not too late. They could still catch him."

They all waited as moments ticked by with agonizing slowness. Finally, the officers searching for the kidnapper called to say that they hadn't found him.

Tony dropped the phone back in its cradle and looked up at Sharon, Ben, Anne, and Lynda, who were all clustered in the arched doorway of the living room.

"They lost him?" Sharon cried. "Are they looking around the area? Did they block off the neighborhood around the phone booth? Maybe he has the girls with him!"

"They're still searching the area," Larry said. "But with this storm, it's unlikely that there were any witnesses."

"But you've got to *do* something!"

Tony rewound the tape of the phone call and looked up at Ben through the door. Ben was still leaning with his forehead against the wall, weeping. Anne was staring at them with a look of shock on her face.

They played the tape again, hoping Ben would recognize the voice, but he couldn't place it. Sharon was near the breaking point. Gritting her teeth, she turned to Ben and shoved him.

"Tell him where it is!" she shouted through her teeth. "Give him what he wants!"

"I don't know what he wants!" Ben cried. "How many times do I have to say it?"

"No more times," she shouted. "Just give it to him!"

"Please, Ben!" Anne threw in, and began to sob into her hands.

He turned to her, then back to Sharon. "Do you really think that I'd put my family through this for some stupid secret?"

"Why not?" Sharon shouted. "You've done it before. Once you even *destroyed* your family over a stupid secret!"

"I have never intentionally hurt my family," he said, quieter now, though his voice trembled. "I've always tried to do the best I could."

"It was the best you could do when you left your wife and children for another woman?" she screamed. "You had no regard for them then, and I don't believe you have any regard for them now."

"Shut up!" Anne cried. "You don't know how he felt! You don't have a clue what was going on—"

Ben broke in, raising his voice over his wife's. "So what do you think is going on here now, Sharon? Do you think I have something that could ransom our children, but I'd rather sacrifice them than turn it over? Is that really what you think of me?"

"Stop it!" Lynda shouted. "All of you."

All three of them turned to look at Lynda, sobs racking them as they glared at her.

"I think I know what he wants," Lynda said. "The Marazzio, Ben. I think it's time to seriously consider that what you found may not have been a reproduction."

CHAPTER THIRTY

hristy woke with a start and shivered from the cold. The night-light must have gone out, she thought, and Mommy must have forgotten to leave on the hall light. But as those thoughts came to her, she realized she was not at home, but lying on a dirt floor in the tool shed where the man had left them.

Emily still slept, her head resting on Christy's shoulder. For a moment, Christy didn't move, for fear of waking her. But as she sat staring into the darkness, feeling the cold creeping around them, despair fell over her. She began to cry quietly.

The feeling that she would never be found, that she and Emily would never get out, panicked her, and she suddenly felt the urgency to try to get out. She gently slid out from under Emily's weight, then helped her to lie down on the cold dirt floor. Emily curled up in the fetal position, trying to get warm, her thumb stuck in her mouth.

Christy tried to reach the shelves to look for something to cover her with, but they were at least four feet higher than she could reach.

Her stomach ached with hunger, and she felt shaky and weak, but she went to the door and tested it again, as if hoping it had miraculously come unlocked during the night. They were still bolted in.

She sank down and listened to the sounds of the rain still pounding against the roof. Was Mommy out looking for her? Was Daddy? Had they called the police?

She wiped the tears from her face and set her hand down on the dirt by the wall. It was wet there. The rain was seeping under the walls, making the dirt floors soft. An idea came to her.

She felt around for a tool of some kind, anything she might dig with, but there was nothing. She tried using the heel of her loafer to start a hole in the dirt. It came loose, so she dug more, until she reached the softer, wetter earth underneath. Getting on her knees, she began to dig with her hands, raking away small handfuls.

"Mommy!" Emily woke, looked around, and began to scream. "Mommy!"

Christy grabbed her. "Emily, it's me. Christy. We're here, remember? In this place?"

Emily's wailing just got worse. "I want my mommy! Moooommmy!"

"She can't hear you," Christy said sullenly. "But I think I've found a way out. You have to help me. Now stop crying and look."

Emily hiccuped her sobs, but grew quieter.

"Look," Christy said, going back to the hole she'd been digging. "Help me dig under the wall, and we can get out."

"Dig with what?" Emily asked.

"Our hands," Christy told her.

Emily looked down at her hands. "I don't want to."

"Do you want to be here when that man comes back?" Christy asked her. "Or do you want to get out so we can go get help and call home?"

"Get out," Emily whimpered.

"Then help me."

Slowly, Emily moved over to the hole and began to help half-heartedly.

"If we dig deep enough, and get under the wall, we can run real fast into the woods."

"I'm scared of the woods," Emily said. "It has wolves and bobcats and alligators."

Christy hadn't thought of that. "Well . . . maybe we'll find a house. Maybe some nice grandma lives there, and she can give us some food. Maybe she has a phone."

Emily liked that idea better. "Okay, but I hope she has a heater. It's cold in here."

Together, they began to dig with their fingers, desperately trying to make a way to escape.

CHAPTER THIRTY-ONE

Sharon didn't know what to do with herself, so she set about to do something, anything, for Christy. First, she washed all her clothes. Then she pulled out a ready-made roll of dough and began to make cookies. The smell that filled the house made her feel that her child would be home by the time they were done.

But when she took them out of the oven, the children were still just as lost as they'd been before.

The house was deathly quiet, though she knew the two police officers sat in her dining room waiting for the phone to ring again. Larry and Tony had taken Ben to the gallery to look, once again, for the mystery painting, and two officers she'd never met were taking their place here while they were gone. The fact that they played a hand of cards in the dining room riled her, for she couldn't stand the thought that they were wasting time when they could be looking for the girls. It didn't matter that other cops—dozens of them—were combing the town for them.

She turned off the oven. Looking around at the clean kitchen, she realized there was nothing more to do. This busyness was crazy, anyway. It wasn't helping to give her any more peace.

She wandered upstairs to Jenny's room and checked on her. Heavily sedated, Jenny was sleeping soundly. Sharon touched her back and felt her rhythmic breathing. At least one of her children was safe. But what if something happened to Christy? Jenny would always blame herself. Her guilt over the kidnapping was overwhelming her already.

Feeling the weight of a couple of tons on her shoulders, Sharon adjusted Jenny's covers and left her bedroom. Slowly, she walked up the hall to Christy's room, trying to recover the feeling that her child was in there, tucked into bed, sleeping soundly. But as she neared the doorway, she was hit with the reality that her child was out in the cold, wet morning someplace, terrified and confused.

She burst into tears as she reached the doorway.

Anne sat there in the rocking chair in Christy's room, her knees hugged to her chest. For a moment the only sound was that of the rain pelting against the windows.

"Oh," Sharon said. "I didn't know you were in here." Anne started to get up, but Sharon stopped her. "It's okay. Stay."

Anne hugged her knees again, and Sharon could see that the misery on the woman's face reflected her own. "Where are they?" Anne asked on a whisper.

Sharon went into the room and sat down on the bed. She picked up one of the dolls propped against the pillow, and smoothed out its hair. "At least they're together."

"Yeah," Anne said. "I was just thinking that. Christy's not that much older than Emily, but she takes care of her. If either of them was alone ..." Her voice trailed off, and she looked out the window again.

"He just wants the painting," Sharon said, trying to reassure herself more than Anne. "He has to keep them alive so he'll have something to bargain with. He can't hurt them. He just can't."

"He already has," Anne whispered. "Just by taking them, he hurt them. The trauma that they're going through ..." She covered her face, and her voice came out in a squeak. "I know God's punishing me."

Sharon stared at her for a long moment, at a loss for what to say. There had been many times since her divorce when she had wished God would punish Anne, but in the last couple of years, those wishes had come less frequently. Why would such punishment come now, and include her own child?

Sharon grew quiet and followed Anne's gaze to the raindrops running down the window. She didn't know what to say.

"Do you remember during yours and Ben's divorce, when you told him that the pain for you was bad enough, but that he had traumatized his children and robbed them of their family? That they'd never be the same because of it?"

"I said a lot of things," Sharon whispered.

"That haunted Ben," Anne went on. "And I never let it haunt me. I thought kids were resilient. That they'd recover. That it wouldn't be a big deal."

Sharon had known that was Anne's attitude. She stiffened a little, wondering where the woman was going with this.

"But sometimes, I think God punishes people by giving them more of the pain they gave somebody else." She swallowed and hiccuped a sob, then kept going. "We traumatized your children, so now he's letting us see how it feels. Only this is even worse."

Sharon stared down at the doll for a moment, running her fingertip across the porcelain face and over the pink lips. "There's one problem with your logic on this, Anne. If it's the way you say it is, why would God make me go through it?"

Anne considered that for a moment, then looked at Sharon. "I don't know. Maybe he's punishing you for something, too."

She dropped the doll and got up. "Maybe you're just wrong about all of it," she said. "Maybe God had nothing to do with any of this. Maybe he's just watching over them. Bringing them back to us."

"They're both so little," Anne said in a tormented whisper.

For a moment Sharon felt a bond with Anne that she had never felt before. The bond of one mother to another.

But she didn't want to feel that bond, and as the contagious agony caught up with her and brought her close to breaking, Sharon left the room, to suffer alone.

CHAPTER THIRTY-TWO

The gallery was almost as it had been the last time Ben left it. The same paintings still graced the walls, the same sculptures stood on their pedestals.

But everything was different.

Ben let his eyes stray to the chalk mark on the floor, and realized for the first time that a man he had respected and depended on, a man he had seen every day for the last five years, was dead. Some murderer had come in here and killed him, and if Dubose had not fired and evicted him, Ben and his family might have been killed, as well. He wondered if that was why Dubose had been in such a hurry to get them out. Did he know he was in danger? Was he trying to spare Ben and his family?

Somehow, that thought made the reality seem more difficult to bear. His eyes teared up, and he turned away.

Tony looked uncomfortable with the show of emotion. "So where was this painting you told us about? How about taking us there and showing us where it was hidden?"

Ben tried to pull himself together and started up the stairs, with Larry and Tony following behind him. He cut through the studio where he'd been the most creative, and looked longingly at the work that leaned against the walls or sat on easels. Without uttering a word, he crossed the room to the office where Dubose had worked.

The little door to the attic was at the back of Dubose's office. Ben turned on the light, and the wooden stairwell lit up.

Slowly, he led them up into the attic. A few bare bulbs hung from the ceiling, casting a weak glare over wrapped and stacked canvases, over empty frames hung haphazardly on the walls.

"It was right over here," he said, and the two cops followed him. "I was up here looking for a frame." He gestured toward all of the old frames, some broken, some just dusty. "I wanted a frame that was obviously old. I was going for the antique look for one of my paintings. I'll show it to you when we go back down. Anyway, I bent down like this to look at that frame over there, and when I stood back up, my head bumped on this compartment, and the painting fell out. It had been rolled up for some time, because when I started to unroll it, the paint cracked a little."

Tony stepped forward and examined the narrow box built into the rafter at the ceiling. The door was hanging open, and he could see how the slanted compartment could have dropped its contents if it hadn't been closed properly. "Any idea where the painting is now?"

"I gave it to Dubose," Ben said. "I never saw it again."

"What might he have done with it?"

"Got me," Ben said. "He may have hidden it someplace else, though I don't really know why he'd go to all that trouble. I mean, it obviously wasn't the original."

Larry took a deep breath. "Well, maybe we'd better look around up here. It could be in a new hiding place."

"But didn't you say that the place had been rifled through? If it was here, the killer would have found it."

"We have to anyway," Tony said. So they set about examining every inch of the dusty, dark attic, moving frames and old cracked canvases, oil paintings that looked as if they'd be better suited to the dumpster outside than the attic, and broken sculptures that Dubose hadn't had the heart to throw away. There were no more hidden compartments, and very little of value there.

As they walked back through the studio, Ben showed them some of the things he'd been working on. "Pretty cushy job you had," Tony said, looking around. "Free rent, nice place to work, steady income whether you sell anything or not."

Ben's face reddened. "I sold plenty. People came from all over the country to buy my work."

"Do you think this is about one of your own paintings?" Larry asked.

Ben shook his head. "Why wouldn't he just call it by name? Describe it? Why the secrecy? Why does he think I know what he's talking about?"

They went through each of his paintings, then headed downstairs, studying each painting for something that gave it more value than the others. Nothing stood out as a work worthy of murder and kidnapping.

"All right, who can we call to find out for sure if that Multitude painting was recovered?" Tony asked.

Ben thought for a moment. "Come to think of it, Louis kept a set of books in his office that have information like that." He started back up the stairs, feeling excited. "I don't know why I didn't think of that before!"

They followed him back up, and he hurried into Dubose's office. "See?" he asked, pointing to the eight volumes on the credenza behind the desk. "*The Dictionary of Painters and Sculptors*. I had almost forgotten. It has information about lost and stolen art, what it's worth now, and all that kind of stuff. Louis used it extensively."

He pulled out one volume and flipped through the pages until he came to Marazzio. "There it is," he said, setting the book down and pointing to the passage so that Tony and Larry could see. "Says *The Multitude* was stolen from a museum in Palermo over ten years ago." He frowned. "I don't get it. It doesn't say it was recovered. These other two that were stolen at other times, they were recovered three years ago, but nothing about *The Multitude*."

"How current are these books?"

"Very current. Louis kept them up-to-date. He just got this set about a month ago."

"Maybe he got *The Multitude* mixed up with one of the ones that really was recovered."

"Or he lied," Larry said.

"If the painting I found was really the original, stolen painting, then it probably is what the kidnapper wants."

"So where is it?"

"I have no idea," Ben said. "Maybe you should search his house . . . his car . . ."

"We searched it after the murder," Larry said, "but we weren't looking for a painting then."

As they drove back to Sharon's house, Tony said, "That painting is the key to whatever is going on here. This painter. Mar—"

"Marazzio," Ben said.

"Yeah, Marazzio. He was pretty famous, huh?"

Ben chuckled, almost condescendingly. "I'd say so. He's considered one of the greats. Who knows? If it was a fake, maybe Dubose was going to doctor the reproduction and try to pass it off as the original, especially if he really did know the painting was still missing. See how many millions he could get for it."

"I'm in the wrong business," Tony muttered, and Larry laughed. "No, really. I'm artistic. I used to draw a mean Bugs Bunny."

"Used to? What happened?"

"I had to trade my crayon in for a gun."

"Tough life, buddy."

"Yeah. But if I'd known the money was in those crayons . . ."

They looked in the backseat. Ben wasn't laughing. But their bantering made him realize one good thing: they no longer considered him the killer.

"So where did Dubose buy most of the original art pieces he found?" Larry asked.

Ben shrugged. "He traveled a lot, went to a lot of auctions. And there were a few dealers he did business with. Some of them spent a lot of time at the gallery."

"Who were they?"

"Well, there were several. He had dealings with people all over the world. But some of the most frequent ones, I guess, were Leon Spatika, Nelson Chamberlain, T. Z. Quarternet. All three of them have bought paintings of mine."

Tony shot Larry a look. "Would their names be in Dubose's Rolodex?"

"Sure. Why?"

"We took it as evidence. Maybe we'll give them a call."

Larry looked over his shoulder. "If Dubose was such a big-time art dealer with all these connections, what was he doing in a little town like St. Clair?"

"He had about ten galleries across the U.S.," Ben said. "They're all as small as this one. It's a good outlet for some of the lower priced paintings he sells. Plus he liked to cultivate up-and-comers. That's what he considered me."

"Then there are other galleries with artists-in-residence?"

"Sure. But I doubt there are any others where the owner has been murdered and the artist's kids have been abducted."

They pulled into Sharon's driveway, but Larry made no move to get out. "Go on in, Ben, and tell John and Nick in there that they'll have to stay a little longer. Tony and I are going to search Dubose's apartment and his car again. Maybe we can find the painting."

"All right," Ben said. "But what if the kidnapper calls back?"

"John and Nick know what to do, and they'll get in touch with us."

"All right." He got out of the car, and headed inside to face the quiet left behind by his two little girls.

CHAPTER THIRTY-THREE

The hole the girls had dug was deep, and though their fingers had developed blisters, they both dug with a zeal that they hadn't felt since they'd come there. At the end of the tunnel they were digging with their hands was freedom. And food. And warmth.

They heard a car pulling up to the shack, its wheels popping on the gravel road.

"Daddy's come!" Emily exclaimed, jumping to her feet. "Daddy! Daddy!"

But Christy clapped a dirty hand over Emily's mouth. "It might be him!" she hissed. "The mean man. Be quiet and help me hide the hole!"

Emily's joy crashed instantly, and she looked around for something to move over the hole. There was nothing.

"I'll sit here over it," Christy said, sitting on the edge of the hole. "You lie down with your head in my lap, and he won't see it."

"What about the pile of dirt we dug out?"

"Lie down in front of it," Christy said. "Maybe he won't see it."

Emily got into place, and Christy could feel her trembling as she laid her head in her lap. "Do I pretend I'm sleeping?" she whispered.

"If you want."

Christy's hand was trembling as she laid it over Emily's arm. "Our hands," Emily said. "When he sees them, he'll know we've been digging."

Christy considered that for a moment. "I'll put mine under you. Put yours between your legs."

Both children hid their hands as the car door slammed. Footsteps came closer to the shed, and keys jingled.

"It's not Daddy, is it?" Emily asked on a whisper.

"No. I think it's *him*."

The door opened, and both girls stiffened. Emily closed her eyes and tried to pretend to be asleep.

The big man stepped inside holding two bags. "I brought you something to eat," he said, and thrust the bags at Christy. She took the bags, forgetting the dirt on her hands. The man didn't seem to notice.

"Thanks, Mister. Are we gonna get to go home today?"

"That depends on how much your daddy wants to keep you alive. It's up to him, kiddo."

Christy's eyes widened as she tried to understand. "It's cold in here. And dark. Real dark, and Emily's afraid of the dark." She started to cry, knowing that it wasn't the right thing to do, but she couldn't stop it. Then Emily's act crumbled, and she began to squint her eyes and cry, too.

"Please let us go home, Mister. We'll tell everybody you were nice to us. We won't tell them about this place."

The man laughed sullenly under his breath. "I told you, it's up to your father. When he gives me what I want, you can go home."

Both girls looked up at him, quiet.

"Eat your food. I don't know when I'll bring you any more."

With that, he closed the door and locked the bolt again.

"McDonald's!" Emily cried, and dug into the bag. "Drinks, too. Look, Christy!"

But Christy wasn't thinking about the food. Her mind was still hung on the fact that her father had the power to get them back, but hadn't done anything about it. More tears ran down the dirt on her face, and she wiped them away with a filthy, blistered hand, smearing mud across her face.

"Aren't you hungry, Christy?" Emily asked.

"Yeah," Christy said and took her drink out of the bag. "Emily, do you think he's ever gonna let us go home?"

Emily bit into her burger, and chewed thoughtfully as she looked at her sister. "If he doesn't, Daddy'll come get us. He'll find us. He always finds me when we play hide-and-seek."

"This isn't hide-and-seek," Christy said miserably. "He doesn't know where to look for us. And the man said it was up to him. What if we have to stay here another night?"

"We'll dig out before then," Emily said solemnly. "We'll run away and find that grandma with the telephone."

Christy wiped her eyes again and moved away from the hole. The man hadn't discovered it. Maybe Emily was right. Maybe they could escape soon.

The baby's cry woke Sharon from where she half-dozed with her head in her arms at the kitchen table, and she jumped up. It was morning. That was Christy calling her! She rushed toward the stairs.

But the crying wasn't coming from upstairs, and as the fog from her brain cleared, reality jolted her. It was Bobby, not Christy. Christy was still out there with some maniac who'd already killed at least once.

She grabbed Christy's Simba doll and wished she could at least get it to her somehow, so there would be some measure of comfort for her child.

She walked into the living room, and saw that Tony and Larry had come back and had fallen asleep on the two couches set at right angles to each other in the big living room. Tony stirred slightly, so she backed out and walked toward the sound of the crying baby.

As she grew closer, the crying stopped. She slowed her step and got to the doorway. Anne was there, holding the baby, humming to him and gently rocking him as he whimpered.

Maternal anguish washed over her, overwhelming her with pain. But it wasn't resentment this time, or jealousy. The sight just reminded her that there would be no outlet, none at all, for her emotions until Christy came back.

Then came the miserable, cruel, startling thought. *What if he's killed them? What if they're already dead somewhere? What if they cried and he got impatient? What if I never see Christy again?*

She covered her mouth to muffle her sobs. Rushing back up the hall, her head bent, she slammed right into someone coming toward her.

She caught her breath and yelped once, before she realized it was Tony.

"Are you okay?" he asked, looking down at her.

She covered her face and shook her head viciously. "What if they're dead?"

He pulled her into his arms and held her as she sobbed violently against his rumpled shirt. "They're not dead," he whispered. "You can't think like that. We're going to find them. Come on. Sit down. You're exhausted."

She let him lead her to the couch, and she sat down and allowed him to pull her against him. She laid her head on his shoulder and hiccuped sobs that wouldn't stop as he whispered soothing assurances against her ear. "Go ahead . . . it's okay to cry . . ."

The human contact helped. Slowly, her sobs subsided, and she was left under a blanket of grief. He still didn't let her go.

He stroked her hair back from her face and wiped her cheek with the back of his fingers.

"I dozed off in the kitchen," she whispered. "And the baby cried, and for a minute, I thought it was Christy. Just a split second, where I believed it had been an awful dream, and I was waking up."

"You need to get some real sleep, Sharon. You're not a superwoman."

"I can't," she said. "Some part of me thinks that if I let myself relax even for a minute, that they'll just fade away, and I'll never see my baby again."

There was nothing he could say.

After a while, she pulled out of his arms and sat upright. "I guess I should make everybody some breakfast."

"That's not necessary," Tony said. "You have enough to cope with."

"No," she said. "It's something I can do. You and Larry have been here all night. I want to feel useful somehow. I'm going to do it."

Tony stood up with her. "Are you sure you're up to it?"

"Yeah," she said. "Thanks for the shoulder. You have no idea how much I needed it."

"Any time." Tony watched her disappear back into the kitchen, then went back into the living room where he and Larry had been sleeping.

Larry was sitting up now. "You're getting a little too close to this case, don't you think, Tony?"

Tony shot him a disbelieving look. "You're kidding, right?"

"No, man. You're here to help find her child, not fall in love with her."

"Fall in love?" He almost laughed. "She was upset, and I tried to comfort her."

"Be careful. That can become a habit."

"Yeah, well, you ought to know." He raked a hand through his rumpled hair and wished for a shower.

"I'm serious, Tony. The woman's really vulnerable right now. She's going through a lot. You need to keep your distance."

Tony turned back around and glared at his partner. "That's just hilarious coming from you, Larry. In fact, I can't believe what I'm hearing."

Larry grinned. It was no secret that he had married a woman whose case he'd worked on. It was also no secret that he'd never been happier in his life. "Look, I know what you're thinking."

"I'm thinking that I was telling you the same thing just a few months ago. 'You're getting too involved. You're not being objective.'"

"I was the exception," Larry said with a grin. "But this is different."

"No, it's not different," Tony said. "But don't worry. I'm not gonna get hurt."

"Get hurt?" Larry asked. "Mr. Confirmed Bachelor? I'm not worried about *you* getting hurt!"

Tony gaped at him. "Her? You think I'll hurt her? What kind of lowlife do you think I am?"

"A noncommittal lowlife," Larry said matter-of-factly, though a twinkle of humor shone in his eye.

"Thanks a lot, pal."

Larry pulled on his shoes and got up, stretching. "Speaking of commitment, I think I'll go call my bride."

"Yeah, you do that." Tony sat down and watched his friend go out of the room. And some part of him resented that Larry had been so lucky. Tony hadn't realized he was lonely until he'd seen how happy Larry's marriage had made him. More and more lately, he had wondered if the bachelor life really had all that much to recommend it.

On the other hand, seeing the tangled web of *this* family reminded him that marriage wasn't all it was cracked up to be, either.

T he storm raged on, tormenting those who waited. It had been two hours since the short appearance they'd all made on the news, in which they had pled for the return of their children. In her despair, Sharon had offered a $25,000 reward for information leading to their return. But still, they hadn't heard a word.

Now Sharon wandered in and out of rooms like a phantom, racking her brain for some idea that would get her child back. In her mind, her prayer for Christy and Emily's safety played like a chant, repeating itself in the same cadence over and over. She wondered whether God was even hearing it.

She stepped out onto the porch and looked up through the screen to the cloudy, angry sky. Under this same sky the children were hidden. God knew where they were, and he was the only one she could trust to keep them safe. Tears came to her eyes as she looked up to plead with him, but a voice behind her startled her.

"I thought we'd have them back by now."

She swung around and saw Ben sitting on a bench leaned back against the wall of the house. His voice was hoarse, and she could see that he'd been crying. For a moment, she thought of going back into the house, but the brief connection seemed more important. Besides Anne, Ben was the only person in the world who knew exactly how she felt.

Quietly, she turned back around and looked up at the sky.

"I never thought we'd come to this," he said. "In my worst nightmares, I wouldn't have believed . . ."

Sharon didn't look at him. A million thoughts fled through her mind, thoughts of how he'd brought it on them somehow, how he was being punished for all the cruelty he'd inflicted on her and their children, and that the kidnapped children were just caught in God's crossfire. But some part of her knew that wasn't true.

"Despite what you might think, Sharon," he went on, his voice raspy and heavy with emotion, "and despite how cruel I was, I never meant to hurt any of you."

If he'd said that two days ago, she would have laughed sarcastically, then reminded him of all the little instances in which his hurting had seemed deliberate. But the fight had left her now, and all that remained was a dull numbness.

"I thought I'd forgiven you," she whispered. "At church, I even bragged about it. Lectured to other divorced women about letting go and praying for their exes. I told them that God loved their ex-husbands as much as he loved them. Even when I invited you to move in, part of me was patting myself on the back, thinking how everyone would see how I lived out my faith. What it looked like to truly forgive. I had it all worked out. I thought I'd even gotten some peace about it. But I didn't know what a farce it all was."

A long note of silence stretched between them as the cool wind whipped around the house, whispering through the leaves.

"I can't undo what I've done, Sharon," he said from his dark corner of the porch. "This whole week, it's been like my life has passed before my eyes. But it's done."

"That's right," Sharon said. "And none of it really even matters right now. I just want my baby back."

She turned and looked at him now, and saw that his eyes were closed as he struggled to control his emotions. "I guess it would make this a little easier if I thought you and I weren't enemies," he said.

"How could we be enemies, Ben? You're in my house. You're the father of my children."

"Neither of those things qualifies for friendship."

"Oh, is that it?" she asked, her sarcasm returning. "You want to be friends?"

"It'd be nice," he said. "We have a lot in common, you know. We both love our children. And we used to love each other."

She turned away again. "Love dies, Ben. You ought to know that more than anyone."

Before he could answer, Sharon went back into the house and left him alone.

CHAPTER THIRTY-FIVE

"Look, Emily. Light!" Christy clawed at the dirt, ignoring the bloody blisters on her fingers. "We reached the other side!"

"Can we get out now?" Emily asked.

"No. We have to dig the hole bigger! Help me!"

The two girls dug faster, the skin on their fingers raw and bloody and caked with the dirt through which they would escape. More light filled the small shed, giving them hope as the hole got bigger and the pile of dirt next to it piled higher.

"I think it's big enough," Emily said. "I can slide out."

"No, you'll get stuck. It has to be bigger!"

On their knees, they both pulled and clawed at the dirt, getting closer, closer, to the point at which they could slide under the wall and embrace their freedom.

Then they heard the car.

"He's coming!" Christy cried. "He'll see the hole!"

"I'm going now!" Emily fell down on her stomach and started to crawl into the hole.

"He'll see you!"

"But I'll get away," she said. "Come on. Hurry!"

They heard his car door close, and Christy hoped he had parked on the other side of the building. His footsteps in the gravel were growing closer. He was coming around the side to the door, and probably wouldn't see Emily escaping. "Go! Hurry!" she whispered.

Emily burrowed through the hole, then up on the other side, and turned back to help Christy.

Christy went head first into the hole, slithering under the wall, but as she tried to come up on the other side, she heard the door open.

"You brats!" the man thundered. Suddenly she felt a hand grab her feet, and she was jerked backward.

"Run, Emily!" Christy screamed. "Run!" She watched as the terrified five-year-old took off into the woods, screaming in fear.

Christy fought with all her might not to be pulled back into the shed, but he yanked her up, bruising and scraping her back on the bottom of the wall as he got her back inside.

She tried to fight him as he lifted her, but he was too strong. Cursing, he held her sideways with an arm around her middle and bolted out of the building. The car parked outside was different from the one he'd taken them in, and he opened his trunk and threw her in, then slammed it shut, encompassing her in darkness once again.

Terrified, she hunkered in a little ball and covered her mouth with her hand, trying to muffle her sobs for fear he would hurt her if she made too much noise.

And then she began to pray, as hard and as fast and as deeply as she'd ever prayed in her life.

Emily had to get away. It was their only hope.

CHAPTER THIRTY-SIX

I t took only a few phone calls to confirm that the original Marazzio had never been recovered. Dubose had lied.

Larry sat over Dubose's telephone records, which he had finally managed to get from the phone company, and compared them to the names on Dubose's desk calendar. "This one guy keeps coming up," he mumbled, thinking out loud, "Eric Boudreaux. The page torn off of the desk calendar was for the day after Dubose died. From the impression on the next page, I can read the words 'Eric Boudreaux, 2:00.' The phone records show a call from Boudreaux in France the day before the murder." He looked up at Tony, who was studying some documents they'd brought from the gallery. "Have you got anything on him yet?"

"Yeah," Tony said, looking up and resting his chin wearily on the heel of his hand. He shuffled some papers around and checked his notes. "He's a museum curator in France. Nothing unusual came up. No prior arrests."

"Do you think Dubose was planning a telephone meeting, or was he going to meet him in person?"

Tony picked up the phone. "I'll call and ask."

He got the long-distance operator, placed the call, and waited. After several rings, a woman answered in French.

"Eric Boudreaux, please," Tony said.

She returned something in French that he couldn't understand, and he closed his eyes. "Excuse me. Do you speak English?"

"A little," she said in a heavy accent. "Uh ... Monsieur Boudreaux is ... not here ... in town ..."

"He's out of town? Where?"

"*Les Estats Unis*. Florida."

Tony's eyebrows shot up, and he looked up at Larry. "Do you happen to know what town?"

"Non, Monsieur. I could have him . . . phone back? Yes?"

"No, that's okay. Thank you very much." He hung up the phone and looked up at Larry. "Ten to one our boy is in St. Clair as we speak."

"Then you think the appointment was face-to-face?"

"Maybe he moved it up a little," Tony suggested.

Larry thought that over for a moment. "I'd say we need to talk to him."

"Without delay," Tony agreed, getting up. "Call for someone to relieve us while we pay him a visit, and I'll start calling the hotels until I locate him." He picked up the phone and started dialing. "Oh, and ask Ben if he knows anything about this guy. He might know something we don't know. And hurry."

Larry rushed into the kitchen, where Sharon and Ben sat stone-faced and silent over coffee that was turning cold.

"Eric Boudreaux," Larry said, leaning both hands on the table and leaning over it. "What do you know about him?"

Ben shrugged. "He's a well-known art dealer."

"Well-known how?"

"He makes some pretty amazing buys." He sat up straighter as something occurred to him. "A few years ago he found one of the lost Monets."

Larry tried to sort out what that might mean. "Where did he find it?"

"He claimed he bought it at an estate auction. That some deceased person had it, and no one knew how he'd gotten it. No one had realized it was an authentic Monet, one of the missing ones. He knew it immediately and seized the moment."

Larry went to the phone and dialed the number of the precinct. While he waited, he asked, "Did anyone ever check out that story? Confirm where he'd found it?"

"What do you mean?" Ben asked.

"I mean, to make sure he hadn't stolen it himself, or bought stolen goods, or that sort of thing?"

Ben breathed a laugh. "Actually, there was so much hoopla about finding the painting that I don't think too many people were concerned about how he'd found it. Art theft is big business, and it's rarely prosecuted, even when the people are caught. The discovery of a stolen Monet is a very big deal."

Larry turned away long enough to ask for relief officers, then hung up and turned back. He began to pace, trying to figure this out. "Okay, let's just pretend. Let's say that Dubose had some important original. And let's say that he had made contact with this Boudreaux guy to sell it. How much did the book say the original lost Marazzio would sell for?"

"Probably around twenty million."

Larry whistled.

Sharon got up, interested now. "You think this Boudreaux person is the killer? The one who has Christy and Emily?"

"No, now wait. It's a hunch. A possibility."

"But why would he kill Dubose for the painting? Why not just buy it from him?"

"Maybe the profit margin was higher if he did away with the middle man."

Ben thought that over for a long time, silently trying to work it all out in his mind. "So you think Eric Boudreaux is the one?"

"I hope so, man." He saw the squad car pull into the driveway, and Tony came into the kitchen.

"He's at the Biltmore. Let's go."

"I'm coming with you!" Sharon said, heading out the door.

Tony lassoed her with an arm and pulled her back in. "Oh, no, you don't. Let us do our work, Sharon."

"But the children could be there with him!"

"We'll call you immediately if anything breaks," he said gently. "Just trust us."

Reluctantly, she went back in. "Please. Call us if you find out anything!"

"I promise," Tony said, and they headed for their car.

mily heard his footsteps coming closer. Breathless, she kept running. She wove through trees and bushes, leapt over logs, tore through briars and thorns.

She cried as she ran, and kept looking back over her shoulder. She couldn't see him yet, which meant that he couldn't see her. Soon she would be to that grandma's house she and Christy had talked about, and she could go in and call the police, and they would come and get them so they could go home.

But the house never came into sight, only deeper, thicker woods, a forest prison that frightened Emily the farther she ran. But what came behind her frightened her more. She could hear his heavy breathing, his feet hitting the ground with weight and speed . . .

She looked back and still couldn't see him, but she could hear him getting closer. She kept running, slipping under branches and tangled vines.

Then she stopped.

She stood at the edge of a gully, looking down into the stream bubbling by. Would the stream be too deep for her if she slid down into it? No, she couldn't do that—there was no place to hide down in the gully. He would see her, slide after her, and catch her.

Panicked, she turned around and searched for a hiding place. There was a tree with low branches beside the ravine. Without thinking, she began to climb it. She climbed from one big branch to the next, knocking away smaller branches and vines entangling it, climbing higher and higher, where the man would never think to look.

Certain she was hidden by the leaves beneath her and the vines webbing through the tree, she found a sturdy branch and sat still, holding her breath.

Within seconds, the man was beneath her, searching. She saw him reach the edge of the gully and almost fall down, but he caught himself. He stood still for a minute, looking up and down the gully, but then turned back around.

She shrank into a tighter ball as he looked up into the trees. His eyes passed over where she sat, and she breathed a sigh of relief that he had not seen her.

Slowly, he walked back through the trees and brush the way he had come, and she watched until he was out of sight.

She thought she was safe—until she looked down at the branches she had climbed to get there, and didn't know if she'd ever have the nerve to go back down. Would she have to stay here, in this scary tree, even when it got dark? What if no one found her?

And where was Christy? She started to cry again. She had heard Christy scream for her to run, and she had, but then she hadn't heard anything more from her sister. What if the man had caught her? What if he had hurt her?

She put her filthy, bloody thumb into her mouth, then quickly spat it out. Wiping a smear of dirt and blood on her shirt, she tried again. The dirty thumb gave her some comfort, but only enough to make her cry harder.

Daddy would find her somehow, she told herself. This was harder than hide-and-seek, but it was more important. He had to rescue them both. He had to.

Hurry, Daddy. Hurry.

CHAPTER THIRTY-EIGHT

There was no answer at the door to the room at the Biltmore where Eric Boudreaux was staying. Larry and Tony knocked again, then looked at the manager who had accompanied them up. "We have a warrant to search his room," Larry said, flashing the paper they had gotten from a judge on the way to the hotel. "Could you let us in, please?"

"Sure. But he isn't here. He checked out." The manager used his key to open the door. Gesturing for them to go in, he asked, "Is this guy in some kind of trouble?"

"We don't know yet," Tony said. "Thanks for your help." Tony looked around at the room. It hadn't been cleaned yet since he'd checked out, but the man had left little behind. He went to the trash can and stooped down next to it, while Larry went into the bathroom.

"At least we have some fingerprints here," Larry said.

Tony nodded as he sorted through the sundry papers that had been dropped into the can. A Delta boarding pass stub, a couple of receipts with credit card numbers, a rolled up newspaper, a small sheet of paper with a phone number on it.

"Hey, Larry," Tony said. "There's a phone number on here. You'll never guess what it is."

"The number of the gallery?" Larry asked.

"You got it."

"Well, that doesn't mean anything. We knew he had an appointment."

"This piece of paper here has the name John Lieber written on it."

"Keep it and we'll check him out." He looked around. "No evidence of any children having been here."

"Nope. If he's got them, he's got them someplace else."

Tony reached for the newspaper and shook it out. It was the edition put out on the day of the murder, and it was folded so that Dubose's picture was on top. "Well, he knows about the murder. No doubt about that."

"Where is he now?" Larry asked.

"Who knows? We'd better check out all the flights leaving in the next few hours. He could be at the airport as we speak."

"What about the children?"

Tony shook his head. "Who knows?"

CHAPTER THIRTY-NINE

E mily had waited what seemed a very long time, but the longer she sat, the more afraid she got. She had seen a TV show once about snakes, and how they loved to hide in trees. Still sucking her thumb, she clung to the trunk and looked around her.

The thought that some unseen creature might be sharing this hiding place with her made her want to get down, but she was still afraid of the man, too. She hadn't heard him since he had walked away into the forest, and she hoped he had given up the search and gone back to the car.

She reached for the next branch with her foot and stepped down onto it. Trembling and perspiring, she made her way to another branch, and then another. She looked around for any sign of snakes and saw a shadow moving across the tree. Quickly, she took another step.

Branch by branch, she made her way down, propelled by fear. A small branch broke under her foot, and she slipped, but grabbed onto another branch in time. She found her footing again and continued her descent.

She breathed relief when her feet hit the ground. Quietly, she crept to the edge of the ravine again. Should she slide down it, hoping the water was shallow, and scramble up the other side? Would that take her deeper into the woods, or out to the road again? Where were those houses she and Christy had talked about, anyway?

She decided to slide into the gully, since she had no intention of going back toward the shed. She looked around for something to sit on as she slid down, but there was nothing that would work. She sat down, scooted to the edge—

Two hands grabbed her from behind, and she let out a high-pitched scream.

"I've got you, you little brat!" Chamberlain said, lifting her and squeezing her under his arm. "I'll teach you to run away from me!"

She kept screaming until he clamped his hand over her mouth and stopped her. She bit him, and he jerked his hand away, allowing her to scream some more.

When his hand came back, he shoved a handkerchief into her mouth and clamped his hand over it again. This time she couldn't bite, and she could hardly breathe as his big hand pressed against her nostrils.

He ran through the trees with no regard for the bushes and brambles tearing at her clothes and scratching her skin. When they came to the edge of the woods, she saw the shed and car, but there was no sign of Christy.

They reached the car, and he opened the trunk.

Christy sat up and looked around, eyes squinted, and started to scream. He pushed her back in, and threw Emily in on top of her. When he started to close it, Christy cried, "No, Mister! We'll be good. We promise. We won't run away again. Please don't put us in here!"

"Shut up!" he said through his teeth. "And if you make a sound as I drive through town, I'll pull over and kill you both. Do you believe me?"

Christy and Emily looked up at his searing blue eyes. "Yes," Emily whimpered, and Christy agreed.

"Lie down," he said, and they both did.

He slammed the trunk shut, and seconds later, started the car.

CHAPTER FORTY

ony and Larry had just returned to Sharon's house when the phone rang. The two cops who'd been waiting beside all the equipment turned on the recorder and picked up their own phone to call for a trace, then nodded for Ben to answer.

"Hello?"

"I'm losing patience, and your girls are running out of time."

Ben closed his eyes and nodded to Sharon and Anne that it was him. They both ran into the other room to hear the conversation as it played across the recorder.

"Look, you obviously want a painting of some kind," Ben said. "I'll give you anything I have. Is it the Marazzio?"

The man laughed. "You're amazing."

"If that's it, Dubose took it. I don't know what he did with it."

"You have until 11:30 tonight, Robinson. I'll call you back later with details. Just be ready."

The phone clicked, and one of the officers cursed. "It wasn't enough time! He knows we're tracing him so he's keeping the conversations short."

Ben sank down at the kitchen table. "What am I gonna do?"

"Daddy, was that the kidnapper?"

It was Jenny, standing at the door in her robe, awake for the first time since she had been sedated. Her eyes were red and swollen, and she looked pale. She hadn't eaten in two days, and he doubted she could eat now. Ben stood up and drew her into a hug. "Yes, honey, it was."

"What did he say?" she asked, beginning to cry. "Is he bringing them back?"

"Maybe tonight," he said. He turned back to the cops, hovered around the recording equipment. "It has to be the Marazzio. What if we faked it again? What if I got another painting and pretended that was it? Last time, I didn't know what size or shape the bundle in the garment bag should be. But if it's the Marazzio, I know it was a roll about four feet long. Maybe we could make a switch for the children before he realized it wasn't the right one."

Tony looked at Larry. "It depends, Ben. On a lot of things. One of them is his delivery method. We'd have to make sure that he delivered the kids before he saw the fake, otherwise it could just make him mad enough to . . . retaliate. We don't know where he wants you to take it yet."

"But don't you see, I have no choice!" Ben insisted. "I have to do something. I don't have the painting he wants, so I have to come up with something else."

"He's right, Tony."

"All right," Tony said. "Let's find a painting and get it ready."

Jenny started to cry and threw her arms around her father. "Daddy, I've been praying for you."

"Don't pray for me," he said. "Pray for your sisters."

"I have, Daddy," she said. "I'm so sorry. This is all my fault."

"Honey, I told you. It isn't."

Sharon pulled Jenny away from her dad and held her while he prepared for the next phone call.

Later, Sharon slumped on the couch alone in her den, waiting, as everyone else in the house waited, for the phone to ring. Tony found her there and sat down next to her.

"You okay?" he asked.

"Yeah," she lied. "You?"

"Just getting psyched up for the big chase tonight. We'll get the girls back, Sharon. I know we will."

She let her eyes drift to some invisible spot across the room. "You have to."

He took her hand and fondled her fingers. "You're a strong lady, you know that?"

"What choice do I have?"

"You could fall apart. Believe me, it happens all the time. Most mothers would have passed hysteria by now."

"I'm glad you have a short memory," she said.

"Well, you've had your moments, but you might have had more." He gazed at her for a moment, noting how pretty she was. Her beauty was striking, but not in the way that he usually viewed beauty. There was an intelligence about her beauty, a dignity, and if he hadn't gotten to know her in such a vulnerable state, he probably would have been intimidated by her.

"Tell me about Christy," he said. "Is she smart? Is she athletic?"

"I think she's smart," she said. "She's only in first grade, but she's been reading since she was four."

"I mean, logic smart. Clear-headed smart."

"Yeah, she's got a lot of common sense. You could say she's even a little precocious. Jenny's always been an honor student, and I have a feeling that Christy will follow in her footsteps. She can count to fifteen in Spanish, to ten in French . . . and she knows all of the states in alphabetical order, because Jenny taught her a song about it. They're working on the presidents."

"Learning them?" Tony asked, amazed. "In the first grade, they learn all the presidents?"

"No," she said. "Jenny's teaching her. She's really good at memory work."

"She sounds like a kid who could take care of herself if she had to."

Sharon's eyes misted. "I think she could," she whispered. "She's strong. She climbs all the time, getting up to her tree house. She runs really fast, and she's a strong swimmer."

Tony smiled. "Good. That's what I wanted to hear. She sounds like a real interesting kid."

"She is. You'd really like her."

"Well, I hope after all this is over, and she's back safe and sound, that you'll give me the chance to get to know her."

"Of course. If you really want to."

"I do." He looked down at her hand, laced his fingers through hers.

She gazed up at him, her eyes serious, haunted. "Who are you, Tony Danks? Are you attached? Detached?"

He breathed a laugh. "None of the above."

"Why not? Why haven't you ever married?"

"Never found the right person," he said. "Besides, marriage hasn't had much appeal to me. Every cop I know who's gotten married has wound up divorced. With the exception of Larry, but he's a newlywed. Give him time."

"Uh-oh. A cynic."

"Not really," he said, hating that she saw him that way. "I'm a realist. I don't like to believe in things that can let me down."

"And here you are asking me to believe in you."

He grinned. "Well, that's because I won't let you down. You can put your faith in me and know I'll do my very best."

"But you can't control everything," she said, her face slackening again. "There are too many factors out of your control. So I can't put any real faith in you."

He looked hurt, but she persisted. "I can't put faith in anyone who's not in control."

"Well, no one is really in control here, except for the kidnapper."

"No. He just thinks he is."

"You *have* to believe in somebody."

"I believe in God. He knows where the children are."

He let that declaration hang in the air for a moment before asking, "Then how come you still don't have any peace?"

"Because I'm weak," she whispered.

Tony got up and walked to the window. He looked out on the news truck that waited outside for some sign of drama. "I'm not much of a believer in God, Sharon," he admitted. "I've had to do too many things on my own."

"You may have thought you were doing them on your own. But God was still God, whether you believed or not."

He turned back to her. "What if we don't find the girls, Sharon? What if this ends badly? Are you still going to believe that God was in control?"

He hadn't realized how biting that remark would be, but she looked up at him with horrified eyes. "It can't end badly, Tony. You see? Already you're giving up. And you expect me to believe in you."

"No, I'm not giving up. It won't end badly. I'm just trying to make a point. What about all the other parents who've lost children? Was God in control there, too?"

She wiped away a tear. "Yes, I believe he was."

"Was he in control when that man was luring your child into his car?"

It was almost as if he wanted her to break, to scream out that God wasn't in control, that the world had fallen out of God's grasp and chaos ruled.

"I don't know what you want me to say, Tony," she said in a shaky voice. "The fact that I'm a basket case doesn't take one iota away from God's power. It just proves how fragile my faith can be. It's an indictment of me, not God."

"Fragile faith?" he asked, his voice softening as he realized he was being too harsh. "Your faith isn't fragile. It's as strong as a rock."

"No," she whispered. "If it were, I'd be asking more directly for his will to be done. But I'm not sure I can do that yet, because I don't know what his will is." She began to cry harder and covered her mouth. "I'm just not to the point where I can trust God to take my child from me, even if there's a big, divine purpose. I don't want to lose my baby!"

He sat back down and pulled her against him, holding her while she wept. For the first time since he was a kid, he thought of praying. But then he wondered what he would say. *God, I don't even think I believe in you, but Sharon does, so if you're listening . . .*

Right. As if God would be open to listening to a prayer like that. But the feeling that his prayers were no good, that there was no way he could appeal to the Creator Sharon put all her faith in, made him feel too helpless.

He dropped his chin on the crown of her head as her tears soaked the front of his shirt, and feeling more humble the harder she cried, he closed his eyes. *Give us a miracle, Lord. Bring the children back. For Sharon.*

If there was a God, wouldn't he answer a prayer for Sharon, who believed so deeply in him?

But didn't bad things happen to Christians? Didn't tragedies befall them, just like everyone else? Weren't they frequent customers at hospitals and funeral homes, just like the regular joes were? Weren't some of their prayers not being answered?

He hated the thought that her faith might not make any difference. It would be nice if it did. After all these years of going it alone, he could use something to believe in. If he just had a sign . . .

But he couldn't rely on God to bring the children home. He could rely only on himself, and his experience, and the gun he carried in the holster under his arm. He could rely only on good luck and solid planning.

Sharon pulled herself back and wiped her eyes. "I never do this."

"Do what?"

"Cry. Openly, in front of a stranger, like I have with you. It seems like every time I've been around you, I've broken down. I don't want you to think this is the real me."

"Isn't it?" he asked perceptively. "You're not really a sweet, loving, feminine beauty who loves her children more than she loves herself?"

She smiled through her tears. "You're good, you know that?" She sat up straight and shook her head. "I don't know why I feel comfortable enough with you to bare my soul like this."

"Because you have to be a tough guy for the others in the house," he said.

"Oh, is that it?" she asked, sniffing. "Why would that be?"

"Well, you can't be vulnerable around your ex-husband. That would be too painful, given your history. You have to keep that wall up, for your own protection, I would imagine."

She cocked her head and gave him a narrow look. "Is that right, Dr. Freud?"

"Yes," he said with certainty. "And you can't let your guard down around Anne, because you don't want to feel her pain. Then you'd have to be compassionate toward her, and you need to hold onto your bitterness. That's a defense mechanism, too."

She stood up. "Oh, that's ridiculous. You're forgetting that my daughter is in the house, too. Do I have deep-seated bitterness about her, too?"

"No. But around her you have to be strong, so she doesn't shrivel. I've seen you come close to cracking with Lynda Barrett, but you held back. I think it may have been because Ben and Anne and everybody were around."

"So I picked you by default? I could have fallen apart with any cop, right? It could have been Larry?"

"I'm cuter," Tony said.

She couldn't help smiling. "While I find your whole scenario to be a lot of baloney, I think you're selling yourself a little short. The fact is that you have a way about you. I've felt I could be myself with you. You've understood."

"Some of it, maybe," he said. "But I'm glad you've felt comfortable with me. Sit down."

Slowly, she sank back down with a giant sigh. He began to massage her shoulders, working out the tension that had hardened itself in her neck and upper back. "There are some things a woman just shouldn't have to face alone," he whispered.

Her face sobered again, and tears pushed to her eyes once more as she relaxed against his ministrations. It felt so good to be pampered, she thought, to be touched with gentle hands, to be spoken to in soft, masculine tones. Part of her wanted to curl up in the warmth and comfort of it, to hide in the strength of it. But another part of her told her it was a fantasy, because he was not a believer. They had little in common.

Larry came into the room, and started at the sight of them. "Excuse me," he said. "I didn't mean to interrupt anything."

"I was just massaging her shoulders," Tony said, letting her go. "No big deal."

Larry glared at him for a moment. "Can I have a word with you, Tony? In the dining room?"

"Sure." Tony stood up and winked at Sharon as he followed Larry out of the room.

Larry was fuming by the time they reached the dining room. "What in the world do you think you're doing?"

Tony looked around innocently. "What are you talking about?"

"Sitting in there with her like that, rubbing her shoulders . . ."

"She's tense and upset. I was trying to help"

"You were trying to seduce her, Tony," Larry whispered. "And I think that's reprehensible. Her child has been kidnapped, and she's not thinking straight. How could you even think of taking advantage of a woman in that state of mind?"

Tony couldn't believe his ears. He gaped at his partner as his face reddened. "You've got a lot of nerve. If I remember correctly, you're the one who gets involved with victims, not me. Check out that ring on your finger if you've forgotten!"

"I've never taken advantage of anyone, Tony. I don't hit them when they're down."

"No, but you've sure offered your shoulder for them to cry on. How come when I do it it's womanizing? Did you ever think for a minute that I might feel genuine compassion for her? That I might have some of the same instincts you've had, to comfort someone who's at her wit's end?"

"Don't get involved with the victims, Tony. That's what you've always told me."

"Yeah, and when's the last time you listened?" Tony turned around to start out of the room, but stopped at the door and turned back. "You make me sick, you know that? You think just because you're some big Christian, that your motives are pure and mine aren't. You think that if *you* comfort someone, it's because you're a good Samaritan, but if I do it, I'm trying to get them into bed." Furious, he shoved a chair under the table, then lowered his voice to a harsh whisper and went on.

"Well, here's a news flash for you, pal. I can feel the same compassion you can! And my motives can be just as pure! That woman in there is broken and hurting, and anyone who took advantage of her right now would be the scum of the earth in my book. I'm not going to let your paranoias keep me from giving her a little comfort when she needs it. Look around and tell me if there's anyone else in this house who can give it to her!"

Larry only stood there, his hands in his pockets, staring at Tony. After a moment, he looked down at his sneaker-clad feet. "All right, maybe I jumped to conclusions. This case has me in knots."

"Think how *she* feels," Tony said, and headed back to the den to find Sharon.

CHAPTER FORTY-ONE

Emily was wailing, and Christy put her arms around her and pressed her sister's face against her chest. The car was going over something rough, like railroad tracks, Christy thought as they took the jarring jolts in the trunk.

"Shhh, Emily," Christy whispered. "He told us to be quiet. He'll kill us if we're not."

"He's gonna kill us anyway," Emily cried against Christy's shirt. "Christy, Daddy's not coming, is he?"

"Yes, he will," Christy said. "And if he doesn't, my mommy will. She won't let anything happen to us."

"But your mommy doesn't like me," Emily moaned.

"Who says?"

"My mom. She says your mommy hates us. That's why she didn't want me going to church with you."

"My mommy doesn't hate anybody!" Christy said.

The car came to a stop, and quickly, Christy put her hand over Emily's mouth. "He's stopping. Emily, if you get another chance, run again. We'll go in different directions. He can't come after both of us."

"But I'm scared!" she whimpered. "I want to get out of here. I want to go home."

The car started rolling again, this time on gravel, and Christy shook her sister's shoulder. "Hush! You sound like a baby!"

"But he hurt my arm when he grabbed me, and I can't move in this stupid place."

"Where did he hurt your arm? Show me."

Emily turned over on her back and, in the darkness, took Christy's hand and ran it along her arm.

"Where does it hurt?"

"All over," Emily said. "It hurts bad."

"It's probably bruised. When Daddy comes, he can look at it."

"He's not gonna come, Christy," Emily said, her panicked voice rising again. "He can't find us, anyway. Maybe he's not even looking." Her crying grew louder, and Christy searched her brain for something to quiet her sister.

"Hush," she said again. "Just listen. I'm gonna teach you a song. It's a real hard song, so you have to listen hard. And I have to whisper so he won't hear."

"I don't want to sing," Emily whined.

"You have to," Christy said. "It'll help you stop crying. Now, listen. It's a song about the states. It goes, 'Alabama, Alaska, Arizona, Arkansas . . .' Now, sing it with me. Whisper. 'Alabama, Alaska, Arizona, Arkansas . . .'"

"I don't want to," said Emily.

"Do it!" Christy insisted. "Alabama, Alaska . . ."

"Arizona, Arkansas," Emily finished on a whisper.

"Good!" Christy said. "The next part is 'California, Colorado . . .'"

Emily was listening, trying now to sing along. The effort of learning the song took her mind off of the cramped quarters of the trunk, the merciless way the wheels bounced on the gravel or over potholes, or the fear of what the man would do with them when they stopped.

They were up to the state of Hawaii before the car finally stopped. They heard the man slam his car door and start back to the trunk.

T he phone rang, and everyone sprang to attention. In the kitchen, Ben put his hand on the phone and looked into the dining room, waiting for the signal. Tony nodded.

Ben picked up the phone. "Hello?"

"May I speak to Detective Danks, please?"

Everyone in the house let out a weary breath as Tony picked up and Ben hung up. "It's for them," Ben told Anne, who had run into the room with Bobby on her hip.

"He's never gonna call!" Anne said, kicking the chair. "When's he gonna call?"

Leaning wearily against the kitchen wall, Sharon watched silently.

Tony was on his feet, reaching for his coat, as he hung up. "We've had a break!" he shouted. "They found the car the girls were abducted in. It was left back at the rental company with the keys in it last night. It was paid for in advance with a credit card. You'll never guess whose name it was in."

"Whose?" Larry asked.

"Ben Robinson."

"*What?*" Ben asked. "I never left the house last night! Everyone saw me!"

"Don't panic. The guy who checked the car out to him gave us a description, and it matches the kidnapper, *sans* hat and glasses. He's talking our artist through a composite sketch right now." He stopped at the door and turned back. "If this pans out, Ben, then we know how he got a gun in your name."

"But none of my credit cards were stolen. He would have needed it days before the murder to get a gun."

"He probably had counterfeit IDs and credit cards made. It happens."

Sharon let out a long-held breath. "Thank goodness, we're getting somewhere."

Tony started out the door. "Larry'll stay here in case the kidnapper calls."

"I'm going with you," Ben said.

"No! You have to stay here in case he calls! As soon as we get a composite done, I'll bring it back to you."

"Fax it!" Sharon said. "Maybe Ben will recognize the guy!" She ran to grab a piece of paper and a pen. "Here's my fax number. It'll come straight into the house."

Tony grabbed the number. "I'll fax it as soon as it's done. Larry'll call me if you guys hear anything." Not waiting for an answer, Tony rushed out.

Albert Gates was a forty-two-year-old car rental agent who hadn't seen such excitement in years. He would never have dreamed that the polished gentleman who had come in here a week ago to rent a car would turn out to be a kidnapper. He couldn't wait to tell the boys at the pool hall.

Albert was suddenly important, someone whose words the cops were hanging on, someone who could make a difference, and he was enjoying every minute of it. Any minute now, the news teams would probably show up.

"The car was really dirty when we got it back," he was saying as the policemen took notes and the artist tried to sketch the description he'd already given. "It looked like he'd been driving on dirt roads. Red clay all over the fender."

The detective who'd just bolted in asked, "Is it still on the car?"

"No," Albert said apologetically. "I had it washed first thing. That's what I always do, to get it ready to go out again."

"Where is the car?" Tony asked. "I want to see it."

"It's the blue Taurus parked by the curb just outside the door."

Tony started back out of the room. "How long before that composite is ready?"

"We're almost there," the artist said, still sketching.

"All right. I'll be right back."

Tony went outside and looked the car over. Just as Albert said, the car had been washed clean. One officer was inside it, dusting for prints, so he leaned in the window. "Find anything?"

"Yeah, I'm getting some prints. But this car's been rented out four times already this month. Plus the agents here and their clean-up staff have all been through it. These prints could be anybody's."

Tony sighed and looked in the backseat. Nothing had been left. He reached through the driver's side window and punched the button to release the trunk. He walked back there and pulled the trunk open.

Nothing.

He stood back and tried to think. Dirt roads. Red clay. He got down on his knees and looked under the car. Just as he'd hoped, it was still dirty. Red clumps of clay still clung to the belly of the car. He reached under and scratched some off.

There were only a few rural places left in St. Clair. Like so much of the Tampa Bay area, it had been overbuilt. He got up and sat back on his heels, examining the red clay on his fingers.

It could be from a building site, he thought, but that was doubtful. Most of the building sites were too visible. Besides that, a single lot wouldn't be large enough to get that much mud caked on the car. It had to be a rural area.

He thought of the few farms still remaining on the east side of St. Clair, and the cover of woods that surrounded some of them. Maybe the kidnapper had taken the children there.

Dusting his hands off, he went back inside to ask about the mileage. Maybe it would give him some clue as to whether he'd left town.

"His eyes were a very pale blue," Arthur was saying. "He was a nice-looking man. And his nose was a little different than what you've done. . . ."

The artist followed the descriptions and made the necessary changes on the sketch.

"Yeah, that's real close. Only I think his lips were thinner. And his eyebrows were thicker."

Tony waited, watching, as the face emerged.

"That's it," the man said finally. "I'm sure. That's what he looked like. Isn't it amazing that you can do that just from my description? I've always wondered how that worked."

Tony leaned over the desk. "You're sure? Absolutely positive?"

"Oh, yeah," he said. "It's him."

"All right." Tony held out a hand. "Let me have it. Where's your fax machine?"

"Over there," Albert said, getting more excited. "Who are you faxing it to?"

"Somebody I hope can identify him," Tony said. He took the sketch and pulled the number out of his pocket. Quickly, he dialed Sharon's fax number, and fed the picture through.

The moment the fax machine rang in Sharon's study, they all dashed for it.

They watched, breath held, as the face slowly emerged.

Ben waited until the machine had cut the page, then inverted it and studied it. "Oh, it can't be ..."

"You know him?" Sharon asked.

Anne pushed closer to see the picture, and her face paled. "Ben, is that ... ?"

"Nelson Chamberlain," Ben said, turning back to Larry, who stood behind him. "It can't be him! He was Louis's best friend. He's the one who posted my bond. Why would he help get me out of jail if he's the one setting me up?"

"Because you have something he wants," Larry said. "You obviously couldn't give it to him from a jail cell."

"But he's been in England. He couldn't be the one—" He blew out a helpless breath. "He knows Emily. She knows him—"

"That's why she went with him!" Anne cried. "Ben, don't you see?"

"But I trusted him." He studied the face again. "It just doesn't make sense. If he's the one who planted all that evidence against me, he was hoping I'd take the fall for the murder. Why'd he post my bond? He stood to lose that money."

Larry picked up the phone and dialed the car agency. "That was a small investment compared to what he stands to make. And it threw us off his scent for a while." The phone was answered, and he asked for Tony.

He waited until Tony picked up. "It's Nelson Chamberlain," Larry said. "One of the art dealers we've been trying to get in touch with. He's supposed to have been in England."

Weakly, Ben lowered into a chair.

"Red clay?" Larry asked. "What do you make of that?"

Sharon stepped closer, hoping they were on to something.

"Yeah, that wouldn't hurt. We need to search his house, and any other property he owns here. Maybe it'll lead us to them."

Tony was just coming in when Larry's number rang. He snapped it up. "Yeah? All right, shoot. Okay, I'm on my way. Get somebody over here to relieve us in case the guy calls."

He grabbed his windbreaker and jumped up as he hung up the phone. "They found some property Chamberlain owns on the east side of town. It's a few acres of wooded area. I'll go over there to see if there's a building anywhere around there where he could have the kids. Then I'll check his house."

"I'm going with you!" Sharon cried.

This time, Tony knew they couldn't stop her.

"What if he calls?" Ben asked, practically chasing them to the door.

"Hopefully we'll get him before he has the chance!" Tony called back. "But if he does, just get his instructions. Play along, like you have what he wants." He saw the police car already turning into their driveway. "They're here. They know what to do if he calls."

Sharon followed Tony at a trot, and Anne ran out behind them. "Tony, Larry! I'm coming, too."

"No, it's not a good idea," Larry said.

"But my little girl could be out there!" Anne cried. "I have to be there when you find her! She'll need me!"

Sharon looked beseechingly at Tony. This time, she said, "Let her come."

He shrugged and got into the car. "All right, get in."

The ride to the other side of town was fifteen minutes or so. Sharon and Anne sat in the backseat, watching out the window, both of them tense and hopeful.

"Turn left here," Larry said. "Yeah, that's it. I think this is the edge of his property."

In the distance, Sharon heard a police siren. "Won't he hear us coming? Shouldn't they turn off the siren?"

Almost as if in answer to that, the siren hushed.

They drove up a long dirt road, and Sharon scanned the trees for any sign of a structure where the children could be. There were no buildings, no houses, only this red dirt road and the dense forest beside it.

"What's that?" Larry asked as they followed the dirt road around a cluster of trees.

Tony leaned forward. "A shed," he said. "And there are fresh tire tracks. Bingo!"

Sharon felt the blood running out of her face. The children couldn't be in there. Not in a four-by-six dirt shack out in the middle of nowhere!

"Stay here!" Tony ordered. "It doesn't look like he's here, but he could be. We'll look first."

Sharon nodded. Anne sat paralyzed, staring toward the shed as the men got out, wielding their guns, and surrounded the little building.

The men shouted something, but there was no reply.

They heard the door being kicked in, and both women jumped.

After a moment, Tony came back around the building, shaking his head.

"They're not there," Anne said, and started to cry.

Sharon, too, covered her face and tried to cope with the horror of it. She got out of the car, not knowing which way to go. "But the fresh tire tracks. It's his property, isn't it?"

Tony looked down at the tire tracks. "Somebody was here, all right. Maybe even today."

Larry came out of the little shed. "Hey, Tony. Come look at this!"

They all rushed to the door. "McDonald's bags," Larry said. "Two cups."

"They were here!" Sharon cried. "He locked them in this dark place? They must have been terrified!"

"Where are they now?" Anne almost screamed.

"It looks like they dug a hole under the wall."

Tony went back out and checked the other side. "Look, footprints," he said. "It looks like one of the kids may have gotten away."

Anne and Sharon stared down at the beloved little footprint. "It's Emily," Anne cried. "She had on tennis shoes."

"She's right," Sharon confirmed. "Christy was wearing loafers."

By now, the other cops were following the prints, trying to trace the steps of the child and the bigger steps of the man who had taken them.

Anne turned back to the woods, the direction the footsteps led. "She ran in there! She's still in there! I know it." She ran into the woods, unstoppable, calling, "Emily! Emily, it's Mommy! Honey, don't be afraid. Just tell us where you are!"

Sharon followed behind her, praying that Christy was with her. But there were no footsteps for Christy.

Frantic, Anne came to the drop-off and looked down into the gully where a stream of water ran. Had Emily tried to cross it? Had she fallen in?

She turned back, looking with horror at Sharon. "Where *is* she? Where *is* she?"

She was beginning to tremble from her head to her feet, and Sharon began to cry with her. They weren't here, and there were only two possibilities. They had either been caught by the kidnapper and taken somewhere else, or they were at the bottom of that gully somewhere, washed downstream.

"Emily!" Anne screamed. "Emily! WHERE ARE YOU?"

Feeling the same anguish Anne felt, Sharon stood motionless, fragmenting piece by piece until there was nothing left of her control.

"They're not here!" Anne screamed. "Sharon, they're not here!"

Sharon took a step toward her and put her arms around the weeping woman. Anne fell against her, heaving with sobs. "If we'd just come earlier. We could have saved them. We could have saved them."

Sharon wept, too, clinging to Anne like a sister, knowing that she was the only other woman on the face of the earth who knew exactly how Sharon felt.

Tony stood back, deeply frustrated that this lead had led nowhere. Yet this picture, of two enemies embracing, touched him in a place that he rarely visited.

Larry came up behind him and saw the women. When Tony looked up at him, Larry saw that his eyes were moist. Neither of the men wanted to look at the other.

"He must have rented another car," Larry said quietly. "I sent the others to check out all the cars that have been rented from other rental car agencies in town. We're getting the sketch printed up, so they'll be taking copies with them. Soon enough we'll know what he's driving."

Tony touched the shoulders of both women to coax them apart. "We'd better get back to Sharon's. He probably doesn't know we know who he is, so he'll be calling soon. Come on, we need to go," he said.

Sobbing, they separated and slowly made their way back to the car.

Nelson Chamberlain drove the streets of St. Clair, desperately seeking someplace else to hide the children. He couldn't take them back to the shed, not after they'd escaped from there once. His home was out of the question, since he was supposed to be out of town. He hadn't gone near his own house since before the murder. He couldn't take them to his hotel, for there was no way to get them inside without their being seen. Their pictures were posted everywhere, and he had no doubt that the St. Clair police were searching everywhere for them and the kidnapper who had abducted them. He hadn't even tried to threaten the Robinsons against involving the police—that would have been a fantasy. The police always got involved, whether overtly or covertly. The fact that they'd been camped in Sharon Robinson's home since the children disappeared was something he could watch and stay on top of.

But where should he take the children now? He couldn't leave them in the trunk all day. The fact was, even though he needed them for leverage to make Ben Robinson act, they were really more trouble than they were worth. He had counted on keeping them in the little shed until their father capitulated and handed over the painting, but the little brats had ruined that.

He saw a pay phone at a convenience store, and inched the car as close as he could so that the cord would reach inside the car. Inserting a quarter, he dialed the phone number of the Biltmore.

He asked for Boudreaux's room. When the clerk responded that Boudreaux had checked out, Nelson's heart crashed. He couldn't have left! Not without the painting!

He searched his pockets for the number of Boudreaux's museum in France, and inserted a fistful of quarters. He thought briefly about using the cellular phone he carried in his briefcase, but quickly thought better of it. If his name did ever come up as a suspect, it wouldn't do to have records on his cellular phone bill that showed he had made calls to Boudreaux, Ben Robinson, or anyone else that could incriminate him. Especially not when he was still supposed to be in England. No, he'd just have to stick with the pay phones.

A French woman answered, and he said, "Excuse me. My name is John Lieber, and I'm a friend of Monsieur Boudreaux's. I was to meet him here in St. Clair, but I'm afraid I missed him. Do you have any word on where he might be?"

"Oui, Monsieur," she said. "Monsieur Boudreaux has a message for you. He has moved to Holiday Inn downtown Tampa and is using the name Passons."

"Very good, very good," Nelson said, breathless. "Excellent. I'll call him right away."

He hung up and breathed out a gigantic sigh of relief, inserted some more quarters, and dialed information. He got the number, dialed it, then asked to be connected with Eric Passons's room.

He listened through two rings. "Hello?"

"Hello, Eric, how are you?" It was his most professional business voice, and he knew Eric recognized him immediately.

"Not well," the Frenchman said. "Very disappointed."

His temples were perspiring, and he pulled a handkerchief out of his coat pocket and dabbed at them. "Eric, has something happened?"

"Oui," the man said. "Some American phoned my secretary earlier asking where I was. I feared being drawn into this ... uh ... investigation. I changed my name and location."

"That was wise," Nelson said. "I'm glad you left the information for me." He paused. "Look, Eric, I can promise you that I'll have the painting by tomorrow morning. Surely you can understand how the circumstances of Dubose's death have complicated things."

Eric laughed sardonically. "Complicated things? After all this time, you still do not have the painting?"

"I know precisely where it is," Nelson countered, his face reddening. "But I don't have to tell you how delicate these matters are. I have to be very careful how and when I retrieve it. And then there's the matter of transporting it."

"You understand, do you not, that I have a buyer for it? The longer I make him wait, the less likely he is to buy it. I really must not wait any longer."

Nelson sat back hard on his seat. He could hear low, muffled voices in the trunk. The children were singing something. He looked around to make sure no one was close enough to hear it.

"Will you give me until morning, Eric? We both know that the wait will be worth it in the long run."

"Not if I am . . . how you say . . . arrested? The picture would be taken from me. And with the murder, and now the kidnapping of Ben Robinson's children, I must tell you I have grave reservations. Perhaps later, in a year or two, after the suspicions have died down."

"In a year or two I can guarantee I'll have another buyer. One who might even pay more than you're offering. Your buyer could hide it for a period of time, until he's comfortable. But unless you act now, someone else will profit from it."

That did make the man hesitate. "Very well, Monsieur Lieber. If I wait until morning, and the picture is delivered, I will proceed with our bargain. But if I do not have it by noon, I will be on my way back to LeMans."

"You'll have it by morning." Nelson cleared his throat and wiped his perspiring face again. "You do understand, now, that there will be some restoration involved? The painting has been rolled up since its theft—"

"Which often means there are cracks in the paint. I understand that, Monsieur Lieber. My price has allowed for that. But if it is an authentic Marazzio, and you do indeed deliver it to me, I am certain that it can be restored to its previous condition. Now, about this investigation."

The singing had stopped, and he heard them talking. Didn't they ever shut up? He revved his engine, hoping the noise would overpower the voices.

"I am concerned in my mind as to who killed Dubose." He hesitated, as if choosing his words carefully. "It has occurred to me that you may have been involved."

Nelson laughed too loudly. "Me? Why on earth would I be the one?"

"The money we've agreed upon is quite a lot of motive, would you not agree? Perhaps you wished to dispose of Dubose so that the money would not be divided."

"That's ludicrous," Nelson bit out. "This is a clean, painless, harmless deal. People do not murder over art."

"*Pardon*, my friend," Boudreaux said. "But there have been many murders over the last decades, precisely over art. Money is a powerful motivator."

Nelson laughed again. "I assure you that Dubose's death was as much a surprise to me as it was to anyone. He was a dear friend of mine. I don't know what I'll do without him."

"Indeed," Eric said, not convinced. "My . . . what you say . . . instincts . . . warn me to return to France."

"Then your instincts are wrong. This whole endeavor will make you a richer man," Nelson said. "I'm not a fool, Eric. I'm well aware that you could sell the painting for a third more than what you're paying me. There are museums in Italy that would sell entire roomfuls of art to raise the funds for this one picture. As for the murder and the kidnapping, I can assure you that they have nothing to do with this transaction. My theory is that Ben Robinson was involved in drug trafficking, and he was probably the real target for the murder—that is, if he didn't do it himself. Robinson is a very complex, dubious man. Very dishonest. A marvelous painter, and quite a gifted restorer. What he had going on outside of the gallery, I don't know. But I feel sure it will all come to light very soon. You'll see. And you'll be very glad you didn't miss the opportunity to find the most important piece of lost art this century."

"Do you think Robinson has any knowledge of this painting?"

"No," Nelson said, as if with certainty. "Not at all. It was very carefully hidden."

When he'd finally convinced Boudreaux to wait, he hung up the telephone and rolled his window back up. The children had grown quieter now, and he racked his brain to think of the location of a pay phone where he could call Ben Robinson and let him talk to at least one of the girls. That might remind him of the urgency here. But all of the pay phones were too public, and someone might see the child. Not only that, but one of them might do something unpredictable to call attention to herself. He couldn't take that chance.

Once again he thought longingly of his cellular, but it just wasn't worth the risk. He would wait until dark, and then take one of the children with him to make the call.

Until then, he had to find some place to put them.

A thought occurred to him as he drove across the Spanish Trail Bridge, out to the eastern edge of St. Clair, where there were still a few small farms and some old dilapidated buildings that were boarded up. There was one in particular he remembered seeing a couple of days ago on the way to his own property. An old abandoned store. That was just the place, he thought, and headed toward it.

The car cut off, and Emily clung to Christy in fear. "We've stopped, Christy!"

"Shhh. Just be quiet."

They heard his car door slam, and braced themselves. In a moment, they heard keys jangling at the back of the trunk, and suddenly the trunk came open, letting in a harsh flood of light that made them squint.

The two grimy little girls sat up and looked fearfully at their kidnapper.

He grabbed them each by one arm and bent down close to their ears. "If either one of you so much as breathes hard while I'm moving you, I'll throw you off the St. Clair pier into the Gulf and your parents won't find you until you wash up on shore—after the sharks are through with you."

Both children trembled and allowed him to move them out of the car.

As he herded them from the car toward the dilapidated building, Christy searched frantically, though quietly, for someone who might see them. But there was no one anywhere around.

He opened the door. This building was much bigger than the last one, and it had a concrete floor. He acted like this was the first time he had been here, and he left the front door open, providing light as he dragged them in.

"No, not here!" Emily cried. "It might have rats! Please! Not here! I want to go home! I want my daddy!"

Nelson Chamberlain squatted down in front of her, his big, threatening finger pointing at her nose. "What did I tell you about making a sound?"

She tried to keep her lips shut, but she began to cry, and the sound wouldn't be muffled easily.

"Mister, we need to go to the bathroom," Christy whispered. "Is there a bathroom here?"

That seemed to give him an idea, and he got back up, still holding each of them by their upper arms. "Up those stairs, and we'll see," he told them. "Come on now."

Emily was crying harder, biting her lip and trembling as they took each step. Some light shone in through a window that had been shot out about fifteen feet up, but it cast only enough light to show the degree of dust and filth that had accumulated since this place was last inhabited. Dead hanging plants covered with spiderwebs dangled from slimy, fungus-covered macramé hangers. The place might have been pretty once, but now it was a study in filth and decomposition.

The man nodded toward a door in the back corner of the dusty room. "There."

"No!" Emily cried again, but he jerked them toward it.

The door opened into Emily's worst nightmare. There was a filthy, cracked commode with only half a seat on it; warped and rotting boards made up the floor. The sink had long ago been torn off the wall, leaving a gaping hole that revealed rusted plumbing—the perfect place for rats to lurk. Above it all, at least ten feet up, was another broken-out window too high for them to reach, and a dozen or so dead hanging plants just like the ones on the other side, with long, brown vines laced with spiderwebs that seemed to reach down and grab for them.

"Mister, can't you leave us your flashlight?" Christy asked.

"No. The dark will keep you from trying to find some way out again."

"But..." Christy's voice broke, and she started to cry, but she tried to keep her voice steady. As her mother had told her more than once, whining got you nowhere. "Those dead plants have spiders, and there are rats in that wall, I can hear them. Can't you? If we're in the dark and we hear something or ... feel something ..." She sobbed and reached for Emily's hand. Her sister was trembling so hard she could hardly hold it still. "We might scream by accident ... And somebody might hear us. If you want us to stay quiet, we promise we will if you'll just give us the flashlight."

The man was quiet for a moment. "All right," he said finally. "The batteries won't last long, anyway."

He handed Christy the small flashlight. "Now, go on. Get in there."

"It stinks," Emily squealed. "I'm scared."

"Mister, couldn't we stay out here, in this room?" Christy asked, crying fully now. "Please ... We promise not to make any noise ..."

He thrust them in and shut the door behind them.

Christy and Emily hunkered in a corner with the flashlight illuminating the nightmarish sights around them. Outside the door, they could hear him moving things to bar them in, since he didn't have a lock.

Emily buried her face against Christy's chest, and tried not to cry loudly. But Christy was having trouble herself. Her fingers, still filthy from digging, were hurting from where they'd blistered and bled as they'd dug. She knew that sores needed to be cleaned to keep them from getting infected, but she suspected that that was just one more thing she had to worry about now. She wondered what Jenny was doing. She wondered if Mommy was worried, if she and Anne were fighting. She wondered if Daddy was looking for them.

They heard something in the wall, and Emily's voice went an octave higher, though she kept her mouth muffled against Christy's shirt. Christy shone her light toward the sound, hoping to frighten whatever it was away, but she squeezed her eyes shut to keep from seeing it herself.

"Pray," she whimpered. "Pray hard. Now."

Emily only trembled, and Christy knew she couldn't count on her to pray. She'd have to do it herself. "Dear God," she squeaked. "We're so scared"

"It doesn't work!" Emily cried. "It doesn't work, Christy! We tried, remember?"

"It does work," Christy said. "It has to. Mommy said it works."

"Then why didn't it work before? Why didn't Daddy find us?"

"He will," Christy sobbed. "I know he will. We just have to pray harder. Now, either pray with me, or be quiet."

Emily chose to be quiet as Christy started praying again.

CHAPTER FORTY-FOUR

elson Chamberlain needed a drink. For a while, he drove around near the abandoned store, making sure there was no reason for anyone to get close to the building where he had hidden the children. They wouldn't be discovered there, he decided finally. The building was too old and dilapidated, and those who drove past it daily would never notice that anything was different about the old building. The girls were stuck there until he went back to get them. Now all he had to do was decide what his next step would be.

He drove into town to a trendy bar called Steppin' Out and pulled into the parking lot as it filled up with happy hour traffic. The bar was popular this time of day, he thought with relief. He could blend in, and no one would notice him. He walked into the noisy room decorated with twenties memorabilia, found a seat at the bar, and ordered a scotch. It calmed him as it went down, and he told himself that things were going to work out after all. Yes, a lot had to fall into place, but the more he drank, the more confident he became.

The music seemed to be growing louder, an unidentifiable blend of guitars and drums, drowned out by the chatter of the after-work crowd. He looked around, through the haze of cigarette smoke, at the silk suits and designer dresses, the perfectly coifed locks of young professional women, the moussed hair of lawyers and accountants and consultants of every kind. He was comfortable here, as he was in bars like it all over the world. In ways, it was his sanctuary, the place where he knew he could come at any time for sustenance or comfort. Even now, as he nursed his scotch, he felt that comfort seeping through him.

It would all work out. It had to. So much was at stake. He had held onto the painting for over ten years now, after daring to take it himself from a museum in Palermo. In Italy, the statute of limitations for art theft was ten years, so he was out of the woods as far as prosecution there was concerned. He'd finally decided a few months ago that it was time to begin searching for a buyer.

But it wasn't his style to do it himself. He liked to stay detached from the particulars of such exchanges, so that if any of his deals went sour, they couldn't be traced back to him. Dubose had been the perfect liaison. With his contacts in the art world, and his legitimate role as owner of several small galleries, he was in a good position to find a buyer. Of all the art thefts Nelson Chamberlain had been involved in, this was by far of the greatest value. It was the *coup de gras*, the one that would make world news—though his name would never be mentioned in connection with it. The fact that it would make him a fortune was enough.

But once the contact had been established, Dubose had gotten greedy. He had demanded half of what Chamberlain would be paid for the painting, though Dubose had not been involved in the theft in any way. Because Dubose already had the painting and because he needed Dubose to make the exchange with the buyer, Nelson reluctantly agreed—until he realized that Dubose was not being honest with him about the price the dealer was willing to pay. He was getting more for it than he had reported to Chamberlain, and was keeping the bigger portion for himself.

That was bad enough, but when Ben Robinson discovered the canvas, Chamberlain's concerns had grown even more inflamed. What kind of fool hid something worth millions in a wooden compartment of a cold, damp attic, where anyone could stumble upon it? There was nothing to do, he thought, except to get the middleman out of the way, and handle things himself. He had to do away with Dubose to ensure that his own interests weren't violated. What a shock, he reminded himself ruefully, after he'd gotten rid of Dubose, to discover that the painting wasn't where it was supposed to be.

There was no doubt in his mind that Ben Robinson had it; Ben was the only other person who had known that it was there. What he couldn't understand was why the man hadn't agreed to turn it over to him after the first phone call. Maybe the police were trying to make him play cat-and-mouse games with him to draw him out. He only hoped that taking his children had made Ben think better of it.

He heard a loud round of cackling laughter, and looked up to see a woman dressed in a tight red sweater and tight black jeans with four-inch heels, flirting with a group of men half her age. She was obviously in her fifties, yet here she was competing with women in their twenties.

"You are just too much!" she was saying in a deep Texas drawl to one of the men standing beside her. Her voice carried over the crowd, as if to draw attention to herself. "For heaven's sake, you have to eat!"

Was she hitting on that man who was young enough to be her son? Chamberlain wondered, amused. There was no telling, he thought. He watched her as she pretended to pout, then pranced over to the bar, pushing between two patrons, and got the bartender's attention. "Excuse me. You over there. Yes, you."

The bartender finished mixing the drinks he was mixing, and leaned toward her. "Can I help you?"

"Doris Stevens here," she said, holding out her hand with inch-long fake nails. The man shook halfheartedly. "I came in here to see if you'd let me put these posters up of those little kidnapped girls." As she spoke, she dug through her huge purse, and brought out a few copies of the posters. "Bless their hearts, they're friends of mine. Little Chrissy and Judy. The sweetest little girls you ever laid eyes on. And now somebody's kidnapped them, and well, I'm doing everything in my power to help find them."

The bartender took one of the posters. "A $25,000 reward, huh?"

Doris waved that off. "Their safe return would be payment enough."

"But the reward money wouldn't hurt, would it?"

She shrugged. "I guess I'd take it, if they insisted. Heck, if I find those kids, I'd deserve the money. And how much is that really, when you consider the value of these two beautiful little girls? Can I put 'em up or what?"

"Sure. Go ahead."

She took the posters back and clicked around the room, tacking and taping the posters, while simultaneously flirting with anyone nearby.

Chamberlain felt his body go tense as the faces of the girls stared out at him. Quickly, he turned away. No one suspected him. His plan was flawless. He was going to get the painting tonight, and he'd be out of town before anyone knew what had hit them. This was one crime the police would never solve.

But the painting was the key, and he had to have it tonight. There simply was no choice. If he didn't deliver it to Eric by tomorrow, he would have to wait another year or two before he could safely approach another buyer. This time he had no middleman. His own hands had gotten dirty for the first time, but it was worth it—as long as the deal went through.

Chamberlain downed his drink and ordered another.

A telephone rang somewhere close to him, and he watched as the man sitting on the stool next to his reached into his coat pocket and withdrew a small cellular flip phone. He answered it, and Chamberlain listened, half-interested, as the man took care of business from his bar stool.

When he hung the phone up, the man set it on the counter next to his drink, and resumed reading the stock market page of the newspaper.

The waiter brought Chamberlain his scotch, and he sipped it as he listened to conversations around him. The news was playing on a television screen up in the corner of the room, and he saw the pictures of the two Robinson girls flash across it. He tried to listen to what was being said, but it was difficult over the voices in the crowd. Nothing new, he surmised from what he could hear. They didn't have any leads yet.

He smiled. The Keystone cops of St. Clair, Florida, were going to have to get their act together if they wanted to figure him out.

Feeling almost an ecstatic energy after his two doubles and the news report that said virtually nothing, he glanced at the pay phone on the wall and wondered if he dared call Ben Robinson from here. No, he thought, someone might overhear. And if they traced the call, he might not be able to get out of the parking lot fast enough before the cops showed up to find him.

Besides, he really needed to get one of the kids to talk to their father tonight, just to drive home his point that time was running out. Robinson needed to know that he wasn't playing games. Either he turned over the painting tonight, or the kids were history.

The cellular phone rang again, and the man next to him snapped it up and answered. As he spoke, three of his colleagues came in the door, and he waved toward them. They clustered behind his stool, crowding Chamberlain as well. The man took care of the call, then hung up and set the phone back on the bar. He turned his back to Chamberlain to talk to his friends in a con-spiratorial huddle.

Nelson stared at the cellular phone, unattended on the bar. He couldn't use his own cellular phone, for fear that the call would be traced, but he could use someone else's!

He looked up at the television, pretending to be absorbed in the news, and quickly put his hand over the flip phone. In one swift motion, he slipped it into his pocket. Quickly, he dropped a couple of bills onto the counter and headed for the door.

He was out of the parking lot when the phone rang again, and Chamberlain began to laugh. He wondered if the man had even noticed yet that his phone was missing. He let it ring as he headed for the building where the children were. After a moment, it stopped.

Another perfect twist in a perfect crime, he thought. All he had to do now was figure out where to have Ben Robinson drop the painting.

He headed for the old abandoned store, but before he reached the road heading toward it, a train stopped him. It was slowing, and he watched as boxcar after boxcar passed, traveling no faster than twenty miles per hour. Slow enough to jump on, retrieve something, and get back off a few miles down the tracks.

Perfect. If Robinson put the painting on a boxcar when it was stopped, Chamberlain could be waiting a significant distance down the tracks, jump on, then jump off, and no one would ever be able to catch him.

He picked up the flip phone, called information, and asked for the number of the railroad office. Quickly, he dialed it and asked for information about when the next few trains would come through today. He was told that one was due to come through around ten o'clock. It would remain for two hours to reload, then would depart again at 12:30.

Elated and anxious, he drove the rest of the way to the abandoned store, dropped the phone into his coat pocket, got out of the car, and reached down on the seat for his other flashlight. Then, treading warily, he went back into the dark, eerie building, and headed up the stairs for the children.

He heard their voices as he came inside and went up the creaky steps. Rodents scurried and scratched in the walls and in the dark corners of the room. He kept the flashlight circle in front of him, hoping the sound of his shoes would frighten them away.

The voices hushed as they heard him coming. He reached the bathroom. Grunting from the effort, he moved aside the steel drum, old machinery, and a long, heavy bench that he'd used to block them in.

The door creaked as he pushed it open.

His light shone around the filthy bathroom, until the circle spotlighted the children, hunkered so tightly together that it was difficult to even tell that there were two of them. They both looked up at him with their grimy faces, and he remembered that he hadn't fed them since morning. He'd have to take care of that later.

"Are you going to let us out of here now, Mister?" the older one asked him in a weak, raspy voice.

"No, not yet," he said, trying not to look at them. He pulled the phone out of his pocket. "We're going to make a phone call, to your father. I want you both to talk to him, to let him know you're okay. If you do as I say, he'll come to get you tonight, and you can go home with him. But if you don't do as I say, you'll never see him again."

"We'll do what you say," the little one, the escape artist, said as her eyes got as round as quarters.

"First, you don't tell him who I am. If you do, you'll be dead in five minutes, do you understand me?"

The older one frowned. "I don't know who you are, anyway."

But the little one, Emily, piped up. "I do. You're Mr. Chamberlain. You come to the gallery sometimes and buy my daddy's paintings."

He knew that the minute she went back to her father, she'd be able to tell who he was. He couldn't let that happen. Somehow, the children would just have to disappear from the whole equation. But he needed them long enough to manipulate Ben.

"I'm going to talk to him for a minute," he said, "and I want absolute silence. When I tell you, you can say hello to your father, and that's it. You tell him that you want him to hurry and get you home, but you don't say anything about where you are, or who I am, do you understand?"

"Yes, sir."

"All right. Now, quiet. If you do this right, I'll bring you some food."

Both children sat in the corner, still huddled in fear, as he dialed the number.

CHAPTER FORTY-FIVE

The phone rang, and Ben bolted for it. He waited until Tony gave him the signal from the other room. Sharon, Anne, and Jenny hurried into the dining room where they could hear the conversation.

"Hello?"

"Are you ready, Ben?" the voice asked.

Ben hesitated. "Yes."

"Then tonight's the night."

In the dining room, Tony waited on the other line for the tracing to be completed.

"What have you done with my daughters?"

"They're fine, Robinson. You're lucky I haven't killed the sniveling little brats."

"How do I know you haven't?" Ben asked, his voice cracking.

"Well, you can find out for yourself. It might even give you a little more incentive. You see, if you don't deliver the painting when and where I tell you, or if you try something foolish, or if you pull what you pulled at the airport, you'll never see these girls again."

"So help me, if you hurt them, I'll find you. I'll track you down if it takes the rest of my life ..."

Chamberlain laughed. "I'm trembling, Robinson. Say hello to your daughter."

There was a muffled sound, a shifting, and then Emily's weak, high voice on the line. "Daddy?"

Anne dropped to a seat at the table in front of the reel-to-reel tape recorder from which she could hear her child's voice. In the kitchen, Ben pressed his face against the wall. "Emily, honey, are you all right?"

"Daddy, I want to go home," she squeaked. "Please, Daddy—"

The phone was jerked from her, and then Christy was on the line. Her lower, raspy voice sounded breathy, weak. "Daddy?"

"Christy." He caught his breath on a sob. "We're looking for you, honey. We're trying to get you back. Can you tell me where you are? Any clue? Just a word?"

She hesitated. "Daddy, we're scared. It's dark and old and there are rats . . ."

He closed his eyes. "Honey, we're going to find you. We're doing everything we can to get you back tonight. Just hold on, okay? Take care of each other."

The man's voice interrupted. "It's your choice, Robinson. Either deliver, or say good-bye."

"I'll deliver," Ben said, glancing back at Larry who was watching him as he listened to the conversation. "Just tell me where."

"Midnight," the man said. "At the railroad station. There will be a train leaving at 12:30. I'll have a red handkerchief hanging in the opening of one of the boxcars between the Franklin Street and the Alethea Street intersections. Find it and put the painting in there."

"What about the children?"

"When I have the picture, I'll let you know where they are. And I'll know it when I see it. If you try to deceive me, Robinson, the children are dead."

Tony shook his head, signaling to Ben.

"No," Ben said. "You'll have to do better than that. Why should I trust you?"

"Because you have no choice. Midnight, Robinson. I wouldn't be late, if I were you. And I mean it. If you try to put a fake past me, you'll regret it. I'll know at first glance."

The phone went dead, and Ben stood holding it for a moment, frowning and looking bewildered and despondent. He looked into the dining room where the two cops were still trying to find the source of the call, and he saw his wife slumped down on the table, sobbing into the circle of her arms. He hung up the phone and went toward her. Sharon was sitting at the table, her face in her hands, weeping.

Ben went to Anne and touched her hair. She looked up at him and fell into his arms. He held her for a long time, crying with her.

Tony longed to reach out, to at least touch Sharon's hand, to comfort her as Ben was comforting Anne. But he held himself back, waiting for Larry to finish the trace.

Larry was on another line, frowning, as though things weren't working out. "What do you mean? Well, can you get the cellular phone's number? It's got to be Chamberlain's."

He waited several more moments, then wilted. "All right. So some guy named Stu Miegel owns that phone. Find him and question him. Maybe he's working with Chamberlain." His frown got deeper. "You're kidding. Well, that's just great."

He slammed down the phone. "You're not gonna believe this."

Tony had heard most of it. "It's not his phone. So whose is it?"

"Some guy who reported his phone stolen out of a bar about half an hour ago."

Tony rubbed his forehead. "What bar?"

"Your stomping ground. Steppin' Out. He said he set it on the bar, and the next thing he knew, it was gone."

"Did anybody show him a picture of Chamberlain?"

"He said he didn't recognize him. But that he hadn't looked around much, so anybody could have been there."

Tony was getting tired. He rubbed his eyes and looked at Ben, huddled with his wife, still in tears. "All right, Ben. Looks like we're going to have to deliver something. He's got to be bluffing about recognizing it at first glance."

"He's not," Ben said. "If I know him, he'd have memorized every stroke."

"We'll just have to take that chance. Is there any place we can quickly get a close reproduction?"

Ben thought for a moment. "What did he say, exactly? Could you rewind it and let me hear?"

"Sure." Larry flicked a knob, rewound the tape, then played it again.

Ben tried hard to focus his thoughts, though the despair over his terrified daughters lingered in his mind.

He groaned and flopped back. "I can't believe Dubose was involved with him, but he must have been. That's why he was so anxious to convince me it was a fake. Then he fired me because he thought I would ruin the deal, or give his secret away! We've got to find that painting. Maybe I can give him another painting of the same size ... and just hope it's dark enough that he can't see it right away until they catch him."

"No!" Sharon cried. "You can't do that! He'll kill them. He said so. And what if the police don't catch him? What if he gets away?"

"Sharon, what choice do we have?" Tony asked.

"I don't know!" she shouted. "But you have to do better than that!"

"She's right," Anne said.

Larry began to pace, trying to think. "Dubose moves the painting after Ben discovers it—and when Chamberlain doesn't find the painting where it's supposed to be, he naturally assumes that Ben has it."

"We've looked all over that gallery and Dubose's house."

"Could he have given it to a friend? Sent it to someone?"

Ben stared at the wall for a moment, remembering that last day, before Dubose had fired him. He had been preoccupied, busy with something.

"I remember him getting a package ready to mail out," Ben said. "It was a cylinder, about four feet long. I never thought of it then, but it could have been the Marazzio. *The Multitude* was four feet by seven feet."

Tony was practically on top of the table as he leaned over to prod Ben. "How did he mail it? U.S. Post Office, Fedex?"

"UPS," Ben said. "He always sent things UPS." His breath was short as he looked hopefully at both of them. "I know where he kept those receipts. It'll have the address he mailed it to."

Tony grabbed his sport coat. "Let's go."

Ben followed him to the door, but Sharon ran after them. "What can I do? I can't just sit here."

"Pray," Larry said over his shoulder. "Pray hard."

CHAPTER FORTY-SIX

Why hasn't Daddy come yet?" Emily's voice was hoarse and raspy. Her lips were getting dry from thirst. She sat close to Christy, afraid to venture too far across the floor, for fear of what might lurk there.

"He will. Didn't you hear the man? He said tonight. Daddy will come tonight."

"What if he can't find us?"

"He will. I know he will."

Hearing a scratching sound in the wall, they tensed up and huddled closer. "What's that?" Christy asked.

Emily covered her face with both hands, but then dropped them, for they hurt too badly. The dirt from all the digging was still caked on them, but the sores they'd rubbed while digging were beginning to get infected. Christy had the same problem, except that she also had that cut on her head and the scrapes on her back from where she'd been jerked out from under the wall in the shed.

"It's a rat, isn't it?" Emily asked weakly.

Christy began to cry quietly. "Let's pray some more," she said. "We have to pray that God will keep the rats from coming in here. We have to tell him how scared we are."

Emily bowed her head without protest.

"Dear God," Christy whispered, "could you please help us, please, and make those rats go away so we won't be so scared? We would appreciate it very much."

The scratching sounded again, and Christy stomped her foot on the floor and let out a loud yell, hoping to frighten whatever it was away. The sound grew quiet.

"I scared it," she whispered.

They heard a sound up above them, another scratching sound, but this one came from the window at the very top of the bathroom, probably fifteen feet up.

"What's that?" Christy asked.

Emily turned on the flashlight and shone it up. The light was weak because the battery was running out. The faint circle of light hit the window, and they saw something standing on the sill looking down at them.

"It's a—"

Before Emily could get the words out, it leaped from the windowsill to the floor.

Both girls screamed and backed further against the corner. Something furry grazed Christy's leg, and she screamed louder, harder. Then they heard a sound they hadn't expected.

"Meeeeooouw."

Emily caught her breath and shone the light on the animal. "Christy, it's a cat. Look!"

Christy opened her eyes and began to laugh with relief at the big yellow tomcat. "A cat? Come here, kitty. You scared me."

It was a good-natured cat, and it rubbed against Christy's leg and allowed her to pick it up. "Look, Emily. He's so sweet."

Emily giggled and petted him. "How did he get in? It's so high up."

"There must be a tree outside the window. See? I told you God would answer our prayer."

"What?" Emily asked. "We didn't ask for a cat."

"No, but he'll scare the rats off. And he'll keep us company, so we won't be scared."

Emily thought about that for a moment. "Yeah. Maybe he'll stay here until Daddy comes to get us."

"He'll have to," Christy said. "He can't get back out until someone opens the door."

"He's a good answer to our prayers," Emily giggled, rubbing her face in the purring cat's fur. "How did God know?"

"God knows what we need better than we do," Christy said matter-of-factly. "My mommy always says that."

"Has God ever sent *her* a cat?"

"Nope. Other things. It's always something different."

"So praying really works?"

"It worked this time, didn't it?"

Emily smiled as the cat curled up on her lap and lay down, purring.

CHAPTER FORTY-SEVEN

elson Chamberlain sat on a small hill near the train tracks, waiting for the 10:30 train to arrive. As he sat, he wove the red handkerchief through his fingers, in and out, until it ran out. Then, unwinding it, he looked up the tracks.

He could hear the sound of a distant train, and knew that it would be here any moment. He would be glad. He didn't like getting dirty, and it wasn't his style to sit on a heap of dirt waiting for a train to come by. His work was clean—never-get-your-hands-dirty work. But lately, he'd been getting his hands dirty more and more. It made him uncomfortable, but he supposed it would all be worth it when he had exchanged the painting with Boudreaux and was on his way to England.

The train grew closer, and he saw its headlight coming up the tracks. He watched as it slowed and passed him, and he counted one boxcar after another. The train slowed even more, until it finally came to a halt, creaking and crawling by in front of him.

He sat still until he was sure it had stopped, then waited another ten minutes before picking out the car where he wanted the painting delivered. There was one not far from where he'd been sitting that had an open door and nothing inside. If they set the painting at the back right corner of that one, as he'd told them to, it would be safe.

He got to his feet, dusted off his pants, and checked to make sure no one was around who would find him suspicious. The first car, where the engineer sat, was around a curve, and no one in it was able to see him. He slipped his handkerchief over the pipe that held the door in place, and tied it there. Then he checked it, made sure it was secure and could be seen.

Jumping off the car, he looked up the tracks. He was going to drive his car to a place about two miles from here, then walk back up the tracks for about a mile. When the train left at 12:30, after Ben had delivered *The Multitude,* he would watch for that car, jump on it while the train was still moving slowly, get the painting, then jump off near where his car was parked.

It was foolproof. They could, of course, station cops on the train when Ben put the painting on board. But they wouldn't dare try to grab him before he told them where the children were. Besides that, they wouldn't know where his car was parked, and once he jumped off the train and fled, they'd never be able to find or identify him. He would be home free after he got the painting and was back in his car on the way to the airport, where Boudreaux had agreed to meet him.

He laughed as he went back over the hill to his car, which was parked behind some trees so it couldn't be seen. Just a couple more hours of this nightmare, and he would finally be on his way to ending it.

CHAPTER FORTY-EIGHT

he UPS receipts were exactly where Ben thought they would be. Louis Dubose had been a master organizer. He kept his office immaculate and always filed away everything so it wouldn't clutter his desk.

The receipt they were looking for was at the front of the file. Victoriously, Ben pulled it out. "It's got the address as clear as day."

Tony looked it over. "Are you sure this is the right item?"

"Positive," Ben said. "Look, he mailed it out of town, but not too far away . . . in St. Petersburg. And it says it's a cylinder. It has to be it," Ben said. "Come on. We don't have much time if we're going to get it."

They flew across St. Clair and into St. Pete, checking their map to find the street the address was on. When they found it, they saw that it was a small shop called "Home Address." A sign in the window said, "Open till 10." "It's only 9:30," Tony said. "Somebody's on our side."

Tony, Larry, and Ben burst in. "Do you have mailboxes here, where people can send things?"

"Yes," the man said, gesturing toward an entire wall of postal boxes. "Do you need one?"

"No." Tony took out his badge and flashed it to the man. "We're with the St. Clair PD. We need to confiscate the contents of Suite 320."

"It's over there. It's really a post office box, but we call them suites so it'll make people look like they have offices. Do you have a warrant?"

"No," Tony said. "But there are two children in trouble right now, and if we take the time to get one, they could wind up dead."

"But I can't hand over some other guy's mail to you."

"Look, all we want is a cylinder that's in there. It's going to save the lives of this man's two little girls, who've been kidnapped. Now, you can make me go get a warrant, but you're coming with me, got that? I'll take you in and question you for a couple of days on how you knew the guy who rented this box, and what your connection might be in his murder and the kidnapping of the two little girls."

The man looked a little stunned, then quickly reached behind the counter for the key. "All right. Open it."

Tony took the key and opened it. "It's a cylinder all right. Return address . . . your gallery."

Ben breathed out a sigh of relief. "Open it. Let's make sure it's the right painting."

Carefully, Tony opened the box and laid it on the counter, while the manager watched with awe. He opened the cylinder and slid out the contents.

"See?" Ben said. "That's it, all right." He took it with careful hands and unrolled it partially. "That's *The Multitude*."

"All right," Larry said. "We don't have any more time to waste. We have to go by the station to report to the captain before we make the drop. We'll need a lot of help on this one."

They thanked the tense manager, then rushed out with the package and drove as fast as they could drive back to St. Clair.

CHAPTER FORTY-NINE

Anne put Bobby to bed, then sat for a while in the rocking chair, thinking about her lost child. Where were Emily and Christy? Would they really get them back tonight?

Unable to sit still, she got up and walked through the house. She headed up the stairs, wanting to go into Christy's room, wanting to be among the things Emily had left there. She stepped into the doorway and saw Sharon and Jenny sitting on the bed, huddled together. They both looked up at her.

"Excuse me," she said, wiping her tears. "I didn't know you were in here." She backed away, but Sharon stopped her.

"Anne, wait."

Anne looked at her questioningly.

"We were praying for the girls, and for Ben. Would you come pray with us?"

Anne hesitated. "I'm not much of a prayer. If there's a God, I'm not sure he'd listen to a prayer that came from me."

"The fact that he ever listens to any of us is just evidence of his grace," Sharon said. "Come on."

Anne came into the room and sat down on the edge of the bed.

"Turn around, Anne," Jenny said. "Let's sit in a circle and hold hands. Jesus said that whenever two or more of us are gathered in his name, he would be among us."

"Really?" Anne asked. "He said that?"

"Yes," Sharon said. "We've got to pray for them."

"Okay," Anne whispered.

Sharon reached for Anne's left hand and held it tightly. Jenny took the other, as mother and daughter held hands, as well. And Sharon began to pray.

CHAPTER FIFTY

A cross town, in Lynda Barrett's home, she and Jake sat on the couch in her living room, with fifteen other friends of Sharon's from their church. Sharon hadn't been told they were meeting, but it didn't matter if she knew or not. Lynda had called them right after she'd gotten the call from Sharon about an exchange being made that night. Lynda had known there was only one thing to do.

The fifteen held hands and prayed one by one, earnestly, deeply . . .

It was Jake's turn, and he grew emotional as he began to speak. "Lord, you said that you would intercede for us, with groanings too deep for words . . . when we don't even know how to pray. I don't know where those little girls are, Lord, or what they need, or what danger they're in, but you can see them. You know. Lord, please take care of them. Surround them with your presence. Don't let any harm come to them. They're so little . . . And Ben . . . he's out there looking for that painting . . . something he can give to the man who has them. Let him find it, Lord. And I pray for the kidnapper, that you'll work on him, as well. Foil him, Lord. Get in his way. Convict him . . . I know you can answer this prayer, Lord. I've seen your answers before. But not our will, but thine. You know what's best . . ."

And so the prayers went on into the night as the group interceded for the family that was in such turmoil.

CHAPTER FIFTY-ONE

The girls fell asleep with the cat lying across their laps. They were so exhausted that they didn't wake when the cat sprang up after hearing a scratching on the wall. His night eyes spotted the small head jerking out of the hole in the wall where the sink had been. He hissed, but the rat wasn't daunted.

His ears stretched tightly back on his head, teeth bared, back hunched, until the rat had quietly made its way out of the hole and down the wall. It had scarcely hit the floor when the cat attacked.

In seconds, the rat was dead, and the cat dragged it to the corner of the room, behind the rusty, stinking toilet. There he left it, and went back to the girls. Neither of them had stirred.

Satisfied, he crawled back onto their laps, began to purr again, and went back to sleep.

A ll right," the captain, Sam Richter, said as he paced in front of the roomful of cops waiting to spring into action. "We have men posted at the tracks already, trying to catch him when he hangs the handkerchief. If we don't get him then, we go ahead as planned. Everybody has their posts. You know what to do. The minute Chamberlain has the painting, apprehend him and bring him in."

"No!" Tony stood up and looked back at his partner for help. "Captain, that would be a mistake. We have to give him time to call about the kids."

"What if he doesn't?" Sam asked. "What if he heads straight for the airport and leaves on the next plane out?"

"He has no incentive to call," one of the cops said. "If he has the painting, he's not going to be worried about those kids."

"Maybe he'll worry because he's a human being," Tony said. "Maybe he'll keep his end of the bargain."

"The man is a criminal," Larry said. "He doesn't care about keeping his word."

Tony swung around, gaping at him. "Whose side are you on, anyway?"

"I'm on the kids' side," Larry said. "And if we go ahead and collar him, maybe we can make some kind of deal to get him to tell us where they are."

"There's one thing you're all forgetting," the captain said. "One of those little girls knows the kidnapper. He won't want her to identify him. So we face the danger of his going back to kill the kids if we don't find him right away. That is, if he hasn't already done it."

"He hasn't," Tony said. "And if he goes back, that's great. He's led us to them. We can collar him there before he has the chance to do anything. I'm not suggesting letting him go, Captain. Just give him some time after he gets the painting. Let's see if he leads us to them or calls the parents to tell them where to look."

The captain sat down on the table at the front of the room, a deep frown clefting his forehead. "All right, then what if he doesn't call or lead us to them? How far do we follow him before we take him?"

"As far as we need to."

"Even as far as the airport?"

"Yes!" Tony said. "Maybe he would call from there."

"What if he gets on a plane?" the captain asked. "Do we allow that?"

"Yes!" Tony said. "We go with him. We watch. We alert authorities at the destination to be prepared to apprehend him the minute he gets off."

The captain gave him a disbelieving look. "And what would that serve?"

"It would give him time, Captain," Tony said, his face reddening with the effort of persuasion. "Time to make a call from the plane. It might be the only place he feels safe doing it. Think about it. He'll think he got away without being followed, if we do our job right. Then when the plane takes off, he'll be breathing easier, thinking he made a clean escape. At that point, it would be logical that he would call the family from the phone on the plane."

"You have to have a credit card to make a call from the air. You really think he's going to mess up and use his own credit card to make a call, when he's gone to such lengths to keep from being traced?"

"He's resourceful. We already know he has cards in at least two other names. But if we grab him before he talks, he may *never* tell us where the girls are."

"Oh, he'll tell us," the captain assured him. "I'll see to that."

"What are you gonna do? Beat it out of him? Let him scream police brutality and get the whole case dropped for civil rights violations?" Tony dropped back into his chair. "Look, all I know is that there's a family out there who is sick with worry over their children. We're down to the wire now. Let's not mess it up."

The captain took a few deep breaths and checked his watch. It was 11:30. They would need to leave in just a few minutes to make the drop by midnight. He looked from Larry to Tony, then strolled to the window of the conference room. Outside, Ben Robinson was sitting at Larry's desk, calling his family to tell them they'd found the painting. He was crying quietly.

The captain turned back around. "All right, guys. Here's what we're gonna do. We're gonna let him get the painting, let him make his escape. Whoever gets close enough can follow him, but keep in close contact with me. If he heads for the airport, you follow him in."

Tony breathed a sigh of relief. "Thank you, Captain."

"Wait a minute. I didn't finish. Follow him in, but do not let him get on a plane. Do you hear me? Do not let him get on the plane."

"Captain, that's a mistake—"

"Apprehend him before he boards. That will give him ample time to call the family. If he hasn't done it by then, we have to assume that he's not going to. We'll play heck getting the information out of him if he's apprehended in Atlanta—or, worse yet, in Mexico City or someplace like that. We need to find those kids tonight."

Tony slammed a fist on the table and got up. "Captain—"

"You've got my orders, Danks. Don't violate them."

"Fine!" he said through his teeth, heading for the door. "I just hope those orders don't ruin any chance we have of finding those girls."

241

CHAPTER FIFTY-THREE

I t was nearing midnight when Tony, Larry, and Ben went back to Sharon's house, and Ben got into his own car with the painting. The cops stationed at the track had not spotted Chamberlain or the handkerchief yet, so Larry and Tony would follow Ben at a distance to the railroad tracks, and let him look for the marking and deliver the painting to the boxcar alone. Even if they spotted Chamberlain hanging the handkerchief, the cops watching for him had been instructed not to act until he had the painting in his hand.

There were no lights in the area of the railroad tracks that Chamberlain had designated, so it was difficult for Tony and Larry to see from where their car was hidden. They quietly got out of the car. Tony watched with night glasses as Ben walked along the tracks, the multimillion-dollar painting in its cylinder clamped beneath his arm, looking for the boxcar with the red handkerchief.

"Has he found it yet?" Larry asked Tony.

Tony shook his head. "No. And I don't see it. What if he hasn't marked it yet?"

His voice stopped cold when he saw Ben hesitate. There, above the door of one of the cars, was a handkerchief flapping in the wind. Ben glanced in both directions, then jumped into the car. Seconds later, he jumped out and headed back to his car.

"All right," Tony said, shoving the night glasses back into their pouch on his belt. "If we cross here, and come up behind the train, it should be dark enough that we won't be seen. The painting's hidden on the eighth car from here. You take the one before it, number seven, and I'll take the one after it. That way we can watch from both sides."

They crossed the tracks, stepping over a joint between two boxcars, and ran hunched over, counting cars. Larry jumped into the one directly behind the marked car, and Tony ran ahead and quietly climbed into the one in front of it.

Crossing the car, he sat by the opposite door, his body carefully hidden in the darkness so that he would have a clear view when Chamberlain came to get the painting. He knew that other plain-clothed officers circled the area, searching for the rental car they had discovered Chamberlain was using now. They had been told not to act if they found it. Just to stay in place so they could follow it when he made his escape.

Tony sat so still that his muscles ached, and he wondered if Sharon was holding up all right. She was at her wit's end. And he couldn't blame her. If they messed up tonight, if the children weren't found, or if they were found but they weren't alive . . .

His heart ached, and he told himself that they just had to be alive. He couldn't accept the possibility that they weren't. He couldn't stand the thought of telling her.

Time ticked slowly by, and no one came for the painting. He began to wonder if they had put it in the wrong car, or if this was all just some kind of hoax, if maybe he was a sitting duck for Chamberlain's warped sense of humor.

He looked up at the sky. Stars sparkled with an uncanny brilliance, like white paint splattered in fine drops on a black canvas. But he doubted even Marazzio could have duplicated it tonight. It was beautiful, and seemed to testify to such peace, that for a moment he found himself wondering if there really was someone up there beyond it, keeping the earth spinning on its axis, the moon circling the planet, the stars suspended where they were.

For the first time, the thought that there was seemed infinitely more comforting than what he had always chosen to believe. If there wasn't a creator, and the earth spun on its own, and the moon controlled its own destiny, and the stars were all there by coincidence—then the world truly was formed out of chaos, and nothing could be predictable, and he might be sitting here wasting his time while those children were in grave danger.

Maybe there was a God. And maybe he did answer prayers. Intelligent people prayed to him all the time. They seemed to think he answered. Even when things went bad, as they had with Jake Stevens and Lynda Barrett, they still seemed to believe that God was with them, working it all out.

He knew that two cars back, Larry was probably praying right now. They were probably all praying. Sharon, Jenny, Lynda, Jake ... everybody. Heck, they probably had all their church friends praying on one of those prayer chains. Half the town of St. Clair, at least those who believed, were probably praying for him and for this whole operation right now. It was a little intimidating. And a little comforting.

He looked up at the stars again. *God, is it you?* he asked silently. *Are you really there? Or are they just talking to air? I've never been one to accept things on faith. That's for dreamers. I'm a realist.*

Then why was he talking to the sky? he asked himself wryly.

The car bumped, and he sprang to attention, ready for something to happen. He looked outside, but saw no one, then wondered if he'd missed it. Had Chamberlain gotten into the car behind his, jarring the car?

But then the car bumped again, and he realized this time that the train was moving. Slowly, inch by inch, it began to creep down the tracks. He checked his watch and pushed the indiglo button to light the digital readout. It was 12:30. Time for the train to leave.

It was all right, though. He had thought of this. He and Larry had agreed that Chamberlain might be waiting a little way down the tracks, prepared to jump on the car to get the painting, then off before the train picked up any speed. It would be the most foolproof way to keep from getting caught.

He braced himself as the train began to move, the noise of the wheels grinding on the tracks sending up a roar. Knowing he wouldn't be heard now, he pulled out his walkie-talkie and turned it on. "We're moving, guys," he told the other cops who were stationed at various intervals at the intersections down the tracks. "Keep your eyes peeled."

The train moved about fifteen miles per hour down the track, slow to someone waiting to cross the tracks, but too fast for someone inside waiting to catch a killer. He stayed in the shadows, watching, watching, as they passed intersection after intersection.

Where was he? Surely he didn't plan to wait until the train's next stop. He must know they'd have people waiting there, ready to catch him. No, the best bet would be to come onto the train from some unpredictable place—anywhere but a stopping point—and jump off before anyone could be the wiser.

"Bingo." It was Larry's voice, and Tony held the walkie-talkie close to his ear.

"What?" he asked.

"I see a guy with a flashlight checking the boxcars," he said. "I think we've got our man."

Tony turned off the walkie-talkie and set it back in his coat pocket. Suddenly he saw the flashlight beam searching the door-way of his boxcar. It moved onto the next, then the beam cut off—no doubt because Chamberlain had seen the handkerchief.

He watched, carefully, as a man ran alongside the tracks, right next to his own car, looking back behind him for the perfect moment to jump on board. He fell behind, in pace with the marked car, then disappeared.

"He's on," Tony whispered to himself. He inched closer to the door, and waited for him to jump back off. Nothing happened.

What was he doing? Was he checking the painting before he got off? Was he going to ride it to the next town?

Before he had time to panic, he saw the man jump back out and roll down the bank of grass. Time for action.

Tony watched him run toward a dark intersection, where a black car was parked off the street, near some trees. He let the train take him a couple hundred feet down the tracks, then jumped off himself. Larry followed.

Tony pulled the walkie-talkie back out and turned it on. "He's at the tracks at Gray Street, guys. The black Ford Tempo."

"We see him," one of the cops radioed back.

"Don't let him see you. And keep me posted. Somebody pick Larry and me up at the same intersection in about three minutes."

Larry was dusting himself off. "Are you all right?"

"Yeah, no problem. I'm just hoping this guy has an ounce of compassion inside him. Maybe he doesn't want to abandon those kids."

"Let's hope so." They jogged back up the track to the intersection Chamberlain had left moments ago.

A car was waiting there for them, and they drove back to the car they had parked miles up the track.

CHAPTER FIFTY-FOUR

B en walked into the quiet house, wondering where everyone was. His hands were shaking, and he went to the cabinets, searching for something strong to drink. Something that would calm him and make the wait less excruciating.

But he found nothing, and he realized idly that Sharon never kept alcohol in the house. If ever there was a need for some, it was now. How was she coping without it?

He sat down at the table and pressed his fist against his mouth as tears came to his eyes. What had happened after he left? Had they gotten Chamberlain? Had he told them where the kids were?

He couldn't sit still, so he jumped up again and went through the house looking for his wife or his daughter—or even his ex. They weren't downstairs.

Had something happened to them? Anxious, he ran up the stairs. The world had gone haywire, and someone had come in here and taken them, too—

And then he heard voices in Christy's bedroom.

He hurried to the door. Inside, he saw his daughter Jenny, with both of the mothers of his children, sitting in a circle on Christy's bed, holding hands and praying.

He sucked in a sob, and they all looked up.

"Daddy!" Jenny lunged off the bed. "Daddy, did you see him? Did you find Christy and Emily?"

"Not yet," he said, wiping his eyes. She pulled him to the bed and he sat down next to Anne, who put her arms around him and dropped her forehead against his shoulder. "I delivered the painting. They . . . they told me to come home and wait for him to call and tell us where they are."

He felt himself losing control even as he spoke, and he collapsed against his wife and broke down completely. She got on her knees on the bed and held him, and Sharon sat back and watched her former adversary comfort the man who used to be her husband.

And it was all right.

"We were praying, Ben," Sharon whispered, reaching for his hand. "We have to keep praying. There's a phone in here. We'll hear if he calls."

He nodded, unable to speak, and kept leaning against his wife as they began to pray again.

CHAPTER FIFTY-FIVE

elson Chamberlain navigated the back roads of St. Clair, making his way to the interstate where he could head for the Tampa Airport. So far, he saw no one following him, and he laughed out loud. He had gotten away with it.

He patted the long cylinder on the seat next to him. He had already checked it, back in the boxcar by flashlight, so he knew that it was just what he'd expected—*The Multitude*, a priceless masterpiece by one of the greatest Italian painters who'd ever lived.

He reached into the box on the floor. There was a fake mustache and goatee, tinted glasses, and a black fedora. As he drove, he fit the mustache above his lip, pressed the adhesive tightly, then applied the goatee. He saved the glasses and hat until he was ready to get out. The garment bag sat in the backseat. When he got to the airport, where he'd told Boudreaux to meet him, all he would have to do is slip the long tube into the garment bag, make the exchange with Boudreaux, and get on the next flight to England. Boudreaux would head back to France. No one would find the children where he'd left them, and they would probably starve to death. But that was just as well. He couldn't risk having them identify him and ruin what was turning out to be the perfect crime.

CHAPTER FIFTY-SIX

W hat have you got, guys? Anything yet?" Larry held the
walkie-talkie close to his ear as Tony drove.

"Nothing," John Hampton answered. "He's
headed for the airport so fast I'm afraid the Tampa
police are gonna pull him over."

"All right. We're on our way there now. If he stops to make
the call, don't let him see you."

He looked at Tony as he took the ramp onto the interstate.
Tony looked as tense as he'd ever seen him. "What do you think?
Will he call?"

"He has to," Tony said.

CHAPTER FIFTY-SEVEN

The pain in Christy's hands woke her, and she looked down at them, barely able to see them in the darkness. They were swollen and still grimy, and the open sores from where she'd rubbed the skin off were wet and painful. Besides that, she didn't feel good. She had a bad headache, and her back was aching. And her throat burned with thirst.

She moved the cat off her lap and got on all fours to crawl to the broken pipes where the sink had been. Maybe there was a leak there. Maybe something a little wet, that she could catch on her tongue . . .

Her hand grazed something hairy, and she jumped back with a scream.

Emily jumped up. "What is it? What's wrong, Christy?"

Christy pressed back against the wall and felt around for the flashlight. Her fingers were almost in too much pain to turn the switch on, but she managed. "Over there, in the corner," she cried. "I can't look! Look and see what it is."

Emily took the flashlight, wincing as she moved the circle of light slowly across the floor. When she saw the dead rat, she yelped.

"What?" Christy asked. "What is it?"

"A rat!" Emily cried.

The cat, awakened by all the commotion, pranced over to the rat and picked it up, demonstrating that it was dead. Then he dropped it back in the corner.

"He killed it! It's dead," Christy said, still crying.

"I don't want to look anymore," Emily said weakly. She shone the flashlight on her hands. Hers, too, were oozing and swollen and grimy. "My hands hurt."

"Mine, too."

"Are they 'fected? Mommy says if you don't clean a sore, it'll get 'fected."

"I think so," Christy said.

"What will happen? What does that mean?"

"I don't know," Christy said. "All I know is it hurts. I want to get out of here. I want to go home."

They started to cry harder. Finally, Emily asked, "When do you think Daddy will come? He said tonight. He promised."

"Maybe he couldn't keep his promise."

"But Mr. Chamberlain said he would kill us if Daddy didn't do what he wanted. Do you think he's gonna kill us tonight?"

Christy thought that over for a moment. Her first instinct was to say no, that he wasn't going to kill them, but then she realized that it could be likely. He hadn't fed them all day or brought them anything to drink. He had left them here with the rats. Why wouldn't a man like that kill them?

"I wish we had a phone," Emily said matter-of-factly. "I'd call 911."

"I wish we had a ladder," Christy said. "I'd climb out that window up there."

The cat purred and rubbed up against Christy. "Well, we have a cat. And we're together. When he put me in that trunk by myself when you ran away, I was scared I'd be alone."

Emily whimpered, laying her head against Christy's shoulder. "Do you think Mommy and Daddy know we haven't eaten? Do you think they know he might kill us?"

"They know," Christy whispered. "They just can't find us."

The cat purred and snuggled deeper into their laps.

"I wish I remembered that story," Emily whispered.

"What story?"

"The one your mom told us that night. About Beth."

"Beth and her tree cottage?" Christy asked. "You don't have to remember. You just have to make it up. I'll tell it to you. You can help."

"Okay," Emily said.

"Once upon a time, a mean man came and stole Beth out of her tree house."

"And he put her in a dark, scary place," Emily added quietly.

"But Beth was very brave. And she was smart. Real smart."

"Could she read when she was four?" Emily asked on a weak whisper.

"Yes. And she knew that song with all the states."

"What happened to her?" Emily asked.

"Well, she watched and waited, and found a way to escape."

"What way?" Emily asked without much hope.

"There was a secret door in the dark place," Christy said. "A secret door that only the nice people could see. The bad man couldn't see it at all. And at first she didn't see it, because she was too upset."

"But then she saw it?" Emily whispered.

"Yes," Christy said. "And she tiptoed to it. But it needed a key to open it. And she didn't know where the key was."

"What did she do?"

Christy was getting sleepy even as she spoke. She yawned. "I don't know. I need to think about it."

Emily didn't answer, and Christy saw that her eyes had closed. Christy rested her head against the wall and surrendered to sweet, merciful sleep. Her last thought before drifting off was, *God, please help Beth find the key.*

CHAPTER FIFTY-EIGHT

The portable light on their dashboard flashed as Tony drove at breakneck speed to the Tampa Airport. He didn't want to pass Chamberlain along the way, so he'd chosen an alternate route. Larry was on the radio with the cops who were tailing Chamberlain.

"Where are you now?"

"Nearing the airport exit," they said. "So far, nothing. There's no cellular antenna on his car. Could he be using a flip phone or something to call them?"

"No," Larry said. "I checked. They haven't heard anything yet. Just don't lose him, and don't let him see you. Let him think he's home free. Remember: There are two little girls whose lives depend on us."

CHAPTER FIFTY-NINE

Nelson Chamberlain pulled off the exit ramp of the interstate and headed toward the airport. Almost there.

He turned toward the rental car return. His first instinct, to abandon the car at the curb of the Delta terminal, had been a bad idea. As far as he knew, they hadn't yet traced this crime to him. Even though he'd rented this car under the name John Lieber, he didn't want any suspicions to arise that Lieber might not be who he said he was.

Someone met him at the parking lot as he pulled his car in. "Can I help you, sir?"

"Yeah," Chamberlain said, jumping out of the car and grabbing the garment bag. "I'm late for my flight. Could you take care of this?"

"No sir. You have to go inside."

"I can't!" He reached into his pocket and pulled out a hundred-dollar bill. "This should cover whatever I might still owe. Just take care of it, and you can keep the rest."

The man hesitated. "Well, all right. The shuttle to the terminal is right over there. It's almost ready to leave."

Chamberlain leaped onto the shuttle. "Delta," he told the driver. "And hurry."

The other two passengers on the shuttle gave him indolent glances, then turned their gazes out the window. The shuttle started to leave.

"Wait!" Two men outside yelled at the bus driver, and he stopped.

They jumped on, breathless. "We almost missed you. Thanks for waiting."

One of them slid his duffel bag under the seat and sat next to Chamberlain as the shuttle started to leave; the other sat across from him, a garment bag slung over his shoulder.

Chamberlain dug his ticket out of his coat pocket and looked down to make sure that he wasn't late for his meeting with Boudreaux, and that he still had enough time to make the flight.

"What terminal?" the driver asked.

"Delta," Chamberlain said.

"Same here," one of the two men called out.

CHAPTER SIXTY

So where is he now?" Larry asked via radio as he and Tony approached the airport and took the ramp heading for the terminals.

"On the rental car shuttle," a cop said. "Nick and John are on there with him. They're plain-clothed, so he won't know who they are."

"Good going," Larry said. "We're almost at the terminals now. Any idea which one he's headed for?"

"Not yet," the cop said. "But we'll have all of them covered. We have a couple of guys going over the rental car as we speak. Maybe we'll find some clues there."

Tony pulled over to wait for the rental car shuttle to come around. Moments later, it passed them and stopped at American. One passenger got off. Then it went a few feet to the TWA terminal. Another passenger got off.

"They're stopping at Delta," Larry said into the radio seconds later. "Three men are getting off. Yep. John and Nick are two of them. The other one doesn't look like him, but it's got to be. There's nobody else on the bus. He's wearing a black mustache and a goatee, a hat, and tinted glasses. Carrying a garment bag over his shoulder. Give him a chance to check in and make the call. He still might do it."

Abandoning their car, they both followed through the door where Chamberlain had gone. They saw the man up ahead, closely followed by the two cops.

"Come on," Tony whispered. "Go to the pay phone. Make the call."

257

But the man headed, instead, toward the gate where his plane would soon be boarding. He checked in at the desk, and they all waited from a distance to see if he'd still turn and make that call. Instead, he turned and, still carrying the garment bag over his shoulder, went into a bar several yards down. He hesitated at the doorway, looked around, then approached a well-dressed man sitting at the back in a booth by himself.

Larry and Tony watched as the other man stood up, and the two shook hands. Chamberlain slipped into the booth, and for a moment, they could only see the back of his head.

"All right," Tony told Larry. "This must be the buyer for the painting. Let's just hang back and take it easy. If we play our cards right, we'll kill two birds with one stone. We'll get him *and* the buyer."

They waited as seconds ticked off, and as the time grew closer for Chamberlain's plane to take off.

CHAPTER SIXTY-ONE

In the booth at the back of the bar, where they were hidden by two half-walls with planters full of greenery, Chamberlain unzipped the bag, pulled out the cylinder, and handed the awkward package across the table to Boudreaux. The man's eyes were huge and awestruck as he carefully removed the contents. The canvas covered the width of the table; unrolled, it extended two feet beyond the edge. Chamberlain helped him hold it uncurled as Boudreaux gazed down at *The Multitude*.

"It's magnificent," Boudreaux said, breathless. "Just as I remember it." He was beginning to perspire, and he pulled a handkerchief out of his pocket and wiped his forehead.

"Where's the money?" Chamberlain asked.

"Fifteen million," Boudreaux told him. "It is safely in a bank account in Switzerland. The account was opened under the name John Lieber." He pulled an envelope out of his breast pocket. "All of the necessary documents are here. In fact, if you wish to call the bank to make sure the funds are there—" He checked his watch. "I believe you would have no problem."

Chamberlain pulled the documents out and studied them. "Yes, I would like to call."

"All right," Boudreaux said, carefully holding the rolled canvas. "Here is the security code for that account, as well as the account number. The telephone number is on the front of the document."

"Stay here," Chamberlain said. He got up and asked the bartender if he could use his phone to make a credit card call. The man slid the phone across the counter.

CHAPTER SIXTY-TWO

From outside the restaurant, Tony watched Chamberlain pick up the phone. "He's calling!"

"Maybe," Larry agreed. "But we can't apprehend him until we've confirmed it. I'll go call our guys over at the Robinson's and make sure that's who he's talking to."

"All right," Tony said. "Meanwhile, I'm going to get as close as I can. He doesn't know me. Let me know the second you have confirmation, and tell all the others to stand by."

Tony couldn't get close enough to hear the telephone conversation, but he found a place at a table that Chamberlain would have to pass on his way out of the bar. He sat down and strained to hear, but the classical music playing over the sound system was too loud, and Chamberlain was turned away from him.

Let him tell them, he prayed without even realizing it.

He was on the phone longer than Tony would have imagined, but Tony sat patiently, waiting for him to finish. He saw the man turn back toward the phone, as if preparing to hang up, and Tony slipped his hand under his sport coat, ready to draw his gun.

Chamberlain hung up and turned back to the table. The other man rose again, shook his hand, and slipped the painting back into the garment bag.

Tony began to sweat. Where was Larry? It was the perfect time, the perfect place to arrest both men without drawing undue attention. If they got out of the restaurant, it would make everything more difficult.

Chamberlain checked his watch. Then he paid his bill with the credit card that probably had Ben Robinson's or John Lieber's name on it so there would still be no trace that Chamberlain had ever returned from London.

Tony got up and glanced out into the corridor, where people hurried past. Sweat began to trickle down his temples.

And then he saw Larry rush up to the doorway of the place, shaking his head and mouthing, "No."

Tony gaped at him. "No?" he mouthed back.

Chamberlain started out of the restaurant, and Tony had no choice but to follow him. Other plain-clothed cops were coming in with their eyes on Boudreaux, prepared to arrest him and confiscate the painting as soon as Chamberlain was gone.

Tony followed him through the crowds, only feet behind him. Larry caught up with him.

"What's the story?" Tony demanded in a low voice.

"He didn't call. They haven't heard from him."

Tony let a curse fly under his breath. "I still say he's going to wait until he's on the plane."

"We've got to get him *before* he gets on the plane, Tony. We have no choice. You know our orders."

Tony saw Chamberlain heading for the Delta concourse, and he hurried to stay close behind him. Chamberlain was hurrying— almost running, and the faster he went, the more people seemed to gravitate between them. Tony broke into a run, bumped into a man, and almost knocked him down. He didn't stop, just kept pushing on, no longer depending on Larry or John or Nick or any of the others who waited for his signal.

As if he sensed he was being followed, Chamberlain zigzagged through people, trying to blend. At Gate 16, the flight was already boarding, and Chamberlain shot up to the flight attendant taking the tickets.

Tony bolted forward, grabbed the man, and flung him back against the wall. "Where are they? Where did you leave them?"

Chamberlain was visibly shocked. Had this guy really thought he'd get away with it? Tony wondered. "What?" Chamberlain asked.

"Where are they?" Tony screamed.

"I don't know what you're talking about," Chamberlain bit out.

"Where are the girls, Chamberlain?" Tony's eyes stung as he took the man by the collar and shoved him again. "The ones you kidnapped?"

"I didn't kidnap anyone."

Tony flung him into the wall, face first, then ripped his goatee off and threw it down. Getting a handful of his hair, he asked, *"Where are the children?"*

Chamberlain closed his eyes. "I don't know. I had nothing to do with any children."

Tony slammed Chamberlain's face into the wall again, then Larry pulled him off. "OK, Tony, get a grip!"

"Where are they?" Tony yelled. *"What did you do with them, slimeball!"*

But it was no use. Chamberlain wasn't talking.

"Read him his rights," Larry said to the other cops as he tried to calm Tony. "We're gonna go get some air. We'll meet you back at the station."

CHAPTER SIXTY-THREE

W here are the children?" Tony Danks's question was posed with more calculated calmness now as he stood over the table where Nelson Chamberlain sat in the interrogation room of the St. Clair Police Department. But the look on his face belied that calm tone. He looked like a man who could rip Chamberlain's head off with his bare hands.

Larry sat across from Chamberlain, playing the good-guy to Tony's bad-guy routine. But tonight, Tony's behavior was no act. "Calm down, Tony," Larry said in a quieter voice. "Let the man talk."

But Chamberlain wasn't interested in talking. He studied his well-groomed fingernails, leaned back, crossed his ankle over his knee, and didn't say a word.

Larry tried again. "Look, it's not going to do you any good to leave those kids out there all alone. The jig's up, Chamberlain. You've been caught. Tell us where to find the kids, and the DA might show some leniency."

Chamberlain breathed a sardonic laugh. "I'm charged with murder, kidnapping, and theft. Do you honestly think they're just going to let me go if I talk? My reputation is already ruined. The way you keystone cops arrested me right in public in the airport, it's guaranteed to be all over the news by morning. It might even be grounds for a lawsuit after I'm acquitted. Defamation of character."

"You bet I'll defame your character," Tony bit out. "CNN has been following the kidnapping. They're right outside this office door as we speak, waiting to get a shot of the monster they've been speculating about."

Larry gestured for Tony to calm down again. "Why won't you tell us?" he asked. "Those kids are innocent. They haven't done anything."

"Why won't I talk?" Chamberlain asked flippantly. "Because I don't know anything about a kidnapping. This is all a very stupid mistake."

Tony kicked the chair next to Larry. The sound made Chamberlain jump, and when Tony grabbed Chamberlain's collar and pulled him face-to-face, he dropped his flippant look. "You had the painting, Chamberlain. The painting that you exchanged for information about the kids. We know you know where they are."

"I told you. I don't know anything."

All three men were starting to sweat. Tony let the man go, and he jerked free and straightened his shirt, which was dirty from his roll down the hill after he jumped out of the train.

Larry leaned forward on the table and fixed his eyes on Chamberlain's. "Are they dead or alive?"

"I'm not saying anything else until I've got a lawyer sitting beside me."

Tony snapped. In one swift motion, he grabbed Chamberlain and threw him back against the wall, knocking his chair over.

"You're not in control here, Chamberlain! You got that? You're not calling the shots here. You have a choice. Either you talk, or I'll see to it that that well-groomed profile of yours is drastically altered. You like art, Chamberlain? You're gonna need an artist to repair your face when I get through with you."

"Where are the kids?" Larry asked again, louder.

Chamberlain closed his eyes but didn't answer. Tony flung him a few feet, letting him drop to the floor. "I've had it with this low-life. I'm throwing the book at him. And I'm locking him in the old wing. Let him sit in the dark, in the damp for a while, and see if he can remember where he put those kids."

Larry looked alarmed. "Tony, that wing is condemned. It's infested with rats. Captain told us not to put any more prisoners there."

Chamberlain looked up at them, wide-eyed, from his position on the floor. "I want a lawyer. Now."

"You've already called one," Tony said. "It's not my fault he's out-of-pocket. Guess your luck is just going bad." He jerked him back up off the floor and pulled him toward the door. "I'll get him processed. That's when they strip you down, Nelson, old boy, and they search you real thoroughly. And then they give you some nice prison duds. You'll like them. 'Course that bright orange seems to attract the rats, rather than repel them. But you don't have a problem with that, do you?"

Chamberlain was sweating heavily now, and trembling slightly.

Larry stood up and stopped them at the door. "Tony, let me talk to him a minute. Just the two of us. You go outside and calm down."

Tony paused a moment, then finally agreed. He shoved Chamberlain back in, and slammed the door as he stormed out.

"Anything?" the captain asked, coming out of his office into the hallway.

"Nothing yet," Tony said. He rushed around to the two-way mirror and watched as Larry kindly told Chamberlain to sit back down. He asked him if he was thirsty, then poured him some water, and waited quietly while he drank.

The captain joined Tony at the window. "So you played the insane cop about to snap and tear into him?"

Tony nodded without taking his eyes off of the criminal. "Only it wasn't an act."

Chamberlain drooped over the table, raking his hands through his short-cropped hair. "Tony's a little high-strung," Larry said in a quiet, soothing voice. "He sometimes flies off the handle. I've seen him do worse than that to a suspect before. He just loses it, somehow, and he doesn't care what the rules are, or what kind of trouble he might get into. He has a one-track mind. I apologize for his behavior."

Tony couldn't help his slight grin as the captain chuckled.

"I'm not sure I can keep him from doing any of what he threatened, though, and just between you and me, he can be pretty tough. One suspect reported him from the hospital, and Internal Affairs got hold of it—"

"Hospital?" Chamberlain asked.

Larry paused and nodded. "Yeah. It was real ugly. Anyway, I'd hate to have you be another statistic, when all you'd have to do is just come clean. Keeping those kids' hiding place secret is not going to help you at all. It's only going to hurt you."

"I'm not going to prison for kidnapping."

"Even without the kidnapping, we have murder. It's a cut-and-dried case, Chamberlain. You could get the chair for that. But if you cooperate and let us know where Christy and Emily are, maybe the judge will go easier on you. Maybe he'd even let you out on bond."

"Where's the painting?" Chamberlain asked. "What did you do with it?"

"It's being tagged as evidence."

"It's priceless, you know. And I own it. When they find me innocent, it will be returned to me, won't it?"

"Certainly. As long as we can verify that it wasn't a stolen painting, and that you indeed have proof of ownership."

Chamberlain didn't answer.

"So tell us where they are, Chamberlain. Tell me where the kids are."

"I don't know where they are. I had nothing to do with their kidnapping."

"So you're not going to tell us? You're going to leave them there? Let them die before their parents can find them? What kind of man are you?"

Chamberlain was silent.

"Did you feed them, Chamberlain? Have you taken care of them? They're only five and six years old. Did you hurt them in any way?"

Chamberlain was mute as he stared back at Larry.

Tony moaned. They weren't getting anywhere with this guy. It was going to be a long night.

CHAPTER SIXTY-FOUR

It was almost morning when Tony made his way back to Sharon's house. There was no real need for him to be there anymore. They had their kidnapper, and didn't expect any more ransom calls. Larry had gone home to shower and have breakfast with his wife. But the fact that those children were still out there made it impossible for Tony to relax.

He knocked lightly on the door to the kitchen, and it was quickly opened. Lynda Barrett stood there, looking as tired as he did. "Tony. Any word?"

He shook his head. "He won't talk. I've tried everything. Boudreaux doesn't know anything about the kids. My gut tells me that Chamberlain acted alone, but he won't tell us a thing." She ushered him in. Jake was leaning against the counter next to Ben, and Sharon sat listlessly at the table, her eyes swollen from tears and exhaustion.

"He wouldn't tell you *anything?*" Sharon asked, looking up at him. "Are they alive? Are they with anyone? Are they being taken care of?"

"They said there were rats there and that it was dark!" Anne blurted from the doorway. "It didn't sound like anyone was with them. They're all alone, and he's going to let them die there!"

Sharon got up and set her hands on Tony's shoulders. "Tony, we've got to find them," she said, her voice pleading. ""We can't just leave them there. You've got to help us."

He nodded. "I was thinking. Maybe it's time to call a press conference. We need to get the whole community involved. Maybe somebody knows something."

"Good idea," Lynda said. "I'll set it up right now."

Sharon looked hopeful. "You can use my office. There's a phone book in the bottom drawer."

Lynda and Jake went into the office.

Tony looked down at Sharon, wishing he had the magic that would bring her child back. "Sharon, you need to get some sleep. You haven't slept in days."

"Neither have you."

"That's not really true," he said. "I slept on your couch while I was here. You've got to rest. There's nothing you can do right now."

"You think they're dead, don't you?" Anne asked in a raspy, breathy voice.

He frowned and turned around. "No. I don't."

"But they could be. That may be why he won't tell you. There's no urgency, because they're dead, and—"

"They're *not* dead!" Sharon cried. "I know they're not. If Christy were dead, I'd know it. I'd feel it, somehow. But she's out there!"

Ben pushed off from the counter and faced Tony squarely. "I want to talk to him. Maybe he'd listen. Maybe he'd tell me."

"Ben, I'm telling you. I've worked on him all night. I've done everything short of beating it out of him."

"Well, *I* could beat it out of him!" Ben shouted.

"No, you couldn't. He's a stubborn man. It's only going to hurt him tomorrow at his arraignment, and I'm hoping the judge will put enough fear into him to make him talk, but we can't wait. I've got him in the worst holding cell the city owns," he told them. "Not a nice place. Then again, it's not nearly as bad as I'd like for it to be, but there are laws about cruel and unusual punishment."

"You ought to have him in a cage, chained to the bars," Ben grumbled.

Sharon shook her head and went to the stove. "I made breakfast for everybody, Tony," she whispered miserably. "But no one was very hungry. Do you want some? It's still hot."

He had to admit that he was hungry. "Yeah, I'll take some, if it's not too much trouble."

Sharon seemed relieved to have something to do. She dipped out some scrambled eggs and bacon and pulled some biscuits out of the oven. Tony watched as she poured him some orange juice and set it on the table. "This is Christy's favorite breakfast," she whispered. "We have it every Saturday morning. I made it thinking . . . hoping . . . that she'd be home to eat it."

Her voice cut off, and she covered her face.

"I was thinking," Tony said quietly. "When you have your press conference, maybe we could ask anyone who's willing to help look for the children to meet at, say, ten o'clock, and with some supervised effort, we could go over St. Clair with a fine-tooth comb. Search every abandoned building in town. Every hotel room. Knock on doors, ask questions . . ."

Sharon looked hopeful. "Do you think anyone would come?"

"Are you kidding? As bad as your church friends have wanted to do something, I'd say that we'll have so many people we won't know what to do with them. Until now, all they could do was pray. Now they can start doing something useful."

Sharon's expression didn't change as she watched him for a moment. "Prayer is useful, Tony," she said quietly. "It's the most useful thing they could do. Bar none."

He looked up from his plate. "Well, I know. I mean . . . you obviously believe that . . . but I just mean . . ."

"God's listening," Sharon said. "Whether we can see what he's doing about it or not. He is listening."

Anne and Ben were stone quiet as they all looked at her, wanting some of her reassurance, desperate for the faith that she still held.

Tony ate quietly for a moment, not sure what to say. Prayer had never seemed more useful to him than action. It was a foreign concept, even though Larry had told him many times how prayer had helped him with things that were out of his control. Sharon, like Larry, seemed too intelligent to fit Tony's preconceptions of the prayer-and-Bible-study crowd.

Lynda and Jake came back into the room in a few minutes. "All right, Sharon," she said. "The press conference is set for 9:00 A.M., on your front lawn. I called Paige, my secretary, and she's going to call all of the television stations in the Tampa Bay area, as well as the newspapers and radio news directors. This is big news, so I think there will be a phenomenal turnout."

Sharon looked up at the clock, then ran her fingers through her hair. "We're going to ask people to meet at ten o'clock to start an organized search."

"Good idea," Jake said. "I was thinking about going up in the plane again. I could direct people to sparsely populated rural areas from the air. It might help."

"Right now we're going to have some new posters made," Lynda said. "These will have the girls' pictures, as well as Chamberlain's. Maybe someone has seen him, and they'll remember. Every member of the media who shows up will want a picture, and we'll need to pass them out to everyone who helps. And we'll need a number people can call to report anything they know. Are your phones still hooked up here, Tony?"

"Yeah," he said. "We can get someone to man them."

"All right. Then we're in business." She started for the door, with Jake behind her.

Sharon sighed. "Thank you, Lynda. Thanks, Jake."

"We're gonna find your kids," Jake told the three forlorn parents in the room. "Hopefully before the sun goes down today."

While the others stacked flyers and planned what to say to the press, Tony hooked up a second VCR to the television and watched a video of the girls, looking for thirty-second clips of both girls to edit out for distribution to all of the television stations. They had already distributed photographs, but now it seemed that the public needed to see the children moving, laughing. Maybe it would pull their heartstrings, as it did his. He sat on a chair right in front of the television, his elbows propped on his knees, and his chin on his clamped fists as Christy and Emily climbed on a sliding board at a park, laughing and waving to the camera.

Their size startled him, and he told himself that he had seen them before they were kidnapped, and they hadn't seemed so tiny then. But now they were in such huge danger. He watched as little Christy slid down, then turned and walked back up the slide, all the while singing, "Zacchaeus was a wee little man, a wee little man was he..." She stood at the top of the slide, then took a leap, and fell into sand. She looked as if she'd hurt herself and quickly got up, dusted off her knee, and looked up at the camera as though she wished her father would cut it off.

"I don't feel like performing right now," she said, lips trembling. "Turn it off."

He did, and it quickly flashed to another scene, where she was "performing," both she and Emily decked out in Anne's clothes, high heels, and jewelry as they sang a song they had made up, complete with bad choreography.

Christy seemed to be singing, or imagining, or laughing in every frame, and he sat helpless for a moment as tears sprang to his eyes. Was she singing or imagining or laughing now? What must be going through those little girls' minds?

The thought that they could already be dead hit him like a sledgehammer between the eyes, and he shook his head and swallowed hard. They couldn't be. They had to be alive. If he was any kind of cop, he'd find them.

The scene switched to a Christmas shot, when they were both sitting on the floor opening presents, with Jenny behind them. It must have been a Christmas that Sharon had spent alone. He wondered how she had filled it, and wished he had been there to help. He had been lonely last Christmas, too.

The perfect shot of the girls came when they were outside on Christmas morning, both donning their new roller blades, and trying to stand straight without falling as they wrapped their arms around each other and smiled at the camera. He pressed "pause" and froze the scene, and for a moment, just stared at those two little happy, innocent faces.

It was almost more than he could bear, and he sat still, fighting the tears in his eyes, fighting the fears in his heart.

Just hang on a little longer, girls, he told them silently. *I'm gonna find you real soon.*

Then, trying to pull himself together, he quickly turned on the second VCR and copied the scene to be splashed across television screens, both locally and nationally, until they were able to find the children.

CHAPTER SIXTY-FIVE

Both children were getting weaker, and Christy could feel Emily's fever as she leaned her head against her. Christy, herself, was having chills, even though the cat was helping her to battle them.

Her lips felt like scabs, and she saw as the light came through the window overhead that Emily's were cracked. The five-year-old looked deathly pale. Her eyes seemed sunken in.

What had happened to Daddy? Why hadn't the man come back?

She looked around the filthy bathroom and saw the dead rat that the cat had killed last night. She turned her eyes away from it, unwilling to look at it any longer. The cat purred on her lap, and she stroked him. "You did good," she whispered weakly.

She looked up at the broken window through which the cat had come, and wished she could climb up there. She was a good climber, she thought. But both of their hands were so tender, and they didn't have much energy.

The cat meowed and looked up at the window, as if wishing he could get out.

"It's too far, boy," Christy said, though she didn't know what gender the cat was. "You can get down from there, but not back up."

But the cat got off her lap and sat back on its haunches, as if readying itself to pounce. It leaped onto the commode tank, and from there fixed its eyes on the closest plant a few feet up. He pounced, then bobbed in the hanging pot of dried leaves and dirt for a moment, shook off a spiderweb, then looked up, evaluating its next move.

It leaped again to the next plant, sending it swinging, then to the next higher one, and the one above that. In moments, the cat had reached the window.

Christy's eyes widened. She sat up, and shook Emily. "Emily, wake up."

Emily stirred slightly, but was too lethargic. "Emily! I have to show you something!"

Emily opened her eyes. "What?"

"The cat. It climbed back up and got out the window. Maybe we could climb, too." She stood up and, feeling dizzy, leaned back against the commode. After a moment, she recovered her balance and took a step toward the wall where the cat had found the first foothold. "I think I can do it. I'm a good climber. You are, too, Emily."

Emily surveyed the wide space between the plants. "I'm not that good. That's high, Christy. Besides, we're too heavy. What if they won't hold us?"

"They will," Christy said. "They have to. I can do it, and if I make it, I can come around and get you out. Or go for help."

"No," Emily whined. "Don't leave me here by myself. I'm scared."

"I promise I won't leave you," Christy said.

"But what if you can't move the stuff in front of the door?"

"I will," Christy said. "I'm strong. Daddy always says so."

"But if you get out, and you can't move the stuff, you won't be able to get back in. I'll be all by myself."

"You're what they call a pestimist," Christy said.

"I am not! What is that, anyway?"

"It's somebody who thinks of so many bad things that they become a pest."

"I am not a pest! I'm just scared!"

"Yeah, well, you're a scaredy-cat, too."

Emily started to cry, and Christy was instantly filled with remorse. She went and sat back down beside her, and put her arm around her. Emily was burning with fever. "I'm a scaredy-cat, too," she admitted. "That's why I want out. But don't worry. I won't go. I'll stay here with you."

Emily rubbed the tears from her eyes and looked up at the window. "I wish the cat could talk, and he could tell somebody we were here."

"I wish he could bring us some food and something to drink."

"I wish he would come back and keep me warm. I'm so cold."

"I wish he would come back and keep you company while I climb out."

"Maybe he will come back," Emily whispered weakly. "Maybe he just had to go to the bathroom. You promise you won't leave me?"

The conversation was exhausting Christy. Looking at the window, she wondered if she could make it even if she wanted to. "I promise not to do it right now."

Emily didn't need more. She just laid her head against her sister's shoulder, and waited. . . .

Sharon couldn't believe the number of people that had convened on her front lawn in less than an hour. Through her living-room window she saw television vans, setting up local, live broadcasts. A conglomeration of cords all led to a cluster of microphones on the front steps of her home. She turned back to Anne and Ben.

"This is a little unnerving," she said quietly. "But the publicity has to help."

"It will," Ben assured her. "Somebody has seen something. If we can just get the word out, we'll find them. I know we will."

"I guess we can each say a few words. Which one of us should go first?"

"You go first," Anne said quickly. Tears came to her eyes, and she pinched the bridge of her nose. "I don't think I can get anything out. You're the professional. You're so good at talking to people . . . you'll say the right thing."

Sharon looked at Ben. "But Ben, you'll speak, won't you?"

He nodded. "Yeah. You go first."

Lynda came in the side door. "Are you ready?"

"Yes," Sharon said. "Are they?"

"It looks like it. One of the stations told me they're doing a feed to CNN. This is going to be national news."

"Really?" Sharon asked. "Why?"

"Look at it from a news directors' point of view. A kidnapper is caught before he tells where the kids are. Every heart in America will be wrenched over this, and someone will be able to tell us something. Let's get to it."

Sharon sighed and almost wished she had changed clothes and put on some make-up, but she just wasn't up to it. She called into the other room. "Jenny? Are you ready?"

Jenny came in carrying Bobby. "Mom, do we have to go out there? There are so many of them."

"Yes," Sharon said. "The whole family's doing this. We're in this together."

Sharon took a breath, bracing herself, and opened the front door. The crowd began to hush as she walked up to the cluster of microphones. Slowly, Anne and Ben came out behind her, then Jenny and Bobby, then Lynda.

Sharon stepped up to the mikes and cleared her throat. "We called you all to come here today, because . . ." She stopped, cleared her throat again. "Because our children, Christy and Emily Robinson, have been kidnapped. As you know, their kidnapper was apprehended early this morning. But he has yet to reveal the location or the condition of our little girls."

Her voice cracked, but she struggled on. "We have every reason to believe they're alive . . . and we need the help of the community to find them. If you've seen anything, please call 555–3367 and report it. If you know of any place in your area that might be a good hiding place, please call. We're depending on this community to get our little girls back. They've been missing for days now, and we don't know if they've eaten, or if they're being taken care of. But we do know that the person we believe to be the sole kidnapper is not taking care of them anymore. Time could be running out . . ." She stopped, braced herself, and got too emotional to go on.

Ben stepped up to the microphones and touched her shoulder gently as she turned away. "I'm Ben Robinson, the father of Christy and Emily. We're asking anyone who can take the time today to please meet at Roosevelt Park at 10 A.M. We're going to start a citywide search for the girls. And girls, if you can hear me, please know that Daddy is looking for you. We're going to find you . . ."

His voice broke, and he stepped back and hugged Anne, who was beside herself already.

Questions broke out from the crowd. "Mr. Robinson, does this kidnapping have anything to do with the murder charges that have been filed against you?"

"I'll take that." Tony came out of the crowd and trotted up the steps. "I'm Tony Danks with the St. Clair PD, and I can tell you that the charges against Mr. Robinson have been officially dropped as of this morning. The kidnapper is our primary suspect in this murder, and if you'll read the statement that I passed out to you, you'll see what the ransom demand was and how it fits into this kidnapping. Again, we will begin a citywide search at 10:00 A.M. this morning, at Roosevelt Park. We need everyone who can come to help us find these children."

He stepped back, and Lynda Barrett took his place. "As an added note, I've been asked to speak for the family to tell you that the $25,000 reward is still being offered to the person who finds and returns these children."

"Are you still trying to get the information out of the kidnapper?" someone asked.

"Yes, of course," Tony said. "He just isn't being very forthcoming."

"Mr. Robinson, is it true that these children are half-sisters?"

Ben stepped forward. "Yes. Christy is my daughter with Sharon. Emily is my daughter with Anne. But they're only a year apart in age. They're very close."

Sharon looked at him and saw the shame, the remorse, on his face at having to admit that their family was such a tangled web. She, too, hated the way it looked. Instantly, they would be labeled a "dysfunctional family." It was a term she hated even more than the word "divorce."

They stood there for a few moments longer as questions were fired at them from the crowd. Enlarged photographs of the girls were passed out to everyone, videos were copied and distributed to the television stations, and finally, the family went back in as Lynda and Tony fielded the rest of the questions.

Two hours later, as Larry and Jenny and Lynda manned the phone lines, Sharon, Anne, and Ben joined Tony and what looked like the rest of the town of St. Clair at Roosevelt Park. Hundreds of people had turned out to search for the children, and a mob of reporters, even more than she'd met on the front lawn of her house, recorded the event.

Sharon was so moved as they drove up that she couldn't speak. Tony saw the emotion on her face, and reached for her hand. "Are you all right?"

"Yes," she whispered. "I'm just surprised."

"St. Clair has a great community spirit," he said. "I knew they'd come."

Anne and Ben got out of the car, but Sharon held back.

"Are you sure you're all right, Sharon?" Tony asked her.

She sat there for a moment, not answering, just staring at the mob of people waiting to find her child. "I guess that ... I'm just afraid ... of what they might find." She wiped her tears away.

Tony scooted closer to her on the seat and wiped a tear rolling down her cheek. "Sharon, last night you said that they weren't dead. You said you would have known it. You trusted. Don't you still feel that?"

"Yes," she cried. "But maybe that's just what I *want* to feel. What if they're dead? I just don't want to know."

"They're not dead," Tony whispered. "Chamberlain is a high-brow art dealer. It would go against his nature to kill two little girls."

"It was in his nature to kill Dubose."

"But this is different. He would have no reason to kill them."

"When he left them, he knew they could identify him. He may have wanted to make sure that they didn't."

Tony grew quiet for a moment. He'd thought of that himself. "Sharon, those children need you right now. They need your faith. Now, I'm not even sure I believe in the same things you do, but I've got to tell you. Your faith has been a comfort to me during this whole thing. I may not believe in God, but I believe in your faith in God. What was it you said just yesterday, about God knowing where they are?"

She leaned her head back on the seat and closed her eyes as more tears poured out. "They're in the palm of his hand."

"Maybe he'll show us where they are," Tony whispered. "Now, come on."

They got out of the car and pushed through the crowd to the raised platform where Anne and Ben were already standing.

Jake Stevens was in the crowd, passing out flyers and pictures of the girls. His mother, Doris Stevens, who'd developed a reputation around town for being a Porsche-driving-teenager-in-a-fifty-five-year-old-woman's-body, was standing in a crowd of people telling the tidbits she knew that no one else knew.

"Jake, my boy, is good friends with the parents, ya see, and he says that the daddy and his family moved in with wife number one on account of that bum murder rap they pinned on him, so the girls were together with their older sister when she went to the grocery store . . . You know, this was all over a painting, and that man, Somebody Nelson, the kidnapper, he killed that Dupuis fella who ran the art gallery . . ."

Tony couldn't help grinning slightly, but Sharon was too focused on starting the hunt.

She stepped up on the platform, and looked at Ben. "Who's gonna do the talking?"

"I will," Ben said.

He stepped up to the microphone and tapped it. There was instant feedback, and someone adjusted it as the crowd got quiet.

"I really appreciate you all coming here today," he said, his voice wobbling. "Some pictures of my girls, Christy and Emily, are being passed out right now, along with the phone number to call if you see anything or think of anything that might help us. Uh . . ." He stopped, cleared his throat. "Christy's six, and she's real bright and real strong. And Emily is five . . . not as athletic as Christy, or as daring. But they're survivors. We . . . uh. . . . don't know how long since they've eaten. And the weather's been getting colder . . . they didn't have their coats . . ." His voice broke and he stepped back, unable to go on.

Tony gave them a few more instructions, organized the groups into sections of the city to cover, then escorted them all back to the car.

"I think the three of you should go home now," he said. "Let these people look for them."

"No," Sharon said. "I'm going to look, too. I can't sit in that house any longer doing nothing."

"But what if someone finds them? You'll need to be home."

"I can take my cellular phone with me. I'm going, Tony. Don't even try to talk me out of it."

"Take us home," Ben said. "We're going, too, but we'll take our own car."

"All right," Tony said, and headed back to Sharon's.

CHAPTER SIXTY-SEVEN

They searched the town high and low, from abandoned buildings to hotel rooms. Tony spent five more hours trying to intimidate the information out of Chamberlain, but to no avail. Even at his arraignment, when the judge ordered him to tell where the children were or be held in the same cell until the Grand Jury investigation, Chamberlain maintained that he knew nothing about them.

Sharon searched in the most destitute part of town, where crack dealers and druggies and prostitutes loitered on the streets. She searched the buildings there with a vengeance, calling out the girls' names at the top of her lungs, until she was too hoarse to be heard any longer.

She had no luck, and her cellular phone never rang. Hourly, she checked at home to see if anyone had given them any leads at all, but any that had been given had already been checked out.

Finally, she drove to the beach, to her favorite spot where she often took the girls, and sat in the car, staring out across the sand and the blue waters of the Gulf.

Why aren't you answering, God? Why have you turned away?

The mighty pounding of the waves were her answer, each white-topped crest tipping toward her like an indictment. For a long while she sat, staring at those angry waves, searching her own heart and mind for the answers she needed.

She had come close to admitting the problem with Ben once, when they'd stood out on that porch and she'd told him of her ulterior motives in inviting him to live in her home. She had con-

282

fessed, partially, to him, though it hadn't been a confession that sought forgiveness. It had been merely a statement, without heart, without much remorse. It had even been flung out in anger.

Now she wondered if it had been enough. God was dealing with her, she thought. He had something to teach her about her own faults, her own shortcomings, her own sins.

"Oh, God, help me to see what you see," she whispered. "I really want to be pleasing to you."

And then she knew.

She started the car and headed home. Maybe if she got her heart right, once and for all, she could pray effectively, she told herself. Maybe then she wouldn't feel this wall between herself and her Savior.

It was late afternoon when she finally returned home, not ready to give up, but desperately needing some cleansing.

The house was quiet—the phone wasn't ringing. Jenny's eyes were swollen as she sat in front of the telephone, waiting for something, anything, to happen. Lynda was studying a map of the town, trying to figure out any places that had yet to be searched.

"Have Larry or Tony called in?" Sharon asked.

"No," Lynda said. "They're apparently not having any luck with Chamberlain."

Her eyes filled with tears. "I wish they would let me at him. I'd get the information out of him!"

Sobbing quietly, Jenny lowered her face into the circle of her arms. Sharon softened and went to hug her. "Honey, have you eaten?"

"No," she said. "But neither have you. And neither have they . . . at least not since Chamberlain was found." She looked up at her mother. "Mom, why didn't he get me, too? Why didn't he just take me with them? Then I could be there taking care of them, making sure they were all right."

"You are taking care of them," Sharon said. "You're here, doing everything you can."

"Mom, I'm so afraid they're dead!" she said in a high-pitched voice. She fell into her mother's arms, and they clung to each other for a moment.

The phone rang, and Jenny jumped for it.

"I'll get it," Lynda said, but Jenny jerked it up. "Hello?"

She wilted as the caller spoke, then said, "Okay. I'll tell them."

She hung up. "It was Tony. He wanted to check on you. He said he's on his way over."

Sharon went cold. "Does he have news?"

"No," Jenny said. "He said he didn't. But they're still looking."

Sharon leaned heavily back against the wall. "Where are your father and Anne?"

"They got back about half an hour ago. Anne's taking care of Bobby, and Daddy's out on the back porch."

Sharon glanced through the den and to the back door. Sighing, she said, "I need to go talk to him."

She left them there and headed back through her house, to the back porch where Ben stood against the screen, gazing out at the tree house where he had sat with his little girls just days ago.

He heard her coming out and turned his head. She came to stand beside him and looked at it, too. "We were going to paint the tree house," he said quietly. "Since I wasn't here for the building of it, I thought I could at least do that. They wanted to paint a mural."

Sharon swallowed. "God willing, you'll still have the chance."

"Well, that's just it," Ben said. "I don't know if God is willing. I haven't done much for him."

She looked down at the tiles beneath her feet.

"You have, though," he whispered. "I guess I'm counting on him listening to you. You always did the praying for both of us."

Sharon shook her head. "It's occurred to me that maybe my prayers are worthless," she whispered on the edge of tears.

Now he looked fully at her. "Worthless? Why?"

"Because I'm still holding so much against you."

He breathed a mirthless laugh. "Yeah, well, I guess you deserve to." He turned away from the screen and went to sit down on one of the cushioned patio chairs. "You know, it's strange, looking back on what I did to you. It didn't seem so bad at the time."

Sharon couldn't look at him. She kept her eyes on the floor.

"You were doing so great professionally, and I was struggling. You weren't that naive little woman who used to look up at me like I was the one who hung the moon."

"I found out you weren't," she admitted.

"I missed having someone to look up to me," he said. "And when I met Anne—"

Sharon shook her head, unable to bear the explanation again. "Don't, Ben. You don't have to do this."

"Yes, I do," he said.

"Why? I didn't bring it up so we could salt old wounds. I came out here to forgive you."

"Is it really forgiveness, Sharon, when you can't even discuss it?" He rubbed his face and looked at her over his fingertips. "I really need to say these things to you."

She glanced at the door back into the house and wondered if she could make a clean exit. But he was right. That was no kind of forgiveness.

"My children live in two different families because of what I did, Sharon. Two of them I only get to see on weekends. Moving in here and seeing how unnatural everything is . . . well, it started me thinking about how drastically I've altered all of our lives." He looked up at her, struggling with the words. "Sharon, I never meant to hurt you. But even worse, I never meant to hurt Jenny or Christy. When I think of leaving you when she was just a little baby . . . giving up that daily experience of watching her grow . . ."

"You were the one you hurt," she whispered.

He nodded, as if he knew that was true. "I told myself that you were strong. And you prospered so over the years. I mean, look at this house. You did it yourself."

"I didn't do it myself," she whispered. "I leaned on God, and he took care of me. He does that. He makes provision."

"There have been times, over the years, when I looked back on my affair with Anne, and I realized how I deceived myself, and you, and her. There were really no winners. Everybody had to pay."

"That's divorce," Sharon said.

285

A long moment of silence stretched between them, and she looked down at her former husband, collapsed on the chair, in turmoil over the present, and in just as much turmoil over the past.

"I'm gonna say something that isn't easy for me," she said, sitting down opposite him and leaning her elbows on her knees as she knitted her fingers together.

"What?" he asked.

"It wasn't just you. I had a part in ending our marriage."

Wind whipped through the screen, ruffling his long hair. "How do you figure that?" he asked. "You were faithful."

"That's true. I never cheated on you. Not with a person. But with my work. And with my affections. Maybe it was my job to keep looking at you the way I had in the beginning. Maybe I set myself up for an Anne to come along." She swallowed, and made herself look at him. "All those times you wanted affection, and I was distant, cold . . . I told myself you were just a passionate artist, that your feelings didn't have to be taken seriously."

His face changed as he gazed at her. "I never in a million years thought I'd hear you say this."

"I should have said it a long time ago, Ben. Yes, you hurt our family when you left. But I hurt them, too. Maybe I left the marriage long before you did."

He struggled with the emotion twisting his face.

"I forgive you, Ben," she whispered. "I hope you can forgive me."

"I do." They were the words he'd spoken on the day they'd exchanged vows, and now they were spoken to heal them of their broken vows. He got up and hugged her, tightly, desperately, then quickly let her go.

"Now maybe God will listen to me," she whispered. "Maybe he had to bring us through this to get us to this point. Come in with me. We'll get Anne and Jenny, and start praying again."

He rubbed his red eyes and followed her in.

CHAPTER SIXTY-EIGHT

ony pulled into Sharon's driveway and sat for a moment in his car, wishing with all his heart that he had some good news for her. He hated to go in there empty-handed again, but he felt a compulsion to be here with her, as though he had some part in this loss they shared.

He got out of the car and walked to the door, but before knocking, decided to walk back to the gate that led into the back-yard. He opened it and went through, and looked around the yard at all the signs of the little girl who lived here. Her Barbie bike with glittery iridescent ribbons streaming from the handlebars stood on the patio next to a little toy stroller. Across the yard, her tire swing sat motionless, empty. He walked across the lawn to the tree house, and looked up. Something drew him up there, so he shrugged off his sport coat, dropped it on the ground, and began to climb the ladder.

He opened the hatch at the top of the ladder and went in to the little room where she'd stored so many treasures. Milk cartons and shoe boxes and rolls of string and glue . . .

He could just imagine the little rascals up here playing to their hearts' content, never worried that some stranger might come along and rock their world.

Unable to handle the emotions suddenly coursing through him, he slipped out the hatch and climbed back down. He grabbed his coat and hurried across the yard.

When he knocked on the door, Lynda let him in. "Any word?" she asked hopefully.

Tony shook his head and sighed. "No. Chamberlain's not saying a word. And now he's got this bigshot lawyer with him trying to strike a deal."

"What kind of deal?"

"Well, it's real nebulous, since the man is swearing he had nothing to do with the kidnapping, but what I'm gathering is that if we give him clemency, he might tell us where they are. But remember, all of this is being conveyed through hints—he still claims to be innocent. The DA says he's going to go for the death penalty, and the judge has done everything but torture him to make him talk. Still nothing."

She groaned.

"Where's Sharon?" he asked.

"Upstairs in Christy's room. She's a wreck. They all are."

"I'll go talk to her before I get back to the hunt," he whispered.

He went up the stairs quietly, since the house seemed so still. It felt strange disturbing it. He saw the pink walls in the room down the hall, and assumed that was Christy's room. Quietly, he went to the door.

There were Sharon, Jenny, Ben, and Anne, huddled on the bed with their arms around each other and their heads bowed, praying out loud for God's help in delivering those kids.

Something about the scene touched his heart . . . *broke* his heart. They were enemies . . . adversaries . . . Their pasts had shipwrecked their futures. Yet here they were, bound by their love for those little girls, acting as a family under the eyes of God.

Tears came to his eyes, and he stumbled backward, quietly, because he didn't want them to hear him. What if they looked up and invited him to join them? He hadn't really prayed since his "Now I lay me down to sleep" days as a boy . . . and he wasn't ready to do it now.

He rushed back down the stairs, feeling like a coward—the big, bad cop who could put the fear into everyone but Nelson Chamberlain, the one who was afraid of nothing—running from the idea of getting caught in a prayer.

He slipped out the door before Lynda could see him and got quickly into his car. He'd cranked the engine and pulled out of the driveway before the first tears stung his eyes.

He had never felt more helpless in his life. Two children were out there who he was powerless to help, and a man sat in jail who wasn't afraid enough of him to talk. Always before, there had been some way of working toward a solution. This time, however, everything seemed out of his hands.

Was Sharon right? Was God really in control? Was there even a God at all?

He drove until it began to get dark, and the stars began to appear, revealing the majesty of the Creator who was artist, astronomer, and physicist. To Sharon, he was a comforter. He was in control. He knew where those children were.

He pulled his car off the road, looked up at the dark sky, and asked himself for the first time in a very long time if he really believed. He wasn't sure. But Sharon's faith, her graciousness with her ex-husband and his wife, sure seemed real. And she was an intelligent woman, not some superstitious soul who would fall for anything. She'd been through fires and come out of them still believing.

His eyes were full of tears as he looked up through his dirty windshield. "If you're up there, God, I don't know why you'd waste any time on me," he whispered. "I'm not exactly what they call worthy. And I haven't given you more than a passing thought in about the last ten years, except when Larry has hassled me about you. You know Larry—yeah, what am I saying, of course you do."

He didn't know why he was crying. It was crazy. None of this made any sense, but as he spoke, a sense of tremendous waste, monumental loss, overtook him. "I can't believe you can even hear me, if you're there, but I figure it's worth a try, anyway. There's probably nothing that could have made me come to you, God, except maybe two little girls out there alone . . . and their grieving mother who believes in you."

He rubbed his eyes, angry at himself for losing control like this. "God, you've gotta help us. You've gotta help them. Not for me . . . not because of anything I've done . . . but do it for them. Those helpless little—"

He sobbed into his hand, then tried to pull himself together again. "I'll make a deal with you, God. If you bring them back safely to their parents . . . I'm yours. I'll be the best believer you've ever seen. I'll do anything you say . . . I'll even pray and read the Bible, even though what I've seen of it I've never understood. But I'll take classes and learn. I'll do all the stuff Larry does, and more. I'll even start being one of those people who gives money to poor people, and visits prisoners, and God, that's a big promise, because I don't have much compassion for the people I lock up . . ."

He sighed and wiped his face. "I think if you could work enough miracles to get Sharon and Ben and Anne praying together, then you can give me that kind of compassion. And you can help us find those kids."

He didn't quite know how to sign off. "Amen" seemed so trite, but "Bye" sounded too silly. So he let it hang there . . . wondering if anyone had heard.

Peace gradually washed over him as he pulled back out onto the street and started searching for the children again.

CHAPTER SIXTY-NINE

Emily wasn't acting right. Since the afternoon, all she had wanted to do was sleep. Her lips were cracked and bloody from thirst, and her eyes were sunken deeper into her face, casting dark circles under them. Christy had tried to wake her up, mostly from fear since darkness was beginning to close in again, but she barely stirred.

She had to get help, Christy thought, looking at the window again. She had to make her way out.

She got up and steadied herself as a wave of dizziness washed over her. After a moment, she recovered her equilibrium, and she stepped up on the rim of the commode and climbed to the broken lid. She looked up and found the plant where the cat had first jumped on its way out. The spider had repaired its web, but she shoved that thought out of her mind.

"Help me climb like a cat, God," she whispered. "Help me climb like a cat."

She was a good climber, she reminded herself. It was her favorite thing to do. She could do this, even if it was hard.

She judged the distance between where she stood and the plant, and reached out her foot. It reached, but just barely, and she pressed one hand against the wall and reached for the grimy macramé with the other. She tested her weight on it, felt the stake in the wall give slightly, but she didn't let it stop her. Quickly, she pulled her other foot up. The plant swung from its hanger, creaking with her weight, so she quickly stepped up to the next one.

Her hands throbbed and bled as she clawed at the wall for a hold, measuring her next step. When she'd gotten both feet on the next hanging pot, she began to get dizzy again.

Hold on, she told herself. *Just wait a minute.*

She waited, swinging slightly, until the dizziness passed, then looked up the wall for the next foothold.

She pulled her body up, and looked up at the window again. It was still so far up there, but she could make it, she thought. She just had to take it easy, go slowly, be careful.

Her arms were getting tired, something that never happened, and she told herself it was weakness since she hadn't eaten. She would only get weaker if she didn't find help. She had to get out somehow.

She clawed at the bricks with each foothold, and winced at the pain in her fingers.

She was hot, but she wasn't sweating, and her throat felt as if it was on fire. If she only had some water, she thought. Just a drop . . .

She looked down, and saw her sister lying limply on the floor. She was burning with fever, and looked so weak. What if she died?

She couldn't give up now. She had to make it up.

The next plant was too high, so she grabbed its pot with her hands and tried to climb the bricks, toe hitting grout, one brick at a time, until she was able to step up to the next plant. She grabbed on to the bricks with one aching, infected hand, and held the macramé for dear life with the other.

Just above her was a wooden planter bolted to the wall, and she reached up and grabbed it. She pushed up until she was able to get her weight over it. Once she got her feet on it, she rested and looked up. The window was only a few feet away. She could make it.

She took a deep breath and calculated that three more plants would get her to the window, and she stretched her leg with all her might to reach the next one, then the next one, until finally she could reach the windowsill.

With all her strength, she pulled herself up, but the window wasn't open. The cat had come in through a broken hole in the glass. But she was too big to fit through it.

She tried to plant her feet on the windowsill, and held on to the top casing with one hand while she struggled to raise the window with the other. It was stuck.

She looked down at her sister still lying on the floor. The room was growing darker, but outside it was only dusk. She could see the big tree beside the window, the tree the cat must have climbed to get in. The branches reaching to the window were small, but she could make it, she told herself, if she could just get the window open.

Holding the casing as tightly as she could with her infected hands, she kicked at the glass. Shards fell out and crashed to the dirt outside. She looked down to see if the noise had disturbed Emily, but her sister still lay there, deep in sleep.

The hole looked big enough to get through, so she ducked through it, kicked the broken glass off of the ledge, and carefully sat down to get her bearings. The cool air against her face made her feel stronger. She tried to find a branch big enough to hold her. None of them looked secure. She grabbed the closest one and straddled it with both arms and legs, sliding toward the center.

It swayed downward as if it might break with her weight, but she grabbed the bigger one beneath her, and climbed down to it. It was stronger, and she slid in toward the trunk, then found another, stronger one, and another, until she felt secure.

It was a massive tree, a perfect climbing tree, but it didn't give her the pleasure that climbing usually did. Her hands were bleeding and sore, and she was shaking. She made her way down, one branch at a time.

When she'd made it to the bottom branch, she looked down. It was at least a six-foot jump to the ground from here, and she wasn't sure if she could manage it. But she had no choice. Emily was still in there, all alone, and she had to hurry.

She judged the distance, as the cat had done, then held her breath and leapt. She made a perfect landing.

Now what? she asked, looking around. There were no buildings, no houses, anywhere in sight. Only this lonely road with a ditch on either side, and thick woods.

She went to the road, looked up and down it, but saw nothing. No cars, no people, no houses.

She would have to get Emily out, she thought, and then they could run away as far as they needed to find help. And she had to hurry, in case the man came back.

She ran back to the front door of the dilapidated structure and pushed it open.

The building was getting dark, full of monstrous shadows and scratching noises and creaks that terrified her. But she couldn't be afraid, she told herself. Emily needed her.

She ran up the stairs, careful to avoid the holes in them, and found the bathroom. The man had slid a huge bench against the door and piled a steel drum and other pieces of rusted machinery on it to weigh it down. She tried to slide it back, but it wouldn't budge.

Christy climbed on top of it, and turned backward, pushing her back against the wall and using the force of her legs to try to slide the bench away. But she just wasn't strong enough. It was jammed tightly against the door, and there was no way she would ever get it open.

She thought of calling out to Emily, trying to wake her again, but then she realized that her sister probably needed the blessing of sleep. If she woke to find herself alone, she would fall apart. Until Christy got her help, she didn't want to wake her.

She was trembling now, both from fear and courage, both from despair and hope.

"God, you can help us," she whispered weakly. "You helped me climb like a cat. Please send somebody now."

CHAPTER SEVENTY

Doris Stevens had been dead-set on winning that $25,000 reward money when she'd set out to look for the kidnapped children that day, but after an all-day search, she was getting discouraged. St. Clair was no huge metropolis, but it was bigger than Slapout, Texas. If she had looked for two lost children in Slapout, she could have turned the whole town upside down in two hours flat, and she would have found what she was looking for.

Now she had less than an hour to shower and change for her shift at the diner where she worked, and she wound her Porsche through the backstreets on the outskirts of St. Clair, heading for her trailer, which was parked on the only piece of land she could afford on her salary. It was far out, yes, but it was home. She'd been urged to sell the Porsche and buy a house or a condo, but she couldn't bring herself to do it. She loved that car. It was the only thing of any value she'd ever had.

It was getting dark, so she turned on her headlights and wove around the curves, ignoring the speed limit, since she rarely encountered other cars this far out. Maybe, if she was lucky, the kids wouldn't be found today, and she'd still have a shot at the grand prize tomorrow.

She turned up the radio on her favorite cry-in-your-beer country tune, something about being cheated on in the worst kind of way, something she could relate to many times over. She began to sing along in her nasal, twangy voice, as loud as the speakers blaring in her car. She had always thought she could have made it as a country singer.

A cat dashed across the road in front of her, and she barely missed hitting it, swerving only slightly to avoid losing control. Suddenly alert, she cursed and reached for her cigarette box, shook one out, pressed in the lighter, and stuck the cigarette in her mouth. She waited until the lighter was ready, then reached to get it out to light her cigarette.

From the corner of her eye, she saw something up ahead, and she dropped the lighter on the floor and looked up.

A child stood in the middle of the road, waving her down.

She swerved, slammed on brakes, lost control. The car skidded to the right, into the ditch, kept sliding several hundred feet further, then slammed full force against a tree.

She sat still for a moment, trying to decide if anything was broken. Nothing but the car, she thought in misery. Then she screamed a curse, and slammed her hand against the steering wheel.

She saw movement outside her window and looked up, and saw that child again. Furious, she flung open the door. "You almost got me killed! What in the world were you doin' standin' out in the middle of the street? Where's your mama? I'm gonna march you right home to her and tell her what you did!" She got out and looked at her crumpled Porsche, and stamped one high-heeled foot. "Look what you did! It's ruined! The only thing decent I ever had, and you ruined it!"

The little girl looked like she'd just lost a fight, and she was shivering. "I'm sorry," she said in a hoarse, raspy voice. "But I . . . I need help. My sister's locked in that old building up the road, and I have to get her out 'cause she's sick. Please. Will you help us?"

Doris looked down at the little girl and could tell that she wasn't doing so hot herself. She had a nasty cut on her forehead, and dried blood matted her bangs. The child looked familiar, except for the dark circles beneath her eyes, the ghost-like pallor to her skin, the blistered lips. "Honey, what's your name?"

"Christy Robinson," the child said.

Doris caught her breath. "Oh, my word! You're the kidnapped kid! You're the one we've been lookin' for!"

"You have?" Christy asked.

"Yes!" Doris shouted. "And I found you! Twenty-five grand is mine! I'm goin' to Atlantic City, that's what I'm gonna do! I'm gonna get me a fancy dress and stay in some fancy room with a hot tub—"

The little girl seemed to be dizzy, and she leaned against the car to steady herself. Doris instantly shut up. "Okay, kiddo. First things first. If only I had a car phone. I mean, there's one in the car, but I couldn't afford to pay for it, so I disconnected it. Heck, I can barely afford to put gas in it, but it doesn't matter now, does it? It's gone. Well, at least it does have insurance. That's somethin'." She saw the half-bottle of Coke sitting in the drink holder, undisturbed even though the front of the car was smashed in. "Honey, you look thirsty. You want this?"

Christy's eyes widened and she took the Coke and finished most of it off in one gulp. She probably hadn't had anything to drink in a while, Doris assumed.

She stopped when there was about two inches left in the bottle. "My sister needs the rest of this," she said. "We have to hurry. The man might come back, and if he finds me gone, he might hurt Emily."

"The man?" Doris asked. "That Nelson Chamberlain fella? Oh, no. He's not comin' back. He's in jail."

Christy looked up at her with those dull, lethargic eyes. "Really?"

"That's right, and honey, your parents are sick with worry over you. They've been lookin' everywhere. Come on, let's go get your little sister."

"Do you have a flashlight?" Christy asked. "We might need it. She has one, but she's not awake. And she's locked in a bathroom, and there's all this stuff shoved in front of it, only it's too heavy and I can't move it. I climbed out the window, but Emily's not as good a climber, and she won't wake up."

"Oh, blazes," Doris said, realizing the urgency of the situation. She went to her trunk, opened it, and found the flashlight and hydraulic jack that Jake had put there. She took them both out, thinking that she might need the jack if the door was barricaded as thoroughly as Christy said.

Christy led her back up the road to the building that was encased in darkness now. It was the old country store that she passed every day. Why she hadn't thought to look there earlier, she didn't know. But the front door was always open, and windows were broken out, and she had just assumed that if anyone were hidden there, the door wouldn't be open.

She shivered at the thought of going in there, and turned on the flashlight. It lit up the downstairs. "I gotta tell you, kiddo. I ain't much of one for bravery. This ain't the kind of place I like to go."

"Me, either," Christy said. "But it's okay. Come on. We have to get to Emily."

Every muscle in her body was rigid with tension as she made her way up the creaky stairs and saw the door barricaded with that big bench, a steel drum, and some other equipment.

She set down the jack and tried to pull the bench away, but she wasn't strong enough. "All right," she said, grabbing the jack. "Never fear. This'll move it right out of the way." She wedged it the best she could between one of the pieces of machinery and the wall, then began to pump it. It immediately began to expand, pushing the bench inch by inch back from the door.

"That's good! I can open it now," Christy said. She slipped between the bench and the door, and opened it.

Emily was still sleeping deeply on the floor. "There she is!" Christy said. "I think she's sick."

Doris slipped into the filthy place and knelt next to the tiny child. She touched her head. "She's burning up with fever," she said. "Poor little thing." She picked her up in her arms, and handed the flashlight to Christy. "Here, I'll carry her, and you lead us back out with the light."

Emily didn't stir as they hurried out of the building.

"Where will we go?" Christy asked.

"My place," Doris said. "It's only about a mile up the road. I can call your mama and daddy from there, and get you somethin' to eat. Give me that Coke, will ya?"

Christy handed it to her, and watched as she poured a couple of drops on Emily's lips, then a couple more. She saw Emily swallow. "Come on, darlin'," Doris said. "Drink some of this, for Doris. It'll make you feel better."

Slowly, Emily's eyes began to open, and she raised her head enough to drink. When the bottle was empty, Doris said, "Okay, let's go."

They walked for what seemed an eternity, and her high heels began to cut into her feet, rubbing blisters and making her ankles ache. But she had the kids, she thought. That was the main thing. That and the money.

"Did that man hurt you, honey?" she asked as they trudged along.

Christy shrugged. "He locked us up."

"But did he . . . *do* anything? Are you all right?"

"I'm hungry," Christy whispered. "And my hands hurt. And I'm cold."

Emily stirred in Doris's arms. "Christy?" she whispered.

Christy looked over at Emily. "Yeah."

"Did God answer our prayers with her?" she whispered weakly.

Christy smiled. "Yeah, he did."

Doris didn't know quite what to say to that. She'd never been the answer to a prayer before.

"Is Daddy coming to get us?" Emily asked.

"You bet he is, darlin'," Doris said. "As soon as I can get us to a phone. Look. See right up there? That's my trailer."

Christy looked so relieved that she stopped for a moment and just took in the sight, before pushing herself on.

CHAPTER SEVENTY-ONE

Tony went back to the house, unable to rest or go home until he'd found the children. Lynda had already left, and Sharon, Jenny, Anne, and Ben all sat around the kitchen table, waiting that excruciating wait that seemed almost pointless.

He joined them at the table, feeling so helpless, so ineffective as a police officer, so inept as a human being.

And then the phone rang. Jenny sprang for it. "Hello?"

"Yes . . . uh . . . is this the Robinson's residence?" a woman with a deep southern drawl asked.

"Yes, it is."

"Well, this is Doris Stevens—Jake Stevens' mama? You know my boy, don't you?"

"Yes," Jenny said.

"I've got some good news for you, honey."

"What?" Jenny asked cautiously.

"I've found your kids."

Jenny sprang out of her seat and grabbed her father's arm. "Are . . . are you sure? Christy and Emily? You have them?"

Everyone sprang up from the table, and Ben grabbed the phone away from her. "This is Ben Robinson. You've found my girls?"

"Sure have," Doris said. "Here's Christy. She can tell you for herself."

He waited a moment, then heard Christy's hoarse, weak voice. "Daddy?"

"Honey!" He burst into tears. "Where are you?"

"With Miss Doris. Daddy, will you come get us now? I want to go home."

"Of course!" he shouted. "Are you all right?"

"I don't feel good, Daddy," Christy said. "And Emily's real sick. She has fever."

"Put the lady back on."

Doris took the phone back. "Hello? I can give you directions if you've got a pencil. I'd bring 'em to you, but I'm afraid I wrecked my car to keep from hittin' your daughter."

He jotted down the directions, and they all jumped into the car.

C hristy ate a piece of cold chicken and watched out Doris's window for any sign of her father, but it had only been a few minutes since she'd talked to him. Doris said it would be at least fifteen before he'd be here.

Doris was holding Emily like a baby and coaxing her to drink. The child's fever was too high, and she hoped with all her heart that they'd be able to stop it in time. "Come on, honey. Drink some more for Doris. You don't want your daddy to be all worried about you, do you? He's on his way, you know."

Emily's eyes fluttered open, and she drank a little more.

"My heavens, look at these hands," Doris said. "Honey, you need to go back to that pan of water and soak your hands," she told Christy. "Get some of that dirt off. They're all infected. And this child's whole hands are swollen. I'm gonna have to let the doctor clean hers. I can't bear to hurt her when she's this sick. You know, you're a hero."

"Me?" Christy asked, turning around. "What did I do?"

"You may have saved your baby sister's life."

"You did that," Christy said. "I prayed that God would send help. He sent you."

"Oh, now, I don't know about none of that superstitious stuff. I prob'ly woulda seen you anyway."

Christy smiled knowingly and shook her head. "Nope. He sent you."

"Wouldn't I know it if God had sent me?"

"Maybe not," Christy said. "But he sent you just like he sent the cat."

"What cat?"

"The cat who protected us from the rats."

Doris shivered. What had these poor children endured for the last few days? Her heart ached as she looked down at the pale, weak child in her arms. No baby should have to go through such things.

"I hope they sling that man up by his toenails and make him eat mud," she muttered. "Treatin' two beautiful little girls like this. It just breaks my heart." She dabbed at the tears in her eyes.

Christy saw headlights, and began to jump up and down. "They're here! They're here!"

Doris peered out the window and saw the station wagon, followed by two or three other cars, some of them police squad cars and a television news van. "Blazes," she muttered. "Wish I'd had time to wash my hair. Go let your daddy in, honey."

Christy ran to the door and down the steps, and straight into Ben's arms as he bolted out of the car. Then Sharon took her from him, and the child clung to her mother.

Anne ran past them and into the house, and found Emily lying weak and feverish in Doris's arms. Sobbing, Anne took her quickly from the woman, kissed the child's face, and began whispering to her.

Tony's eyes were red with emotion as he stepped into the trailer, followed by Ben and Christy and Sharon. Doris wiped her eyes at the reunion as the mothers cried over their children.

"She's burning up," Anne shouted up to Ben.

"Her hands are infected, too," Doris pointed out. "And she ain't eaten a bite. I tried to feed her, but all she'd do was drink a little."

"Christy's feverish, too," Sharon said. "We've got to get them to the hospital."

"The squad car will escort you," Tony said. "Go ahead and take them."

Photographers were gathering and cameras rolled as the children were rushed out to the car and driven away with a flashing escort. Doris ran out and grabbed Tony as he started to get in his car, ignoring the reporters who were trying to get her to stop and give them an interview about how she'd found the children. "Can you drive me to the hospital?" she asked. "I really want to know how the little things are."

Tony looked surprised. "Sure. We're going to need a statement from you, anyway. How did you find them?"

Doris started to say that it was a fluke, that the child had just appeared in her headlights. But then she thought better of it. "Well, accordin' to that little Christy, God sent me to 'em. She swears up-an'-down that I'm an answered prayer."

Tony's eyes welled with tears, and he smiled. "You know what, Doris? Christy's absolutely right."

CHAPTER SEVENTY-THREE

The children were kept overnight in the hospital, with IVs to battle their dehydration, and antibiotics to fight the infections originating in their hands. Both girls had their hands bandaged, and Christy had a bandage over her forehead.

Anne and Sharon requested that they be allowed to share a room, so that Ben could see both children at once. Jenny came in as soon as someone from their church had come to relieve her from taking care of Bobby, and tears sprang into her eyes at the sight of her two sleeping sisters. "Oh, Mom . . . Anne . . . I'm so sorry for letting this happen to them."

Sharon pulled her older daughter into a hug. "Honey, it's not your fault. And they're going to be fine."

"Really? Are you sure?"

"Yes."

"Were they . . . abused in any way? Molested, I mean?"

"No," Sharon said with certainty. It was one of the first things the doctor had looked for.

She walked Jenny back out of the room, knowing that Anne would keep an eye on Christy if she woke. "Honey, I know you're still blaming yourself for all this, but I want you to know that some good did come out of it."

"What?" she asked. "How?"

"God used it, to make me confront the fact that I'd never really forgiven your father. Or Anne. In my heart, I think I really hated them."

"You couldn't have hated them, Mom. You let them move in with us."

"Well, I had several different motives for that. One of them was to look good to you. The more generous I looked, the worse they looked. But there sure wasn't any love involved."

"What about now?"

She glanced back in the room. "Anne's a mother, just like me. She loves her kids every bit as much. And she's been a good stepmother to you and Christy. I haven't made it easy for her. And your father . . . he's not a bad man. He made some mistakes, and his mistakes hurt me, and you, too. But I was far from perfect myself, Jenny."

Jenny wiped her eyes. "Me, too."

"God forgives our mistakes," Sharon said.

"He's awesome," Jenny whispered. "So awesome."

Sharon hugged her daughter again, and saw Tony standing across the hall. He'd heard everything. "Tell you what," she told Jenny. "Why don't you stay with Christy for a while, and I'll go get something to eat. I haven't had much in the last few days, myself, and I'm starting to feel a little hungry."

"Okay," Jenny whispered, and went back into the room.

Sharon went out of the room and looked up at Tony—who looked as tired and relieved as she did. "You've been great, Tony. Really great."

He seemed to struggle with emotion as he looked down at his feet. Unable to say what was on his mind, he nodded toward the waiting room. "Doris is the real hero. She's in the waiting room."

Sharon took his hand and they went to the waiting room. Doris was in there with Jake and Lynda, chattering ninety-to-nothing about how she'd found the girls. When she saw Sharon, she sprang to her feet. "How are they, hon?" she asked.

"They're great," Sharon said, hugging the woman who'd saved her daughter. "They'll both get to go home tomorrow. I just don't know how to thank you enough. The reward doesn't even begin to cover it." She wiped her eyes. "I'll write you a check tonight before you leave."

Doris glanced at Lynda and Jake, then let out a heavy sigh. "Oh, heck, I can't take your money. At first, when I was lookin' for 'em, I thought I could. I mean, they were just pictures on a flyer, ya know? But now that I know 'em, and I seen what they've been goin' through ... well, I can't take money for it. It just doesn't seem right. Not when Christy's so sure that God was usin' me to find 'em. I can't imagine why. Not like he's ever been able to use me before! Out of the mouths of babes. Who am I to dispute it? But no money."

"But your car," Sharon said. "It's totaled. Let me at least help you ..."

Doris raised her hand to stem the woman's offer. "My insurance will pay for the car. It was fun while it lasted, sure. But I think I'm gonna take the insurance money and get me a little second-hand car of some kind, and use the rest of the money for a down payment on a nicer place to live. That trailer's too far out. It's time I did that, anyway."

Jake hugged his mother. "Mama got a call from Oprah Winfrey a few minutes ago," he said with a grin. "She's going on her show next week."

Sharon laughed. "Really?"

"Yeah," Doris said, waving a hand as if it meant nothing. "Somethin' about modern-day heroes. Can you imagine?"

A flock of reporters rushed to the door of the waiting room and descended on Sharon, but she pointed them to Doris. "She's the one who found the children," she said. "Sacrificed her Porsche to do it."

They all surrounded her as Sharon and Tony slipped out of the room.

Downstairs, Sharon and Tony sat sipping coffee over empty plates. Neither of them had realized how ravished they had been after not eating much for several days. A feeling of utmost peace seemed to fill Tony in a way that he'd never before experienced.

"Something weird happened to me today," he said, not able to look at Sharon as he spoke.

"What?" she asked.

He shrugged. "Well, I don't know. I was ... sort of ... under the fig tree."

Her eyebrows shot up. "You prayed?"

He couldn't meet her eyes. "I sort of made a deal with God."

"Uh-oh," Sharon said. "You're not supposed to bargain with God."

He smiled. "He took me up on it. I told him that if he brought the girls home safely, that I'd be a believer, and that I'd be the best Christian he had ever seen."

Sharon couldn't believe her ears. "And?"

"And I'm keeping my end of the bargain," he said. "He did it, didn't he? He really answered." He swallowed and looked up at her. "See, I've been struggling with this. Some voice in my head keeps saying, well, he may have answered, but why'd he let it happen in the first place? And then I heard you and Jenny talking, and I realized that he really may have created good out of it. In a lot of ways. For one, I never dreamed Doris Stevens would turn down the money. That's a miracle in itself. And this afternoon . . ." He wiped his eyes. "I saw you and Ben and Anne praying together . . . you had just put away your problems, your differences, all that baggage . . . and you went to God. That was good, wasn't it?"

She smiled. "Yeah. It was good."

"And it worked." He propped his chin on his hand and looked at her with probing eyes. "God may not have caused the kidnapping. I don't know. But I do know that he used it to knock me in the head. He used it for a lot of things."

She smiled as tears formed in her eyes. "Then it was worth it."

Gently, he took her hand. "Sharon, would you consider going out with me when all this is over? We were supposed to have had dinner. We never got to."

She smiled poignantly. "A real date?"

He nodded, feeling like that awkward teenager again. "I would consider it an honor to spend as much time with you as you're willing to spend with me."

"I would love to," she said, squeezing his hand. "As a matter of fact, why don't you come to church with me Sunday?"

He nodded. "This time, there's nothing I'd like more."

AFTERWORD

Recently, when I was reading the book of Zechariah, something jumped out at me that I had not understood before. It was in chapter 7, when the people came to the prophet and asked him to inquire of God whether they should continue observing the fast to commemorate the destruction of Jerusalem, since Jerusalem was now being rebuilt. God answered their question with a question. He asked them if they were fasting for him, or for themselves. And then he added something that seemed unrelated to their question. "Administer true justice; show mercy and compassion to one another. Do not oppress the widow or the fatherless, the alien or the poor. In your hearts do not think evil of each other." The people must have frowned at one another and thought, "Did God misunderstand the question? We asked about fasting on a particular day, and he answers us with all this stuff about justice, compassion, and our hearts."

I've read that before and it has gone right over my head, but this time, it shone in my face like a beacon illuminating my own sins. I go to God expecting a pat on the back for all the good deeds I've done, all the people I've helped, all the enemies I've forgiven, all the worship I've sacrificed my time to offer. And God says, "Get real, Terri. Who were you doing those things for? Me or yourself?"

It's as if I look up at God and say, "Well, if that's not enough, what do you want?"

And he replies, "I want your heart pure. Your good deeds amount to nothing but filthy rags if your heart isn't pure. If worshiping me is a sacrifice, and if your good deeds are nothing more than markings on the scoresheet of your life, then you still don't get it."

Like the chicken-and-the-egg question, I guess it all comes down to the question we Christians continually have to ask ourselves.

Which came first, the righteous heart or the good works? Do good works give us a righteous heart, or does our righteous heart lead us to do good works? Which would God rather see?

I know the answer, and most of you do, as well. God doesn't ask for a scoresheet or a legalistic report card. He's already done all the work to save us. He sent his Son to die on the cross for all of our sins and to demonstrate our inheritance in his Resurrection. All he asks is that we give him our hearts. All of our hearts.

So many times I've run myself ragged trying to do things that I believe are pleasing to God, only to realize sometime later that I've neglected my prayer life and my Bible study—in fact, I've left God out of it entirely. "Was it really for me you fasted?" God asked. Interesting question. And a painful one, as well.

And God sits quietly, watching and shaking his head, wondering when we will learn.

Thank God that he doesn't wash his hands of us. Thank God that he asks those probing, painful questions that remind us what is important. Thank God that he never stops teaching us.

May our hearts be so pure, so full of his righteousness, so Christlike, that our good deeds burst forth as acts of worship, rather than sacrifice.

And may God never stop working on me.

God bless you all,

Terri Blackstock

Presumption
of Guilt

*This book is lovingly dedicated
to the Nazarene*

ACKNOWLEDGMENTS

I can't end this series without thanking the people who have shared my vision for it since the beginning. I'd like to thank my agent, Greg Johnson, for believing in what I was doing and sharing my enthusiasm. And I'd like to thank my Zondervan friends who have worked tirelessly beside me: Dave Lambert, the best editor I've ever worked with (and I've worked with plenty); Lori Walburg, the second best editor I've ever worked with; Sue Brower, who believed in the books enough to go to great lengths to get them into the hands of readers; and all of the others at Zondervan who have been such a pleasure to work with.

Thanks, also, to Bob Anderson from the attorney general's office in my state, for answering important law questions for me.

And thanks to you, all of the readers who have followed this series to the very end. You've been God's way of telling me over and over that this is where I'm supposed to be!

CHAPTER ONE

T he Buick had been tailing Beth Wright for miles. She had first noticed it weaving in and out of traffic too closely behind her on the Courtney-Campbell Causeway, the driver making no attempt to hide the fact that he was after her. Now, nearing St. Clair, they had left most of the traffic behind, but he was still there. She pressed the accelerator harder, checking her rearview mirror.

It didn't take a genius to figure out who it was. She had known that, if word got out that she was doing the story on the St. Clair Children's Home, Bill Brandon would come after her. What he would do once he caught her was open to speculation, but she didn't want to find out.

The Buick sped up and switched lanes, cutting in front of a motorcycle, forcing it to swerve, and then pulled up beside her, as if trying to run her off the road. He must have found out somehow that she had interviewed his sister, and he didn't like it. Marlene had warned her that he wouldn't take it well, but Beth hadn't needed warning.

The Buick swerved sharply to the right, almost hitting Beth's car, and she caught her breath and rammed her right foot to the floor. Her car burst forward, leaving the Buick behind. If he ran her off the road, he would kill her. If he was desperate enough to chase her down on a state highway with other drivers watching, then he was desperate enough to commit murder.

Her hand trembled as she reached for her cellular phone. It had fallen to the floor, so she bent forward, groping for it. The Buick jolted her rear bumper, and she swerved onto the shoulder.

Grabbing the wheel, she pulled it quickly back into the right lane. The few other cars on the highway had begun pulling off the roadway to let her car and the Buick go by, probably alarmed by the Buick's erratic driving. Maybe someone had already called this in to the police.

She reached again into the darkness in front of the passenger seat for the phone, and this time her hand touched it. She picked it up and dialed 911 with her thumb.

"911, may I help you?"

"There's someone after me!" she cried. "He's trying to kill me!"

"What's your address?"

"No! I'm in my car! He's following me. We're on Highway 19 between St. Petersburg and St. Clair. I just passed the Ship's End restaurant. Please hurry!"

"What is he driving, ma'am?"

"A dark Buick—I'm not sure of the color."

He bumped the rear corner of her bumper again, and she screamed as her car veered to the shoulder. "He's ramming my car! Please, have you sent someone?"

"Yes," the dispatcher said. "We have a car on its way—"

But while the woman was still talking, Beth punched the "end" button, cutting her off, so she could pay attention to Bill Brandon's Buick. The stretch of road between St. Petersburg and St. Clair wasn't as busy as the others they'd been on. If there was a patrol car in the area, he'd spot them immediately—but if not, she might be dead before they showed up. To her right, she could see the beach, the turbulent waves smashing against the sand. If he stopped her, he could easily make her disappear in the Gulf Coast—and he wouldn't think twice about it. She looked in her rearview mirror. There was a car's distance between them now, but he was gaining. No other cars were in sight behind them. Where were the police?

Nick, she thought. *I have to call Nick.* He was expecting her to come straight to his house, to let him know what she'd found out from Marlene. But with this maniac following her, she might never get there. She'd better tell him what she'd learned—just in case.

She punched out his number and waited as it rang. "Come on, Nick," she whispered.

The answering machine picked up. "Hello, you have reached the home of Nick Hutchins . . ."

The Buick bumped her again, and tears sprang to her eyes. She punched off the phone and tried to think. *Where are you, Nick? You're supposed to be waiting for me!*

A message, she thought. *He must have left a message.* Maybe he'd called to tell her to meet him somewhere else instead. Her hand trembled, making it difficult, but she managed to punch out her own number, then waited for her machine to answer so that she could punch in her code and get her messages.

"Hello?"

It was the voice of a boy.

Startled, she asked, "Who is this?"

There was a long pause. "Who do you want?"

She turned on her bright lights, looking for a road, any road, that she could turn down in hopes of losing him. "I thought I was calling my own house," she said.

"You must have the wrong number."

Confused, she punched the "end" button, and followed the road's curve along the edge of the beach. The Buick did the same, right on her bumper. *Where were the police?* And what number had she just dialed? She punched "recall" and saw the digital readout. It was her number. So who had answered the phone at her house?

Her car jolted again, and she saw the Buick in the lane next to her. He was trying to force her off the road now. She had to get help—he would kill her if she didn't lose him.

She pressed "redial" and checked the number on her read-out. She had dialed right the first time. She pressed "send" and waited as her own number rang again. This time, it rang on and on. The machine, which normally picked up on the fourth ring, never answered.

What's going on?

The car edged over, pushing her toward a drop-off. She looked in her rearview mirror and saw that no one was behind her. No witnesses, no one to notice if he sent her tumbling over a seawall.

She saw a road sign up ahead, and quickly breathed a prayer. Then, waiting for just the right moment, she slammed on her brakes until she was behind the Buick and screeched into a left turn, skidding around the corner onto a side street. She stomped on the accelerator and made another turn, and another, until she was completely out of his reach, hidden by trees.

She eased up on the accelerator only slightly, checking her rearview mirror every few seconds. It was more than fifteen minutes before she was certain that she had lost him; only then did she feel that she could safely try to make it home—hoping he hadn't figured out where that was yet. She had intentionally rented the little house out in the woods because it would be hard for unwelcome guests to find. So far, she'd kept herself insulated from him, but now she knew that interviewing Marlene had been a mistake. Bill Brandon was too smart and too suspicious not to keep close tabs on the sister who had once worked with him. He must have found out about the interview somehow, and followed Beth from Marlene's house.

So maybe he still didn't know where she lived. Maybe her little house in the woods was still a safe haven.

CHAPTER TWO

The car phone in the Buick rang, and Bill Brandon snatched it up. "Yeah, what is it?"

"Bill, it's me." The boy's voice was shaky and frightened.

"What are you doing?" the man asked. "Where are you?"

"Still in her house," the boy said in a half-whisper. "But I can't find any of the papers or any tapes. I've looked everywhere."

Bill cursed. "Does she have a desk? A file cabinet? Did you check her computer?"

"Yes. I looked in all those places, and I couldn't find anything on the computer. She has millions of directories, and I don't know what to look for."

"Well, keep trying. And hurry. You don't have much more time."

"Are you still following her?"

"No, I lost her."

There was a pause again. "She just called here."

"She *what?* What do you mean she called?" Bill's face darkened as he held the phone to his ear, taking it in. He heard the sirens, and quickly pulled off the road, cut his lights, and stopped behind a rickety-looking body shop.

"She called. I picked up the phone 'cause you told me you were gonna call and warn me when she was coming home. I thought it was you."

"You idiot! What did she say?"

"I made like she called the wrong number. She called back, and I just let it ring."

"Well, you'd better get out of there, you fool! She's on her way home!"

"I thought you were gonna stop her!"

"I didn't," he snapped. He saw the reflections of blue lights flashing against the trees and junk cars surrounding the body shop. He wiped his sweating temple as the lights continued on up the road. "You blew it already, kid. Next time I'll find someone else who can do the job without botching it up."

"But Bill, I tried—"

"That's not good enough!" Bill shouted. "I'll deal with you when we get home! Now, get out of there!"

"Where will I go?" the boy asked in a voice on the verge of tears.

"Go to the Fraser Gas Station on Banton Street. I'll pick you up."

"But that's five miles away, Bill! Will you wait for me?"

"I told you I'd pick you up, didn't I? Now don't let anyone see you. If anybody does, you don't say a word, you understand me? You don't know anything."

"Okay, Bill."

Bill slammed the phone down and cursed again as he pulled out of his hiding place and headed for the gas station.

CHAPTER THREE

As he hung up the phone, ten-year-old Jimmy Westin heard tires on the gravel outside the house. Headlights swept through the windows of the darkened house, and the small red-haired boy froze, wondering which of the side doors she would come in, which door he could safely leave through. The little cocker spaniel at his feet yelped up at him, wanting to play. He shouldn't have given it so much attention when he'd first come in, but he'd never had a dog of his own, and he hadn't expected to find it here. Bill hadn't said anything about it.

"Shhh," he whispered, trying to quiet it. "I have to go."

He heard the car door slam in front of the house. Her keys rattled in the door.

Now it was too late to go out *any* of the doors. He would have to hide. He looked around frantically, then dashed up the stairs, leaving the fat, young puppy yelping after him. Halfway up, he looked back and saw it struggling to climb the first step. He left it behind, and hurried up to the woman's loft office, where he'd searched for the papers and tapes Bill wanted. There was a door there, next to a closet. He opened it.

It was a floored walk-in attic. He slipped in and closed the door quietly, just as he heard the door downstairs closing behind her. Instantly, he was surrounded by darkness, thicker darkness than that downstairs. Downstairs, there had been a night-light over the stove, and a small lamp she had left on. In here, the darkness was opaque, smothering...

He trembled as he shrugged off the black backpack he wore, unzipped it, and pulled out his flashlight. The beam revealed boxes against the walls—tall ones, short ones, empty ones, packed ones. Across the floor was a window. Perfect. He could get out that way. He walked softly, trying to make it to the window, but the floor creaked beneath him. He froze, afraid to take another step. What if she heard? What if he got caught? What would they do with him?

He was sweating, and his breath came harder. All of the heat of Florida seemed contained in this attic, locked in with no escape, just like him.

He stood there, motionless, listening. He could hear her downstairs, doors closing, footsteps moving across the floor. Was she looking for him? Had she figured out that the voice on the phone wasn't a wrong number? What if the puppy somehow led her to him?

He shone the beam around him again, looking for a hiding place, and he saw lots of them. Places where mice, too, could hide. Spiders. Snakes, even. There was no telling what could be in an attic in such an old house.

He eyed the window again, and tried taking another step. It didn't creak. Taking a deep breath, he tiptoed across the floor, walking as lightly, as quietly as he could, until he reached the window. He unlocked it and tried to slide it up, but it was stuck. With all his might he tugged, but it didn't budge.

For a panicked moment, he thought of breaking the glass and making a run for it, but it was a long way down. By the time he figured out a way to get to the ground without breaking both legs, she would have the whole police force surrounding the place.

He was stuck here. Stuck until she went to sleep. Then, if he was very careful, and the floor didn't creak, and the dog didn't bark, maybe he could get out. Bill would be furious that he hadn't made it to the gas station on time, and Jimmy would probably have to make it all the way back to the children's home on foot—unless he could get to a phone and call for someone to come get him. He reached into his empty pocket, wishing he had a quarter. Maybe the lady who lived here had one lying around somewhere. Maybe he could find it before he left.

Maybe.

He wondered what Bill would do to him for messing this up. Quickly, he shifted his thoughts. He couldn't dwell on that. He had to go back, and that was that. Lisa would bear the brunt of his punishment if he didn't. He couldn't let that happen.

He heard footsteps coming up the stairs, and quickly dove behind a box in the corner. He held his breath and listened. Her footsteps moved across the office floor; she was going to her desk. He realized that he had forgotten to turn the answering machine back on. How could he be so stupid?

He should have worn gloves. Could they trace the fingerprints of ten-year-old boys? And once they found him, would they put him in jail or send him to the detention center? Did they really have that room with the black walls and only a slit that they slid bread through—the room Bill had warned him about? Is that where they would keep him locked up until he was old enough for prison?

He closed his eyes and leaned back against the wall. He could hear her out there, doing something in her office, moving around. He heard her saying something to the puppy, heard the little animal yelp and scratch on the floor. Would the dog lead her to him?

"Please don't let her find me," he whispered. "Please . . ."

CHAPTER FOUR

Nick Hutchins stuffed the duffel bag full of the clothes the two frightened little boys—six and eight years old—would need, and wished they didn't have to listen to the string of expletives flying from the foul mouth of their drug-dealer father, who stood handcuffed in the corner of the living room. His wife, also involved in the family business, screamed over his curses that they couldn't take her children away. Tony Danks and Larry Millsaps, the cops who had called Nick to come take the children into state custody, ignored her pleas and continued recording the evidence they'd compiled. There was enough crack cocaine in the house to ruin the lives of everyone in St. Clair.

It wasn't an unusual event, but Nick had never gotten used to it. He zipped up the bag and went back into the living room where the two boys sat huddled together.

"My daddy didn't do anything!" the older child cried. "Neither did my mom. Why don't you just leave us alone?"

"Please don't take my kids!" their mother cried. "I didn't know nothing about what he was doing. He did it behind my back! Please!"

Nick glanced hopefully at Larry. If there was some way they could avoid arresting the mother tonight, then he could spare the children the trauma of being taken from their home, at least temporarily. But Larry shook his head.

"We caught her dealing on videotape," Larry said. "And with all the stuff we found in the back room, there's no way she didn't know what was going on."

Nick looked at the distraught woman. "Do you have any relatives we can call? Someone who can take the kids tonight?"

"No, my parents are dead," she cried. "And we don't even know where his parents are."

"Any cousins or aunts or uncles? Sisters or brothers? Anyone?"

"No!" she cried, struggling to make him understand. "So you *have* to let me stay with them. They don't have anybody to take care of them."

Wearily, Nick slid the strap of the duffel bag over his shoulder, then took the children's hands. "We'll see that they're cared for."

"But *I* can take care of them! Please don't take them."

"Come on, kids," Nick said. "Let's go."

The woman screamed and fought to get to her children, but the officers restrained her. "You're making this harder on them!" Tony shouted over her cries. "If you love them, help them through this."

"You're not—taking—my kids!" she screamed, fighting to break free.

The children pulled out of Nick's hands and ran to their mother, but with her hands cuffed, she couldn't hold them. As they screamed, Nick wrenched them away and hurried them out to his car and into the front seat. He positioned one wailing child in the middle of the bench seat, hooked his seat belt, then hooked the other one in on the passenger side. Agency policy was to put kids in the backseat, but Nick could imagine how lonely the backseat could be when you didn't know where you were going.

For a few moments after he got in, he could hardly speak. He cranked the car and pulled out of the driveway to get them away from the house as quickly as possible. Then he looked down at the kids, who were still sobbing quietly.

"My name's Nick," he said, patting the leg of the boy next to him. "And I promise you, this isn't going to be so bad, okay? We'll just find you a place to stay tonight, and you're going to be all right."

"But I want to stay at home tonight," the younger one cried. "I want my mom!"

"Are you taking them to jail?" the older child asked in a shaky voice. "For a long time?"

"I can't answer that, because I don't know," Nick said. "But you don't have to worry, because you'll be taken care of."

The children cried quietly now, tears glistening on their faces. His heart ached for them, but that voice that played like a tape in his mind reminded him not to get involved. His job was to find a place to put them tonight; tomorrow, he would try to find a more permanent temporary home. There was no rational reason for the guilt and grief that he felt; it wasn't his fault that these two boys were becoming wards of the state of Florida. He just wished their parents had thought about their kids before they'd started dealing drugs.

A few minutes later, Nick parked in front of his office. The building, a branch of the Department of Health and Rehabilitative Services, or HRS, was small, dirty, and structurally unsound, but it was all they could afford on their small budget. He dreamed of the day they could get a nicer place, with a playroom to cheer up broken-hearted kids as they waited to be processed. He unhooked the apprehensive boys and slid them across the seat and out of the car.

"Please, mister. Take us back to our mom. She's really nice." The eight-year-old wiped his face and hiccuped a sob. "She won't do anything bad or nothing."

Nick stooped in front of them and wiped the tears on both their faces. "The police have your parents," he said softly. "I can't do anything about that, and I can't make any promises about what's going to happen. But I can promise that we'll take good care of you and find you someplace nice to stay."

The boys clung together, weeping, and Nick stroked both of their heads. He couldn't mend their broken hearts or erase the trauma their parents' arrest had caused. But he could help with some of the uncertainty. "This is just my office, okay? Let's go in and see if I can find you a coke or something, maybe a couple of candy bars."

"We're not allowed to take candy from strangers."

The irony. Drug dealers for parents, and they'd managed to teach these kids not to take candy from strangers. "Then I'll give you each fifty cents and let you get it out of the vending machine yourself. And while you eat it, I'll make some phone calls and find a nice family who'll let you spend the night with them tonight. Sound fair?"

The boys shrugged.

No, you're right, Nick thought. *None of it is fair.* "Call me Nick," he said. "And I'll call you Matthew and Christopher, okay?"

"Matt and Chris," the little one corrected through his tears.

"Okay, Matt and Chris. Let's go on in. Nothing in there for you to be afraid of—just an ugly office and me." He glanced up at the other car parked next to his. "And it looks like my boss is here, too. But that's all. No big bad wolves."

He led them in and saw Sheila Axelrod, his supervisor, sitting at her desk, talking on the telephone. In a car seat on her desktop lay a screaming baby that couldn't have been more than three months old. She hung up the phone as Nick came in. "There's got to be a better way to make a living," she said listlessly.

Nick fished some quarters out of his pockets for the vending machine. "Who've you got there?"

"Abused baby," she said. "Police intervened in a domestic fight and saw her. Cigarette burns on her little legs prove the abuse. But it'll take a miracle to find anyone to take her tonight." She nodded toward the two still-crying boys beside him. "You're lucky. At least they're old enough for SCCH. I've got to go down the list until I find a taker."

SCCH—the St. Clair Children's Home—was the only private children's home in town. It had once been Nick's first choice in cases like this, but not anymore.

"I'm not calling SCCH," he said, going to the car seat and lifting the crying baby out. Instantly, the child grew quiet and lay her head on Nick's shoulder. He felt a wave of gratification—and concern—flood through him.

"What do you mean you're not calling them? Who will you call?"

Still holding the baby, Nick ushered the two little boys to the vending machine and handed them some quarters. They took them grudgingly and chose their candy. The baby on his shoulder whimpered softly as her eyes slowly closed.

"Did that baby's mom get arrested, too?" the younger boy, Matt, asked.

"I don't know," Nick evaded. "But it looks like she's in the same boat you're in. Tell you what, guys. You're older than she is. If you'll calm down and not look like we're sending you to the dungeon, maybe she'll quit feeling like something bad is about to happen. What do you say?"

Chris shrugged. "What's SCCH? Is that where we're going?"

"No."

Sheila had the phone to her ear, but she put her hand over the receiver and asked, "Why not, Nick? They have a whole cottage just for temporaries. It's the easiest thing, and if this is long term, that's probably where they'll end up anyway."

"I told you, I have too many suspicions about some things going on at the home. Until I can give the place a clean bill of health, I'm not going to send any more kids to them."

Her face hardened, and her voice changed. "Nick, those two kids have to be placed tonight. You'll send them where I tell you to!"

He touched the baby's head again, trying to keep it calm in spite of Sheila's ranting. "Sheila, if I can find a home to take them tonight, what difference does it make to you?"

"Because I'm trying to find someone to take the baby. It's not likely that we can find more than one family this late to take them, and nobody's gonna take all three!"

"Let me try," he said. "That's all I ask, Sheila. Just give me a while to try."

She moaned. "If you don't send them to the home, you might have to split them up."

One of the boys gasped, and the other burst into tears again. "No! Please don't do that."

"We won't," Nick assured quietly. He pulled a tissue out and wiped the little boy's nose as he shot Sheila a look. "Sheila, why don't you let me take care of this, and you go on home? I can handle it."

"Really?" She looked at him as if he'd just offered her a week's vacation. Then she seemed to deflate. "I can't. Not until they're placed. I'll give you an hour to try to find a family to take them. If you don't, I'm taking them to SCCH myself. I'll work on the paperwork, and you work on the phone calling. Here, give me the baby."

"No, she's fine," he said softly. The baby was relaxing on his shoulder, and he could feel that she was close to falling asleep. "I can call while I hold her. And if I need a hand, my buddies here can help me, can't you, guys?"

The boys nodded quietly.

"All right," she said. "I'll be in here. Buzz if you need me."

He ushered them down the hall to the corner of the building he sometimes shared with two other caseworkers—except that they had both quit in the last month and hadn't yet been replaced. He looked over the baby's head to the boys. "You gonna eat that candy, or just let it melt in your hands?"

Matt put it into his mouth, but Chris just sat there. "Do we have to go anywhere with her?"

Most of the kids didn't like Sheila, which didn't surprise Nick. She could be cold sometimes, but he knew her coldness was stress-induced. She'd been at it longer than he had, and it was a job that got to you over the years. He sat down and leaned back in his chair, still stroking the baby's head. "I'll try to find a place for you myself, guys. And if I can, then I'll take you there."

"Why can't we stay with you?" the little one asked.

Nick smiled and messed up the boy's hair. "Because I'm not home much, kiddo. I couldn't watch you."

"We can watch ourselves. We'd be okay. We do it all the time."

"No can do. But trust me with this." He picked up the phone, breathed a silent prayer for help, and dialed the number of his first choice—a family he'd saddled with four new kids just this past week.

When they turned him down, he tried the next one on the list, and then the next, until he had almost given up. Little Matt had lain down on the small, garage-sale sofa against the wall, and had gone to sleep with his head in his brother's lap. The baby slept soundly, too. Chris just stared back at him with red, dismal eyes.

Not the St. Clair Children's Home, Nick prayed. *There's got to be somebody else.*

Holding the phone between ear and shoulder, he dialed the next number—a new family on their list. A retired couple who had volunteered to be foster parents, they had just today completed all the requirements to be accepted into the program. This would be their first placement call. He wondered if dumping three children on them this late at night their first time might frighten them away. He had no choice but to try.

"Hello?" The woman sounded kind—a good sign. He hadn't been the caseworker assigned to her—Sheila had done it—so he hadn't met her before. He hoped her voice wasn't deceiving.

"Mrs. Miller? This is Nick Hutchins with HRS. I have three children I need to place temporarily tonight. They're from two different families, so if you can't take all of them, we can give you one or two of them. But I'd at least like to keep the brothers together—"

"We'd be delighted to have them!" the woman said, then put her hand on the receiver and shouted, "Honey, they're bringing some children tonight." She came back to Nick. "Please, bring all three of them. What ages are they?"

Nick couldn't believe his ears. "The baby girl is probably three months, and then I have two brothers, six and eight. The baby's an abuse case, and the boys' parents are in police custody."

"Oh, the poor little things. Please, bring them right over. We'll have their beds all ready when you get here. I'll tell Vernon to get the crib out of the attic. We'll get it all dusted."

Nick mouthed "thank you" to the ceiling as he hung up the phone. He hurried to Sheila's door. "I found someone to take all three, Sheila. Grace and Vernon Miller. She's even excited about it."

Sheila didn't look impressed. "I wasn't planning to give them a trial by fire. I was going to ease them in. But I guess it can't be helped. Remind her not to get emotionally involved with them, Nick. They're new at this."

"I will," he said. But in his heart, he hoped they'd get a little involved. These kids were going to need someone who cared about them.

CHAPTER FIVE

Beth ignored her puppy as he whimpered and scratched at the attic door. Instead, she stared down at the answering machine. Why was it turned off? She had left it on; she was sure of it. Maybe the power had flickered, and the machine hadn't come back on.

Maybe. But that didn't explain the person who had answered the phone when she'd called.

Maybe the cellular phone company had mixed the signals. She'd heard of it happening. The fact that she was being followed at the time had made it all seem suspicious, but that didn't mean that the two events had anything to do with each other. She was probably being paranoid.

She started to turn the machine back on, but the yelping puppy distracted her. She scooped him up and stroked his head. "What's the matter, boy? You want to play?" He wiggled in her hands and reached up to lick her face. "We'll go down and play in a minute," she said, walking to the window near the apex of her roof. She peered out into the night, looking for headlights, any sign that Bill Brandon was out there, waiting, watching, ready to pounce.

No, of course he wasn't out there. She'd chosen this house very carefully. No one could just accidentally find it, and no one would be able to look her up, either. Her address was a post office box. It wasn't listed in the phone book, and it wasn't even in her files at school or the paper. Since she rented, there was no public record of where she lived. The only way to find her house would be to follow her here.

But a nagging voice in the back of her mind reminded her: *Bill Brandon has ways of finding out anything he wants. Everyone who knows him discovers that.*

Shivering, she carried the puppy back down the stairs, set him down, and went back to the phone to try Nick's office. Just as she picked up the phone, she heard a car on the gravel outside. She froze. Keeping her eyes on the door, she dropped the phone back in its cradle, pulled open a drawer in the end table, and grabbed the pistol she kept there. The doorbell rang, and the puppy erupted into a round of high-pitched barks.

He's here, she thought, holding the pistol aimed at the door. Her heart flipped into a triple-time cadence, and adrenaline pulsed through her.

The bell rang again, and a knock followed. "Beth? It's me, Nick!"

Nick. Not Bill.

She let out a huge breath of relief and lowered the gun. Feeling dizzy from the sheer terror that had gripped her, she headed for the door and opened it. "Nick, you scared me. I didn't know it was you. Where have you been? I tried to call."

Nick came in, his brown, slightly wavy hair tousled by the warm wind. His face looked tired, and the stubble on his jaw added to the picture of fatigue. "Didn't you get my message?"

"What message?"

"On your machine. Telling you I had an emergency and couldn't meet you at my house, that I would just come over here." He frowned as he saw the gun. "What's wrong?"

"I just got a little spooked, that's all." Embarrassed, she put the gun back into the drawer and closed it.

"Did something happen? Did the interview turn out badly?"

"No, no. It was fine." She shoved her hand through her short honey-colored hair and looked up the stairs toward the answering machine that had been off when she'd checked it. "It's just . . . a little weird."

"What is?"

"That you left a message. My machine was off when I got home. Are you sure it was on when you called?"

"Positive," he said. "I left a message that the police had just done a drug bust, and there were these two boys—their parents were dealing cocaine. I had to go get the children and place them in foster care tonight until we could find some relatives."

Her face whitened. "You didn't put them at SCCH, did you?"

"No," he said. "My supervisor would have, but I put them with a retired couple new to the foster-care program. They'll be okay." He paused and studied her for a moment. "Beth, you're pale. What is it?"

She breathed a self-conscious laugh and tried to calm herself. "Nothing, really. The interview went great. Better than I could have dreamed." She sank down on her couch and covered her face, and Nick sat down next to her.

She didn't really know Nick all that well, having met him just a few days ago when she'd called to interview him about his take on the children's home. Her questions had immediately piqued his interest because he'd also had suspicions about the home. So he'd spent a lot of time with Beth since that first meeting, trying to help her put the pieces together.

Although Beth tried to deny it or, better yet, ignore it, there was something about Nick Hutchins that made her feel safe. Her life up to this point had been anything but secure—ironically, that meant she distrusted nothing more than feelings of safety and security.

Still, something about Nick invited her trust. Maybe it was that he seemed to genuinely care about the children he watched over. It had been her experience that most social workers were so overburdened that they had little time to care about the people whose lives they affected. Nick seemed different.

She drew her mind back to the conversation. "Marlene was ready to talk," she said. "I taped our conversation. It was fascinating. She confirmed everything. Bill Brandon uses some of the kids in his care in a crime ring that breaks into people's homes and businesses and steals things. He has a central warehouse where he stores things until he can sell them—or until his people can sell them. Apparently, there are more people than just Bill and the kids involved. In fact, she said he has someone big running interference for him. Like someone on the police force or in government.

That's how he's gotten away with it. She didn't know any names or where the stuff is stored, but she said that he uses horrible tactics to force the kids into cooperating. Besides the abuse that you've suspected, he threatens them with harm to their sisters and brothers, their parents if they're living, or he makes them believe that they're as guilty as he is—that they're the ones breaking in, that his hands are clean, so if anyone goes down for the crime, it'll be the kids. And they have no way of knowing otherwise, so they cooperate."

Angered, Nick bolted up and paced across the floor, his fatigue evident. He needed to shave, and his light brown hair was tousled as though he hadn't given it a thought all day. Looking at his reddened eyes, she wondered if he ever got much sleep.

"We've got to put him away, Beth. We've got to get those kids out of there. Sheila, my supervisor, says I don't have enough evidence to start relocating the children. She thinks I'm nuts and Bill Brandon is a saint. I think she just can't face all the work it would take to relocate the kids. But it *has* to be done, and I don't care about the work."

Beth tried to think clearly. "First, we have to have enough evidence to convince the court. Maybe if you got some of the kids alone and told them you already knew what was going on, some of them would talk."

"I've tried. They all get this terrible look on their faces—fear, that's all I know to call it—and insist that they've never been happier and they've never been treated better."

"It's fear, all right. But we need more evidence. Marlene's statements are good, but she's just one person."

Nick frowned. "Why did she talk to you, anyway?"

Beth hesitated. "Well, I already knew she wasn't part of his organization anymore. She said that her life has changed in the past year. She seemed to genuinely care about the kids now, and she didn't want to sit by and let Bill do what he was doing."

"Are you sure you can trust her? What if she's just baiting you to see what you know?"

"She told me things I didn't know. It was real, Nick."

Nick sat slowly down and leaned forward. "Does Bill Brandon know that she talked?"

She was unsure how much to tell him. "Yes. I mean, I'm pretty sure he does. He—or someone in a dark Buick—was following me most of the way home."

"*What?*"

"Chasing me is more like it," she said, standing up again and setting her fists defiantly on her hips, as if the stance could erase the image of helpless victim. "It's okay. I made sure I lost him, so he couldn't follow me home. My car's got a few dents, though."

"He *hit* you? What was he trying to do?"

"Run me off the road," she said. "Near the seawalls."

"Beth, this is getting out of hand. He could have killed you!"

She went to the window, peered out through the blinds. "He almost did. I called the police, but it took them forever. By the time they came, I had lost him."

Nick went to stand behind her, and she turned around and looked up at him. "Beth, how do you know it wasn't a setup? The whole Marlene thing—all her deep confessions, and then her brother chasing you down and trying to kill you? What if they planned this together—"

"I don't think so," Beth said. "Marlene seemed scared herself. And she was sincere. She really was."

He blew out a frustrated breath. "No wonder you had a gun when you answered the door."

"It was stupid, really," she said. "He doesn't know where I live."

"Are you sure?"

"Positive," she said weakly.

"Then why do you keep looking out the window?"

"Just being careful. I mean, really, I can't even be sure it was him. I'm just assuming it was. Who else would come after me right after that interview? It had to be either him or someone who works for him."

"Beth, this is getting dangerous. You have to call the police again. Tell them who you think was following you."

She shook her head and plopped down on the couch. The puppy put its paws up on her shin, panting happily. She leaned over and picked him up. "I don't want to call them again. I did it before because I was desperate. But now that it's over, I don't think I want to bring them into this yet."

"Why not?" he asked. "Why would you wait?"

Determination tightened her features. "Because this is *my* story," she said, "and I don't want every paper in the state getting it before I can get the *whole* story out. If I call the police, it'll be public knowledge by morning. There'll be a barrage of articles, none with much meat, and Bill Brandon will clean up his act for a while and walk straight, and they won't catch him at anything, and everyone will write it off as hearsay and rumor, and go back to thinking he's the clean-cut, unsung hero who molds broken young kids into model citizens. I want to get him, Nick. And I'm not going to depend on the cops to do it."

He shook his head. "And how long will all this take?"

"I'm going to stay up late tonight transcribing the tapes of my conversation with Marlene. I'll start writing the story. Maybe tomorrow I can track down some other witnesses. If I could just find out where that warehouse is—and who he has in government working with him—"

"Beth, if you take too long, he's going to catch up with you. Then what?"

"I won't take too long," she said. "I'm as anxious to get this story out as you are. You have a list of kids in the home, don't you?"

"Yeah."

"Then start making plans to move them. I promise you, the story will be out within a week."

"I hope that's not too late. Especially now that he knows something's up."

She thought that over. "Maybe I can get it finished by tomorrow. If so, we could print it the day after—if I can convince my editor. Remember, I'm still just a grunt around there. The college kid, always looking for a front-page story. If he's going to print it, it has to be great."

Nick wasn't reassured. "What if he comes after you again? What if he *does* find where you live?"

"I can protect myself, Nick. I've done it for a long time."

He breathed a laugh. "Right. You're a junior in college. How old? Twenty?"

"Twenty-one."

"How long could you possibly have done it?"

"I'll be all right, Nick." She couldn't help the slight edge in her voice. "Now, why don't you go on home? You look really tired."

"I am tired," he said, "but I could sack out here. Make sure he doesn't show up. I'm really afraid to leave you."

She smiled slightly. "Spend the night, huh? I don't think so."

He shook his head again. "Not like that, Beth. That's not my style."

"Mine either."

"You have any objection to a guy wanting to watch out for you?"

"You have enough people to watch out for, Nick. Don't worry about me. If I can't take a little heat, I have no business being a reporter."

"That's what I figured," he said. "You're a hundred-ten-pound tough guy. What do you have for protection? Karate? Brass knuckles?"

"I have my wits," she said with a half-smile. "And the .22 in that drawer. Oh, and I have my dog." She set the puppy down, and he wagged over to Nick.

"Yeah, right." He bent down and petted the puppy, who instantly made a puddle on the floor. "Uh-oh. You're not walking him enough."

"We're working on the house-breaking thing," she said with a soft laugh as she ran to the kitchen to grab a towel. "I don't know if he's training me or if I'm training him. But he's only six weeks old. What can you expect, huh, Dodger?"

"Dodger?"

"Yeah. Like the Artful Dodger in *Oliver*."

"Any chance that name came from the story you're working on?"

She stood back up. "Yeah, I guess so. That and the fact that he loves stealing socks out of my laundry hamper. He chewed a hole in the side of it so he could get to them."

He chuckled and went to the door, opened it, and peered out into the woods surrounding the house. "It's kind of creepy out here. Are you sure you're not afraid?"

"One person's creepy is another person's refuge," she said. "He won't find me here, and very few people have the address. Reporters have to take certain precautions."

He turned back. "I guess I should feel honored that you gave it to me."

She smiled a little self-consciously, and looked down at the puppy. "Actually, you should. I don't even know why I did."

"I like to think it was my trustworthy eyes."

"They are pretty trustworthy," she said, bringing hers back to them again. For a moment, their eyes locked, and finally, she looked away, realizing her face was getting warm. "Look, I'll call you tomorrow and let you know what's happening. If you find out anything, let me know, too, okay?"

"All right."

He looked at her for a second, as if considering something else to say. "See you later."

"Yeah. Later."

She watched as he walked across the gravel, examined the dents in her car, then, shaking his head, went to his own vehicle. She checked the shadows of the trees on both sides of the house with a growing sense of unease, then shuddered and closed the door. She bolted it shut, then turned back to the puppy, who was curled up on a rug. "Yeah, that's right," she told him. "Go to sleep, just when the hard work is about to start. Never mind, I'll do it myself. Your spelling's pretty lousy, anyway."

CHAPTER SIX

ick tried to shake the uneasy feeling taking hold of him as he pulled off the dirt road leading to her property and back onto the paved street where occasional cars drove by. She was tough, that was certain, but it didn't make him feel any better. A man like Bill Brandon had ways of breaking down toughness.

On the other hand, Bill was used to dealing with children. Maybe he'd not yet met the likes of Beth Wright.

Nick knew *he* hadn't. She had blown into his life like an answered prayer, one that he was still reeling from. Just when he'd felt so helpless and frustrated that he wanted to quit his job, she had come along with some answers and the encouragement he had sorely needed.

It hadn't even been two weeks ago that he'd gotten the phone call from the distraught mother who'd had visitation with her son at the children's home that afternoon and had found him bruised from a beating that the child told her had come from Bill Brandon. Since the mother was a drug addict going through rehab, Nick hadn't taken what she said at face value. Instead, he had ordered a medical exam of the child. The doctors confirmed that he *had* suffered a beating.

Finally, Nick had confronted Bill Brandon about it. Brandon told him that the child had been fine when he'd left for visitation, but that the mother herself must have beaten him. Bill had launched from there into an impassioned argument that parental visitations were detrimental to the healthy environment he tried to provide for "his" kids.

There were obvious problems with Bill's story. Why would the mother have called attention to abuse she'd inflicted herself? Besides, Nick had heard the despair in her voice, the urgency, the worry. Yes, her child had been taken from her due to neglect and drug addiction—but now she was clean. The sound of maternal worry in her voice had been authentic. Much more authentic than Bill Brandon's arguments.

Sheila, Nick's supervisor, had blown the whole thing off, convinced that Bill Brandon was right and that the mother was just trying to cover up for something she knew would be discovered eventually. She suggested they file to revoke the mother's visitation privileges.

Nick had allowed her to believe he would take care of it, but he hadn't. Something about Bill's and Sheila's rationales didn't ring true. Something about the mother's pleas did.

He had begun to look deeper into problems at the home. He had gone to the public school where Bill Brandon's children were sent, and had studied the records of the SCCH kids. He saw a repeating pattern of children falling asleep in class, over and over and over. When he spoke to their teachers—no small feat since it was summer and some of them had been difficult to locate—he was told that they had contacted Brandon about the problem, only to be told that he would "take care of it" when the kids got home from school. Fearing what Brandon's punishment might be, and sensing the terror on the kids' faces when they thought they were being reported to him, most of the teachers had fallen into a routine of letting it slide without calling the home. They, too, suspected that things might not be all they seemed at the home, but they had little evidence to back it up. There had also been a few reports of some SCCH kids being caught committing crimes, but everyone had written those incidents off to bad parenting or to the typical rebellion of low-status, high-risk kids. None of his suspicions, none of the facts he'd compiled, added up to enough evidence to close down the home, or even to start an official investigation.

He'd been at a dead end—and then he'd gotten a phone call from a young woman who had identified herself as a reporter with the *St. Clair News* and said she was working on a story about some alleged abuses in the St. Clair Children's Home. It had been just the encouragement he'd needed to convince him he was on the right track. But when Beth had told him that she suspected Brandon was using the children in a crime ring that worked in areas within a two-hour radius of St. Clair, Nick had been stunned. Was that why the children were so sleep-deprived?

The idea had been so far-fetched that it was almost unbelievable—yet some part of him believed it. First, he had beaten himself up about placing so many children in the home. Then, he'd determined to get them all out. But first he had to get enough proof.

He'd met with Beth, told her everything he knew, and promised to help her in any way he could. Since then, she'd been busy putting together the story that would outline all of Brandon's alleged crimes. Now they could add to it his attempt to run her off the road—if they could somehow prove that he was the driver.

Nick thought back over the things she'd said tonight, the look on her face when he'd frightened her, the shakiness with which she'd revealed, little by little, how she had been followed from the interview. She hadn't looked so tough then. She was scared.

I might regret this, he told himself as he made a U-turn. But the fear in Beth's eyes haunted him.

He pulled his car into a metered space in front of the St. Clair Police Department. Larry Millsaps and Tony Danks were probably still there processing the parents of the boys Nick had placed earlier. Maybe they'd have time to give him a minute.

The station was noisy, as usual, and smelled of sweat and booze from some of those who waited in handcuffs to be booked. He scanned the desks where cops answered phones and did paperwork. Tony Danks sat tapping at his computer keys, probably getting a history on the couple who sold dope for a living. Nick ambled over.

"Man, don't you ever go home?"

Tony looked up and grinned. "Don't *you*? You look tireder than I do, Nick. How are those kids? Get them placed okay?"

"Yeah, no problem. They were a little scared, but I think they'll be all right. That's not why I'm here." He took the chair across from Tony's desk, crossed his legs and slumped back until his neck almost rested on the top back of the chair. "You got a minute?"

"Sure," Tony said, turning away from his computer and leaning on his desk. "You want Larry in on this?"

Nick glanced over at Larry's desk, saw that he was filling out reports. "Yeah, if he can spare a minute. I just need some police advice."

"You came to the right place." He half stood and yelled, "Larry!" over the din, and Larry looked up. He saw Nick sitting there and got up to head over.

"You get those kids placed?" Larry asked as he approached the desk.

"Yeah," Nick said. "But there's something else I need to ask you. Off the record."

Larry's eyebrows lifted, and he sat down on the edge of Tony's desk. "Okay, shoot."

Nick dropped his foot and leaned forward, bracing his elbows on his knees. "I have this friend. A woman. She's a reporter, and was doing an important interview tonight, and she got followed most of the way home until she lost him. She thinks she knows who it was, and she thinks it has to do with the story she's working on. Basically, he wants to shut her up, so I don't know what he might do to her. But she's convinced he doesn't know where she lives."

"You're not convinced?" Tony asked.

"Well, I can't be sure. This guy's shrewd, and he has a lot to lose. And I'm not entirely convinced that the whole interview wasn't a setup. Anyway, she didn't want to involve the police for fear of having the story come out before she breaks it—you know, the competition might get it—but I'm not sure waiting is a good idea."

"It's not illegal to follow someone," Tony said. "And it could have been a coincidence. Did he do anything to her? Ram her fender? Try to force her off the road? Anything to indicate ill intent?"

"Absolutely. She has at least two dents on her car where he tried to run her off the road."

"Then he did break a law. Would she be willing to file a complaint?"

"No, she won't. Not yet."

Larry shook his head dolefully. "Sorry, Nick. Nothing we can do."

"Officially, no," Nick said. "But what about unofficially? Could you kind of keep an eye on her tonight? Watch over her so that nothing happens?"

Larry and Tony exchanged looks. Tony rubbed his eyes. "Truth is, we're a little busy here tonight, Nick. We could send a squad car to patrol her house every hour or so, but we can't leave anyone there all night."

"Well, maybe that would be enough. Anything you could do would help. And I'd prefer that you told the cop who does it not to pull all the way down the dirt road leading to her house. Just far enough to get a look at the house and make sure no other cars are there. Seeing headlights would scare her to death. Besides, I don't want her to know I came to you. She wouldn't like it."

Larry stared at him for a moment, then broke into a sly grin. "Who is this girl, Nick? She sounds important. Something you haven't told us?"

Nick rubbed his stubbled jaw. "Actually, I just met her a few days ago. But yeah, I like her. She's a little young. Only twenty-one—"

"And you're an old man at . . . what? Thirty?"

Nick grinned. "Not quite."

Tony had to laugh. "Nick Hutchins, the guy who's too busy for a woman. Looks like he's clearing some time."

"Don't get carried away," Nick said. "I've just been trying to help her out some. She's nice. Smart. Savvy. Different than the other women I know."

"Uh-oh. Famous last words," Tony teased.

Nick got to his feet, fighting his own grin. "All right, guys. I'm just worried about the lady, that's all." He grabbed a pen off Tony's desk and jotted her address on a pad. "If you could get someone to patrol around there, just watching for anything suspicious—a dark Buick in particular—I'd really appreciate it."

Larry looked down at the pad. "All right. No guarantees, though."

"Didn't expect any."

He gave them both friendly handshakes, then walked out of the police station, wishing he could rest easy now. But he knew he wouldn't—it would be a long night for him.

And it wouldn't be any better for Beth.

CHAPTER SEVEN

Beth loaded her tape recorder and began to play back the tapes of her conversation with Marlene, quickly typing the words into her laptop computer. Beside her, Dodger slept, his little rhythmic snore making her wish she could lie down herself. But she had to get this done—and she was too tense to sleep anyway.

She heard something creak over her head. Lifting her hands from the keyboard, she looked at the ceiling. Was it her imagination, or had the floor squeaked upstairs? She cut off the tape recorder and listened.

There it was again. Quickly, she grabbed for the gun she kept in the table beside the couch. She went to the stairs and stared up at the top. Nothing there. She started to go up, then thought better of it. Still aiming at the stairs, she backed up and groped for the telephone. She snatched it up and dialed 911.

Her voice trembled as she tried to get the words out quietly. "There's someone in my house. Please—send someone right away. It's on Kramer Road, the number 343 is on the mailbox at the beginning of a long dirt road. Turn in there, and you'll see my house about a quarter of a mile in. Please hurry."

She hung up, but kept the gun aimed at the stairs. If he came down, she would shoot him. She had no choice. If Bill Brandon had found her, if he had broken into her home, then he was planning to kill her. Her only hope was to kill him first.

At the police station, one of the sergeants grabbed Tony on his way out. "Hey, Danks. That address you gave us to patrol? We just

347

got a call from the lady who lives there. Says someone's in her house."

Surprised, Tony glanced over his shoulder at Larry, then back at the sergeant. "Have you sent a car out?"

"Yeah, there was one real close. In fact, he'd just made a swing by there and didn't see anything. Jane sent him back."

"We'll head over there, too," Larry said.

"Should we call Nick?" Tony asked as they hurried out to their car.

Larry shook his head grimly. "Let's see what's up first."

CHAPTER EIGHT

The Fraser Gas Station was closed this time of night, and Bill Brandon sat in the shadows of the pumps with his headlights off, waiting for the kid to get there. It shouldn't have taken Jimmy this long to make it the five miles from her house to the gas pumps. What if he'd gotten caught? What if he'd made an even bigger mess of this?

He should have expected it. Jimmy was too soft, too young. Bill knew he should have used one of the more experienced kids. But this should have been an easy job, and Jimmy was so small for his age that slipping him in through the small bathroom window they'd found unlocked had been a snap. Besides, Jimmy was a whiz when it came to computers, and he knew that if anyone could handle the computer end of the job, it would be him.

Yeah, that was the way it was *supposed* to have gone. That was the plan. Send Jimmy in through a window, then the kid gets all the tapes and papers he can find, copies her files onto a disk, then erases her hard drive. Then everything went wrong. Bill had planned to stop her from getting home, but she'd gotten away from him. And then the stupid kid had picked up the phone. He'd pay for that.

Bill cranked his car, turned on the lights, and started back toward her house, hoping he'd see Jimmy on the road somewhere. He drove slowly, scanning the trees, watching, waiting. The kid had been trained too well to be seen easily, but Bill hoped he'd recognize the Buick and show himself.

Nothing.

He pulled over to the side of the road and thought for a moment, trying to build a strategy. Maybe he needed to go back to the house, look into the windows, see if she was home.

He pulled back onto the street and headed for her dirt road.

But before he reached it, he heard a siren, then saw a police car's lights flickering through the trees. The squad car turned onto her dirt road.

She called the police, he thought, driving quickly past. *Which means the kid got caught. Now what?*

He wiped the sweat from his brow with his sleeve and decided to return to the home. The cops would probably call him to report that they had one of his kids in custody, and he'd better be there to take the call. He'd pretend that the kid had escaped through a window when Bill thought he was sleeping, that he always had trouble with this one.

Jimmy wouldn't dare tell them differently. Bill had done too good a job preparing him for a time like this.

Upstairs in Beth's house, the boy heard the sound of a siren approaching outside, and he strained to see through the window without moving. He saw blue lights flashing against the glass, a pale flicker illuminating the shadows of the attic. Did she know he was here? Had she called the police?

He heard the front door open, the dog yelping, and the lady's voice outside. With no one downstairs to hear him, he ran across the floor to the biggest box he could find, pulled out a four-foot Christmas tree, climbed into the box, then pulled the tree in on top of him. Trying to settle his breathing, he curled into as tight a ball as he could and waited.

It didn't take long. The door opened and a light came on, a light that seemed to flood through the attic, lighting every crack, every shadow, every particle of dust. He was sure it exposed him, too. Could they see him? Could they tell where he was hiding?

He heard voices—several of them—as they filed through the attic, searching. He squeezed his eyes shut and chanted in his mind, *Don't let them find me . . . don't let them find me . . .*

"There's nobody here," one of the men said. "Maybe she heard a mouse or something."

Someone else's feet creaked as he came closer to the Christmas tree box. Jimmy braced himself. "Yeah, this house is pretty old. Probably wouldn't take more than a mouse to make the floor squeak."

"But what about the guy following her, Tony? You don't think this is a coincidence?"

"Didn't seem like it at first. But there's nobody here. Are you sure you checked thoroughly downstairs?"

"Positive."

"Well, she's probably jumpy because of what happened in the car. Maybe she just needs a little reassurance. We can tell her we'll step up our patrols of her house. Maybe that'll put her mind to rest."

"Let's look again, just in case."

He heard them shuffling boxes near him, and suddenly panicked: he had left his backpack out, lying on top of a box. They would see it and know, and then they'd empty out all of the boxes until he came tumbling out . . .

"I give up," one of the cops said, finally. "Cut the light, will you?"

The light went out, and Jimmy sat paralyzed as the door closed. He was soaked with sweat, trembling, and the tree was cutting into his arm and the back of his neck, but he didn't dare move. What if they heard him? What if they came back? Even after they left, *she* could still hear him and call them back.

A tear rolled out of his eye, a tear that Bill would not have tolerated. He managed to wipe his wet face on his shoulder. This was hopeless. He was never going to get out of here.

Downstairs, Beth tried to find comfort in Larry and Tony's assurances that no one was in her house. "I'm really sorry to bother you guys. I guess I'm just getting paranoid."

"I can understand that," Larry said. "And don't apologize. It's our job to check things like this out."

"Yeah, but I didn't expect two detectives when I called."

Larry and Tony looked at each other, and finally, Larry decided to come clean. "The truth is that Nick Hutchins was worried about you and asked us to keep an eye on you."

Her eyebrows rose. "Nick? What did he tell you?"

Tony looked apologetic. "He said you were followed home tonight—and when we drove up, we saw the dents on your car. It's no wonder you would be nervous after that."

Her face tightened, and she looked down at the puppy. "I told him I could protect myself."

"That's what he said, but since we're here—why don't you file a complaint? Give us an idea who followed you so we can arrest him."

"He'd be out by morning. Besides, I can't prove it. I can only guess who it was."

"If you give us a name and he has complementary dents in his car, that'll be proof enough."

She thought it over for a moment as she peered off into the trees surrounding her yard. There were risks either way. If they could keep him in jail for a day or two, that might help her finish her investigation. "It's Bill Brandon. He runs the St. Clair Children's Home."

Tony wrote down the name. "I've heard of him."

"Yeah. Probably as a hero and protector of children. All lies."

"Why do you say that?"

She thought of telling them everything, but she just didn't have enough evidence yet. Alerting them to part of the problem might do more harm than good. "It'll all come out in the paper in the next couple of days, detectives. Then you'll see."

"So that's why you think it was him? Because you're doing some kind of story on him?"

"You got it."

"Would you be willing to file a complaint against him tonight?"

She considered that, then shook her head. "No, I'd rather hit him with the big guns in a couple of days. There's a lot at stake."

She walked them to the door, and the little dog bounded out into the night, its tail wagging. She grabbed his leash and hurried after him, clipped it to his collar, and watched as he found a bush to do his business. "Thanks for coming," she told the cops.

Larry held back. "I'd feel better if you were locked in before we left."

"Yeah, I guess I would, too." She waited for the puppy to finish, then hustled him back inside. "Thanks again."

She locked and bolted the door, then watched out the window as the car drove out of sight. She was losing it, she told herself. Calling the police just because the house creaked. Of course it creaked. It was old. It had probably creaked every day since she'd moved in. But that was before she'd taken on Bill Brandon. Now, everything was suspect.

But she was okay, she reminded herself. He couldn't find her here.

CHAPTER NINE

Marlene Brandon lay awake in bed, her mind reeling with the confessions she'd made to Beth tonight. She'd had to do it. It was the only way to set things right. Her newfound faith required it of her. It wasn't enough to simply believe; she had to put feet to that belief. Even if those feet led her into danger.

She looked at the clock and realized she had been lying here for two hours without closing her eyes. That uneasy feeling that had gripped her all day was almost strangling her now.

She turned over, fluffed her pillow, adjusted the covers, and tried to push her conversation with Beth out of her mind. Marlene had told her things that, most likely, would land her in jail, unless the prosecutor granted her immunity for testifying against her brother. The thought covered her in cold sweat.

I do not give to you as the world gives. Let not your heart be troubled, and do not be afraid. The remembered words brought her comfort, wrapping themselves around her heart. A strange, unexpected peace washed over her, and she began to think that she might sleep tonight, after all.

Her mind shifted back to Beth, so young and bright, so ambitious, so alone. She was proud of the way Beth was supporting herself through college by working at the small-town newspaper. Only twenty-one, but she'd come so far. And she was living a clean life with a pure heart, going to church faithfully and trying to follow the letter of God's law. Marlene only hoped that Beth would learn about his grace, as well. Maybe she should have made sure. Maybe she would call her tomorrow and do just that.

Her eyes began to drift shut, and her mind released its hold on her troubles as sleep pulled her under.

"Hello, Marlene."

She sat bolt upright in bed at the voice, and saw the silhouette of her brother standing in the doorway of her bedroom. "Bill!"

"Surprised?" he asked with that sinister amusement she'd heard so often when he spoke to the children. She had learned it from him, and had gotten good at using it herself over the years.

"How did you get in here?" she asked, pulling her covers up over her as though they could shield her from his wrath.

He laughed then, that condescending laugh that had crushed the spirits of young and old alike. "Marlene, Marlene. You know there isn't a lock anywhere that can keep me out." He came in and sat on the foot of her bed, gazing at her. "I'm hurt, you know. I always thought that, of all people, I could trust my sister."

"You don't trust anyone," she said, sliding back against her headboard.

His face was half lit by the hall night-light, half shadowed by the darkness in her room. "That's true, I guess. Sad, but true. It's hard to trust, Marlene, when people betray you left and right."

She swallowed, and her mind searched for the comfort of Scripture she'd recalled moments ago. *Let not your heart be troubled . . .*

"You want to talk betrayal, Bill, let's talk about what you're doing to those children."

He leaned back against the post at the foot of her bed. "I'm teaching them a trade, Marlene. One they can use all their lives."

"One that can ruin their lives and land them in prison when they're older. You're warping their minds, Bill; you're dragging them into hell. You'll pay for it. You'll be accountable for it someday."

"Is that what they tell you down at that church you've been going to? That some invisible force out there is going to swoop down and strike me dead?"

The fear seemed to have fled, and in its place was a boldness she had rarely felt around her brother. "You'll pay, Bill."

"And so will you."

"Yes, I was a part of it. I'm prepared to suffer the consequences. But I've been forgiven."

"What did you tell her, Marlene?"

His voice sliced like a knife through her words. She swallowed. "Very little that she didn't already know. She's going to expose you, Bill. She's not afraid of you."

"She should be. And so should you."

He pulled his hand out of his pocket, and she saw the shiny metal of the pistol as the hall light fell upon it. He got up and came closer; he aimed the gun at her forehead. Even so, that peace hung on, and so did the boldness. She wasn't afraid to die. "What are you going to do, Bill? Kill all of us? One by one? Me? Beth? Her editors? All the adults who grew up in your home, the ones who know the real story? The children who are working as your little slaves now?"

"Maybe," he said. "But I think for now I'll just settle for you."

CHAPTER TEN

I n Cottage B on the back side of the St. Clair Children's Home campus, seven-year-old Lisa Westin lay still in her bed, clutching her threadbare teddy bear with one arm. She stared up at the ceiling and forced her ears to listen hard, so hard that she'd hear her brother when he finally came home. But some long-held fear told her that he wasn't coming home.

She squeezed her eyes shut, trying to hold in the tears and block out the memories of three years ago. She had been only four, and Jimmy told her often that she was too young to remember, that she had gotten it all wrong, but she knew he was just trying to make the memories seem like a misty dream that hadn't really happened. But she knew better. They weren't her first memories—there were others, but they came more in sensations and scents, feelings that seemed warm and sad, tiny glimpses of happiness that she knew she'd felt then. The memory she had of what happened that day—the day their mother hadn't come home—was more vivid, more distinct. She remembered harsh faces of policemen, words that she didn't understand: neglect, abandonment, addiction. She remembered the realization, after two whole days of going without food, that their mother had forgotten them. And she remembered the inescapable panic, the what's-going-to-happen-to-us terror. Jimmy had seemed so much older than seven at the time; he had been the rock she had clung to, her big brother. But he had been the age then that she was now. He had promised her, as the policemen had carted them off to become wards of the state, that he wouldn't allow them to be separated—that, even though no one else in their lives had stuck around, he would never leave her.

She wiped her tears, held back the sob pulling at her throat, and slid out of bed, careful not to wake the other little girls sleeping in the beds around her. The home was supposed to look and feel like a real home, with ruffly bedspreads donated by local church groups, and frilly little dolls that no one was allowed to play with. But Lisa suspected that real homes weren't filled with fear, as this place was. Her long white gown dragged the floor as she padded barefoot across the carpet and peered out the window. Maybe Jimmy was out with Bill, doing that job he had said was so important. But she had heard Bill's car a few minutes ago, and had gotten up then to see if Jimmy was with him. When she saw under the streetlight in front of Bill's cottage that he was alone, she had known something was wrong.

Still clinging to one last fragment of hope, she padded out of the room and into the hall, past Stella, their house mother, whose loud snores reassured Lisa that Stella was asleep, and to the big room where all the boys in this cottage stayed. She tiptoed close to Jimmy's bed. Maybe he had come in quietly, not wanting to wake anyone. Maybe he didn't know she had waited and waited...

But the bed was still neatly made. Jimmy wasn't there.

She looked around for some of his belongings, wondering if he'd packed them. Then she'd know if he had planned to leave her.

She got down on her knees and peered under his bed, and found the box in which he kept everything in the world he owned. As quietly as she could, she slid it out. In it, she saw his baseball glove, his ball, the Atlanta Braves cap he'd gotten somewhere...

And she saw the envelope with the snapshots of them taken a few years ago, snapshots he kept because he said he always wanted to remember that they were sister and brother.

Wouldn't he have taken those if he'd intended to leave? Or had he left them here for her, so she could remember even though he'd chosen to forget?

"What are you doing in here?"

The harsh whisper startled her, and she swung around and saw Brad, one of Jimmy's roommates, sitting up in bed.

She put her finger to her lips to quiet him, and quickly slid the box back under the bed. But she kept the envelope of snapshots.

"I'm telling," he whispered louder. "I'm telling Stella. And I'm gonna tell Jimmy when he comes back. You're not supposed to be in his stuff!"

Another of the boys stirred. "Will you shut up? This is the first night I've been able to sleep all week!"

"That little creep is going through Jimmy's stuff."

"I am not," she whispered back. "I was looking for something that's mine. He was keeping it for me."

"What is it?" Brad taunted. "A pacifier?"

"I don't suck a pacifier!" Lisa flung back, struggling to hold her tears back. She got to her feet and headed for the door.

"I'm still telling!" he whispered.

She ignored him and tiptoed out into the hallway and past Stella's room. Her snoring hadn't changed its rhythm, and Lisa breathed a grateful sigh of relief. Maybe Brad wouldn't tell. If he did, Stella would spank her, then send her to Bill for further punishment. She'd never been sent to Bill before, but Jimmy had. She had seen the bruises herself.

She got back into bed and lay down, staring at the ceiling as she clutched the pictures to her chest. What would she do if Jimmy didn't come back?

Now she let the tears come, heavily, deeply. She turned over and buried her face in her pillow, muffling her sobs.

A dusty ray of sunlight from the attic window woke Jimmy the next morning, and it took a moment for him to realize where he was. He was hiding at the bottom of an old Christmas tree box, and the prickly tree still covered him.

But he hadn't been found.

He reached above him to move the tree and tried to stand up. Quietly, he set it down beside the box and stretched to his full height. It felt so good to stretch after a whole night crammed into that box. He listened . . .

Was the lady home, or had she gone to work? If she had, he could escape. He could get back to the home, let Bill punish him, and get back to normal.

He heard a television downstairs, and his heart sank. She was still here.

He sank back into the box, afraid to move. He needed to go to the bathroom, and he was hungry, and his body ached, and it was getting hotter in here.

When would she ever leave?

CHAPTER ELEVEN

B eth sat at her kitchen table. Spread out in front of her were the documents she'd collected from Nick about the things the children's teachers had said, as well as the statistics on the rise of burglaries in St. Clair and surrounding cities, and the few citizens who'd mentioned seeing children breaking in. She had spent most of the night transcribing Marlene's interview from the tape, and now she sat with a highlighter pen, marking off quotes she'd use in her story and trying to decide what her lead would be.

The television in the living room was on, and the Tampa news anchor droned on about last night's city council meeting, a fire in Oldsmar, a murder . . .

She tuned it all out and sipped her coffee as she reviewed the transcript of her conversation with Marlene.

"The victim was identified as fifty-one-year-old Marlene Brandon . . ."

Beth looked up, stunned. Through the doorway of the living room, the television flickered, showing footage of the police cars surrounding the house where she'd been last night. Slowly, she got to her feet.

"The murder was a result of an apparent burglary. Ms. Brandon's body was discovered early this morning by a neighbor . . ."

Gasping, Beth dove for the telephone and punched out the number of the newspaper. When her editor answered, she cried, "She was murdered, Phil! The woman I interviewed last night was murdered! Marlene Brandon. What do you know so far?"

"That was the woman you interviewed?" he asked, astounded. "Wow, Beth, all we have is that it was a burglary. The house was ransacked, according to the police."

"She was murdered because she talked to me!" Beth shouted. "Her brother did it, Phil!"

"Now, wait, Beth—unless you have proof, something we can take to the police . . ."

The floor above her squeaked again, this time twice in a row, and Dodger started barking. Catching her breath, she turned toward the staircase, the phone still clutched to her ear. "Phil, I'll call you back. No! Better yet, you hang on. I keep thinking I hear someone in my house. I'm going upstairs to look, but if I don't come back to the phone in a few minutes—"

"Beth, you're going off the deep end. You're overreacting a little, don't you think?"

"I'm not overreacting, Phil. The woman is dead. If he killed his own sister, he'll come after me next. Now, hold on, and call the police if I don't come back."

She set the phone down—and heard the squeak again. She grabbed her gun out of the drawer and, hand trembling, aimed it toward the top of the stairs as she started up.

Dodger tried to follow her, his fat stomach making it nearly impossible for him to pull himself up from one step to the next. His yelping gave her some degree of comfort, though. As long as she could hear it, she felt grounded in reality.

She swallowed as she got to the top of the stairs, crossed her little office, and flung the attic door open.

"All right," she said, beginning to sweat and tremble as she clutched the gun. "I know you're in here. I've heard you, and you're not going to get away with it, so you might as well come out and show yourself now, or I'm going to start shooting. I mean it!"

She looked around. Everything looked undisturbed. There was no sign of anyone. Mentally, she tried to calculate exactly where she'd heard the squeak. She'd been standing at the telephone, near her kitchen table; directly over that would be that back corner, where the Christmas tree box sat. Was that tree sticking further out than it had been last night?

Her heart pounded in her ears as she stepped closer to the box, breathing so loud that whoever was hiding there would know how terrified she was. *Someone* was in that box. Bill Brandon? Was he in here playing with her, trying to frighten her to death? Was she going to be his next victim?

Terror overwhelmed her, and she cocked the pistol. "I'm giving you to the count of three to come out, and then I'm going to start shooting. One.... two ... three ...."

Nothing happened, so she slipped her finger over the trigger. "I warned you," she said through her teeth. "You're underestimating me, Bill."

She heard a noise behind her and swung around. The gun went off.

The puppy yelped and squirted a puddle onto the floor. He had made it up the stairs, but now he stood there trembling just inches from the bullet hole.

She had almost shot her dog.

For a moment, she thought of dropping the gun and comforting the puppy, but someone was still here. She turned back around, took a step closer to the box, grabbed a branch of the Christmas tree, and in one quick motion jerked the tree out.

The box was empty.

Drenched in sweat now, she backed away, so relieved that she wanted to cry. The puppy got between her feet, almost knocking her over. She picked him up and gave the attic one last look around. Maybe she was losing her mind. Maybe what she'd heard was an opossum on the roof, or a squirrel, or even a rat. Any of those things would be preferable to Bill Brandon.

She left the attic and closed the door behind her, then hurried down to get a towel to clean up the dog's puddle. On her way to the kitchen, she went back to the phone. "Phil? Are you there?"

"Yeah, Beth. What's going on there? Did I hear a gunshot?"

"It was me. I thought I heard someone, but it was a false alarm. Maybe I am a little paranoid. But Marlene Brandon is still dead. I have to go to the police. Who's covering her story, Phil?"

"I don't even know if we're going to print anything about it, Beth. It was all the way in Tampa, and our St. Clair readers wouldn't be that interested. Besides, they're saying it was just a routine burglary."

"It was *not* a routine burglary, Phil!" she shouted. "She was the sister of Bill Brandon, who's the subject of the story I'm working on. She got killed right after telling me everything. You really think that's a coincidence?"

"Well—okay, no. But what do you want to do? Do *you* want to cover it?"

She hesitated and tried to slow her thoughts. "I don't know . . . yes. I guess I should go and see what I can find out."

"If what you're saying is true, Beth, then don't you think your time would be better served by finishing the story? Then the murder of Marlene Brandon will tie in and make more sense."

Confused, she sat for a moment, eyes fixed on the ceiling. "Yeah, I guess you're right. But would you put someone else on it? It's important, Phil. We have to know everything about her murder."

"All right. I'll send Todd."

"Good. Let me know everything you find out. Even if it seems insignificant."

"And you finish that story."

"I'll have it there this afternoon."

She hung up and started for the kitchen to splash water on her face, but the doorbell rang, startling her again. She snatched up the gun and peeked through the curtain. It was two police officers. Breathing a sigh of relief, she shoved the gun back into its drawer and answered it.

"Can I help you?" she asked, wondering if they noticed how badly she was still shaking.

"Yes," one of them said. "Are you Beth Wright?"

"Yes."

He introduced himself and showed her his badge. They were not from St. Clair, but from Tampa. "We'd like to come in and ask you a few questions about the murder of Marlene Brandon."

CHAPTER TWELVE

he two police officers looked around her house as she ushered them in. She wondered if they had been there when she'd fired her gun. "I just heard about the murder," she said. "On the news." Her eyes welled with tears. "I couldn't believe it."

"We understand that you were the last one to see her alive."

She sat down and gestured for them to take the couch. "Obviously someone saw her after I did. How did you know I was there, anyway?"

"Her pastor."

"Her what?"

"Her pastor spoke to her after you left. Apparently she called him. He said she seemed exhilarated, because she had confessed some things to you. What we'd like to know from you is whether you saw anyone hanging around the house, a strange car, or someone walking up the street. Anything at all."

She closed her eyes and tried to think. "I didn't see anything, at least not at her house. But I was followed most of the way home."

"Followed?"

"Yeah. Someone was after me. I called 911, but I lost him before the police got there. And when I got home, I kept thinking someone was in my house. I even had the St. Clair police come out last night to check."

One of the cops began to jot that down. "Who were the officers?"

"Well, there were several, but I remember Larry Millsaps and Tony Danks."

They jotted the names down. "What time was that?"

"Around midnight, I think."

"Miss Wright, do you have any idea who could have followed you home?"

She hesitated, glancing at the table with so much evidence waiting to be printed. If she told them too much, and word got out, the rest of the media would jump on it before she had the chance to get her story into print. Because she was the last one to see Marlene alive, other reporters would piece it together, until they discovered more than she wanted them to know. Still, if she could get Bill Brandon off the streets . . .

"She mentioned that she wasn't getting along too well with her brother, Bill Brandon. And the things she confessed to me—they had a lot to do with him. Have you questioned him?"

"Yes. Ms. Brandon's pastor indicated that she and her brother were on the outs. But he was home last night. Several people, employees of his, confirmed it."

"I'll bet they did. Officers, if I were you, I'd check his story out with someone besides his employees."

"Why? Do you have reason to believe he wasn't at home?"

"I'm just saying that she told me she was afraid of her brother. He had warned her not to talk to me."

"About what, Miss Wright? What is the story you were interviewing her about?"

She glanced at the table again and swallowed. "I'm doing a story about children's homes. She used to work with her brother at the St. Clair Children's Home, but I learned that they had parted ways, and I wondered why. They'd had some philosophical differences, and her brother was still hot over her leaving." It was part of the truth, she thought, even if it wasn't all of it.

"Hot enough to kill over?" the officer asked.

"Maybe. I'm just telling you what I think."

The two cops exchanged looks, and finally, one asked, "Miss Wright, where were you around eleven last night?"

"Right here," she said. "I got home at about ten."

"Did you talk to anyone? See anyone?"

366

"I told you, I saw the police around midnight."

"Before that, was there anyone?"

She couldn't believe they were asking for her alibi, but she took it seriously. "Yes, as a matter of fact. Right after I got home, Nick Hutchins stopped by. Call him and ask him. He was here about half an hour."

They didn't write the name down. "Nick Hutchins. Could you give us a number where we can reach him, please?"

"Yes," she said, anxious to clear this up. "You can call him from my phone if you want. Check me out. Then maybe you can get out of here and arrest the real murderer."

CHAPTER THIRTEEN

immy hadn't moved a muscle since the lady had left. He'd been sure she was going to shoot him. He had walked over to the window and had been trying desperately to open it when he'd heard her coming up the stairs. So he had jumped behind a stack of old newspapers and balled himself up as small as he could get himself, and luckily she hadn't seen him. He had heard her say that she would shoot, and then he'd heard her pull out the Christmas tree—and even though he'd braced himself, expecting the gunshot, he had still wet himself when the gun went off. He'd been sure she was about to find him, but she hadn't.

Now he wondered who was downstairs with her. He had heard the doorbell, and there were voices down there. He half expected it to be Bill—but when he got up enough courage to creep a little closer to the window and look out, he saw a Tampa police car instead. Tampa? Were *they* looking for him? Had they tied him to any of the Tampa burglaries?

He had to get out of here. Somehow, he had to make a break for it.

If only he could use her bathroom and get a drink of water.

He heard the door close downstairs, and looked out the window to see the two cops going back to their car. She was out there, too, walking the dog, and he wished she'd walk up the dirt road, far enough that he could escape. But she hung around the front door, as if afraid to get too far from it.

He slid back down the wall, hopeless, helpless.

What was Bill doing about all this? Would he try to come after him and get him out? Or would he just leave him here to rot?

And what was Lisa thinking?

He closed his eyes and tried to come up with a plan, but there wasn't one. Until she left, he was stuck here.

Outside, Beth watched the police car drive away as the puppy tugged at the leash and sprinkled every leaf and bush he could find. She didn't want to get too far from the house, for fear that Bill Brandon would jump out of nowhere.

Her eyes drifted up to the window in her attic, and she tried to tell herself that no one was there. She had searched it, and the police had searched last night. Anyone would be paranoid after the events of the last few days.

But what was that? Something moving in the darkness beyond the dusty window. She stepped further back from the house and tried to focus better. Was it a reflection from the sun through the trees, or had she seen movement?

She stepped to the side, trying to see it without the glare of sunlight on it, and stared at the glass.

Then she saw it again. The slightest, slowest movement of something rising up, then jerking back down.

Someone's in there! They're watching me!

She jerked the puppy back into the house by its leash and grabbed her gun again. This time, with bold, renewed anger, she ran up the steps and burst into the attic. She kicked at the box beside the window, knocked over the four-foot stack of newspapers in the corner, clutching the gun in front of her.

"I saw you, you sleazeball! I know you're in here!"

She was shaking so hard she could hardly hold the gun, but she swung around, knocked over more boxes, kicked at others, shoved things aside.

Then she saw, on the far wall, the shadow cast by the light coming in from the window.

She took one step cautiously closer, then another, and cocked the pistol. He was behind that box in the corner, she told herself. Crouching like a coward, waiting to pounce on her or run like the wind . . .

"Don't move!" she screamed as she trained the gun on him and kicked the box away.

A little boy with red hair looked up at her with frightened green eyes, frozen like a doe in the glare of headlights. "Don't shoot, lady," he whimpered.

She caught her breath and stepped back, lowering the gun instantly. "You're—you're a kid! Just a kid! I almost shot you!"

"I know."

"What are you doing here?" she asked, breathless. "How did you get in?"

He slowly rose to his full height, no more than four-feet-four. The front of his black jeans were wet, and he was soaked with perspiration. "I was . . . uh . . . I was lost, and I saw your house . . . I knocked, but no one was home. I came in through a window downstairs just so I could call my mom . . . that's all I wanted to do . . . but then you came home and I got scared . . ."

"You've been here since last night?"

"Yeah."

"Why didn't you let me know you were here? I would have helped you."

"I was too scared."

She tried to stop trembling. She reached for his hand—it was dirty and rough—and pulled him around the box. "Come on, we'll call her now. She must be worried sick about you."

He grabbed up his backpack as she led him out of the attic, into the full light of her loft. "How did you get lost, anyway? What's a kid your age doing out alone at night?"

"It's a long story," he evaded. "Can I use your bathroom?"

"Of course." She glanced at the wet spot on his jeans. "If you'd like to change, you could probably wear a pair of my shorts. They'd be baggy, but—"

"That's okay," he said, embarrassed. "I don't need 'em." She led him downstairs and showed him the bathroom. He went in quickly and tried to bolt the door behind him.

"The lock's broken," she said through the door. "Tell me your number, and I'll call your mother."

There was no answer. In a moment, she heard a scraping sound, and realized he was raising the window—probably the same one he'd come through last night.

She burst through the door and caught him halfway out.

And suddenly it dawned on her. Black jeans. Black shirt. Black backpack. This child had been put here deliberately, planted in her house to rob her or spy on her or maybe even hurt her—

She grabbed him and wrestled him back in, her face reddening with escalating anger. "You lied to me," she said through her teeth. "You're not some lost kid. You're from SCCH. You're one of Bill Brandon's kids, aren't you?"

The kid looked stunned, and she knew instantly that she was right.

"Answer me," she demanded. "Did he make you break in here? What was he looking for? Papers? Tapes?"

He lowered his worried eyes to the floor, and she turned him around and yanked off his backpack.

"Answer me!" she bit out as she unzipped it and examined the contents.

"I didn't get anything!" he said. "You came home—"

"What *would* you have gotten?" she asked, jerking up his chin. "What did he tell you to get?"

The fear in his eyes was real. Instantly, she let him go, but she didn't break that lock she had on his eyes.

"He's gonna kill me," the boy whispered.

Her anger crashed. She knew that fear, understood that certainty.

"What's your name?"

"Jimmy," he muttered.

"How long have you been there, Jimmy? At the home?"

"Three years," he said. "Me and my sister. Lady, if you report me, they're gonna put me in the juvenile center, and there won't be anybody left to take care of my sister. She's only seven."

But the words weren't penetrating. She was too caught up in the realization that if this kid had gotten into her house, it was because Bill Brandon knew where she lived and how to get in. The fact that she wasn't already dead was a miracle.

"How did he know where I live?"

Jimmy shrugged. "How does he know where anybody lives? I don't know. He doesn't tell me stuff like that."

"So what *did* he tell you?"

He looked miserable as he struggled with the truth, and she knew that he wondered if any of his mission was salvageable now. He was probably hoping to get out, go back to the home, and act as though he'd never been caught.

"Come on, Jimmy. I'm not going to let that man hurt you."

"You can't stop him."

"I sure can. And he knows it. That's why he made you come here. He wants to stop me from telling what I know."

His eyes were raging as tears filled them. "He *will* stop you. He's mean, and he doesn't give up. He woulda stopped you last night if you hadn't lost him."

She caught her breath. "How do you know that?" Then her face changed as she remembered the phone call, the boy's voice . . . "That was you on the phone, wasn't it?"

He swiped at the tears spilling down his face. "He told me he'd call to warn me you were coming home. I thought it was him. It was stupid. I shouldn't have answered. Man, he's gonna kill me."

"No, he's not. Because you're not going back there."

His face began to redden now, and he looked up at her with pleading eyes. "I *gotta* go back. You don't understand. Lisa's still there. He told me the sins of the brothers are visited on the siblings. It's in the Bible."

"That's not in the Bible, Jimmy. That's something he made up."

"He'll still hurt Lisa if he thinks I ratted on him. He swore he would, and I know it's true."

"Jimmy, even if you did go back, don't you know Bill's going to go ballistic when he sees you after this botched-up break-in?"

"He hates mistakes," he whispered, leaning back against the wall and clutching his head. "But at least he'll go off on me and not Lisa. She didn't do anything. She doesn't even know about all the stuff Bill makes us do. I don't want her to know."

"But don't you want Bill stopped? Wouldn't it be great if he could get caught and arrested for what he's done?"

"No!" he shouted. "*I'll* get arrested, too. Bill didn't break into anybody's house. *I* did. I'll be the one they put in prison. Not him."

"Jimmy, that's all just a lie. He tells you that to keep you doing what he wants. He wants you to be afraid. But the truth is that they don't put little kids in prison. How old are you, anyway? Eight, nine?"

"I'm ten," he said, insulted. "I'm just . . . short for my age."

"Probably why he chose you. You can fit into small places. But Jimmy, they don't put ten-year-olds in prison. And if they stop Bill, they'll put you and Lisa and all the other kids into a decent place—"

"That *is* a decent place," he screamed. "Don't you get it?"

"Just because something is familiar, Jimmy, it doesn't mean it's good."

"It doesn't *have* to be good."

She rubbed her face, wondering what she should do. Call the police? Or Nick Hutchins? Go against this kid's will and turn him in, or let him go back?

He was afraid that he would go to prison, and she couldn't blame him. Bill had probably pounded that threat into his brain.

She took his arm and led him to the kitchen, picked up the phone, and started dialing.

"Who are you calling?" he asked.

"My friend, Nick Hutchins. He's a social worker. He'll know what to do."

"No!" The kid jerked away from her. "Are you crazy? No social workers! I'm tellin' you, he'll beat the daylights out of Lisa, just to get back at me."

"Maybe Nick can get your sister out of there."

"Nick? The one who *put* us in there? No way! Lady, you're gonna ruin everything!"

"Jimmy, I want you to call me Beth," she said. "I'm going to help you."

Tears came to his eyes, and he swatted them away. Under his breath, Jimmy muttered, "I ain't calling you nothing."

Beth heard what he said but ignored him. Of course he was angry. Of course he was afraid. So was she.

She breathed a sigh of relief when Nick answered the phone. "Nick, I was wondering if you could come over. I need to see you."

At the other end of the line, Nick hesitated. "I could get there in a couple of hours or so. I'm kind of tied up right now."

"It's really important." She glanced at the boy. "There's something I need for you to see."

"What is it? You're not going to keep me in suspense until I can get there, are you?"

"I have to," she said. "Nick, come as soon as you can."

"Is it the article? Have you finished it?"

"No," she said. "I got a little sidetracked. I'm still working on it, though."

"Are you all right?"

"Yes. For now, yes."

She could almost hear the wheels turning in Nick's head. "Beth, just hold tight. I'll be there as soon as I can tie up some loose ends here."

"All right, I'll see you then." She hung up the phone and gave Jimmy a look.

"I thought you were gonna tell him," he said, wiping his face.

"Not over the phone. I want him to see you in person. He's a nice guy, Jimmy. He cares about you."

"He doesn't care about me! None of them do! I *hate* social workers. They don't care if they separate sisters and brothers, or if they take you out of one place to put you in a worse place. They don't care about nothing."

Her heart ached for this jaded child. "Jimmy, you've obviously had some bad breaks. But Nick is going to change your opinion of social workers. I promise you."

"Yeah, I've heard promises before, too," he said. "Let's face it, lady. I'm sunk. The sooner we get this whole thing over with, the better."

CHAPTER FOURTEEN

While they waited for Nick, Beth made breakfast for the boy, who attacked the food as if he'd been starving to death. She sat with him as he ate, sipping on her coffee and studying him.

"What did Bill tell you about me?" she asked.

He hesitated, then shrugged. "Nothing. Just told me to come in here and get the papers and tapes. And dump the files about us on your computer."

She frowned. "He didn't say why?"

"Said you were gonna write a story about us. That we'd all go to jail if you did."

"I'm writing a story about *him*. He's the only one going to jail—he and the other adults working with him. But not the kids, Jimmy. I'm not out to get the kids." She wiped the wet ring from his glass off her table, then looked up at him again. "Did you find anything?"

"No, nothing."

"That's because I had most of it with me, and I hadn't put anything on the computer yet. I imagine he was planning to kill me before I got home, and then he would have destroyed any evidence I had with me." She thought about that for a moment. "Why do you think he *didn't* come out here last night? If he knew where I was, and that you were still here, why didn't he come?"

"I don't know. I kept thinking he would. Maybe he thought I got away, and that you called the police after he followed you. Maybe he was too scared to come."

"Bill Brandon, scared? I don't think so."

The boy looked up and stared at her for a moment. "You know him, don't you?"

She met his eyes, then looked away. The doorbell rang, and she got up, grateful for the chance to evade the question. "Maybe that's Nick," she said.

"Or maybe it's Bill."

She stopped halfway to the door, reached into her table drawer, and pulled out her pistol. *It's not as if Jimmy doesn't know I have one*, she thought, *I almost shot him with it an hour ago.*

Peeking through the curtain, she saw Nick, and quickly put the gun away before opening the door. "Nick, you got here sooner than I thought."

"Had to. You had me so curious." He stepped into the house and saw the little freckle-faced boy with a milk mustache, his red hair tousled and unkempt. "Who's this?"

Beth drew in a deep breath. "Nick, this is Jimmy. A very interesting kid, with a very interesting story. Why don't you sit down? This could take a while."

When he'd heard Jimmy's story, Nick seemed ready to burst with excitement. "He's just what we need! A witness, from the inside."

"They're not gonna listen to me. I'm just a kid," Jimmy said. "And none of the others will talk. They're too scared."

"They *will* listen to you," Nick said. "Once we get your story into the paper, the police will be banging down the doors of that home."

"And the kids will be scattered all over the state," Jimmy added, "and brothers and sisters will be separated, and some of us will be in awful places . . ."

Nick hesitated, giving Jimmy a long look. "Jimmy, don't you want out of that home? Don't you realize what he's done to you? He's not only risking your life, he's using you to commit crimes, training you and the others to be crooks. That's child abuse."

"Can you get Lisa out? Can you keep us together? If you can't, I'm not telling anything. Nothing. You can find another witness."

"Jimmy, I can try my best to keep the two of you together. But Lisa's going to be better off no matter where we put her."

"Bull!" Jimmy shouted, his eyes filling with angry tears. "She depends on me. She's probably worried to death right now. She thinks I left her, just like—" The word fell off, and he turned away. "When can you get her out?"

"As soon as I relate all this to the police." Nick paused and shot Beth an eloquent look. "I know you want to get the story done first, but do you think you can finish it in the next couple of hours? If Brandon thinks you're ready to go public, we don't have a lot of time. I want to get those kids out of there."

She looked at all her evidence scattered across the table. "I think I might be able to pull something together by then. But then my editor—"

"Great. Beth, do you realize that this is the break I've been looking for? That we might really be able to shut down that home?"

"Yes," she said softly, touching Jimmy's shoulder, though he shook her hand away. "I realize it. It's a dream of mine, too."

"Oh, man. Jimmy," Nick said, "you could be a hero because of this. A regular celebrity. And your life of crime is over. Nobody's going to make you break into people's homes ever again."

But Jimmy didn't look so sure.

"Hey, why don't you come with me, Jimmy? We could hang out while Beth finishes the story."

"I don't want to go anywhere with you."

"He can stay here," Beth said. "He can just watch TV or something while I work. It'll be all right. He's quiet as a mouse. Proved that last night. My only fear is that Brandon will show up."

"Don't worry about that. I think I'll pay him a visit right now."

"What for?"

"I'm allowed to make impromptu inspections whenever I want. I'll just hang around there, inspecting the cottages and all. That way we can be sure he stays where he is."

"Okay," Beth said. "I'll do the best I can. But are you going to mention Jimmy? Should we call the police about finding him?"

Nick considered that. "No, I don't think so. They'd just report it to Sheila or me. Let's keep this just between us for now. I could lose my job, but I'll risk it. And I can't wait to see how Bill handles Jimmy's disappearance."

He patted Jimmy's shoulder. "Jimmy, you just relax, all right? I'll try to check on Lisa while I'm there."

"Will you tell her I'm okay? That I haven't left her?"

Nick hesitated. "I don't think that's a good idea, Jimmy. It might put her in danger. If she tells anyone, Bill could hear about it."

"She keeps secrets," he said. "She won't tell."

"She might do it without meaning to. But relax. In a little while, we can go in there and get her out for good."

That wasn't good enough for Jimmy. Brooding, he slumped on the couch.

"I'll call you in a couple of hours, Beth," Nick said, rising.

Beth walked him to the door and bolted it behind him.

CHAPTER FIFTEEN

L ock the door, Brad."

Bill's order was clipped and direct. The eleven-year-old boy could tell from Bill's voice and from the look on his face that this was going to be one of those meetings Brad would wish he hadn't attended. Not that he had a choice. He locked the door when the last of the dozen kids in Bill's group of "favorites" filed in, then took his seat beside his best friend, Keith.

The faces of the children were solemn—even frightened. Bill didn't often call them together in broad daylight. It drew too much attention from the other kids. But this morning he had made them all get up early, even though it was summer and they didn't have school, and file into the meeting room next to Bill's office for what he called a "briefing."

Something had happened, Brad thought, and he was sure it had something to do with Jimmy Westin.

Bill's face was angry as he paced in front of the dead-silent children, tapping a metal ruler against his palm and examining their faces one by one. "We've had a development, people," he said. "A rather upsetting development. I thought I should prepare you so you'd know what to expect." Suddenly he slammed the ruler down on a table, making all of them jump. "Jimmy Westin was arrested last night."

A collective gasp sounded in the room, and the children gaped up at him for more details.

"He got sloppy," he went on. "Let himself get caught during a mission. Now he's paying for it."

Brad whispered a curse, and anger surged inside him that his friend could be so stupid. He had always thought that Jimmy wasn't careful enough. He hadn't worked at it, like Brad had.

The boy looked up at Bill and struggled with the question weighing on his mind. "Was it adult jail, or the detention center?" Either way, it was bad, but in their room late at night, the boys sometimes speculated about what would happen if they got caught.

"I hate to say it," Bill said, "but they're holding him in the adult facility. A year ago, he may have gone to juvenile hall, but after the last election, Florida passed the Adult Crime-Adult Time Law. You do a grown-up crime—and they do include burglary—and you serve with the meanest, toughest criminals in the state.

"I wish I could tell you that I could get him out. But I'm afraid it doesn't work that way. Because he's a ward of the state, he's considered high risk, which means that—according to HRS—if I can't make something out of him, he's probably a lost cause. So they're processing him into the justice system, where he's likely to stay for at least ten or twenty years."

Brad wasn't sure he followed all of this. He often had a hard time understanding much of what Bill said. But the ten-to-twenty-years part didn't escape him. That was practically Jimmy's whole life.

"I think you all know what this means," Bill said, slapping his palm with the ruler again. "It means that every one of you is in trouble. If Jimmy Westin talks, you might go down with him."

Brad tried to imagine what Jimmy might say if he was tortured or threatened. Would he drag them all down with him? Or would he hang tough and keep his mouth shut?

"I don't think he'll talk," Bill went on, as if he'd read Brad's mind. "We have Lisa. As long as Jimmy knows that his sins will be visited on his sister, we'll be all right. And just to make sure *she* doesn't talk, I'm going to get her to replace Jimmy, and put a little fear into her myself."

Silence hung in the air as everyone imagined what he might mean by that.

"Okay, listen up. People are going to be coming around here, asking questions about Jimmy. Those people are *not* our friends;

they'll be out to get us. Until I tell you differently, I want you to pretend Jimmy's still here. If HRS comes snooping around, act like he just left the cottage, or the playground, or wherever you are. You just saw him a minute ago. Got it?"

One of the girls frowned. "Won't they *know* where he is?"

Bill shook his head. "Not necessarily. 'The right hand knows not what the left hand doeth.'" None of them knew what that meant, but it sounded biblical, and thus, scary. "HRS is not in touch that much with the police. And I don't want them to know that one of *my* kids is a jailbird. Besides, they might start looking at each of you, one at a time. I don't want you to wind up where Jimmy is."

He paced the room again, this time walking between their perches on arms of sofas, tabletops, or on the floor. "But we can overcome this obstacle, if we try. Are you people up for it?"

A weak chorus of yeses sounded around the room.

"I can't hear you!"

"Yes!" they shouted.

"You're not ordinary kids! You're gifted with special skills. As the Good Book says, 'Many are called, but few are chosen.' You are the chosen. *My* chosen. You're called to a higher purpose—a mission that isn't for the faint of heart. You're called to excellence, people. And you *are* excellent. That's why I chose you. That's why you are my hands and my feet. That's why you are favored among God and men!"

It didn't matter that his words made little sense to Brad or the others. It sounded good and hopeful, and it elevated them to something more than orphaned children. It made them special.

When the children had gone back to their cottages, Bill went through his office into the room where closed-circuit television screens showed him what was happening around the campus. He watched the children going back to their cottages. Some whispered among themselves, but he knew those conversations would be harmless, so he let it go. Seeing no cause for concern, he went back into his office, sat down behind his desk, and thought over the things he'd told them. They'd believed everything. It was so easy to manipulate them. "Adult Crime-Adult Time Law"—what a laugh. There was no such thing.

He just hoped that dirty-faced brat didn't turn on him. And why had no one called him about the boy yet? If he was in police custody, wouldn't they have reported it to him?

He looked at the phone and wondered if *he* should call *them* and act like a concerned guardian worried about a missing child. But then he would have to explain why it had taken him so long to report the disappearance. He could say that he'd put the boy to bed himself—but that Jimmy had sneaked away during the night, so that he hadn't known Jimmy was missing until this morning.

It might work. And it would certainly cover him in the event that Jimmy *did* talk.

But maybe he was jumping to conclusions here. What if the kid wasn't in custody? Calling could open a whole can of worms that Bill didn't want to open. Investigations, news reports, posters all over town . . .

No, he couldn't chance it. He'd have to wait. If the police did have the boy and if they showed up to ask him about Jimmy, he could say that he'd been duped. After all, the police were always quick to assume the worst about these parentless, high-risk kids, who'd been products of alcohol, drugs, selfishness. The police, like everyone else, expected the children to continue the pattern set by their parents. As Bill himself was often quick to remind the police and others, you could take the kid out of the trash, but you couldn't take the trash out of the kid. And no one ever argued with him about it.

Yes, his best bet was to do nothing, then plead ignorance if the police called. It was the safest course.

CHAPTER SIXTEEN

he old Western on TV didn't hold Jimmy's attention, nor did the puppy who kept wanting to play tug-of-war with him. He could hear Beth's fingers on the keyboard upstairs as she wrote the story that would bring the walls of the St. Clair Children's Home tumbling down— exactly what Bill had sent him here to prevent.

He let the puppy win the tug-of-war with the sock, then watched him curl up on the floor to chew on it. Jimmy's eyes strayed up the open stairway. With just a slight lean, she could see him, and she'd kept a close watch on him all morning. He had kept an eye on her, too. Up there, disks were lying around. Papers. All the things that Bill wanted. If he took those things back to Bill, maybe Bill would go easy on him. Maybe Lisa wouldn't have to suffer.

But Beth wouldn't let that stop her; she would write the story anyway. Besides, she had been nice to him, and he didn't want to rip her off now. She could have reported him to the police, but she hadn't. It was like she believed he was a good person when she hardly even knew him—like she thought the bad things he had done weren't his fault. Anyone else would have hung a guilty sign on him and handed him over to the cops.

No, he couldn't turn on her now. But he still worried about Lisa. If there was just some way that he could talk to her, tell her to hold on, that he hadn't just left her.

His eyes strayed to the telephone. Could he get away with just calling her? Clicking the remote control, he turned up the television as the shoot-out raged louder. He picked up the phone, then took it to a part of the living room where he was just out of her sight. Quickly he dialed the direct number to his and Lisa's cottage. It rang, and Stella, the housemother, answered.

He tried to disguise his voice. "Can I speak to Lisa, please?"

"Who is this?" Stella asked. "Jimmy, is that you? Where in blue blazes are you?"

As if it had stung his hand, he hung up the phone quickly and backed away from it. Oh, great. Now Stella would tell Bill that he had called, and Bill would be madder than ever that he'd been near a phone and hadn't tried to reach him. When he found out Jimmy had tried to reach Lisa, Bill would fly into a rage—and when he finally found Jimmy, as he would eventually, he would get even.

The worst part was that Lisa still wouldn't know that her brother hadn't abandoned her just like every other person she'd ever loved had done.

CHAPTER SEVENTEEN

B ill didn't like Nick Hutchins. The social worker seemed to have it in for him. Nick had been giving him too much grief lately. His monthly inspections of the home had stepped up to twice monthly, and he seemed too curious about the children, especially those who'd been caught in petty crimes. Bill had tried to explain to him that he wasn't responsible for the value systems of these kids before they came to his home, but that he did the best he could with what he got. If one of them occasionally got himself into trouble, it wasn't Bill's fault.

Now, as Bill followed the man from cottage to cottage, as if Nick expected to find some horrible violation that would warrant a severe reprimand from the state, he wondered what Nick was looking for. Did this impromptu inspection have anything to do with Jimmy's disappearance?

"Are all the kids on the premises right now?" Nick asked casually, walking into a playroom and scanning the children playing games.

So, he does know that Jimmy's missing. Bill struggled with the idea of candidly admitting to the kid's disappearance. But he couldn't understand why Nick was being so secretive. Why didn't Nick just come out and ask him where Jimmy was, and how long the boy had been missing? No, maybe he was just being paranoid. He decided not to mention it yet. "No, actually," he said. "We took a vanload to the library this morning. Some of the others had swimming lessons at the Y."

Nick peered at him skeptically.

They had just turned up the hall so that Nick could snoop in the bedrooms when Stella, the housemother of Cottage B, burst in. "Uh, Bill, could I have a word with you, please?"

"Certainly," Bill said. "Nick, you'll excuse me for a moment, won't you?"

Nick nodded but didn't say anything, and Bill felt the man's eyes on the back of his neck as he followed Stella out of earshot.

"What is it?"

"It's Jimmy. He called just now, trying to disguise his voice. He wanted to speak to Lisa."

His eyebrows shot up. "Where is he?"

"I don't know. He hung up before I could—"

"I'll find out. Go back in there and keep that jerk from doing us any harm. I have to go to my office for a minute."

He rushed out of the cottage and across the lawn to his office and bolted inside. He unlocked a closet and checked the Caller ID he kept so that he could monitor the origin of calls coming into each of the cottages. When he'd opened the home, he had had an extension to each line installed right here in his office. He also taped all of the calls made on any campus telephone, either incoming or outgoing. It was what he called quality control. You never really knew whom you could trust. And of course no one, not even his "inner circle" of staff, knew what was in this closet.

He checked the Caller ID for Cottage B—and saw the name *E. J. Wright*. Bill's heart jumped. Elizabeth Wright. Beth. Jimmy was still in her house? Was he nuts? Hadn't he told that kid to get out of there? But Jimmy hadn't asked to speak to Bill, who could come and get him, but he'd asked instead for Lisa—and in a disguised voice.

Something was wrong. Jimmy had turned on him.

What was he telling Beth? Bill rubbed his forehead and found it cool and wet with sweat. Was Jimmy giving her more fodder for her story? That little twerp knew enough to bring down his whole operation.

Bill hadn't had a lot of time to think this morning—first the cops had come to tell him about Marlene's death and ask a ton of questions, and then Nick Hutchins had shown up. But this situation didn't require a lot of thought.

He was going to have to kill both Beth and Jimmy, before she could turn that story in.

His face hardened with violent determination as he cut back across the lawn to the playground behind Cottage B. He saw Lisa, Jimmy's little sister, sitting alone on a swing, drawing figures in the dirt with the tip of her toe. Her strawberry-blonde hair strung down in her eyes, and he could see from her red eyes that she'd been crying.

He approached her, and she looked up fearfully. "Come here, darlin'," he said, taking her hand. "Come with me."

Her innocent eyes widened. "Where?"

"We got some trainin' to do. I'm about to promote you from orphan to executive. What do you think about that?"

He could see that she didn't have a clue what he was talking about. "I don't know."

"See, since Jimmy's gone and got himself in trouble, I'm giving you his job. It was a real important job. You think you're smart enough for it?"

Tears filled her eyes, but she nodded bravely. "When is Jimmy coming back?" she managed to ask through trembling lips.

"Good question," he said. "Probably never."

CHAPTER EIGHTEEN

ill didn't like to get his hands dirty. That was why he always used the children. It kept him nice and distant, and if the children were ever caught breaking and entering, he could throw up his hands and insist that he'd tried as hard as he could to keep tabs on them, but children would be children, and there wasn't a lot he could do about kids who'd been born among criminals—except love them and show them compassion and hope that some good would rub off on them.

Sure, Bill had compassion. So much compassion that he really wished he could see the look on Beth and Jimmy's faces as they opened the cigar box he was "doctoring" for them.

"Know what this is, darlin'?" he asked Lisa, gesturing toward the cigar box open on the desk before him.

"No, sir."

"It's a little package we're sending to a friend," he said. "A friend who's been real good to me. And I'm gonna let you deliver it for me."

She didn't say anything, just sat in the corner, trying hard not to move.

He set the explosives in carefully, then rigged up the detonator caps so that the bomb would go off the moment the box was opened. He'd never done this before, actually, but he'd read all about it in articles on the Internet about the Unabomber. It was no secret, and he and some of his partners had discussed the precise methods more than once. He couldn't believe how perfectly this would work out—except that those two traitors wouldn't get this little present until tomorrow, which could be a problem if Beth finished her story and turned it in to her editor before that. In that case, he'd have to make sure the newspaper didn't get his story out by then. In any event, if there were any questions about Bill's involvement in the explosion, he would be able to prove that he was miles away when the explosion occurred.

He closed the box carefully and wrapped it, then addressed it to Beth Wright and affixed an Express Mail waybill.

"You ready to deliver this for me, darlin'?"

Lisa hesitated. "Where?"

"The post office. You're big enough to take something in by yourself, aren't you? You don't even have to talk to anybody. Just drop it in the slot, and my friend will have it by tomorrow."

She nodded.

"If you do a good job, Lisa, honey, I'll give you a more important job, like the kind I gave Jimmy. And if you do a bad job . . . well . . ." He propped his chin on his hand and smiled. "Remember that time Jimmy had to stay in bed for two days because he couldn't walk so good? Remember those bruises?"

She seemed frozen.

"Well, just don't do a bad job, darlin'." He took the package and her hand and led her out to his pickup. He'd parked his Buick in a toolshed at the back of the property; even a stupid cop would be able to match the dents and paint scratches on it to the marks on Beth's car, so he didn't plan to drive it until some of his staff had painted it.

Across the lawn, he saw Nick coming out of one of the cottages—and heading toward him.

He cursed. "Get in, Lisa, and put the package under the seat."

She did as she was told, and Bill closed the door and walked around to the driver's side. "You about finished snooping, Nick?" he asked in a pseudo-jovial voice.

"Maybe," Nick said. "I just wondered where you're taking her."

"To a birthday party," he said. "One of her little friends at school. Don't think a kid should miss all the fun just because they're wards of the state, do you?"

Nick looked down at the little girl, and Bill wondered if he knew who she was. He wished she didn't look quite so fragile.

"She's a little worried 'cause she's late. I clean forgot about it, but no harm done. She'll get there before they blow out the candles if we hurry."

Nick backed away from the truck. Bill could see that he was trying to think of a way to detain him. What was Nick up to?

"When will you be back, Bill? I want to talk to you."

"Won't be long. Haven't we talked enough? Don't you have something constructive to do? The state isn't paying you to hang around here all day, are they?"

Nick wasn't intimidated. "Get somebody else to take her, Bill. I'm not finished with you."

Bill groaned and got out of the truck. "All right, hold on. I'll get Stella, but I'll have to make sure somebody's watching the kids before she comes." He looked at Lisa with an apologetic face. "Sugar, you're gonna be a little bit late, but we'll get you there somehow."

Lisa looked perplexed.

He helped Lisa out of the truck and took her into his office to make sure that Nick didn't speak privately with her. He called over to Cottage B. "Stella, I need you to come run an errand for me. If you run into Nick, tell him that you're taking Lisa to a birthday party, but don't mention her name. Call her Susan. He might know about Jimmy, and her name might ring a bell."

"Doesn't he already know her?"

"It's been three years since he's dealt with either of them. He won't remember."

"Where am I really going?" she asked.

"To the post office. Drop Lisa off at the corner and let her put the package in the 'express' slot."

"Is Lisa going to be one of your regulars now?" she asked. "Isn't she a little young?"

"She's perfect. Just get over here. And don't botch this up. I've had enough problems lately, and I'm not in a good mood. If you mess this up, everything could blow up in our faces."

He hung up and took in a deep breath. "If that man asks your name, you tell him it's Susan. Do you hear me?"

Lisa nodded, her eyes big.

"You put the package in the Express Mail slot, and if anyone asks you what it is, you say it's a book for your grandma. Got it?"

She nodded.

"Just do as I say, and when you get back, I'll have a surprise for you."

Her eyebrows shot up. "Will Jimmy be home then?"

He decided he might need that leverage. "He might just be, darlin'."

He led her back outside as Stella hurried across the lawn. "Come on, sugar. Let's get you to that party."

CHAPTER NINETEEN

eth sat back in her squeaky desk chair and sighed. Her article was finished—complete with the quotes by Marlene and Jimmy, along with the sad and suggestive news that Marlene had been murdered immediately after giving the interview. She wished she had another hour to tweak it, but she sensed that time was tight. Sitting forward again, she sent it by modem into the paper, then e-mailed her editor to look for it and call her back. As an afterthought, she electronically transferred the transcribed conversation with Marlene so that it would be on file at the newspaper office.

She went downstairs. Jimmy and the puppy were lying on the area rug in front of the television, curled up together as if they were old friends. She stepped around them and saw that they were both sound asleep.

She smiled. How exhausted Jimmy must be, after spending the night in terror in the attic.

The telephone rang, and she snapped it up. "Hello?"

"Beth, I got your article." It was Phil, her editor.

"Read it yet?"

"Yep. Interesting. Very interesting. Sure is going to cause a big stir."

"Phil, this is headline material. You'll print it in the Saturday edition tomorrow, won't you?"

He hesitated. "I don't know, Beth. I'm a little reluctant."

"Why?" she asked. "What's wrong with it?"

"I'd like a few more quotes. The only two people quoted are a dead woman and a little kid who might just have a vivid imagination."

"Was it my imagination that the kid broke into my house last night, Phil? I didn't make that up. He's here now."

"Still, I'd feel better if you could get another quote or two. Somebody who's not dead or a juvenile delinquent."

"Juvenile delinquent? How do you figure that?"

"Hey, don't get defensive. I'm just pointing out how it's going to look to a skeptical public. He did break into your house."

"Didn't you read the article? He was *forced* to. And Marlene's dead *because* of the article."

"The kid's story is suspect, Beth. Sorry, but that's the truth. And you *say* the woman died because of your interview; the police haven't concluded that yet. We need more. Maybe you can find someone who grew up in Brandon's home, someone who's not under his thumb anymore. Maybe they'd be willing to talk. That would be just what we need. And call the police stations in all of the towns within a two-hour radius. Find out how often there was evidence that kids had done it. You know, fingerprints, footprints, maybe they saw them but didn't catch them, that sort of thing."

She closed her eyes and started to feel sick. "If I compiled all that today, Phil, would you print it tomorrow? It's crucial. This whole thing is taking on a life of its own. Something has to be done with Jimmy, and he's worried about his little sister—with good reason—but we can't get the kids out of there until there's enough evidence. But if I turn him over to the police, *he* may suffer instead of Bill Brandon—"

"Yes, Beth," Phil cut in. "Get me what I asked for and I'll run it. You have my word."

She let out a heavy breath and dropped the phone in its cradle. What was she going to do?

She closed her eyes and asked herself if she had the guts to do what was necessary. The right thing never seemed that easy, and it had an awful lot of conditions attached.

But she had spent the last three years trying to make something of herself. She had found a church, and now she went every Sunday. She tried hard to live by the Ten Commandments—don't lie, don't covet, don't commit adultery. In fact, some people thought she followed God's laws to a fault, but she figured she had enough sin in her life that it would take fifty years of walking the straight and narrow to get to the point where she'd come close to making herself worthy of God.

But this was hard. Writing this story Phil's way meant digging deeper than she'd wanted to dig, exposing things she hadn't wanted exposed . . .

And it meant that she would need advice about the law.

She picked up the phone and dialed the number of Lynda Barrett's law office. Lynda, a devoted Christian and respected lawyer, was one of the teachers in Beth's Sunday school class. Maybe she could help.

Paige, Lynda's secretary and another friend from church, put Beth right through to Lynda.

"Hi, Beth. What's up?"

"Hi, Lynda. Uh . . . I'm sorry to bother you. I just . . . I wondered if you could come by and see me today. It's pretty important. I need some advice, and I need it quickly."

"Legal advice?"

"Yes. It has to do with a story I'm working on. It involves a little boy. I'd rather tell you about it in person, if you have time, and I'd rather not come there."

"I could come right now. I was supposed to be in court this afternoon, but it was postponed, so I'm free."

"Great. Oh, and bring Jake if you want. My little friend might like to meet him. Kids love pilots."

CHAPTER TWENTY

Stella let the truck idle at the corner near the post office. "All right, Lisa. Take the package and go. Put it in the Express Mail slot. Then hurry back to the truck. Try not to talk to anybody."

Lisa got the package from under the seat. It was heavier than it looked, but she dared not complain. She got out of the pickup, clutching the package against her chest, and backed into the door to close it.

Walking rapidly, she hurried toward the post office door. Shifting the package to one arm, she tried to open the door, but it was heavy and she almost dropped it.

A man came to the door and opened it for her. "There you go, honey."

"Thank you," she said almost inaudibly. She stood inside the post office, looking around at the boxes and stamp vending machines and slots. Through some glass doors were the postal workers, and a dozen people waited in line.

The package was getting heavier, so she shifted it again, trying to get a more comfortable hold on it. Stella had said to put it in a slot. She saw the slots marked "local" and "stamped" and "metered." He'd said to put it in Express Mail, but she didn't see that one.

It was too heavy for her to hold any longer, so she went to the "metered" slot and tried to fit it through the small opening. It wouldn't fit.

"That's not where you want to put that, pumpkin," one of the postal workers walking through told her. "That'll have to go in Express Mail over there."

"Oh." She headed across the room to where he pointed, and looked up at the lever, which was too high for her.

"Here, sweetheart, I'll get it," the postman said. He opened the small door and took the package from her. The weight surprised him. "Boy, this is heavy. Whatcha got in here, anyway?"

She tried to speak, but her voice wouldn't come. Clearing her throat, she tried again. "A book for my grandma," she said just under her breath.

He smiled and let the door close. "I'll just take it on back, pumpkin."

She only stood staring at him for a moment, not sure what to do. Finally, she decided she'd better get back to the car before Stella left her. "Thank you," she said again, and walked quickly to the door.

Stella was still waiting at the corner. Lisa ran up the sidewalk and climbed into the pickup.

"What took you so long?" Stella demanded.

"I don't know."

"Well, did you put the package in the Express Mail slot?"

Lisa thought of telling her about the man, but a dread came over her that she might be punished for giving the package to him. "Yes," she said.

"Did you talk to anyone?"

"No."

Stella breathed out a sigh of relief as she turned the corner and headed back to the home. After a moment, she muttered, "I oughta get hazard pay for this."

Lisa turned around and looked out the back window, wondering if the man had really mailed the package, or if he'd opened it and looked inside. She hoped it wasn't anything too awful.

She sat back down and tried to console herself with the thought that Jimmy might be back when she returned to the home. Wouldn't he be proud that she was smart enough to work for Bill now, too?

B eth poured two cups of coffee and brought them to the table where Lynda sat, filling in the notes she had made as Beth told her of the allegations she was about to make concerning the home, and what Jimmy's part had been in it. As Jimmy and Jake sat on the floor playing with the puppy, Beth quietly popped the question she had been waiting to ask.

"I wondered, Lynda, what kind of responsibility Jimmy and the other kids who've worked in Bill Brandon's crime ring will have. In other words, are they accountable for something they were forced to do?"

"You mean, can they be prosecuted?" Lynda asked.

Jimmy looked up, and she knew he'd overheard. She wished she hadn't asked.

"Well, breaking and entering is definitely a crime," Lynda said, "and under ordinary circumstances, a child Jimmy's age who committed a crime like that would be sent to the detention center, depending on the judge's disposition and the number of offenses against the child. But these are extenuating circumstances, and I find it hard to believe that any judge or jury would blame Jimmy or the other kids for being victims of Brandon's control."

Beth looked down at the coffee cup in her hand. "There's someone I know, who I might try to interview. She's someone who was in Brandon's home a few years ago. She's an adult now, and I'm hoping she'll corroborate what I've already uncovered. But she might be worried that she'll be prosecuted if she confesses. Would she?"

"Well, that depends. How old was she when she stopped committing the crimes?"

"Eighteen. She stopped when she left the home."

Lynda blew out a breath, and shook her head. "That's a tough one. A jury might say that she was old enough to know right from wrong."

"But if she'd been doing it since she was ten, and she was scared to death of him, and she knew that she had no choice but to do everything he said . . ."

"It would depend on her lawyer, Beth, and what kind of case he laid out."

"But you think she would *need* a lawyer? That there would be charges against her? Isn't the statute of limitations in Florida three years?"

"Well, yes. Has it been longer than that?"

"Just barely," Beth said. "Does that means she'd be clear?"

"Yes, she would. But any of those legal adults who stole for Bill within that three-year period would be at the judge's mercy."

"What about loopholes? Is there any way they could ignore the statute of limitations and prosecute her anyway?"

"It's possible that they could get her for something else. Something like withholding evidence or aiding and abetting."

"But she hasn't aided or abetted. Not since she left the home."

"Still, just by keeping her mouth shut she was allowing the crimes to go on."

"But that isn't fair! How much can someone be accountable when they've never had free will? When their every thought has been controlled by that man? When they're totally dependent on him for food and clothing and shelter, and they're afraid of his discipline if they don't do what he asks?"

"It may not be fair, Beth, but that's the justice system."

"Well, if that's the case, then it wouldn't be worth her while to talk, would it? Anyone would be better off keeping their mouth shut, even if they were outside the statute of limitations. And even then their reputation could be ruined—future job opportunities, credit, housing . . ."

"Technically, yes. But there's a moral issue that might outweigh all that," Lynda said. "There are children being abused and warped. Without *someone* stepping forward, it'll never end. Is it worth her reputation? I can't answer that. All I know is that God honors those who honor him by doing the right thing."

"When?" Beth asked, staring at the lines of her palm.

"When what?"

"When does God honor the person who honors him? How much of a sacrifice does he demand first?"

Lynda looked a little surprised by the question. "That depends on the person, Beth," Lynda said. "To one man Christ said to sell everything he owned. To another, he just said to go and sin no more. It all depends on what dark thing is in a person's heart, separating them from him. Mostly all he wants is confession and repentance."

"Yeah, that's the part I have trouble with," Beth said. "There are some buried things in life that you just don't want to dig up again."

Lynda's eyes lingered on her for a moment. "Confession is risky, all right. No question. But it's cleansing, Beth. Tell your source that the release that she feels afterward will overshadow anything the justice system can do to her. After repentance, she still might face consequences of some kind, but she won't be alone. God will walk with her and provide for her in all of that."

Beth tried to let it all soak in, but she wasn't sure she bought it.

"So when do you think the story will come out?" Jake asked from the floor.

"Tomorrow, if I can manage to get everything finished. It really has to be tomorrow. We can't wait any longer."

"My sister's there," Jimmy explained.

Lynda and Jake looked fully at Jimmy and saw the concern on his face. "Are you worried about your sister, Jimmy?" Lynda asked.

"Yes. He warned me. He said, 'The sins of the brothers are visited upon their siblings.' He knows the Bible real good."

"That's not in the Bible, kiddo," Jake said.

"I told him that," Beth said. "But Brandon always misquotes Scripture. He rewords verses and gives them a perverted, sinister meaning, and uses them like weapons against the children." She hesitated. "I've heard that from several people."

"Well, the more I hear, the more I think you need to get this story finished no matter what you have to do. Why don't Jake and I take Jimmy to stay with us while you work?"

Jimmy looked hopefully up at her.

"Sure," Jake said. "We could do some guy stuff."

"But we haven't reported finding him. I'm not sure what the police would do. We were just going to hide him until the arrests are made."

Jimmy sprang to his feet. "Please? It'll be all right. Nobody'll see me."

Beth gave Lynda a narrow look. "Are you sure you wouldn't feel compelled to report him?"

"Of course not," Lynda said. "I agree with you. It's best to hide him quietly for a while, as long as HRS knows."

"We could go out to the airport and take him up."

"In an airplane?" Jimmy asked, his eyes huge.

"Sure, in an airplane. Unless you know some other way to fly."

"Can I, Beth? That would be so great! None of the other kids would even believe it!"

Beth couldn't help laughing. "I guess that's all right, if Jake promises he won't crash."

"I beg your pardon," Jake said, insulted.

"It's not like you haven't done it before."

Jake gave a smirk. "It'll never happen again. Jimmy's not scared, are you, Jimmy?"

Jimmy looked a little less exuberant now. "You crashed?"

They all laughed. "It's a long story. We'll tell you about it on the way."

Beth walked them all to the door, said her good-byes to Jimmy, and watched them drive away.

For a moment, she contemplated what Lynda had said, trying to draw it into the core of her heart, her faith. It was too great a risk—yet all those children had no one fighting for them, no one to make things right. *Somebody* had to talk.

She looked through her Rolodex and found her old friend's number. All of the "graduates" of Bill Brandon's home kept unlisted phone numbers and very private addresses, so he couldn't reach them. They all continued to live in fear, to one degree or another. But Maria had trustingly shared her number with Beth, who had never expected to use it for a favor like this.

She picked up the phone and dialed Maria's number at home. Maria had gotten pregnant shortly after leaving the home, and was

now the mother of twin two-year-olds. She had a sweet, support-
ive husband—ten years her senior. Beth hoped that Maria was
happy; she hated to drag all this up now. But Maria was her best
chance for getting cooperation.

"Hello?"

Beth smiled at the sound of her voice. "Maria, hi. It's Beth
Wright. I mean . . . Beth Sullivan." It had been a long time since
she'd used that name.

"Beth! It's good to hear from you. How are you?"

"I'm great," she said, but couldn't manage to work any enthusiasm into her voice. "Listen, I was wondering if you'd have time
to meet me for lunch today. I know you have the kids and all. I
could pick up hamburgers and meet you at the park or something
so they could play. I just need to talk to you about something."

"Sure. I'd love to see you. But what do you need to talk to me
about?"

"It's about Bill Brandon."

Dead silence hung between them for an intense moment.
Finally, Maria said, "What about him?"

"There's just some stuff I need to talk to you about, but I'd
rather do it in person."

"All right. What time?"

Beth didn't know what to expect Maria to look like; it had been
nearly three years since she'd seen her. But the girl looked much
more beautiful now than she had at eighteen. They hugged, and
Beth admired the twins.

"Two babies. Wow."

"We want at least five," Maria said with a laugh as the children went to play in the sandbox. "The family I never had." They
took a bench just a few feet away, so Maria could rescue them if
anything happened. "You dyed your hair! I might not have recognized you if I'd seen you on the street."

"That was the point," Beth said.

Maria touched Beth's honey-colored hair. "Don't you ever
miss being a brunette?"

"Sometimes. But it's worth it. Staying in St. Clair had its
risks, you know."

"Tell me about it. But I was so glad to hear from you. We should stay in touch more. I didn't know how to call. I didn't know you had changed your name."

"Yeah," Beth said, watching the little girls in the sandbox. "I didn't have a husband to give me his name, like you did, so I just made one up. It made me feel more secure to have a different name."

"Maybe if we'd kept in touch, we could have supported each other."

"It's hard," Beth said. "We're both so busy. I've been working myself to death."

"I know, Beth, but I'm real proud of you. How close are you to getting your degree?"

"One more year."

"You're really going to do it, aren't you?"

"Yeah, and I've got huge student loans to prove it," Beth said.

"You always were determined. And working at the paper. I didn't expect you to get a job this soon."

"Yeah, well, they hired me as an intern my freshman year. They don't usually give bylines to interns, but I've worked so hard and dug up such good stuff, that Phil, my editor, has started treating me like a regular staff writer. During the summers, he pays me like one, but believe me, I have to work for it."

"I'm so proud of you, I guess I can forgive you for never calling me."

Beth smiled and squeezed her hand.

"So what's up, Beth? Why did you want to talk to me about Bill?"

Every muscle in Beth's body tensed as she took in a deep breath. "Maria, I've decided to expose him."

Maria's face showed no expression. She merely stared at her. "Are you sure you want to do that? He'll come after you."

"He already has."

Her face grew pale. "You're braver than I am."

Beth almost laughed. She tried to push down her own self-loathing. "It's not bravery," she said. "Not on my part. But I can't stand the thought of Bill abusing those children, training them to be thieves, preparing them for prison. Or worse. But I know that the minute this story comes out, hopefully tomorrow, Bill will be arrested. I'm not worried about him hurting me after that."

Maria stiffened. "Why are you telling me all this?"

Beth shrugged. "Well, I thought you would want to know. And—I thought you might let me interview you. My editor says I need more sources, someone who was there, who's grown now. Someone besides a dead woman and a little kid."

"Dead woman? What are you talking about?"

"Marlene," Beth said. Her mouth trembled slightly, but she managed to add, "She talked to me, and Bill killed her."

Maria threw her hand over her mouth and sprang up. With terror in her eyes, she hurried to the sandbox and picked up one of the twins, then grabbed the other by the hand and started to her car.

"Maria, where are you going?"

"Home!" Maria shouted as tears came to her eyes. "Why didn't you tell me on the phone that Bill knows you're doing this? I never would have come! If he killed Marlene for talking to you, then he'll kill me, too!"

"No, he won't! He's not following me now."

"You don't know that!" Maria shouted. She spun, her face red and raging as she glared at Beth. "I thought better of you, Beth, than to risk my life and the lives of my children. I have a family now! It took me three years to stop being afraid all the time, and now, just when I have some peace, you have to drag me into something that Bill's already killed his sister over?"

"I'm not dragging you into it, Maria. I just want to stop him."

"Then stop him yourself!" she shouted. "You don't need me. We have the same story!"

Beth froze, unable to find an argument to counter Maria's. Her story *was* the same. As much as she tried to deny it, hide it, wipe it from her mind, it was almost identical. "I can't use myself as a source," she choked out. "It wouldn't be objective."

"Are you kidding?" Maria shouted. "You'd probably win a Pulitzer Prize, if you didn't wind up in jail. Is that what you're scared of, Beth? That you'll wind up in jail?"

Beth looked down at her feet. "No. I made sure that I waited long enough. Three years. They can't try us after three years have passed."

"Oh, that's noble." Maria said with a sarcastic laugh. "You were so worried about the kids that you waited three years to make sure your own crimes were covered!"

"So did you!" Beth returned.

"That's right," she said. "Because *my* kids are more important to me right now. But I'm not the one trying to make some noble cause out of the whole thing—all that compassion and concern for those kids, while you were waiting for time to pass so you wouldn't go down with them!"

"No one but Bill is going down, Maria!" Beth bit out through her teeth. "We're not guilty! We didn't do any of it of our own free will. We were just kids."

"I was old enough to be a mother, Beth!"

"But we didn't have a choice! We were wards of the state. They put us in his care. It's *their* fault, not ours."

"Right," Maria said. "Just don't say that to a jury. When you start blaming other people for your own sins, they lose sympathy real fast. We knew that what we were doing was wrong."

Tears came to Beth's eyes, and her face was crimson as she took a step toward her old roommate. "What could we have done?"

"We could have run away," she said. "Or we could have turned him in then."

"He had us brainwashed! He wanted us to think that we would all go to jail. He *still* has us brainwashed!"

"Maybe so," Maria said. "I heard it from the time I was eight years old—that I'd be the one to go to jail, not him. I'm still hearing it. And if it's true, if any part of it is true, Beth, I can't even think about it, statute of limitations or not. I have two babies who need their mother, and I don't want them to grow up knowing I was a thief."

Beth just watched as Maria headed back to her old car. As the car drove off, she sat back down on the bench and stared ahead of her.

Maria was right. It was cowardly to expect her friend to talk, when Beth wouldn't talk herself. What kind of friend was she, anyway?

The hot breeze feathered through her hair, making little wisps stick to her face. What did God think of her, looking down from his throne that seemed so far away? Did he give her any points at all for deciding to go after Bill? Or would some of the points be taken away because she'd waited three years? Would she be docked more points for hesitating to come forward herself?

He must understand that the mere admission that she had been one of Bill's kids would immediately make people presume her guilt—not just in those crimes, but in others. She had once been branded *abandoned, orphaned, trash*—she had outgrown those labels, had overcome them. She didn't want to be known as a thief now.

Maybe she should have left town when she'd left Bill's home—gone somewhere she'd have been free to start over without constant reminders of Bill's presence nearby. But she'd spent her senior year of high school filling out forms for financial aid at St. Clair University, and when the loans and grants had been approved, it had seemed silly to go elsewhere. Now she was bound to St. Clair until she graduated, no matter how she wished she could relocate to someplace where she'd never fear Bill Brandon or think of him again.

It was too late now. She had to think of the children.

And she had to give Phil something he couldn't deny.

She got up from the bench and squinted against the sun in the direction Maria had gone. She had a decision to make. A big one. She only hoped that she had the guts to make the right one.

CHAPTER TWENTY-TWO

S o you were a real pilot? The kind that flies those big planes with hundreds of people on them?" Jimmy asked as he and Jake and Lynda strolled across the tarmac to the Cessna they had rented for the afternoon.

"That's right," Jake said. "A commercial pilot. I thought I was hot stuff."

"You were!" Jimmy cried. "Go to all those cool places, whenever you wanted, and all those people trusted you—"

"And the money," Jake said, winking at Lynda. "Don't forget the money. For a bachelor with no responsibilities, I made pretty good. I was real proud of myself."

Jimmy sighed. "I wish I could learn to fly. I'd fly me and Lisa to Brazil or somewhere far away. We'd have it made."

Lynda smiled as they reached the plane. "Look, Jimmy," she said. "See over there, on Runway 3?"

"Yeah," he said.

"That's where we crashed when our landing gear wouldn't drop."

"Right there?" Jimmy asked. "You really crashed?"

"We were trying to land."

Jimmy gazed out at the runway. "Wow," he said, awestruck. "You almost died right there."

"In a way, I did die," Jake said. "But you know what? That crash was the best thing that ever happened to me."

"Yeah, right."

"No, really. That was when I learned that God's in control of my life, not me. And once I knew that, I really started to live."

Jimmy breathed a laugh that sounded much too cynical for a boy his age. "God's not in control of *my* life. Bill is."

"Not anymore, he's not," Lynda said.

"You watch. He'll get me back, some way. And he'll make me and my sister pay."

Lynda bent down until her face was even with his. He was so small for his age, and his Opie-like expression belied the experiences he'd had. "Jimmy, I know this is easier said than done, but I want you to trust Beth and the others working on this."

But the expression that crossed his face was just the opposite of trust, and he turned away from her to peer out at Runway 3 again. "My mom said that to me once. To trust her." He didn't cry, but the tough look on his face had an amazingly fragile quality. "Are we gonna fly or what?"

Lynda looked at Jake, and silently they agreed to back off.

"All aboard," Jake said, and climbed onto the wing. Bending over, he pulled Jimmy up behind him. "Get ready, Jimmy Westin, to experience the ride of your life."

CHAPTER TWENTY-THREE

Nick sat over the books and files on his desk, trying to find a loophole in the law that would allow him to get Lisa out of the children's home immediately so that he could satisfy Jimmy's—and his own—fears. But there was nothing. Nick's suspicions were unproven, and today's inspection had been fine, even though he'd known that Bill was tap-dancing to cover the fact that all of the children weren't accounted for.

To all outward appearances, SCCH seemed to offer the children a loving, compassionate environment. Taking the kids swimming, to the library, to birthday parties—it was all very impressive, if one didn't know better.

He got up and pulled Jimmy and Lisa's files out of the file cabinet, hoping to find some forgotten aspect of their situation that would offer him some reason to pull her out. He flipped through the file and saw a picture of the two kids. Jimmy a couple of years ago, and his little sister—

It was her. The little girl in the picture was the same one Bill had put into the car to take to the birthday party. She had looked pale, almost afraid. She was shy, Bill had said.

But that was Lisa—and if Jimmy was right, Bill was already taking his anger out on her. No wonder she'd been frightened.

He rubbed his eyes with the heels of his hands. How could he have stood there and not realized that it was her? He had placed them in SCCH, after all. But she'd been three years younger then, and her hair had been short and sparse—she'd been malnourished.

No wonder he hadn't recognized her. They had driven her off right under his nose.

He grabbed his keys off the desk and rushed back out to the truck. He had to go back. He had to see if Lisa was back yet or if they were still claiming she was at the party. He had to make sure she was okay. If something had happened to her today, he would never forgive himself.

And Jimmy and Beth would never forgive him, either.

B ill Brandon was getting angry with him, but Nick didn't care. Bill glared at him from across the lawn as Nick walked toward Cottage B, where he had learned Lisa was assigned. Some children were playing in a playground behind the cottage, and the required number of adults were on hand to supervise. He walked to the fence and scanned the faces.

Stella, the woman who had spirited Lisa off earlier, was sitting in a lawn chair watching the children. She looked up at him as he approached the fence. "Business sure must be slow at HRS, to warrant this much attention from you in one day."

"I thought I might have left something here," he said. "I can't find my favorite pen. It was a Mont Blanc that I got as a gift. You didn't happen to find it, did you?" Actually, he really *had* been given one as a college graduation gift, and it had been lost—for over two years.

"Nope. Sorry."

"So how was that birthday party?" he asked, his eyes still sweeping across the children, looking for Lisa.

"Fine," she said. Her tone was defensive, questioning.

He spotted Lisa now, sitting alone in a corner of the fenced area, leaning her head against one of the posts and peering out to the street, as if watching for someone. Was she looking for Jimmy?

"I was thinking I might have dropped my pen over there," he said, pointing to the area where Lisa was sitting. "Mind if I check?"

She got up then, and looked back over his shoulder. Bill was approaching him from behind.

"Nick, I know you're supposed to do surprise inspections," Bill Brandon said as he got closer, "but don't you think two in one day is a little ridiculous?"

"He left something," Stella said. "A pen."

"A Mont Blanc. I wanted to look around and see if I could find it." As he spoke, he started walking around the fence to where Lisa sat. "I was thinking that I might have dropped it when I came out here—"

Lisa looked up at him as he drew closer. He looked down at her legs and arms, searching for some sign of a bruise or scrape, any indication that she may have been beaten or abused.

Bill was right on his heels, trying to distract him from her. "If you'd dropped it, I'm sure we would have found it by now. If it turns up, we'll call."

Nick bent over the fence. "But I was right over here, and I may have bent over. It could have fallen out of my pocket." He pretended to look on the ground around the fence, then acted surprised as his eyes collided with Lisa's. "Hey, you're the little girl who went to the birthday party. What was your name again?"

She started to answer, but Bill interrupted. "Susan. Her name's Susan."

"Hi, Susan," Nick said. "How was that party?"

Lisa had the same pale, wide eyes as Jimmy. "Fine."

"Good. I love birthday parties. Did you have cake and ice cream?"

She glanced up at Bill, waiting for him to prompt her. Nick couldn't see him, since Bill stood behind him, but he must have signaled for her to say yes. She nodded.

There was no point in pushing it. He was obviously making Lisa uncomfortable. She was here, and she wasn't hurt—at least not that he could see.

Frustrated, he turned and started back toward his car. Bill followed. "Call if you find it, will you? It's a valuable pen. I hate to think I lost it."

"Sure. I'll call," Bill said suspiciously.

Nick headed back around the fence, his eyes scanning the other children, reading their expressions—

He froze as he saw Chris and Matt, the two little boys he'd placed in the Millers' home just last night. They sat huddled

411

together in a corner of the yard, watching the other children with wan, miserable faces.

Nick swung back toward Bill. "Those two boys over there. When did you get them?"

Bill glanced over at them. "They're temporaries. Sheila Axelrod brought them this afternoon."

"Sheila?" Nick asked. "But I put them in a foster home last night."

"Take it up with her, Nick. She brought them to us, and we took them in."

He turned back toward the two boys, fighting the urge to leap over the fence and tell them that he hadn't meant for this to happen. The older boy, Chris, caught his gaze, and his face hardened. He muttered something to his little brother, and they both glared at him.

They think I betrayed them.

With an aching heart, Nick got back into his car and drove away.

But before he'd gone two miles, he pulled over and tried to decide what to do now. Bill and his employees were onto him. Maybe that was good. They wouldn't hurt Lisa as long as they knew he was watching. And maybe they wouldn't hurt Chris or Matt.

But that wasn't good enough. He had to get them all out.

He leaned back on the headrest and looked up at the ceiling. His eyes misted as angry sorrow rose within him. "Lord, you've got to help me. Right now I'm so mad at Sheila Axelrod I could strangle her. How could she have put those two boys there? And why? They were fine with the Millers."

He wrapped his arms around the steering wheel and rested his forehead on them. "This is too much for me," he said. "I can't handle it—without you."

A turbulent peace fell over him—peace that fighting for the kids was the right thing to do, but turbulent because he couldn't rest. God wasn't going to take that anger away from him, not yet. Maybe he was supposed to use it.

He pulled his car back out into traffic and headed to the HRS building. Sheila's car was there, and as he got out, his rage escalated.

She was at her desk, talking on the telephone. She looked up as he entered, and he strode toward her and bent over her desk. "Want to tell me what's going on with the kids I placed last night?"

She rolled her eyes. "Let me call you back, okay?" she said into the phone. She hung up and looked up at Nick, unintimidated. "You got a problem?"

"Yeah. Those kids were welcome in the Millers' home. Why did you take them out?"

"Because the Millers weren't ready for three kids. They still have the baby."

Nick's teeth came together. "I didn't want those kids in SCCH, and you know it."

"And I told you that we're not going to quit placing children there just because you don't like Bill Brandon. I am the supervisor of this office, and I have the final word. If you can't live with that, Nick, you know where the door is."

"And where would that leave you, Sheila? You can't handle this office alone."

"Watch me."

They stared each other down for a long moment. Nick thought of quitting, of insulting her, of reaching across the desk and throttling her. But if he resigned, he couldn't help Beth; he could do nothing for the kids. Working from the inside, he could help bring Bill Brandon down. When Beth's story hit the streets, Sheila would understand.

He straightened and massaged his temples. He was getting a headache. "Sheila, those kids were scared to death. The Millers were nurturing. They made them feel protected."

"It's not my job to make them feel protected, Nick. It's my job to make sure they have a secure place to stay for as long as they're wards of the state."

"It's not just about paperwork, Sheila!"

She laughed bitterly as she got up. "Don't tell me about paperwork, Nick. I've been at this longer than you've been an adult. I've seen cases that would curl your hair."

"You've seen too many," Nick said. "You've lost your compassion."

"Well, maybe it wouldn't hurt for you to do the same. That compassion will kill you, Nick. It'll turn your hair gray and keep you awake nights. And for what? For the peanuts the state pays us?"

"Then why are you still here?"

"Because this is what I was trained to do, and in case you haven't noticed, jobs aren't easy to come by in this state. After a while, you stop worrying. You stop losing sleep. Those things don't help the kids anyway—they just make you miserable. You find ways to stretch a dollar, or you supplement your income selling catalog makeup or magazine subscriptions. And you go on. You do the job, because you're the only one here to do it."

"There's got to be more to it than that, Sheila," Nick said. "I came into this because I believed it was a calling from God."

"Right," she said on a laugh. "Let me tell you something, Nick. If there were a God, there wouldn't be a need for social workers."

Nick's anger faded as he realized how little Sheila understood. "Maybe we *are* the way God's solving the problem. Maybe you and I are like angels to these miserable, abused children."

She snorted. "Yeah, well, I lost my halo a long time ago." She dropped back into her chair and picked up the phone. "This conversation is wearing me out, Nick. And I have about a million phone calls to return."

He watched as she dialed a number and began talking, ignoring him. His anger was gone, but in its place was a sad frustration, so deep that he didn't know how to combat it. Breathing out a defeated sigh, he headed out of the building and got back into his car.

There was nothing he could do for Matt and Chris right now. But there had to be something he could do for Lisa.

He pulled her file out of his briefcase. He hadn't finished studying it earlier. Now he flipped through the many forms that had been filled out to make Lisa and Jimmy wards of the state. Someone else—one of his coworkers who had long ago quit for a less stressful job—had removed them from the home. Then Nick had taken over the case, moving them from temporary foster care into SCCH, so he had never really studied their past.

They were not orphans. The forms revealed that the original social worker had been unable to locate their father. But they still had a mother.

He read intently about the woman who had voluntarily abandoned her children to the state.

Her name was Tracy, and she'd been twenty-five years old at the time. HRS had received reports of neglect, investigated, and found that she was a heavy drug abuser. Shortly after the investigation began, she had left the children, ages four and seven then, home alone for two days while she reveled in an ecstasy binge. The state had taken the children.

Nick ached for the pain those kids must have endured. He sat back in his seat. What would make a mother have such disregard for her children? That precocious little boy, that beautiful little girl—no wonder Jimmy distrusted adults. After a history of abandonment and neglect, Nick—who should have gotten things right—had dumped him from the frying pan into the fire. How many other times had he made the same mistake?

He closed his eyes and leaned his head back against his headrest. Where was that mother now? The papers said she was a resident of St. Clair, but she could have moved on since then. He wondered if her life was still controlled by drug abuse.

He closed his eyes and tried to think. He couldn't get any of the kids out of the home on his own, not until Bill was exposed tomorrow and charges filed. And plenty of things could go wrong. The state could get caught in a mire of bureaucracy and fail to act immediately. That could be a fatal mistake, because as soon as Bill Brandon read Jimmy's quotes in the article, he would be sure to take his vengeance out on Lisa.

Unless . . .

It was a long shot, but—he could at least *try* to track down their mother.

CHAPTER TWENTY-FIVE

B eth spent the afternoon writing the story of a little girl neglected and abused, then placed in what was considered the nicest, most stable home in the state. She wrote of how that child was forcefully recruited into a crime ring at the age of eight, how she was taught to pick locks, slip into small openings in windows, crawl into homes through crawl spaces with garage entrances. She told how the girl learned to unlock jewelry boxes, search for cash, unhook VCRs, TVs, computers. She explained how she had worked for hours each night in her young life of crime, only to fall asleep in class the next day and suffer punishment at the hands of teachers and principals—and then again from Bill Brandon on returning home. And she told of the "tapes" that still played in her mind, tapes of Brandon's voice telling her that *she* was the thief, not he, that she had the dirty hands, that if she ever told this story, she would have to fear not only prison, but death at his vicious hands.

The sun was low in the sky behind the trees when she finished. Just writing this anonymous confession had exhausted her. And it might not even be enough. Phil would want substantiation. He would want a name, and she wasn't ready to give hers.

Drained and depressed, she called her editor. He sounded rushed as he answered. "Yeah, Beth. What's up?"

"Phil, it's about the article. I've finished it, but—"

"But what?"

"But the other source I got. It's anonymous. It's a woman who used to live in Brandon's home and worked in his crime ring . . . but she doesn't want me to use her name."

"You realize, don't you, that we're making some fierce allegations here? If we intend to accuse an upstanding citizen of charges this serious, we have to be prepared to defend them in court, Beth. I can't take the chance of getting the paper sued, because we made allegations that we can't back up."

"We *can* back them up, Phil. It's not my fault that Marlene was murdered, and that Jimmy is a little boy."

"I know that. But you're putting me between a rock and a hard place here."

She slammed her hand on the table, waking Dodger who slept at her feet. "Phil, someone's going to get hurt if we wait! Bill Brandon already knows I'm working on the story. He's going to do everything he can to stop me. The longer we put off printing this story, the more danger I'm in, and the more danger those kids are in."

"You're asking me to ignore my legal counsel."

"I'm asking you to have a little courage, Phil. Get some guts, for heaven's sake!"

He hesitated. "Beth, are you sure that you've gotten the facts right? Are you positive?"

"Phil, I'd stake my life on it. In fact, that's exactly what I'm doing."

She could tell from his sigh that she'd made her point. "All right. Send the story in, and I'll take a look."

She closed her eyes. "Do more than take a look, Phil. Please. This could be the biggest story of the year."

"Sure, it could. It could win you an award. We could also get our pants sued off."

"Forget the awards, Phil. Don't even give me a byline. I don't care. Just print it."

"I'll read it, Beth. We'll see."

"Call me as soon as you decide," she said.

"I will."

She hung up and rested her face in her hands. She'd done her part. Now, if Phil printed the story, her career—even her life—might be ruined. Or Bill might decide to go out in a blazing act of vengeance, and come after her.

She just hoped God hadn't forgotten to record this in her scorebook.

CHAPTER TWENTY-SIX

ick found the woman's apartment building, an old structure with peeling paint, busted-out windows, and trash and old furniture on the front lawn. He found it hard to believe that people lived here; it looked as if it should be torn down.

A toddler played at the bottom of a staircase, wearing nothing but a filthy diaper. As Nick walked from his car across the lawn, he looked for some sign of an adult nearby. Seeing none, he leaned down, hands on knees, and smiled at the child. The baby's face was dirty and sticky, and his nose was runny. He smiled back and reached up to hand Nick a cigarette butt that he'd, no doubt, picked up from the clutter at his feet. His fingers were crusted with filth.

"Hi there." Nick took the butt. "Where's your mommy?"

"Who wants to know?" a hoarse voice said from behind the broken staircase.

Taking a couple of steps, Nick peered around the staircase and saw a girl of no more than fifteen sitting on a cracked slab of concrete, smoking a cigarette. "Hi," Nick said. "I didn't see you there. I thought the baby was out here alone."

"What's it to you?"

He shrugged. "Just worried me, that's all. There are a lot of things around here that could hurt him."

"So what do you want, anyway?" the girl demanded.

"Uh . . ." He looked back down at the dirty toddler. His instinct was to scoop the baby up and take it away to a place where it would be cared for. But he reminded himself, as he had to several times a day, that not every child was his responsibility, and that things weren't always as bad as they seemed. "I was looking for a woman named Tracy Westin. I think she lives upstairs. Do you know her?"

"Yeah, I know her."

"Is she home?"

"I haven't seen her come out."

He looked up the broken staircase. "So she's in that apartment up there?"

"Give the man an award."

Annoyed, Nick started to respond in kind—and then realized that she was, herself, a child, unable to handle the weight of hopelessness that so obviously held her down.

He looked at the baby again, then back at the girl. Sister? Mother? One could never tell. He only hoped that she was a better caretaker than his first impression suggested. He could only hope that she *had* a better caretaker for herself.

He went up the staircase, stepping over the broken steps. A garbage bag with trash spilling out of a gnawed-out hole sat at the top of the steps, and a cat prowled in the refuse. He stepped over it, ignoring the stench, and knocked on the door.

For a moment, he heard nothing, and almost turned to go. Then he heard a voice.

He pressed his ear to the door and knocked again. He heard the voice again, but couldn't make out the words.

He checked the doorknob—unlocked. Slowly, he opened the door.

The apartment was dark and filthy. He stepped inside and looked around. There was little furniture except for an old torn-up card table in the kitchenette, covered, as was the kitchen counter, by dishes piled on dishes, old crud dried on them. There was a mattress in the far corner of the cluttered room.

On the mattress was a woman in shorts and a dirty tank top, curled up in a fetal position, shivering. Her hair was long and red, tangled and matted. He stepped toward her. "Tracy?"

She didn't answer.

"Tracy?" he tried again.

She still didn't respond, so he stepped over the clothes lying on the floor, the sandals, the wadded sheets that had been kicked off the mattress. She looked tiny, anorexic, no more than eighty pounds. And she was sick—that was clear. He knelt beside her and reached out to touch her forehead. It was alarmingly hot.

"Tracy, can you hear me?"

Her eyes, glassy from the fever, focused on him for a second, and she moaned, "Help me."

He wasn't sure if this was drug withdrawal or a real illness, but either way she needed to be in a hospital. He looked around. "Do you have a phone?"

"No," she whispered.

He thought of rushing off to find a pay phone and call an ambulance, but decided that she would get help more quickly if he took her himself. "Tracy, can you get up?"

She only closed her eyes.

"All right," he said. "I'll pick you up. I'm going to carry you out to my car and get you to the hospital, okay?"

No answer.

He scooped her up, surprised at how light she was in his arms. She probably hadn't eaten in days—maybe even weeks. He wondered how long she had been like this.

He carried her out, stepping back over the reeking garbage, and carefully made his way down the stairs. The girl with the baby was still sitting there. She watched him blankly as he carried Tracy out.

"Can you tell me how long Tracy's been sick?" he asked her.

"Do I look like her mother?" the girl responded.

"When's the last time you saw her?"

"I don't know," she said, putting her cigarette out on the concrete. "A week maybe."

"Was she sick then?"

"How should I know?"

Frustrated, he hurried her to his car and laid her in the back seat. She curled back up in a little ball as he jumped into the front, turned on his lights, and drove away.

CHAPTER TWENTY-SEVEN

B eth dove for the phone. "Hello?"

"Beth, it's Phil."

She closed her eyes, bracing herself. "Phil, tell me you're going to print the article. Please. I don't think I can handle it—"

"Relax, I'm printing it. It was great, Beth. Thank your anonymous source for me."

"Then it'll be in tomorrow's paper?"

"Absolutely."

"Yes!" she said, punching the air. "Thank you, Phil. You may have saved my life."

"I wish you didn't mean that literally, but I guess you do."

"You bet I do. Listen, Phil, I know you're not going to go for this, but I'd like to give a copy of the story to the police department tonight."

"No! That's too soon!" he said. "That's our story. I don't want every other newspaper in the area getting it before we do, and that's exactly what will happen if you give it to the police. You know better than that."

"I don't care about being scooped anymore, Phil. Jimmy's little sister is still in that home, and so are a lot of other innocent victims. Not to mention the fact that Bill Brandon is after me. I want him locked up. Now."

He moaned. "All right, Beth. Maybe the other papers still won't get the whole story. Or maybe the police won't act quickly."

"They will. They have to."

He hesitated, and Beth knew that all his editor's instincts told him not to risk losing the scoop. "All right. Do what you have to do."

"I will."

She hung up and immediately clicked her mouse on the "print" button. Watching as the article slid out of her printer, she picked up the phone to call Nick and tell him the good news, but she only got his machine.

She grabbed the printed article, folded it in half, and headed for the door. Dodger was right behind her, begging to go out. She picked him up, clipped on his leash, and put him back down. He scurried out the door the second she opened it and made a puddle on her doorstep.

"Good boy!" she said, petting him. "You're getting the hang of this, aren't you?" When he was finished, she hurried him back into the house.

The sun was setting as she headed to the police station, hoping those two detectives, Larry and Tony, would be there. She wanted to make sure this didn't fall through the cracks.

Larry was on his way out as she came in, and she grabbed his arm and stopped him. "Detective Millsaps?"

He looked down at her, and she could tell that he couldn't place her.

"Beth Wright. You were at my house last night, remember?"

"Oh, yeah," he said. "Nick Hutchins's friend."

"Right. Listen, I need to talk to you about something really important. Do you have a minute?"

He checked his watch. "Yeah, I can give you a few minutes."

He led her back through the maze of desks in the noisy room, and offered a chair in front of his desk. Plopping into his own chair, he asked, "So what's up? Did you hear something in your house again?"

"Yes, I did, as a matter of fact. And I found the culprit. It was a ten-year-old boy."

"A ten-year-old boy?"

"Yes. And Bill Brandon, the man who runs the home where this little boy lives, is the one who forced him to break into my house so that he could find and destroy any evidence I had against him."

"Oh, that's right," Larry said. "You were working on a story about him." He pulled a pen out of his drawer and began to take notes. "You're sure he was behind it?"

"Positive." She handed him the article. "The boy is still with us—Nick knows all about it. Don't you think it's odd that a child is missing from the St. Clair Children's Home and no one there has reported it?"

"Well, yeah . . ."

"Read the article," she said, sitting back and crossing her arms. "I'll wait."

She watched as he read the article, skimming at first, then settling in as a wrinkle of concentration and concern gradually deepened across his forehead. When he'd finished, he looked up at her and rubbed his hand across the stubble around his mouth. "That's some article."

"It's all true."

"So let me see if I got all this. Brandon has a crime ring that might explain dozens of break-ins in St. Clair over the last several years. He's abusing these kids. He probably murdered his sister to keep her quiet. And he ran you off the road—"

"Tried to," she cut in.

"Tried to run you off the road." He shook his head and looked up as he saw Tony hurrying through. "Hey, Tony. Come here."

Tony seemed a little distracted as he headed toward them.

"You got to read this," he said. "It's coming out tomorrow in the *St. Clair News.*"

They both watched as Tony read. As his interest in the article increased, he dropped the sport coat he'd been holding by one finger over his shoulder. "This is bad."

"Then you'll do something about it? Tonight?" Beth asked.

Tony glanced at Larry. "What do you think?"

"Well, we'll have to talk to the kid first . . ."

"Where is he now?" Tony asked.

"With some friends of mine," Beth said. "Lynda Barrett and Jake Stevens."

"Yeah, we know them. We'll head over there and interview him right now."

423

"He's scared to death that something will happen to his sister if an arrest isn't made soon. I think he has reason to be."

"I think *you* have reason to be, if what you're saying is true." She stared at them. "Why would I lie?"

"I'm not suggesting you are," Larry said. "But we have to have more substantial proof than a newspaper article and the word of a little boy who got caught breaking the law. Kids have been known to lie their way out of tight spots."

"He isn't lying! Check the dents on my car! Check out Bill Brandon's alibi the night his sister was murdered! You think it was a coincidence that Jimmy broke into *my* house when I was working on a story about Bill?"

"We're going to check it all out, Beth," Tony said. "We aren't doubting you. We're just doing our job. Now, do you think Nick is up to placing all those kids when we arrest Brandon and take the rest of his staff in for questioning?"

"He's been ready."

"None of us may get any sleep tonight," Larry said.

Tony reached for the phone. "I'll call Sharon and cancel our date tonight."

"Yeah, I'd better call Melissa, too. Beth, if I were you, I'd wait at Lynda's until you hear from us. It's safe there. We can follow you over right now."

"All right," she said. "But you'll call me when you've got him?"

"Sure thing. Come on, Tony, we've got to get all this done so we can catch Judge Wyatt to get a warrant before he leaves for the day."

Tony shrugged on his blazer to conceal his gun. "He's the presiding judge in town," he told her. "This is worth going straight to the top."

As they hurried out ahead of her, she felt a huge weight drop from her shoulders. At last, her case was in good hands.

CHAPTER TWENTY-EIGHT

ick knew all of the emergency room doctors and nurses, because he was called here frequently when injuries to youngsters suggested the possibility of child abuse. As soon as he'd brought Tracy in and told them how he'd found her, they'd rushed her back, intent on finding the reason for her illness. She was in good hands.

While he waited, he went to the pay phone and tried to call Beth. Her machine answered, so he left a message, hung up, and dialed his own number. Beth had left a message that she had gotten approval from the paper, that the story would be out tomorrow, and that she was giving it to the police so they could arrest Bill Brandon tonight.

He grinned and hung up, then dropped into a chair. Part of him wanted to relax, but the other part knew that he needed to be at the office finding qualified foster parents to stay with the kids tonight. He had already thought this through and decided that, instead of scattering them all over the state in private homes, it would be better, at least for the next few days, to get couples to come replace SCCH's employees so the children could stay where they were. That would be less traumatic for the kids, and less work for Sheila and him.

The emergency room physician, a guy he'd played racquetball with a few times, came out and scanned the faces in the waiting room, spotted Nick, and came to take the chair at right angles to his.

"So what is it?" Nick asked. "Drugs?"

"Actually, no. No drugs in her bloodstream at all. What your friend has is probably the worst case of double pneumonia I've ever seen."

"Pneumonia? This time of year?"

"Yeah. She's in bad shape, Nick. She may not pull through. We're admitting her into intensive care right now. Can you fill out the paperwork? Give us her insurance company, that sort of thing?"

He shook his head. "I don't know anything about her other than her name. And I seriously doubt that she has insurance. Judging from the place she lives, I'd say she's indigent. That's why I brought her here."

It was a charity hospital, so he had known that they wouldn't turn her away.

"All right. We'll take care of things," the doctor said. "Do you know if she has any next of kin?"

He thought of Jimmy and Lisa. "She has two kids that were taken away from her. They're seven and ten."

"Any adults?"

"I couldn't tell you."

The doctor suddenly looked very tired. "I'll level with you, Nick. If you hadn't brought her in here when you did, that girl wouldn't have lasted through the night. I hate to see a person that near death, without a person in the world who cares about her."

Nick rubbed his weary eyes. "Yeah, me too."

The doctor slapped his knee and got up. "We've got her on an IV, and we're starting a round of serious antibiotics. ICU doesn't allow nonfamily members to visit, but I'll pull some strings if you want to come back and see her tonight."

He nodded. "Yeah, I'll do that."

"Thanks for bringing her in, man."

Nick checked his watch as he headed out of the emergency room. He wondered if Bill Brandon had been arrested yet—and if Beth was safe.

Walking out into the night, he looked up at the stars spread by the millions across the sky like a paint-spattered canopy. God had been with him today. "Thank you," he whispered, grateful that the Holy Spirit had prompted him to find Tracy, just in the nick of time. There must have been a reason.

It wasn't all hopeless. There was a plan. There were times when Nick *did* act as an angel to a dying world. That realization gave him the energy to keep going tonight.

And he knew he wasn't working alone.

CHAPTER TWENTY-NINE

I can't give you a warrant for Bill Brandon's arrest." Judge Wyatt said the words with such finality as he packed his briefcase that Tony and Larry only stared at him.

"Excuse me, Judge, but did you say you *can't?*" Tony asked.

"No, I can't! Not on such outlandish charges with absolutely nothing to support them."

Larry touched Tony's arm to quiet him, and tried again. "Judge, maybe we didn't make ourselves clear. There's the account given by the boy from the home who was caught breaking into this reporter's house. We just talked to him ourselves. The reporter has another source who used to live in Brandon's home, who corroborated that story. And Marlene Brandon, Bill Brandon's sister, was murdered right after she talked to the reporter. We've been in touch with the Tampa PD, and the only ones backing up Brandon's alibi are his employees, who could also be involved."

"I read the article, gentlemen," the elderly judge said. "But I'm not issuing a warrant for anybody's arrest based on some trumped-up charges by a newspaper that won't print anything unless it's painted yellow!"

"Your honor," Tony tried, hoping a little more respect might calm things a bit, "this isn't yellow journalism. This article matches the facts we do have. We have a lot of unexplained break-ins. Kids have been seen in some of the areas before or after a crime was committed. We have small unidentifiable fingerprints at the scene of some of these crimes. We didn't pursue that angle very hard in our previous investigations of the robberies because it seemed so farfetched. But if this is a professional crime ring—"

"Then where are they keeping the stolen goods?" the judge demanded. "Where are they selling it? Have you gotten down to that, yet?"

"Well, no, not yet. But—"

"Then how do you expect me to give you a warrant for this man's arrest? This is pretty shoddy police work, gentlemen. And I'm not going to wind up with egg on my face when it comes out that a decent, upstanding citizen who provides a good home to so many children was wrongly arrested because of some cockamamie story by an overzealous reporter trying to make a name for herself! Until you come up with something I can see, something other than a kid with a strong imagination who's trying to get himself out of trouble, don't waste my time with this again."

"Judge, you can't be serious—"

"Good-bye, detectives," he said, grabbing up his briefcase and ushering them out. "I have a meeting in twenty minutes, and I don't intend to be late."

"Judge Wyatt, you're acting irresponsibly here!" Tony cried.

The judge swung around. "What did you say?"

Tony's face was red. "I said, you're acting irresponsibly. Children's lives are at stake, for Pete's sake."

"If you don't get off these premises in the next three seconds, detectives, I'll call my bailiff and have you thrown into jail yourselves."

Tony and Larry stood there, stunned, as the judge headed out of the office without another word.

"Great going," Larry bit out. "He's right. We shouldn't have been in such a hurry. We should have gotten more evidence before we came here."

"Then let's go get it now," Tony said. "Time is running out for those kids."

CHAPTER THIRTY

Bill Brandon thanked his source for the tip, hung up his phone, and stared down at his desk for a moment. So the article was scheduled to come out in tomorrow's newspaper. Beth Sullivan—alias Beth Wright, he thought with amusement—actually thought she was going to expose him. But she was so wrong.

He picked up the phone again and dialed the extension for Cottage B. One of the children answered. "Put Stella on the phone," he ordered. He waited a few seconds, then the housemother answered.

"Stella, send the team over for me, pronto. We have a job to do. Oh, and include Lisa Westin."

He went to the closet and pulled the rolled-up blueprints off the top shelf. There was one for City Hall, one for the Police Station, one for the courthouse, one for the St. Clair First National Bank . . . He pulled them out one by one, until he came to the one for the building housing the *St. Clair News*. He put the others back carefully, then went to his desk and opened the blueprint, spreading it out across his desk.

There it was: all of the rooms at the *St. Clair News*, carefully labeled with their purposes and the machinery housed there. His sources were nothing if not thorough.

A knock sounded on the door, and he called, "Come in."

Brad, an eleven-year-old he'd been grooming for the last four years, opened the door. "Bill, you called for us?"

"Yeah, guys, come on in."

Seven boys and four girls, ranging in age from eight to fifteen, filed in quietly and found places around the room. Tailing the group was little Lisa Westin, her big green eyes looking frightened and apprehensive as she stepped into his office.

"What's she doing here?" Brad asked with contempt. "She's too little."

"She's taking Jimmy's place," Bill explained.

"Any word on Jimmy?" Brad asked.

"No. And things don't look good for him."

Bill knew that would give them all images of the child rotting in a jail cell. Enough incentive to keep them from messing things up.

He glanced at Lisa and saw that those big eyes were full of tears. "Lisa's already done one job for me, and she did such a good job that I thought I'd reward her by giving her a little more responsibility."

She didn't look all that proud.

"And she knows that if she botches anything up, Jimmy will be in even worse shape than he is now. You all know I can get to him if I have a point to make. There's not a lock made, even in a jail cell, that I can't open. You know that if you mess up, Lisa, that Jimmy will pay for it, don't you? That's how it works."

She swallowed and nodded her head.

He turned his attention back to the others. "It's come to my attention, people, that there's supposed to be a newspaper article coming out about us in the paper tomorrow. It will point fingers at each of you, exposing you as thieves, and will probably result in the police arresting all of you before daylight."

There was a collective gasp all over the room.

"Bill, what are we gonna do?"

"I don't want to go to jail!"

"Can't you tell them we're not thieves?"

Bill sat back and shrugged. "Wouldn't do any good. They have proof. Some of you have been seen, but that's not the worst of it. Jimmy Westin has turned state's evidence."

"What's that?" Brad asked.

"He's told them everything he knows about our operation."

"No! He wouldn't."

"*Au contraire.*" He chuckled in his sinister way, and met the eyes of each individual kid around the room. Satisfied that he had put sufficient fear in them to manipulate them into doing anything, he smiled. "But don't worry. Bill is going to take care of you. Doesn't he always?"

A few of them nodded.

"I've got a plan. But it's going to require a lot of hard work and a few risks. Somebody might even have to get hurt. But sometimes sacrifices have to be made. As the Good Book says, 'Greater courage hath no man, than to lay down a life for his cause.'"

The children all gazed somberly at him. He had them right where he wanted them.

"Oh, don't worry. I'm not asking any of *you* to lay down your lives. I just want that kind of commitment to this project—that you would if it came to it, which it won't. No, it's not your lives that'll be in danger. But the people in the building . . . well, some things are just in God's hands."

He looked down at the blueprint. "This, my friends, is the blueprint for the newspaper offices. In this big room, here at the back, is the printing press that puts out every copy of the newspaper that will be distributed all over town the first thing in the morning. Your job, should you decide to accept it," he said, drawing on the *Mission Impossible* theme, even though he knew they didn't have the option of refusing it, "is to stop the presses. Literally. That way, the story won't come out, and you won't be arrested."

Some of the kids let out huge breaths of relief, and Bill smiled and said, "I told you I'd take care of things, didn't I? Now, come on over here and get around the desk, so I can show each of you what your job will be. We've still got a few hours before we need to go. That gives us plenty of time to plan every move."

CHAPTER THIRTY-ONE

The waiting room for the family members of those in the Intensive Care Unit was full of rumpled, tired people with lines on their faces and worry in their eyes. Beth followed Nick past the reception desk, where a woman stood consoling a family whose loved one had just been in a car accident. On the desk were two stacks of towels and a sign that said that toilet articles were available if anyone needed them.

"They take showers up here?" Beth asked quietly.

"Yeah. Many of these people are here twenty-four hours a day. They're afraid to leave."

"But I thought visiting hours were only thirty minutes every four hours."

"Right. They sit by the bedside for thirty minutes, then come back to the waiting room and worry for four hours until the next visit."

"Seems cruel."

"Maybe it is. But those short visiting times are usually in the best interest of the patients. They need quiet."

He led her into the huge room lined with vinyl recliners and chairs. Families had nested in certain areas of the room, surrounded by books and little bags with their belongings, Walkmans, and canned drinks. It was easy to distinguish the family members from occasional visitors. They looked more worn, more stressed, more near the breaking point. In one corner, a woman crocheted an afghan furiously, and already it was big enough to cover her legs. Beth wondered when she'd started it. Across the room, someone else worked on a laptop, and next to her, a red-eyed teenaged girl did cross-stitch as if her life depended on getting every stitch exactly in line.

The five telephones on the wall rang constantly, and they were always answered by one of those nearby. Then they would call out, "Smith family" or "Jackson family," and someone would rush to answer it.

"It's like a little community up here," Beth said.

"Yeah. My dad was in ICU for three weeks before he died. I didn't leave the unit except for meals. I ate those downstairs, and only if I had to. A lot of times, churches brought sandwiches and stuff right here to the waiting room."

"But what's the point in staying? I mean, if you can't visit them . . ."

"It's the fear that something will go wrong. That the doctor will need you to help make a decision. Even the irrational fear that if you leave, if you're not there hanging on, they'll slip away."

"I can't imagine being sick and having someone waiting out here that diligently for me."

"What about your mother?" he asked.

"She's dead." The words came so matter-of-factly that she feared Nick would think she was cold. The truth was, if Beth's mother were alive, she wouldn't have waited in the ICU waiting room for Beth anyway. The deep sadness of that fact washed over her. She was really no different than Tracy Westin, lying in there so sick with no one out here in this room, representing her and praying for her, refusing to leave because they had to stay and fight with her.

"I'm sorry."

She didn't say anything, but watched the dynamics of a family in the corner. "Poor Tracy."

Nick looked at her. "What do you mean?"

"She's all alone."

"We're here."

"Yeah, but she doesn't know us. We don't love her."

"Yes, we do. I love her because I'm a Christian. I'm ordered to love her."

Beth smiled grimly at the irony. She hadn't had much experience with love, but she knew *that* was wrong. "Love isn't something you can be ordered to do, Nick. You have to feel something."

"Love is first something you do, Beth," Nick said. "The feelings are important, yes, but love is a verb, not a noun. We're here to love her because no one else is."

Well, there was something in that. She sat quietly for a moment, looking around the room at all the people so steeped in the act of loving. She wondered what it would be like to have people like that caring for her, waiting hours to see her, not willing to leave for fear that she might need them. She couldn't even fathom it.

The crackle of the intercom quieted the room, and a voice said, "ICU visitation will begin now. The following families may go back: Anderson, Aldredge, Burton . . ." Eventually, they came to the name Westin, and Beth and Nick got up and followed the stream of visitors through the double doors into ICU. As he had promised, the doctor had bent the rules to allow Nick and Beth to visit Tracy.

There were no doorways in ICU, only three-sided rooms open to the nursing station so that the nurses could see and hear the patients at all times. Tracy lay on her bed, sitting up at a forty-five degree angle, with an IV in her hand and an oxygen mask on her face. Several cords ran out from under her sheet and hooked to monitors that kept close watch on her vital signs.

She looked so tiny, so emaciated. Beth hesitated at the foot of the bed, feeling like an intruder in this woman's private hell.

Nick went to her bedside and leaned over her. He looked carefully at her face to see if she was sleeping, but her eyes were half opened. "Tracy? Can you hear me?"

"Don't wake her up," Beth said softly.

"I don't think she's asleep," he said. "Tracy, I'm Nick. The one who found you and brought you here."

She looked up then, and met his eyes. "Thank you," she whispered.

"No problem. They're going to do everything they can for you here. Did they tell you you have double pneumonia? You're in ICU so they can watch you real closely."

She closed her eyes.

Nick looked at Beth, not sure what to do. "My friend here, Beth, knows your son. We thought—"

Her eyes fluttered back open, and she tried to rise up. "Jimmy?" she asked weakly.

"Yes," Beth said, stepping forward. "He's a great kid."

Weakly, she dropped back down. "Haven't seen him in three years. I have a little girl—"

"Lisa?" Nick asked.

Her eyes grew rounder. "You know Lisa?"

"Yes, Tracy. That's why I was coming to see you today. I'm a social worker, and I've taken an interest in your kids."

Tears began to roll down her face. "Are they all right?"

"They're good," he said. "Healthy, smart . . ."

Her face contorted in anguish, and she asked, "Do they hate me?"

Nick looked up at Beth, not sure how to answer that. Beth felt her own eyes filling, which rarely happened. She hated herself when she cried. "I don't think they hate you," she whispered.

"I left them, you know . . ." Her voice broke off, and she closed her eyes and covered her face with a scrawny hand that had the IV needle taped in place. "You should have just let me die."

Something about the heartfelt regret touched Beth in a deep place, a place of wounds that had never fully healed. She turned away, blinking back her tears, *ordering* back her tears. When she turned back to the woman on the bed, her eyes were dry. "We don't want you to die, Tracy."

Nick shook his head. "That's right. God might need you to get well so you can help your kids understand why you did it."

"*I* don't understand why," she said.

Nick leaned closer. "Tracy, are you still addicted?"

"No. Been through treatment . . . three times. Always fell back. But this last time . . . clean for two months."

"Do you work? Do you have a job?"

"No."

"Are you on welfare?"

"No. I was living with my husband . . ."

He looked up at Beth, surprised. "Husband? You're married?"

"Six months. Doomed."

"Where is your husband now?"

"Who knows? Gone. He's worse off than I was."

"Do you mean he was sick, too?"

"He's a junkie." She wiped her tear-streaked face with the hand her IV was taped to. "When I got sick, he took off. Couldn't stand to hear me hacking all the time."

"Why didn't you go to the doctor?"

"No money."

"But you could have gone to the health department."

"Too weak."

"You didn't have anyone to take you? No one?"

"No . . . no one."

The nurse came into the room and told them their visiting time was up, and Nick touched Tracy's hand. "Tracy, we have to go now, but we'll be back. You get better, okay? We're praying for you."

She nodded mutely, her face contorted with sorrow and regret.

As they stepped out into the night, Beth felt anguish gaining on her again, sneaking closer to her breaking point, pulling her under. Nick seemed to sense it. He put his arm across her shoulders and said, "Let's not go to the car just yet."

When she didn't protest, he led her down the cobblestone walkway that led through the hospital's courtyard and around the little pond. Moonlight flickered on the surface of the water, lending a sense of peace and beauty to the world that had so much ugly darkness.

"I think she's remorseful," he said. "I don't always see that."

Beth couldn't answer.

"I just hope she lives. Maybe through some miracle we could reunite the kids with her."

"Don't you think you're jumping the gun a little?" Beth asked quietly.

He shrugged. "Maybe. I guess I'm just a believer in miracles."

Beth reached a bench, sank down, and pulled her feet up to hug her knees. "I believe in miracles, too, Nick. But I've learned that you can't custom order them."

Quiet settled between them as he sat down next to her, watching her face. She couldn't look at him, for those tears were slipping up on her again, threatening her. She looked out over the water, trying to sort out the storm of emotions whirling through her mind. Anger, rage, sorrow, loneliness, rejection, frustration, fear ...

"We sure have screwed things up, haven't we?"

"Who?" she asked.

"Us. The human race. God gave us families, such a wonderful gift, and we break them into tiny pieces, reject them, throw them away ..."

"That's it," she whispered, still staring across the water. "Thrown away. That's how those kids feel. And no matter what happens to them, that feeling doesn't quite go away."

"And then there's Tracy."

"Yes. I wonder how Jimmy will feel when we tell him we found his mother."

Nick tried to imagine. "Well, he'll put on a tough-guy act. But deep down, kids love their mothers. Even kids who have been abused and rejected."

"Sometimes there are other things that cover that love so deeply that you can never get back down to it. I don't think we should let him see his mother like that. I don't think we should even tell him we've found her until she's better."

"That's true. Besides, she might die, and then he'd have to grieve for her all over again."

"Again?" she asked, finally looking at him. "I doubt he grieved for her at all. Being taken from her may have been a relief to some extent. And he was probably so hurt, so angry that she left him like that ... So worried for Lisa ..."

"He's still worried for Lisa. Like I said, this isn't the kind of thing God ever meant for a kid to have to worry about. Families are supposed to protect each other. Love each other. When I have kids, nothing in heaven or earth could force me to leave them. And the best thing I'll do for them is to love their mother."

A soft, gentle, wistful smile curved her lips. "I believe you could do that." She watched his face as he propped it on his hand and smiled at her. "Tell me about your family, Nick. Did you have a mother and father who loved you? Did you eat at the table at night, all together, talking about your day?"

He gave her a strange look that told her the question had been too revealing. "Yeah, I guess we did. I had four sisters and brothers, and my parents have been married forty-five years. It was a busy household. What about yours?"

Her smile faded and her eyes drifted back to the water. "My household was very busy, too," she said. "But not like yours. You might say I'm one of the pieces my family broke into."

He gazed at her for a moment, and she wondered if it was pity or disdain she saw on his face. Was he measuring her against himself, finding her flawed and scarred? Did he look at potential mates against a measuring stick of broken families and dysfunctional childhoods, as she sometimes did? She had broken a budding relationship recently when she'd discovered that the man had been raised fatherless. She had told herself that she desperately needed someone who had not suffered the battles she had as a child, someone who had more parts to him than she had to her.

Yet she knew it was a double standard, for if others measured her the same way, she would always be alone.

"I wondered where that tough edge came from," he whispered. "Is that where? From a broken family?"

She smiled. She liked that he'd seen a tough edge in her. She had cultivated it for years. "Maybe."

"I'm sorry if you had to go through pain as a child, Beth. But God works all things for good. And if you had to go through all you did to be who you are today, well, it turned out pretty good, didn't it?"

She sighed. "You don't really know who I am. Not really."

"Then show me."

It was a challenge, and she rarely backed down from challenges. Yet what he was asking was too intimate, too revealing, and she couldn't risk it. He couldn't know that she had once been one of those kids in the homes he monitored, one of the names in the files he kept stacked on his desk. He couldn't know that she had been a trained thief, a practiced liar . . .

"You don't have to show me," he said, finally, when he could see that she struggled with the challenge. "I've seen it. In the way you're fighting for these kids, risking your life, daring to make a change. Not many people would do that."

"Given the proper motivation," she said coolly, "people will do lots of things."

"Yeah, you're real tough," he said with a hint of amusement as he touched her soft, short hair. "But you know what I saw the first time you came to me to get information about the home?"

She looked reluctantly at him. "What?"

"I saw a woman who sent my heart stumbling in triple-time. A beautiful woman with those big, clear blue eyes, and that smile that made me want to sit and stare at it for hours . . . And then I heard you talk, heard how you cared for those kids, how passionate you were about this story . . ."

She smiled uneasily and looked down at her hands. Suddenly they were clammy. Suddenly, she was shaking.

"You cared the way I cared. I had cared about those kids for some time, had worried about them, and I felt a bond with you. I thought that maybe God had crossed our paths for a reason."

She looked at him curiously then. "You see God working in everything, don't you? Nothing's accidental. Nothing's left to chance."

"Absolutely nothing. Don't you believe that?"

"I don't know," she said honestly. "I don't think God's working in my life yet. I haven't done enough. Things are still too off balance."

"What do you mean 'off balance'?"

"You know. I'm sort of behind on this religion thing. I got a late start. I have a lot of work to do before I can expect anything from God. But I'm willing to do what it takes."

"It doesn't take work, Beth. It just takes surrender. Repentance. You just have to give all of yourself to Christ."

"I'm not sure he wants even *some* of me," she said with a self-deprecating smile.

"Trust me. He wants all of you. And you don't have to wait until your good deeds outweigh your bad ones. Look at the thief on the cross."

She looked up at him, stricken. Why had he chosen that example? Did he suspect her past? "What about him?" she asked.

"He told Jesus he believed in him. To remember him when he came into his kingdom. Did Jesus tell him to clean up his act and work hard?"

"No."

"What did he say?"

Her Bible knowledge was shaky, but she did remember that. "He said, 'Today you shall be with me in Paradise.'"

"That's right. He took him just like he was, hanging on a cross for crimes he *had* committed, while Jesus hung there for no crime at all. But that man's sins were transferred to Jesus, and when that thief got to heaven, he was clean. Not because of anything he had done, but because he believed in his heart."

Beth sighed. She had never compared herself to the thief on the cross, not until now. But she'd heard about this concept of *grace* before—they always sang and preached about it at church. Somehow, she doubted that Nick or any of them had it right. There had to be more. It had to be tied into behavior, or none of it made any sense. She couldn't believe that, after everything she'd done, God could just accept her, forgive her, welcome her into heaven—at least not without her first having to *do* something to make up for all of those sins, and that something should be substantial. Because if that was true, if God just accepted and forgave us no matter what we'd done, then . . .

Well, then, someone like Bill Brandon—who professed to believe in Christ but used Scripture for his own evils, and who had ruined the lives of hundreds of children just as he had tried to ruin hers—could be readily accepted into heaven if he made a deathbed conversion.

And that could *never* be true.

"Tell me something, Beth," Nick said. "Look ahead five years, ten years, whatever, and tell me, if you could be everything you think God wants you to be, what will you be doing? Who will you be?"

She shifted on the bench and propped her elbow on the back. "Maybe I'll be married to a wonderful man I don't deserve. And I'll have babies . . ." That smile grew across her face. "Lots of babies. And my husband will love them, and never hurt them, and I'll live my life the way a mother should, so that they'll always trust me and count on me, so that no one will ever be able to take them away."

His smile faded as she spoke, and she realized she had said too much. He was watching her with misty eyes now, hanging on every word.

But she couldn't help going on in a strange, wistful voice. "And that family will be so great. The whole world can fall apart around us, but we'll be so strong, so tightly knit, that nothing will ever break us."

"'What God has joined together let no man put asunder.'"

"Yes!" she said. "I know exactly what that means."

"Do you believe that family you described is the plan God has for you? In other words, that he has good plans for you instead of calamity?"

"Yes," she whispered. "But sometimes we bring calamity on ourselves. Sometimes other people bring it on us." She shrugged. "On the other hand, he may plan for me to be alone. Some people are supposed to be single. Some people never find the right mate."

"That thought has run through my mind a few times, too," he admitted. "But I'd prefer to think that there's a terrific family that's already a snapshot in God's mind, and that I'm standing at the head of it."

"That would be a beautiful snapshot," she said. "Send me a wallet size of it, will you?"

His smile was eloquent, but she couldn't decipher what it could mean. She was too busy wishing she could be in that snapshot.

He touched her face, feather stroking it with gentle fingertips, testing her, as if he thought she might pull away. She didn't. Their eyes met in a startling moment of awareness, and she unconsciously wet her lips.

Slowly, his face moved closer to hers, and those fingertips moved into her hair and pulled her toward him. His lips brushed hers, gently, sweetly, and she felt her heart bursting into a Fourth-of-July display as their kiss deepened.

For a moment, all time was suspended, all tragedy was held at bay, all calamity was delayed. For a moment, she saw herself in that snapshot, standing under his arm with a serene smile on her face, surrounded by children that looked like him.

The joy of that hope brought real tears to her eyes, tears that she didn't try to blink back.

He broke the kiss and pressed his forehead into hers. He wiped one of her tears away with his thumb. For a moment, neither of them could speak.

His mouth seemed engaged in the same emotional struggle as he finally tried to find words. "You're a beautiful woman, Beth. Do you know that?"

She swallowed.

"A very beautiful woman."

He pulled her into his arms then, and held her while her tough facade crumbled and she melted into tears. She didn't remember ever being held like that, not in her life, and as she reveled in that warmth, she feared the ending of it.

Finally, he let her go and stood up, taking her hand. "We'd better go. Tomorrow's going to be a big day."

"Yeah," she whispered. "I guess I do need to get home."

"I'm not taking you home," he said. "It's too dangerous. I'm taking you back to Lynda's."

"But I can't impose on her that way."

"She insisted when we left," he said. "She took me aside and made me promise not to let you go home tonight. She even invited your puppy. Besides, I want to say good night to Jimmy."

"All right, then," she whispered, leaning into him as he slid his arm around her shoulders. "If I can go by and get Dodger."

"Sure. No problem."

Smiling gently, she walked with him to his car.

CHAPTER THIRTY-TWO

The parking lot at the *St. Clair News* was never empty, and tonight was no exception. At least a dozen cars were parked in scattered spaces, testifying to the fact that people were in the building, working to get out the next morning's edition of the paper.

Bill Brandon had timed things just right. Earlier that day, he had phoned the paper and spoken to a building maintenance supervisor. He'd told him that he was teaching a summer class in journalism for the University of Florida—Clearwater Campus's "College for Kids" program, and that he would like to bring a group on a field trip to tour the paper. But he wanted them to see the paper actually being printed.

That was impossible, the supervisor had told him. The paper was printed after midnight, and he doubted that any children's parents would be willing to send their children on a field trip at that hour. Bill had sighed and agreed.

But by the time he got off the phone, he knew exactly where in the building the paper was printed, and what time would be best to strike. Then he'd called one of his associates, who had much to lose if the article was printed and who had agreed to help. Since his associate was a prominent member of St. Clair's government, he would show up at the paper to complain about a political editorial that had been done the week before. Before he left, he would unlock two or three windows, so that later, the kids could get in. He had called back shortly after that with the location of the windows.

The children were quiet as he drove them through the parking lot flanking the building. He pointed down a hill toward a basement door with a light on, and said, "There. You see? That's the area you want to get into. But the windows are unlocked on the other side of the building, second floor. You'll have to go through the building to the right place." He drove around until the other side was in view. Lights glowed on that side of the building, as well, but not in the area where they would break in.

"Take the ladder and go in. Remember, quiet as mice, like I taught you. Space far enough apart that if one of you is seen, everyone else won't be given away. Now, what did I tell you to say if anyone sees you?"

Brad was the first to speak up. "I'm John's boy. He brought me to work with him tonight."

"What if nobody named John works here?" one of them asked.

"Somebody named John works everywhere," Bill said. "There are people scattered all over the building, so they'll accept that without thinking about it. Now stay in the dark places, and follow the route that I gave you. Everybody got their backpacks loaded?"

The team that consisted of four rough-looking boys, and three girls, including Lisa, all clothed in black, was ready.

"Remember," Bill said as they filed out of the van. "If you botch this up, you'll go to jail tomorrow. When that article comes out—"

"We won't botch it up, Bill," one of the kids said.

"All right. Now once you've done what you came to do, you take off through that door and don't waste any time. I'll be waiting."

The kids filed out, one by one, adjusting their backpacks on their shoulders. Three of the boys unloaded the ladder that was tied to the top of the van, the ladder they would leave behind, and carried it quickly to the side of the building where the three windows on the second floor had been unlocked.

They set the ladder under the window, and two of the girls held it while Brad scurried up it and slid the window up. No one said a word as Brad stepped through. Lisa was next. She climbed the ladder carefully, not fast enough, she was sure, but she was terrified of falling, and the weight of the load on her back made it more difficult to keep her balance. She reached the window and slid under. Brad helped her down without a word. It was the quietest she'd ever seen him.

She watched as he took off through the building, exactly the direction Bill had drilled them on. She waited and helped Kevin in, then took off herself, leaving him behind to help the one behind him.

A sense of importance filled her as she took off through the dark hallway to the exit sign that was her first marker. She quietly went through the door, took the stairs down, and came out on the first floor. She saw Brad a little ahead of her, hurrying past lit offices with people working at computers, past a huge room with dozens of cluttered desks, but only two or three people working. She could hear something clicking in there, something like a fast typewriter or printer. Maybe the noise would keep the workers from hearing them.

She looked behind her and saw Kevin gaining on her. She ducked past the door and to the next exit door, and headed down to the basement.

She was big enough to do this, she thought with satisfaction. Wouldn't Bill be proud of her, that she'd taken directions so carefully and hadn't messed it up?

She heard the sound of machines running as she came out of the stairwell into the basement. It was so loud that no one was ever going to hear them. She saw Brad looking around for anyone nearby.

There were two men in one of the rooms, their skin shiny with sweat as they operated the machines. It was hot down here, even though there was air conditioning and the fans overhead hummed. The machines put out a lot of heat. But she knew that it was about to get hotter.

Brad motioned for her to follow him, and she looked behind her and gave the same gesture to the person following her. He pointed to the room where the men were. "Somebody has to go in there," he said, his voice muffled by the drone of the machinery.

"No! They'll see us. We'll get caught," one of the children protested.

"If we don't do it, we're only half doing the job, and the article will come out."

"Send Lisa. She's the littlest. They won't see her."

Lisa's eyes widened. "I'm not going."

"Yes, you are," Brad said. "If you don't, I'll tell Bill. Now go. Head under the machine, and douse it good."

She got tears in her eyes as one of the kids unzipped her backpack and pulled the hose with the trigger spray nozzle out. "We'll be in here. Now hurry."

Lisa wanted to burst into tears, but she knew that if she did, she would be punished. She had to get the job done. It's what Jimmy would have done.

Biting her lip, she went to the edge of the door and peered around the doorway. She could see the sweating men doing something with the gadgets on the machine as the pages of the paper were spat out one by one. The room smelled of sweat, mildew, ink, and paper.

She ducked out of their sight behind the machinery and began to spray the inner workings of the machine, the floor around it, and the paper behind her against the wall awaiting its turn on the printer.

She heard voices. The men were talking to each other, but she couldn't hear what they were saying. Did they smell the gas, or was the artificial wind created by the fan pushing the smell down? Would it blow the fire out as soon as it got started?

She emptied the container of gas on her back, concentrating only on that one side of the machine, since she couldn't get to the other side without the men seeing her. Then she scurried back out of the room.

The others had been busily emptying their own containers, and she smelled the acrid fumes of gasoline soaked into curtains, carpet, dripping on the machinery in every room along the darkened hallway. Brad motioned for them to follow him, and they all ran down the hall to the door through which they would escape, the last person trailing a line of gasoline behind him.

When they reached the outside door, the others sprinted toward the van. But Brad grabbed Lisa and stopped her. "You're not finished," he whispered.

"What?" she asked.

"You get to light the match," he said. "It's your initiation. Bill said."

She didn't know what an initiation was, but she didn't object to it. She took the match from his hand, struck it against the gritty side of the matchbox, and smiled at the flame dancing on the end of the matchstick.

"Throw it in, stupid!" he whispered harshly. "Don't just stand there with it."

She threw the match down in the puddle of gasoline and watched it billow into flames. She caught her breath and jumped back as the fire raced down the hall. Brad grabbed her hand and began to pull her away from the door as the rooms they had doused went up in a quiet conflagration.

Lisa felt a sudden rush of fear. Looking back at the building as Brad pulled her along, she cried, "Those men! Brad, those men were in there!"

"They'll get out," he said. "Everybody will get out as soon as the fire alarm goes off. Now hurry!"

The van was moving as they reached it, and Brad forced Lisa into it, then jumped into it himself and closed the door just as they heard the fire alarm ring out.

Lisa rolled on the van floor, unable to find her footing, as the van accelerated out of the parking lot. But she managed to claw her way up to a window and peer out in time to see people fleeing from the burning building.

CHAPTER THIRTY-THREE

T he trucks that delivered Express Mail for the St. Clair area were lined up against the back of the post office, their rear doors open as graveyard shift postal workers loaded the next day's deliveries. On top of one of the stacks was the package Lisa had delivered earlier that day. The one addressed to Beth Wright, with the return address of Marlene Brandon.

As the sky began to take on the rose tints of dawn, one of the postal workers stopped for a moment to rest. He wiped his sweating brow and opened his thermos for some lukewarm coffee. "Hey, Alice," he called to the woman sitting at the front desk, "has the paper come yet?"

"Nope. Sorry. Looks like the delivery boy slept late today."

The man brooded as he slurped his coffee. Oh, well. He could always read one of the magazines before it got loaded onto a truck for delivery. He grabbed one out of a stack of mail, propped his feet up, and began to flip through.

A ll that night, Beth lay awake in Lynda's guest room, anticipating the arrival of the *St. Clair News* on the front steps of a hundred thousand readers.

She dressed as the first hints of morning began to peek through her window, put her leash on Dodger, and tiptoed past Lynda's room, then past the room where Jimmy slept, sprawled on top of his bedcovers. She went through the living room and kitchen and quietly slipped out the door into the early morning mist. She put Dodger down and walked him around to the front of the house. While he sniffed around in the bushes, she sat on the front porch steps, watching for the paperboy.

A tremendous sense of peace about what had happened with Nick last night enveloped her—only to be offset by a sense of dread about Bill Brandon.

She wondered if Bill had been arrested last night, if they'd found a way to make it stick so that he wouldn't be able to simply talk his way out of jail.

As the warm wind whipped through her hair, she pulled her feet up onto the top step of the porch. The sky was gray, but a faint pink hue crept up over the trees across the street. Maybe what happened today would wash away the sorrow and pain from the past.

Her eyes strayed up the street, where the paperboy should soon appear. She wished he would hurry.

At the end of the street she spotted a jogger dressed in black running shorts and a white tank top. She started to stand up and go inside, for she didn't trust strangers, especially not on this isolated street where no one ever came unless they were invited. And then she saw that the man was Jake.

He waved as he reached the halfway point on the block, then slowed his jog and walked the rest of the way, cooling down. When he reached the driveway, he picked up the towel he'd left on the trunk of his car, threw it around his neck, and came toward her.

"You're up awfully early," he said, his breath still coming hard. He bent down to pet Dodger, who wagged his tail stub and slobbered all over him.

"So are you. I was just waiting for the paperboy. I didn't know you jogged."

"Yeah, for about the last month or so. I'm trying to get in shape for my medical."

"Your what?"

"My medical. I have to get a medical release to get my pilot's license back. This afternoon is the moment of truth."

"Well, that shouldn't be a problem, should it?"

"No, ordinarily it wouldn't." He sat down on the steps next to her and rubbed the sweat from his face. "But this false eye could play against me, so I'm trying to overcompensate with the rest. If I can prove I'm more fit than most people, they might overlook the eye."

Beth narrowed her eyes and stared at him. "I didn't know you had a false eye, Jake. Which one?"

He chuckled. "If you can't tell, I'm not going to."

"Your eyes look just alike. And they move together. I didn't know false eyes could do that."

"They look just like ordinary eyes, but that's not what the licensing board cares about. They want to make sure that I can *see* like I'm supposed to. Half of my peripheral vision is gone now, so I can't fly for the commercial airline I used to fly for. They have pretty high standards. But if I can get my license back, I could buy a small plane and start a chartering service or something."

"That's great, Jake. They'll give it to you, won't they?"

"I think so. I'm just a little nervous. A lot is riding on this."

Thankful for the diversion, she asked, "Like what?"

He smiled and looked off in the direction from which he had just jogged. "Like . . . my relationship with Lynda."

"I thought that was pretty solid."

"It is. But I'd like for it to move forward. Have a little more permanency. I never thought I'd say this, but I don't want Lynda to just be my lady. I want her to be my wife."

Beth grinned. "Does she know this?"

"I'm sure she suspects it. But I haven't said it, straight out. Not when I have so little to offer her."

"Lynda doesn't need much."

"No, but she deserves everything." He sat down next to her on the steps. "I've been out of work and living on savings and odd jobs since the accident. I want to have an income, and be contributing something, before I ask her to marry me."

"That's admirable," Beth said. "I hope somebody will care about me like that one day."

"You're still young. No hurry."

"Yeah," she said. "And there's a lot of unfinished business I have to take care of before then." Her eyes strayed back to the end of the street. Still no paperboy.

"Unfinished business?"

"Yeah. This article is just part of it."

"Well, it should be here soon. But come to think of it, I usually see the paperboy when I'm jogging, and I didn't see him today. He must be running late. Tell you what. I'll go shower, then if it still hasn't come, I'll go pick up one at the closest newsstand. I'm anxious to see it, too." He got up and threw the towel back around his neck.

She smiled and watched him head back around the house and into the garage apartment. She wondered if Lynda had any idea how blessed she was to have a man like that in love with her.

After watching for the paperboy for a few more minutes, she decided not to wait any longer. She went back into the house and got her purse. Lynda was coming up the hall in her robe. "Beth, where are you going so early?"

"To try to find a newspaper," she said. "The paperboy is late. I'm just really anxious to see the article. There's a truck stop near my house that is always one of the earliest to get a paper. I'll go there and see if I can get one. I'll call you from home. Thanks for letting me stay here last night, okay? And tell Jimmy I'll be back to see him this afternoon."

"Okay. He'll be fine."

"Oh, and tell Jake that I'm sorry I couldn't wait."

Beth carried Dodger out to her car as that sense of uneasiness crept over her again. After she'd left Lynda's isolated street, she scanned the driveways for the rolled-up newspapers that always came with the morning. She saw none. She grabbed her car phone and dialed the number of the newspaper, planning to ask someone in circulation if there had been some delay in getting the papers out that morning.

A discordant tone came on instead of the ring, and an operator's recorded voice said that the number was temporarily out of order.

She cut the phone off, frowning, and wove her way through the neighborhood, neat little houses all lined up with no newspapers in the driveways.

Something is wrong.

She dialed the number of the police station and told the sergeant who answered the phone who she was. "I'm checking to see if Bill Brandon was arrested last night. Larry Millsaps and Tony Danks were on the case."

The sergeant checked his records, then came back to the phone. "No, I don't show an arrest made last night for a Brandon."

She closed her eyes. "All right, thanks."

She almost ran a red light, then slammed on her brakes and rubbed her forehead, trying to ease a rapidly escalating headache. What was going on? The telephone at the newspaper out of order, the arrest never carried out—

She whipped a quick U-turn at the intersection and headed back in the direction of the newspaper office.

It took her a few minutes to get to the street on which the *St. Clair News* was housed. And then she saw why the phone was out of order. The building was in shambles, half of it burned to the ground, and the other half, though still standing, only a monument of crumbling brick and slanted beams, with smoke-scalded ceilings and walls, and computer equipment and file cabinets smashed where the building had collapsed on one side.

She sat stunned, staring through her windshield at the smoldering ashes.

She hadn't realized anyone was coming toward her until a police officer knocked on her window.

"Ma'am, you'll have to move your car."

She rolled the window down. "I work here," she said. "What happened?"

"There was a fire last night," he said, as if that wasn't obvious.

"No, I mean, how did it start?"

"We suspect arson, but we're still investigating. Now, if you don't mind moving your car—"

"But the paper! The paper got out this morning, didn't it? The paper will still be delivered!"

"I don't think there's going to be an edition today, ma'am. Most of the machinery is toast."

She sat back hard on her seat and covered her mouth. The article wasn't coming out. Not today. A sense of injustice crashed over her. Familiar injustice. Predictable injustice.

"When did this happen? Did anyone see who started it?"

"No, no one saw anything. Two men who were right in the area where the fire was the most concentrated were killed."

"Killed? Oh, no! Who?"

He checked his clipboard, then asked her, "Are you asking as a member of the press, or a friend?"

"A friend!" she shouted. "Who died?"

"Off the record until we notify next of kin . . . Hank Morland and Stu Singer."

She didn't know them well, but she did know them, and now she closed her eyes and hugged herself as if she might split right down the middle and fall apart. Had her article caused someone's death? Did she have to bear that guilt now, too? She slammed her car into park, cut off the engine, and climbed out. "I need to get in touch with Larry Millsaps or Tony Danks. I need to talk to them now. Get me their home numbers, please!"

"I can't do that, ma'am. But if you have some information about who might have started this fire, you can tell me."

"Of course I know who started the fire!" she shouted. "It was Bill Brandon! You've got to tell them! Please, get in touch with them for me."

He didn't seem anxious to call in such an emotional revelation from a woman who seemed unstable, but he went to his squad car and asked the dispatcher for their home numbers.

Beth was with him when the answer was radioed back, and she bolted out of the squad car.

"Ma'am? Where are you going?"

"To call them," she said. "From my car phone."

He came to stand beside the open door as she punched out Tony's number.

He answered quickly. "Tony? This is Beth Wright."

"Yeah, Beth." His voice was gritty, as if she had awakened him. "I tried to call you last night, but you weren't home."

"What happened?" she demanded. "Why didn't you arrest him?"

"We couldn't get a warrant. Judge Wyatt was really hard-nosed about it. He said we didn't have enough evidence to arrest him."

"Not enough evidence? Are you kidding?" She looked at the building, still smoldering, and cried, "Did you show him my article?"

"I did. But he doesn't have a lot of faith in journalism. He's going to have to see more. We plan to make it our business to get him more so we can get Bill Brandon today. We're stuck with his decision because he's the presiding judge in St. Clair. There's no one higher up to go to."

"Well, if you're looking for evidence that Bill Brandon is too dangerous to be running loose, I've got it right in front of me."

"What do you mean, Beth?"

"I mean that the newspaper article is not going to come out today, Tony, because there's not going to *be* a newspaper today, because Bill Brandon burned the blasted place down last night. He killed two people in the process!"

"What?"

She was about to cry, and she fought it, hating herself for it. "He did it, Tony. You know he did. Somebody told him about the article—he's got lots of connections. So he took care of it."

"You're sure it was him?"

"He didn't sign his name, if that's what you want. He probably didn't even get within fifty feet of the building himself. He

455

probably used his kids to do it, like he does everything. Think of that, Tony—such a dangerous thing, and the kids are so young ..."

His pause told her she was getting too emotional, giving herself away, so she tried to rein in her emotions. "Look, you've got to arrest him before he does anything else. He stopped the presses last night, kept the article from coming out today. Now he has to get to the source of that article, and that, we both know, is me."

"You're right," he said. "Beth, stay there. Larry and I will be there in twenty minutes. Maybe we can find something to prove definitively that Bill Brandon or his kids were behind this. Something we can show Judge Wyatt."

"All right," she said. She glanced at the police officer's name tag. Lt. J.T. Mills. "Tell your friend Lt. Mills, so he'll let me stay."

"Okay. Hand him the phone."

She did, then got out of her car and took a few steps toward the building. Flashes came back to her, flashes of those late-night planning sessions with Bill and the rest of his kids, memorizing of blueprints, the endless drilling on which way they were to turn when they broke in, what they were to take, how they were to escape. She remembered the feel of her heightened senses as he'd let them out of his dark van, the urgency and adrenaline rush as they'd climbed into windows or cut glass out to unlock back doors, the smothering fear as they'd stolen through dark hallways ...

Bill had never asked her to start a fire or take someone's life. But he was getting desperate now, and his crimes were more catastrophic. What guilt those children would live with! She hoped they didn't know they had killed someone last night.

She heard the officer close her car door and come toward her. "You can stay, ma'am, but please stay back. Danks and Millsaps will be here soon."

She nodded her head. Leaning against her car, she watched the smoke softly swirling above the rubble, like prayers that would never find their way to heaven.

CHAPTER THIRTY-FIVE

The television news woke Jimmy. He sat up in bed and looked around, trying to figure out where he was. Oh, yeah. Lynda Barrett's house. Today was the day that Beth's article would come out, and Bill would be arrested, and he'd see Lisa again.

He quickly got dressed, then walked barefoot into the den. Lynda and Jake were glued to the television, and neither of them saw him.

"... suspected arson. The building went up in flames at approximately one A.M. Fire crews were on the scene within five minutes of the alarm going off, but it was too late to save the millions of dollars worth of equipment ... or the lives of the two men who were trapped in the flames ..."

"What building is that?" Jimmy asked, startling them. They both turned around.

"Good morning, Jimmy," Lynda said. "Did you sleep well?"

"Sure, but what building is that?"

"It's the building for the *St. Clair News.*"

"The newspaper building," Jimmy said, staring at the footage of the building engulfed in flames. He felt as if a fist had just whopped him in the stomach, knocking the wind out of him.

Bill's fist. His face reddened, and he tightened his lips to keep them from trembling with the emotion gripping him. "So he did it."

"Who?" Lynda asked.

"Bill. I told you he'd never let it come out." He knew his expression belied his matter-of-fact tone, but he couldn't seem to control it.

Lynda stepped toward him, but he backed away.

"I told you he'd never let Lisa out, either. They're never gonna hang anything on him. He's just gonna keep doing what he does, and now I've blown it and I can't go back, and Lisa's trapped there—"

"Jimmy, we don't know for sure that he was behind this. Even if he was—"

"*I* know for sure," he cut in. "*I* know!"

He ran out of the room, back to the bedroom where he had slept last night, and slammed the door. He sat down on the bed, trying to think. Somehow, he had to reach Lisa.

He went to the phone extension that sat on his bed table and put his trembling hand on it, wondering if he should risk calling her again. Then he wondered if he could risk *not* calling her.

Lisa wasn't safe.

He picked up the phone, punched in the number of Cottage B at the St. Clair Children's Home, and waited, holding his breath.

In Cottage B, Stella stood like a sentry over the children, making sure they all finished every last bite of their cereal. Some of the children woke up more easily than others, but all were awakened at the same time. Those who'd gone out with Bill last night, and had come in smelling of gasoline fumes, could barely hold their heads up, but they could have no one sleeping because that Nick fellow might pop in for an inspection again, and it wouldn't do to have children sleeping in the daylight. To keep up appearances, everyone had to be out of bed at the same time. It was good for them. It would make them tough.

The telephone rang, and Stella picked it up. "Hello?"

Click.

Annoyed, she hung it back up just in time to see Lisa's little head bobbing toward her cereal bowl, as though she might fall asleep right in the milk. "Lisa!" she shouted, startling the child. "Get a grip, would ya?"

The child propped her chin and tried to make her eyes stay open.

Frustrated, Jimmy admitted to himself that he'd never get to talk to Lisa—at least, not by phone. He closed his eyes and tried to think of a way to communicate with her. He wished she had a computer, that he could e-mail her as easily as he did the friends he corresponded with across the country on one of the computers that had been donated to the children's home. Bill had always encouraged Jimmy's interest in computers—after all, he'd been able to use the boy's knowledge on a number of occasions. That was why Jimmy'd been chosen to break into Beth's house; Bill had needed someone who could find Beth's files on SCCH.

No, Lisa didn't have access to the home's computers—but others did. Was there someone he could trust?

Brad. He was Jimmy's best friend, and there was nothing Brad liked more than keeping a secret. It made him feel important. That was why he seemed to thrive on the jobs Bill sent him to do. They were all secrets, and Brad went on all his missions like a miniature spy sent out into the night to risk his life to save his country.

Yes, Brad would keep Jimmy's secret. As loyal as Brad was to Bill, he'd been beaten enough to harbor the same smoldering hatred for him that Jimmy had.

Jimmy found Lynda in the kitchen. "Lynda, do you care if I play on your computer?"

She grinned. "Well, I don't mind, Jimmy, but I don't have any games on there."

"Do you have access to the Internet?"

Lynda couldn't help chuckling. "Yes, as a matter of fact. My modem is hooked to a second phone line, so you can use it all you want. You can probably find some good games on the network I subscribe to."

She told him the name of the network she used, and he smiled. It was the same one they used at the home.

"You're not an Internet addict, are you?" she asked.

"I just like to surf around and see what's there."

"Okay. Sure. I'll show you how to turn it on."

"No, I already know how," he said.

He went into the area of the great room where the computer sat, and turned it on. He found the icon for her network, registered himself as Lynda's guest, and entered his own screen name from the home's system. Quickly, he got on-line and clicked the "compose mail" button.

He sat there a moment, trying to remember what Brad's screen name was. It was something weird, some combination of letters from his name. Darb? Arbd? Drab? Yes, that was it. Drab and some numbers. His age. That was it. Drab11.

He addressed the letter, under "Subject" put "Secret," and then tabbed his cursor down to the body of the letter.

Brad,

It's me, Jimmy. Don't tell anybody you saw me here. I don't know what Bill told you, but I'm okay and I'm staying with a friend. I got caught on my mission the other night, but they were nice and didn't turn me in. If Bill finds me, he'll kill me. You know he will. Please don't tell.

Get a message to Lisa. Tell her I'm okay, and I'm trying to get her out of there. Tell her to be ready. I don't know how I'll do it yet, but I will. She can write me back if she wants. I think I can get my e-mail here.

Don't touch any of my stuff, and don't let anybody else get it. Especially my baseball cards. And if you tell, I'll tell the police everything you've ever done. If you keep my secret, maybe I'll try to get you out, too, and we can all find a boxcar to live in like the kids in that book and have fun from now on. Wouldn't that be cool?

Your friend,
Jimmy

He clicked the "send" button, and sat back. *Please let him see it. Please let him see it.*

"So how's it going?" Lynda asked.

"Good," he said, clicking the network off-line, and cutting the computer off.

"Hungry?"

"Sure."

She led him into the kitchen where a huge breakfast waited. He wished Lisa was here to share it with him.

CHAPTER THIRTY-SIX

B rad sat down at the computer, too tired to go outside where it was hot and muggy. Instead, he'd gotten permission to stay inside and play on the computer. It was one of the perks that the kids in Bill's "inner circle" got.

He turned on the network, got on-line, and checked his e-mail for a message from one of his pen pals in another part of the country, a pen pal who didn't know that he was an orphan, or that he lived in a children's home, or that he was a thief.

There was only one message from someone named JWMan. JWMan? It was familiar, but he couldn't remember who used that name. He clicked "read mail," and saw instantly that it was from Jimmy.

He sat up straighter as he read.

When he was finished, he looked out the window and saw Lisa sitting on a swing on the playground, leaning her head against the chains, as though she might fall asleep and come tumbling off. He went to the door and called out for her. "Lisa!"

She looked up.

"Come here. I have to show you something."

She looked like she didn't want to, but she got up and shuffled to the door. "What?" she asked belligerently.

"I've got a message for you from Jimmy," he whispered, taking her hand and pulling her to the computer.

Her eyebrows popped up. "Where?"

"Here. Look."

Lisa sat down in front of the screen and began to slowly read the letter. She had made A's in reading her first-grade year, but she still had to read slowly and concentrate very hard. Her finger followed the words, and she whispered them as she sounded them out, while Brad stood guard making sure no one came in.

Her eyes widened as she got to the part about him seeing her soon. "He's coming to get me!" she said. "We're gonna live in a boxcar! I want to write him back."

"All right," Brad said. "Hit 'reply' and type it in. It'll be under my screen name, but that's okay."

"Will you type it for me?" she asked.

He glanced toward both doors, then sat back down and put his fingers on the keyboard. "Okay. Tell me what to say."

"Say, 'Dear Jimmy, I miss you.'"

"I'm not typing that," Brad said. "That's gross."

"You said you would. It's my letter. I can say it if I want."

He moaned and typed the words. "What else?"

"Please hurry to get me. Bill gave me your job, and I don't like it."

"Not so fast," Brad said, still hunting and pecking on the word h-u-r-r-y. He made his way through the rest of the sentence.

"I guess that's all," she said, her lips beginning to quiver as tears filled her eyes. "I'm glad he's okay. I thought he wasn't coming back. I thought he left me here."

Brad didn't tell her that he had believed Bill's story about Jimmy being in jail. He might have known it was a lie. The boxcar thing sounded good—real good. They could get somewhere where Bill would never find them. They could get jobs—and until they did they could steal enough to get by. He hoped it would happen soon, before the police tried to arrest all of them.

"Tell me if he writes back," Lisa said.

Typing his own note now, Brad nodded. "Yeah, don't worry, I will."

In his secret room, Bill Brandon scanned the closed-circuit television monitors that kept him informed of everything that went on at SCCH. He watched with mild curiosity as Brad played in the computer room—then with suspicious puzzlement, watched as Brad called Lisa Westin in. They weren't good friends—in fact,

Brad could hardly tolerate the girl. So why the sudden cama-raderie?

He saw Lisa sit down and read something on the computer; Brad shuffled around the door, seeming to stand guard. Whatever was going on here, Bill didn't like it.

He waited, stiff, until the boy had turned off the computer and left the room. Then Bill headed across the campus to the com-puter room. A couple of kids had drifted in since Brad had left. Bill said loudly, "Outside, kids. It's too pretty a day to be playing inside."

They quickly turned off the computers and headed outside, leaving him alone. He locked the doors, then sat down at the com-puter Brad had been using. He turned it on, opened the on-line network he allowed them to use, and typed in Brad's screen name. His list of recent mail came up, but there were only three letters. One from some kid who was under the impression that Brad was the son of a congressman and lived in a mansion with a pool. Bill chuckled with disdain.

He clicked the next message, saw that it was part of a stupid conversation that didn't interest him.

Then he clicked the third. It was from someone going by the name of JWMan. He read the first line and knew that JWMan was Jimmy Westin.

His face reddened, and he clicked open the "Read Mail You've Sent" area, where outgoing messages were held. When Brad's log of messages appeared, Bill clicked the most recent one.

Lisa's letter came up, along with Brad's addition.

After he'd read them, he sat staring at the screen, trying to decide what to do. There was no question that Lisa and Brad should be punished for communicating with Jimmy, but he had to do more. He had to put the fear in them, so that they wouldn't tell the other kids what they'd learned. He hoped it wasn't too late. He looked out the window, saw Brad and Lisa talking quietly together at the back of the playground. Lisa was more animated than he'd seen her in days.

He looked back at the screen. Besides punishing the two of them, he had to find a way to make Jimmy come to him, so that he could put him out of commission. Too much was going wrong;

there were too many people out there who knew too much. HRS people sniffing around, reporters trying to write exposes of his operation, cops trying to get warrants for his arrest . . . Bill's whole world was in danger unless he could do some quick damage control, and Jimmy, little Jimmy, was right in the middle of it all. He had to lure Jimmy in somehow.

He clicked "unsend" on the letter the two kids had sent Jimmy, and waited anxiously to see if it was too late. If Jimmy had already opened it, he couldn't get it back. But if he hadn't . . .

The computer said that the letter had been unsent, and he grinned. He clicked "edit," then made a few changes. He deleted Lisa's portion, then on Brad's typed in, "Lisa's hurt real bad from the beating Bill gave her. Jimmy, you need to come get her before he kills her. I'll leave Stella's window unlocked so you can get in. Please hurry!"

He grinned as he sent the letter across cyberspace. Now all he had to do was be ready when Jimmy came.

He cut off the computer, then went to the back door and called for Brad and Lisa. Reluctantly, apprehensively, they both came in.

He locked the door behind them, then turned around to Brad. His arm swung and he backhanded the boy with a fist across the chest, knocking him down. Then he kicked him twice, once in each side, until the child was balled up in fetal position, moaning and crying and begging Bill to stop.

When he was satisfied that he'd done enough damage, he turned to Lisa. She shrank back against the wall, tears in her eyes and her face as red as the shirt she wore. "I didn't do anything."

"You've been communicating with your brother, and so has Brad," he said in a surprisingly gentle voice. "And I can't have that."

He grabbed her shoulders, shook her violently, then flung her across the room. But he didn't kick her, like he had Brad. Nick or someone else might come around asking about her, and she'd better not have a mark on her. He left Brad lying on the floor, and grabbed Lisa up. Marching her out of the computer room, he dragged her across the campus to another specially built room near his office. This one had been designed for discipline. It had no windows, no lights, and no furniture. Just a bare floor and darkness.

He flung her in there as she screamed in protest, and he locked the door behind her, blocking out the sound of her cries.

Then he sat down behind his desk and tried to catch his breath. No, there wouldn't be a mark on her—at least not on her body. Just on her mind. And if anyone came asking about either of the Westin kids . . . he could get her out of his "special room" quickly and no one would be the wiser.

As for Brad—no one cared about Brad anyway, so he didn't expect anyone to ask. He only hoped the beating had taught the kid a lesson.

He couldn't wait for Jimmy to get his message and show up at the home. With a grin, Bill jumped up and hurried across campus to Cottage B, where he unlocked Stella's window.

CHAPTER THIRTY-SEVEN

A few minutes after he got up that morning, Nick saw the news reports about the burning of the newspaper building, and quickly phoned Lynda's house to see if Beth had heard. When he didn't catch her there or at her own house, he decided to drive to the newspaper building itself. Just as he'd suspected, she stood there in the parking lot, leaning on the fender of her car, staring, stunned, at the smoldering ruins.

He pulled up beside her and got out of the car. "Beth, are you all right?"

She shrugged, then said in a dull monotone, "He stopped us. I knew he would."

"You really think Bill Brandon did this?"

She sighed. "They just found footprints of children's sneakers. They came in that window." She pointed to the part of the building that had not burned to the ground. "There was a ladder left behind, and children's fingerprints all over it."

"But I thought Brandon was arrested last night."

"The stupid judge refused to give them a warrant." Her voice was so flat, so calm, that he could hear the defeat there. "Now two people are dead, and those poor kids have this guilt on their heads."

He looked around. "Have Larry and Tony been out here?"

"Yeah, but they've gone back to try again to get a warrant." She looked up at him. "Nick, I'm worried about the kids. What if one of them was burned in the fire? What if they got too close?"

"I'll go back to SCCH today," he said.

"What good can you do there? They already know you're onto them."

"So I've got nothing to lose. If I'm there, he can't do anything to foil the police's arrest attempts."

"All right," she said. "Do it. Do whatever you have to."

"And you go back to Lynda's."

"No, I can't. I've still got the article on computer. I'm going to take it to the *St. Petersburg Times* today. Somehow, I'll convince them to print it."

"But you can't go to your house, now that Bill knows where it is. It's not safe."

"Nick, I have to. I have to get the disks that the story is on."

"Then I'll go with you."

She sighed. "All right. Follow me. It'll just take a minute."

She climbed into her car, took a moment to greet Dodger, who had been asleep on the front seat, and cranked her engine. Nick followed her closely all the way home.

"It's almost over, Dodger," she said to the puppy. "The article will still come out, regardless of the fire, and Bill will still get arrested, and Jimmy and Lisa and the other kids will be put in safe homes . . ." She tried to believe what she said as she reached the dirt road leading through the trees to her house—but the truth was, Bill had beaten them all. As, deep down, she had known he would.

The house looked undisturbed as she pulled up to it and parked. She got out, put Dodger on the ground, and waited as Nick pulled to a halt beside her car.

Nick insisted on going in first, but Dodger beat him to it. The puppy sniffed around, wagging his tail, and headed for the chew toy lying on the floor. As though he'd never ceased to work on it, he began to chew with his little tail stub wagging.

"It looks all right," Nick said. "Then again, somebody could be hiding in your attic and we'd never know. Is your computer upstairs?"

"Yeah," she said. "I'll just go up and get the disk . . ."

"I'll go first." He went up the stairs, checked around the corner, then motioned for her to follow. He stood with her as she found the disk and her briefcase, in which she had put a hard copy of the article. "Here it is."

"All right, let's go."

She followed him down. "I'll leave Dodger here, I guess. We can come back for him later." She checked the puppy's food supply and water, then locked the door and followed Nick back to her car.

He leaned over and dropped a kiss on her lips. "I'll head over to the home, and you call me when you get back from St. Pete. Go to Lynda's first—not home, okay?"

"All right. Be careful, Nick."

"You too."

With Beth's car in the lead, they headed down the dirt road leading to the street. They were almost to the end of the road when a postal truck turned in. Since the mailman always left Beth's mail in her box out by the street, she assumed he must have a package for her, so she did a quick U-turn and rolled her window down as she came next to Nick. "It's a package. I'd better get it."

He turned his car around and followed her back.

She got out just as the postman began to knock on her door. "Hi," she called up to the house. "Is that for me?"

"Beth Wright?" he asked.

"Yes."

"It's an overnight delivery." He stepped down the porch steps and handed her his clipboard. "Sign here."

She could hear Dodger inside, whimpering and scratching to get out. He didn't like being left any more than she did. She signed the clipboard, then took the package, surprised at the weight of it.

"Thanks," the postman said. "You have a nice day."

"You too."

Dodger began to howl and whine, and rolling her eyes, she shoved the package under one arm. Nick had rolled his window down so he could hear the exchange, and she called back to him, "I have to get Dodger, Nick. He's having a fit in there."

Before he could respond, she stuck the key back into the door and opened it. Dodger panted and jumped up on her calves, as if he hadn't seen her in weeks. "I was coming back, you silly little thing," she said, bending down to pet him. "I wasn't leaving you forever. Come on, let's put your leash back on and you can go with me."

She headed for the kitchen to get the leash. Dodger took the opportunity to dash outside, and she heard Nick's car door slam. "I'll get him!" After a second, he brought the squirming puppy back to the door. "Throw me the leash and I'll walk him. Who's the package from?"

"I'm trying to see." In the kitchen, she took the leash off its hanger and tossed it to Nick. Nick stooped in the doorway and tried to clip it to Dodger's collar, but he slipped free and bolted into the kitchen, his feet sliding on the hardwood floor.

She knelt down to make him quit jumping on her, still looking for the return address. She froze as her eyes located the "From" square. "It can't be."

"What?" Nick asked, leaning against the doorjamb to block it if the dog decided to make a break for it again.

"It's from Marlene Brandon. The woman who was murdered after she talked to me. But it's postmarked in St. Clair." Quickly, she got a knife and began to tear open the wrapping paper as she walked back into the living room. She tore off a strip of it, but the package was heavily taped. The dog frolicked beside her, trying to reach the torn strip hanging down.

"But this was an overnight package," Beth said, puzzled. "How could Marlene have mailed it yesterday? She was dead the night before."

"Maybe she mailed it before you talked. Maybe the post office just took longer than they should have."

She sat down on the couch, and Dodger tried to jump up onto it. She helped him, then slid the box halfway out of the envelope. Had Marlene sent her more documents? Photographs? Tapes?

Before she had the chance to slide it all the way out, Dodger rammed his nose against it, sniffing, and it slipped out of her hands. Dodger slipped off the couch with it as it hit the floor and, playfully, he grabbed a corner of the thick wrapping, the cigar box still held half inside, and dragged it across the room, inviting a game of hide-and-seek or tug-of-war.

Beth stood up as he scurried away from her, his tail wagging. "Dodger, stop that!"

The box slid all the way out of the express envelope, landing on its side, and the top fell open.

The explosion sounded like the end of the world. The last thing that crossed Beth's mind before she blacked out was that Bill had kept his word. He had gotten her. And now she would never be able to tell her story.

CHAPTER THIRTY-EIGHT

When Beth woke she was lying on the dirt outside. She had no idea how long she had been unconscious. Smoke poured through the charred door of her house. Nick crouched over her, his face stained with soot.

"It's okay, Beth," he was whispering. "Just hang on. They're on their way."

She heard a siren and tried to sit up. Her head hurt, and she felt dizzy. She began to cough, calling, "Dodger! Dodger! Nick, where's Dodger?"

But the look on Nick's face was a clear enough answer even without words. Distraught, she sank back against the ground.

"Hang on," he said. "An ambulance is coming."

She became gradually aware that he wasn't simply touching her to reassure her, but rather that he was pressing hard on her chest because she was bleeding. She closed her eyes, feeling nauseous. The fire truck wailed toward her house, getting louder and louder, and she opened her eyes just in time to see it jerk to a halt and the fire crew leap off and begin unwinding the hose. Behind the fire truck came an ambulance, and two EMTs rushed to her. Nick moved aside as the two began to check her vitals.

In minutes, she was in an ambulance racing to the hospital.

When the ambulance reached the hospital and she was whisked inside, she again saw Nick's worried face as he jogged along beside the gurney. Then darkness closed over her.

In the waiting room, Nick stood at the window, staring out at the pond they had sat at just last night. How could he have let her open that package? Why hadn't he realized what it was and snatched it out of her hands? Why hadn't he been clued by the return address of the dead woman?

Smoke inhalation, burns, a chest wound—but Beth could have been killed. If the puppy hadn't knocked the box off the couch, if she'd had it in her lap as Bill Brandon had intended, she would have been. Instead, the dog was blown apart, and she'd been knocked back.

He had dived toward her the moment the bomb had exploded, had dragged her out of the fire started by whatever incendiary device Brandon had included in the box. Then he had scrambled to her car where he knew she kept a phone. He'd been shaking so hard he almost hadn't been able to dial 911.

Thank God she was alive.

The sliding doors to the emergency room opened, and Lynda and Jake burst in, with Jimmy on their heels. He had asked a nurse to call them, for he hadn't had the composure to do it himself.

"How is she?"

"She's in surgery," he said. "She has a pretty bad chest wound. I don't know . . . how bad it is."

"I got hold of Larry Millsaps in his car," Lynda said. "He's heading out to Beth's house with a bomb inspector, and he's determined to get definitive evidence against Bill Brandon. He'll need it—he said they tried again today to get an arrest warrant for Brandon, and Judge Wyatt refused again."

"What is wrong with that judge?" Nick shouted, slamming the heel of his hand against the windowsill. "If he'd issued it last night, there wouldn't have been a fire at the paper, and Beth wouldn't have . . ." He stopped, unable to continue.

"I don't know, Nick. Judge Wyatt is really hard-nosed. I always try to avoid him in the courtroom if I can. He's not the most reasonable man in the world."

"Then what's he doing on the bench?"

"He's a lifetime appointee. Plus, he's the presiding judge. There's no one higher to appeal to unless they go to the prosecutor. He has great job security."

"Even if he's an idiot?"

She sighed. She was still trying to find an answer when the doctor came out and looked around for Nick. "Mr. Hutchins?

She's out of surgery, and she looks good. We were able to clean all the fragments out of her wound—it wasn't as bad as it looked, and her stitches should heal quickly. Thanks to you, her blood loss wasn't bad, nor did she inhale much smoke. You just may have saved her life."

"The dog saved her life," he said.

Jimmy's eyebrows rose. "Dodger saved her? Where is he?"

Nick swallowed. "Jimmy, I'm sorry, but Dodger's—" He stopped, gesturing hopelessly, trying to think of a way to break the news.

Jimmy's face fell. "He's dead, isn't he?"

Nick looked at Lynda and Jake, wishing for someone to say it for him. But there were no takers.

"I'm afraid so. If he hadn't done what he did, Beth might be the one dead instead."

Jimmy tried to plaster on his tough-kid look, and nodded stoically. He turned away from them and went to look out the window. Jake followed him, laying a hand on his shoulders, but the boy shrugged him away.

Nick turned back to the doctor. "When can I see her?"

"In a little while. We've put her in a room, and she should be waking up soon. We'll be keeping her until we're satisfied that there aren't any complications. Maybe she can go home tomorrow."

Home, Nick thought. Her home was in bad shape. She wouldn't be going there.

Lynda patted his back. "We'll wait here, Nick. You go on in and see her."

Nick was grateful that they didn't make him wait.

There was a nurse standing over her bed when she woke up. "Beth, how do you feel?" the nurse asked.

Beth had to think for a minute. "Okay," she whispered, but realized instantly that that wasn't exactly true. "Where is this?"

"The hospital," the nurse said. "You were in an explosion. Do you remember it?"

It started to come back to her in film-clip images . . . the package . . . the tape that was too tough to tear . . . Dodger getting it away from her . . .

472

"You've had some injuries, but you're going to be fine. I'm going to run out for just a minute and let the doctor know that you're awake, okay?"

She watched the nurse leave the room, and lay there for a moment, looking around at the cold, barren room, with nothing in it that belonged to her, and realized how alone she was. Just like Tracy.

She closed her eyes, her mind moving slowly through disjointed images until it called up a time when she was ten, when she'd broken into a huge home of a wealthy businessman. No one had been home, but he'd had a bird that she hadn't been told about. The bird had fluttered in its cage, spooking her, and she'd taken off running. She'd been so spooked that she had run through the sliding glass door to his patio. It had shattered around her, knocking her out and cutting her in a million places. The other kids had quickly carried her out and thrown her into the van.

Bill had refused to take her to the hospital because he was afraid someone would make the connection between the glass door shattered in a robbery attempt and the little girl covered in glass fragments. Then they'd be caught for sure. So he'd kept her in a room by herself at the home, where he had tweezed the fragments out one by one. It had been a slow torture, one he had seemed to enjoy, and he had followed each withdrawal with a swab of alcohol that had stung worse than any pain she'd ever felt before or since. She still had small scars in some places to remind her.

She'd had bruises all over her body from that incident, and must have had a concussion as well, for she'd slept at least three days following the accident.

Lying here in this room alone reminded her of the week she'd spent in bed in that room at SCCH as a child, wondering if anyone out there cared at all about her, wondering if anyone even gave her a thought.

Bill had told her as he picked glass out of her that they had ways of identifying the blood on glass shards, and that he expected them to arrest her at any moment. It was her fault she was in this position, he'd told her, because she shouldn't have panicked. He was trying to protect her by keeping her here, he'd told her, but Bill's kind of caring wasn't the kind she craved. His was a sick, self-centered concern that frightened her to death.

Funny that Bill was behind this injury, as well. He had almost succeeded at keeping her quiet. He had almost killed her along with her story.

Tears rolled down her face. Lying here, alone, she felt like a wasted, discarded, useless body—the way Tracy probably felt. Was God really there, watching out for her, or was he just disgusted by her?

She thought of the lies she'd told about this story, the anonymous confession, the sneaky way she'd tried to get Maria to confess so that she, Beth, wouldn't have to. She thought of the secrets she'd kept from Nick, from Phil, from the law enforcement officers who needed to know the name of the only available adult witness. The secrets she had kept from little Jimmy, who needed to know that there was someone who truly understood his plight as no one else could, someone who had been there and suffered as he was suffering, someone who had survived it—maybe even grown through it.

Could God see through those sins and walk with her now? The consequences of confessing those sins loomed ever bigger in her consciousness, reminding her that there would be a price to pay. But all those children were still paying. Paying and paying, and they would continue to pay as they grew older and broke free of Bill Brandon. They would pay like she was paying until someone broke the cycle.

And that's what she'd been trying to do. But she'd been trying to do it the easy way, the cheap way. Maybe there was no cheap way. Maybe the only way was to accept the possibility of losing her job and her reputation, and to tell the truth. Maybe then she could have a chance with God.

To do that, she'd have to forget the story she'd written so neatly and remotely, and instead offer herself as a witness who could put Bill Brandon away for life. The buck had to stop somewhere, and it was going to stop here. Unless he stopped her first.

She heard a knock on the door, and then it opened. Nick stood there, looking as fragile and shaken as she'd felt lying out on the dirt with her house burning behind her. He tried to smile, but she could see that the effort was almost too great for him.

He came and leaned over her. "Are you all right?" he asked.

Her voice was hoarse, weak. "Yes. Amazingly, I am. I wasn't supposed to be, though. He intended to kill me."

She could see that Nick agreed with her.

"If I could have just gotten the package away from you before you opened it," he whispered. "I should have realized right away . . . I should have taken it and—"

"Shhh," she whispered, reaching up to touch his lips. "Don't. He set us up. He knew I wouldn't be able to resist a package with Marlene's name on it. He's smart, Nick. I told you how smart he is." She closed her eyes, fighting the tears. "Poor Dodger. He didn't know what hit him."

Nick clearly didn't know what to say. He just stroked her hair back from her face, and she closed her eyes.

A memory, white-hot and miserable, came back to her, a memory of another little dog they had found at the home. It had wandered up onto the lawn one day, and they had played with it, then asked Bill if they could keep it. He'd told them no.

She wasn't sure why that little dog had created such a fierce longing in them, why the children had wanted him badly enough to risk Bill's wrath, but someone had suggested that they hide it and keep it anyway, that they could keep it a secret from Bill. They had all agreed.

They had hidden the little dog in a storage shed at the back of the grounds at night, then moved him wherever he was least likely to be found during the day. He had been a kind, gentle secret that bound the children, so unlike the dark, ugly secrets they had shared before.

But one night, when they'd come in from robbing the home of the president of the local college, Bill told them that he'd discovered the puppy, and that he realized how much they must love the dog to work so hard to hide him for so long. He told them that they had worked hard for him, too, and that they deserved something of their own for their labors. He told them they didn't have to hide the puppy anymore.

Eagerly, they had all run out to the shed to get the puppy and bring him in, each of them arguing about which one of them the dog would sleep with that night. They had reached the shed, thrown open the door, flicked on the light—

The puppy lay dead on the floor, shot through the head.

Bill had taught them a valuable lesson.

She wondered how many more "valuable lessons" he had taught to Jimmy and Lisa and all those other children at the home—lessons that might twist and scar them for life. How many times over the years had she fantasized about a rescuer who would come and save them all from Bill. Maybe that was why she had suffered the childhood she had. Maybe God was grooming Beth to be the rescuer of these children. Maybe she was going to be their Esther, groomed "for such a time as this."

"I have to go," she said weakly, trying to sit up. "I have to get out of here."

"You can't leave, Beth. You have to stay, at least overnight."

"No, I can't. I have to talk to Phil, my editor. I have to tell him what happened. I have to tell him some other things."

"I've put too much pressure on you," Nick said, his eyes misting over. "I've made this seem like the most important thing in the world, and you almost got killed. It's not worth it."

"Of course it is! Until I get that story printed, I'm in danger. Once the story's out, it would be too obvious if anything happened to me. He wouldn't dare try anything." She looked up at him. "Nick, tell them I'm okay. That I can go. Please?"

"No," he said. "You're not as strong as you think. You have to lie still, Beth. You have to stay here."

"Then make Phil come to me," she said. "And call Lynda, and Larry Millsaps and Tony Danks at the St. Clair Police Department."

"Lynda's already here," he said. "With Jake and Jimmy. But I'll call the others. I'll tell them to come tomorrow."

"No, not tomorrow. Now! I have something I have to tell all of you, Jake and Jimmy, too. Something important, Nick. Please. It really can't wait."

"Okay," he said finally. "Just calm down. Be still. I'll go call them now."

CHAPTER THIRTY-NINE

The doctors were at first strongly opposed to having such a group in her room so soon after her injuries, but when Beth convinced them that her long-term safety depended on a quick arrest of the one who'd injured her, they finally allowed it.

Phil was the first one in when the group came quietly into her room. "Beth, are you all right?" he asked.

"Yes, for now," she said. "But I need to talk to you. All of you."

Lynda rushed forward and hugged her. "I'm so glad you're okay. And what a miracle that Jimmy wasn't there."

"Yeah," she said. "Where is he?"

"I'm right here," Jimmy said from behind Lynda. He came up to the bed, hands in his pockets, and glanced awkwardly at her. "Bill did this, you know."

She swallowed hard and nodded. "I know."

"But he'll get away with it. He always does."

"Not this time, Jimmy."

Jake bent over the bed and pressed a kiss on her cheek, and she saw Tony and Larry coming in. Nick was last to enter the room, and she held out a hand to him. He came to the bed and held her hand, lending her support he didn't even know she was going to need.

"Thanks for coming, everybody," she said. "I won't keep you long. You've probably all figured out by now that someone's trying to kill me, to keep me from finishing the story I'm working on, about the St. Clair Children's Home. Last night, the *St. Clair News* building was burned down, and this morning, the explosion—Bill Brandon doesn't want it printed." She cleared her throat and looked at her editor.

"Phil, you kept saying you wanted one more quote. Yesterday, I gave you one, but it was from an anonymous source." She hesitated, then forced herself to go on. "But it's time to tell who that source is. The reason this story is such a passion for me is that ... I was the anonymous witness who grew up at SCCH."

Nick looked more stunned than anyone. His mouth fell open. "You what?"

Jimmy gasped, then narrowed his eyes and studied her closely. The others looked first at one another, then at her, shock evident on their faces.

"I didn't want to tell anyone because ... being in Bill's home brings with it some degree of ... guilt."

"Wait a minute," Phil said, scratching his head. "Are you telling me that you've seen these abuses firsthand?"

She closed her eyes again, and Nick tightened his hold on her hand. "I'm telling you that I've been involved in them."

Larry and Tony got up from their chairs and came closer to the bed. "So you were one of the kids in his crime ring? He actually used you to break into homes and steal things?"

"That's right. From the time I was eight years old until I left the home at eighteen." She lifted her chin high, to fight the tears pushing into her eyes, and met Nick's stunned gaze. "I'm sorry, Nick. I should have told you—"

Nick took a few steps closer, his face twisting as he tried to understand. "You were in that home? But I worked for HRS then. I would have seen you."

"No, Sheila Axelrod is the one who processed my release when I turned eighteen. And actually, we did cross paths a couple of times. But I've changed my hair color and cut it, and I changed my name. But I came to you when I decided to expose Bill, because I knew you seemed like someone who would listen. I knew that from the way you treated some of my housemates."

Nick was still gaping, disbelieving, and she turned back to Larry and Tony. "I realize that this confession could get me into trouble, and that's why I've tried not to expose myself in this story.

But Bill Brandon has got to be stopped. An old friend of mine from the home told me yesterday that if I wouldn't even talk, what made me think anyone else would? Well, now I'm talking." She looked at Phil. "You wanted a reliable adult's word? Well, here it is. She's got a name and everything."

"Awesome!" Jimmy said. "No wonder you knew so much about Bill. No wonder he knew so much about you!"

"Wow." Phil slumped back in his chair. "I can't believe this."

"Believe it. It's true. Bill Brandon trained me to be a thief, and for ten years, that's what I was. And as we speak, he's training other kids to be thieves. Maybe worse. Kids were involved in the arson last night. They could have been killed."

"There's more," Tony said, glancing back at Larry. "After the explosion at your house, Nick told us where the package was postmarked, so we went by that post office to see what they could remember about the package. Turns out that one of the postal workers saw a little girl bringing it in."

"A little girl, delivering a bomb?" Beth asked.

"He described her as six or seven, reddish-blonde, shoulder-length hair, big eyes, very polite."

"Lisa," Jimmy said. "It's Lisa."

Nick clenched his jaw. "Tony, Larry, you've got to get this guy. Somebody else is gonna get killed if you don't."

Jimmy's face was reddening, and his lips trembled. "You've got to get Lisa out of there. She doesn't know any better. She's just seven. He's so mean ..."

"All right," Larry said. "We have ample evidence now to arrest Bill Brandon. If Judge Wyatt refuses us a warrant this time, we'll go over his head to the prosecutor. We'll have Brandon locked up by the end of the day."

"I wish the article hadn't been destroyed," Phil said.

"It wasn't," Nick said. "She has a copy in her car, with a disk."

"I was taking it to the *St. Petersburg Times*."

"Good idea. They'll print it, if we can't. If you'll give it to me, I'll make sure of it, Beth."

"I want to make some changes, first. I want to put my own name in there, and write down what I just told you."

"You can dictate it over the phone. I'll call you here when I get to St. Pete."

"What about me?" Jimmy's rough voice surprised them all. "What about Lisa, and all the other kids? Are we gonna go to jail?"

"You leave that to me," Lynda told him. "I'll take care of everything."

"Can either of you lead us to where he warehouses all of the things he steals?"

"No," Beth said. "He never shared that part of the business with us. He just gave us our orders, and we followed them."

"Do you know who else was involved?"

"All of the adults who work for him, according to Marlene. But not all of the kids. Sometimes I didn't even know what other kids were involved. He seemed to pick out the ones he could control the best. The ones who would fear him and try to please him."

"Was there physical abuse involved?"

"Yes. Always. That was how he controlled us."

"Sexual abuse?"

She shook her head. "No, thank God. I was never molested, and I didn't hear about it happening to anyone else. I think Bill considers himself a fine, upstanding, normal citizen who happens to have an unusual hobby."

"How about you, Jimmy? Has Bill ever molested you or any of the other kids?"

"Not me, and not the others as far as I know."

"Just beatings."

"Yeah, and other things."

Other things. She thought about the plate-glass window, and the alcohol, and the puppy with a bullet hole through his head. Bill's cruelties knew no bounds. She wondered what horrors Jimmy had experienced.

"What other things, Jimmy?"

He looked down at his worn sneakers. "One time, Keith Huxtin fell from a ladder when he was breaking into a house, and he broke his leg. We didn't think anybody was home, but somebody was, and they came out and saw us. We had to carry Keith down the street to the van, running as fast as we could to keep from getting caught. Bill wouldn't take him to the hospital because he knew they were looking for a kid who'd been hurt. He made him sweat the pain out for two days. Then he took us to school early and made us carry him in and lay him in the hall. We had to pretend he had fallen at school, so Bill wouldn't be blamed and it would seem like it had happened two days after the break-in. Those idiots bought the whole story, even though his scrapes had already scabbed over."

"This van. What does it look like, and where does he keep it?"

"In the shed at the back of the campus. It's dark green."

Larry's eyebrows rose. "Can *you* take us to the warehouse?"

"No. I don't know where it is. It was always dark, and I was always in the back of the van. Sometimes there was a truck there, loading up. I don't know where they took all the stuff. Somewhere to sell it, I guess."

"There are a lot more people than Bill and the kids involved," Beth said. "I don't know who they are, but there are others."

"All right," Larry said. "We need to take Jimmy down to the station to make another statement, and we'll send someone in here to get Beth's. We'll also post a guard here for protection."

"I'm going with Jimmy," Lynda told Beth. "I'll be back as soon as they're finished with him."

"Nick, we need everything you've already compiled about the home," Tony said. "We're going to throw the book at this guy, and make sure no one drops the ball. We also need you to be there for Jimmy's statement. As long as a representative of HRS is with us, we won't have to get any other bureaucrats involved."

"All right." Nick's voice was distant, and he seemed distracted, preoccupied, as he looked down at Beth. "I'll be back as soon as I get them what they need, okay?"

"Yeah," she said, touching his face. "Just one thing."

"What?"

"Are you disappointed in me?"

"Why would I be disappointed?" he asked.

"Because I lied about my interest in the case. And you didn't know that I was raised breaking into people's homes. You thought I was a normal, healthy woman."

"Hush," he said, stroking her hair back from her face. "Enough of that. You are a normal, healthy woman. And you're courageous. You could have let it all go. But you cared enough about those kids to tell the truth."

"Took me long enough."

He leaned over and kissed her forehead, but she could still see the troubled expression in his eyes. "I'll be back."

When the room had cleared out, Beth lay on her back, staring at the ceiling and wondering what would happen next. Wouldn't there be consequences? Wouldn't the media ask when she'd been old enough to know right from wrong, and to do something about it? Why she hadn't turned Bill in years ago? Maybe the media wouldn't ask—but *she* still had those questions. She pictured that little boy, Keith, who'd broken his leg and suffered for two days. The plate-glass-window incident could have been the last time, if she had found some way to turn Bill in then. Then Keith wouldn't have had to suffer. But no, she'd kept her mouth shut, and gone along, and even after she was out, she'd been so grateful and relieved to be away from Bill Brandon that she hadn't thought much about the kids she'd left behind. Jimmy had come only shortly after she'd left. Because of her silence, he'd suffered.

Now she wondered what her own personal consequences would be. While Nick was too kind to condemn her, did this revelation change the way he felt about her? It wasn't as if she was looking toward marriage, but the thought that Nick might reject her because of this filled her with despair. What if Nick, who dealt with troubled pasts and presents all day every day, decided that he didn't need all her baggage—that she just wasn't the one for him?

She wouldn't blame him at all if he did.

CHAPTER FORTY

J ake was in the Police Department waiting room when Jimmy, Nick, and Lynda came out of the interrogation room. Jimmy had just spent two hours answering questions, and he looked worn out.

Jake stood up as they approached. "How'd it go?"

"Okay, I guess," Jimmy said. "I think I told them what they wanted."

"All they wanted was the truth."

"Well, that's what I gave them." He looked up at Nick. "What now?"

"Nothing yet. We just have to keep you safe until we get Brandon off the streets and start moving the kids from the home. I'll spend the rest of the day trying to line up places to relocate them."

"You'll keep me and Lisa together, won't you?"

"Of course. I'll move heaven and earth to do that, Jimmy."

"Hey, Nick," Jake cut in. "Since you'll be so busy, and Lynda needs to go to the office, how about letting Jimmy spend the afternoon with me? I have some errands to run, and he can help me."

Nick looked down at the kid. "Want to, Jimmy?"

"Sure," he said. "It's better than nothing."

Jake chuckled at the under-enthusiastic response. He kissed Lynda good-bye and ushered him out to his car.

"So where are we going?" Jimmy asked.

"Someplace really important," he said. "Remember I told you I was going to try to get my medical release so I could get my pilot's license back?"

"Yeah."

"Well, it's this afternoon. I thought you might like to come with me."

He shrugged. "Yeah, okay."

"You can't go into the examination room, but you can wait outside, and if they turn me down, you can help carry me out to the car. I'll be too depressed to walk."

"Nervous?" Jimmy asked.

"Were you nervous in there with the cops?"

Jimmy nodded.

"That's about how nervous I am," Jake said. "I have a lot riding on this. I have a flying job lined up that I really want. But no license, no job."

"And you won't ask Lynda to marry you?"

He thought that one over for a moment. "I'm not sure, Jimmy. All I know is that I want to get back on my own two feet before I ask her."

"They'll give you your license back. Why wouldn't they?"

"Well, one of their concerns is my reflexes. Whether my legs have healed enough to react as they should. I think I've got that one in the bag. But the eye thing . . . Sometimes they'll overlook a false eye, if the pilot can convince them that his vision is fine anyway, that he can compensate with the other eye. But it all depends. Sometimes they decide it's just too risky, and they ground you for life."

Jimmy just looked up at him. "I hope you get it, Jake."

"Yeah, me too."

Jimmy sat by the window in the Federal Aviation Administration offices, staring down at the parking lot just in case Bill managed to find him and come after him here. If Bill only knew what he'd told the police, he'd kill him for sure. And if he couldn't kill Jimmy, he'd kill Lisa.

The door opened, startling him, and Jake came out, his face solemn and pale. Jimmy got to his feet. "They turned you down?"

A slow grin stole across Jake's lips. "No! They gave me my license back!"

"All right!" Jimmy said, jumping up and slapping Jake's hand. They both danced a little jig, and then Jake pulled him into a tight hug and almost knocked him over. "I'm glad you were here to share this moment with me, buddy. I don't think I could have done it if I hadn't known you were out here for moral support."

"I didn't do anything."

"You did plenty. You were here!"

Jake practically floated back out to his car, alternately walking fast, then punching the air, then dancing again.

"Wait till you tell Lynda," Jimmy said.

Jake shook his head as he got into the car. "No way. I still don't want her to know. I want to spring the whole thing on her when I ask her to marry me."

"So when will that be?"

"Soon, my boy. Very soon. Let's just hope she says yes."

"She'd be stupid not to."

Jake laughed. "You're a good friend, pal-o-mine. And just as a reward, I think I'll take you for my first post-crash flight without another licensed pilot tagging along. Are you up for it?"

"Yes!" Jimmy said. "Let's go."

At the airport, Mike, the owner, celebrated with Jake over the return of his license, and offered him free use of a rental plane for the afternoon. Jake took Jimmy up, and they flew out over the Gulf, where Jimmy had a bird's-eye view of St. Clair.

The familiar serenity washed over Jake, calming his spirit and making him feel close to Jimmy. "Isn't this beautiful?" he asked.

"Yeah," Jimmy said. "When I grow up, I want to be a pilot."

"I'll teach you myself," he said. "The job I'm hoping for is as a flight instructor. I'll do that part-time, and fly for several ministries around this area on the side. But I'm sure I could make time to teach a bright kid like you how to fly."

"It depends," Jimmy said. "I don't really know where I'll be. I may not even be in St. Clair anymore."

How pressing this worry must be for Jimmy, Jake realized. The low hum of the engine accompanied the thoughts going through both their minds.

"Tell me something," Jake said quietly. "Tell me about your parents."

"They're dead," Jimmy said quickly.

Jake knew that wasn't true, but he wasn't sure that Jimmy knew it. "Do you remember them?"

He shrugged and looked out the window. "My dad was a spy who was killed in France during the war," he said. That was impossible, Jake knew, but it didn't matter—it was a fantasy he could identify with. He'd never known his father either, and had made up similar stories.

"I didn't have a dad," Jake said. "Never knew him." Jimmy didn't change his answer, so Jake pressed on. "What about your mom?"

Jimmy took a little longer to answer that. "She died almost three years ago. That's why they put us in the home."

"What did she die of?" Jake asked.

"Cancer," Jimmy said. "She had cancer."

"I'm sorry, Jimmy. What kind of cancer?"

Jimmy thought for a moment. "Prostate cancer, I think it was."

Jake's eyebrows shot up. "Prostate cancer, huh?"

"Yeah."

"Oh." He almost smiled. "That's rare in women."

"Yeah."

"Do you remember much about her?"

"Sure. She was the greatest mom in the world. She made our lunches, and cooked these great suppers, and we'd all sit at the table and talk about our days. And we always had plenty to eat and warm beds to sleep in and clean clothes . . . and she loved us."

Tears came to Jake's eyes. The memories were sweet, yet the boy thought his mother was dead. What if he found out that she was alive? What if they reintroduced him to her?

He looked at the boy, and saw the solemn, dreamy look that had passed over his face. "Do you ever miss her?"

Jimmy swallowed and shrugged. He couldn't seem to answer, so he only nodded. "Lisa misses her most," he said. "She can't remember her too good. I tell her stories about her. Good stories, about all the things she used to do."

Jake had heard enough from Nick to know that none of those stories were true. But maybe they could be, if they reintroduced the boy to his mother . . .

The thought wouldn't leave his mind, and after they landed, he left Jimmy alone and made a couple of phone calls—to Lynda first, and then to Nick.

Jake didn't mention his phone calls to Jimmy when they got back into the car. Instead, he told him that they were going to the hospital to check on Beth, and that Nick would meet them there. But as he drove, he prayed silently that he was doing the right thing.

CHAPTER FORTY-ONE

Tracy had been moved out of ICU, Jake learned when he got to the hospital and found Nick waiting for him. Nick spoke to Jimmy, then stepped aside with Jake. "Look, if he gets upset or anything..."

"He's out of there. No problem."

"All right."

They went back to where Jimmy waited, and Nick leaned down to Jimmy. "Jimmy, before we go see Beth, while you're here at the hospital, I think there's somebody here you might like to see."

His eyes widened. "Lisa?"

"No, not Lisa. Someone else. A patient who's in here with pneumonia. I found her real sick the other day and brought her here."

Jimmy hesitated. "I'm not too good with sick people."

"It's okay. You don't have to do anything. You don't even have to say anything."

"Then why am I going?"

The elevator doors opened, and Nick led him on. "You'll see. Just wait."

Jake was quiet as he followed Nick and Jimmy off the elevator.

They reached the open door, and Nick peered in. It was a semiprivate room, but the other bed was unoccupied. Tracy lay in bed, IVs still attached to her and an oxygen mask over her face.

Jake touched the back of Jimmy's neck, and followed Nick in. As they came closer to the bed, Nick leaned over her. "Hi," he said. "How're you feeling?"

"Okay," she said weakly.

He looked back at Jimmy, who stood awkwardly back. "Recognize her?"

Jimmy shook his head. "No. Do I know her?"

Nick shot a concerned look at Jake. "I have someone here I wanted you to see, Tracy," he said.

Jimmy froze at the name. "No. Not her." His mouth tightened, tears sprang to his eyes, and he began to back out of the room. "I don't want to see her."

Tracy rose up slightly and saw her son. "Jimmy?"

"No!" he shouted, and the nurse came running. Jake grabbed him, but he shook free and fled from the room. Jake followed him out.

"Jimmy, wait!"

The boy ran to the elevators and began punching the down button, waiting for one to open. His face was crimson and covered with tears, and he turned his face away so Jake couldn't see. Jake squatted in front of him and held him by the shoulders. "Son, you don't have to go back in there. It was a bad idea, okay? We didn't know it would upset you. We thought you'd be happy. Will you forgive us?"

"So you proved I lied. You coulda just told me you knew!"

"I didn't know you lied, Jimmy. I thought you might really think she was dead."

"I know what you're all up to. You're gonna take Lisa out of the home and give us back to her. And it'll be even worse than it was at the home." His voice broke off, and he bent over, weeping, and covered his face with both hands. "I should have known."

"Jimmy, nobody's giving you or Lisa back to your mom."

"Lisa's better off where she is than with that sorry excuse for a mother in there!" Jimmy raged. "At least she has a chance where she is. I can take care of my sister better than *she* can. I was the one who did it, anyway, when we lived with her."

"Jimmy, you've got to trust us."

Jimmy's eyes flashed. "I don't believe anything you say. You're all a bunch of liars! You don't care who gets stuck with who, or what things are like there."

"Jimmy, listen to me, please—"

"I'm not listening anymore," he said. "Just let me go, and I'll handle things myself."

The elevator doors came open, and Jake grabbed Jimmy's shoulder and followed him on. *What a terrible move*, he thought. *What a mistake.*

"Look, son, you don't have to talk to me, but you do have to come with me. And you can just listen, okay?"

Jimmy didn't answer.

"We'll go for a ride. Maybe out to the beach."

Jimmy didn't respond.

The doors opened on the first floor, and Jimmy darted off. Jake caught up to him and grabbed his shoulder. "This way, little buddy," he said, and directed him to his car.

Back in Tracy's room, Nick tried to apologize to her, but the sight of her son had shaken her. She was crying and gasping for breath, and he wanted to kick himself for making such a stupid error in judgment.

"I'm sorry, Tracy," he said. "I thought—I don't know what I thought. That it would help Jimmy to see you, I guess. To know that he still has a mother. That he's not all alone in the world."

"I'm not his mother," she wheezed. "The state took him away. He hates me, and I don't blame him, 'cause I hate myself."

"Don't say that, Tracy," Nick told her. "How can you hate someone God loves?"

"God doesn't love me," she said. "Why would he love me?"

"Because he created you."

"Yeah, and then I destroyed myself."

"Not yet. It's not too late to turn around, Tracy. It's not too late to make your kids love you again, either."

She turned her head to the side and wiped at her eyes. "You don't even know what you're talking about," she said. "Just leave me alone."

Nick started to protest, then thought better of it. "All right," he said quietly. "Listen—if you decide you want to talk in the next hour or so, call me up in Beth Wright's room."

She didn't answer, and he felt a deep self-loathing. He shouldn't have tried it. So stupid. Defeated, he walked out of the room.

CHAPTER FORTY-TWO

ony didn't even bother to sit down when they returned to Judge Wyatt's office. All he wanted was to snatch the warrant and run as fast as he could to SCCH so he could arrest Bill Brandon. "The evidence is overwhelming and conclusive, your honor," he told Judge Wyatt. "We have an adult who was raised in the home who has given us a statement. We have a child who's been participating in Brandon's crime ring recently. We have the murder of Bill Brandon's sister, and we have two attempts on Beth Wright's life—including a package bomb that almost killed her, and we have the arson at the newspaper the night before the article exposing Brandon would have come out."

Judge Wyatt adjusted his glasses and looked over the charges, a deep wrinkle clefting his forehead. He seemed to study it too hard, as if it required much thought, and Larry, who was sitting, shot Tony a disturbed look.

The judge started to get up, almost distractedly, as if he'd forgotten they were in the room. "I'll spend some time looking over these charges tonight," he muttered. "I'll take all of it under advisement and get back to you tomorrow."

"Tomorrow?" Larry sprang out of his chair. "Judge, tomorrow's too late. He's a killer, and he's trying to take out our main witness. She's in the hospital as we speak."

"She'll be safe until tomorrow," the judge said. "No idiot would attempt murder in as public a place as a hospital."

"Give me a break!" Tony cried. "What is the deal here? You've stood in the way every step of this investigation!"

The judge banged his fist down. "It's my job to ensure that you do your job within the bounds of the law, so that my courtroom doesn't fill up with a bunch of lawyers who waste my time with technicalities and loopholes. I will not issue arrest warrants for every Tom, Dick, and Harry you *think* may have committed a crime!"

"Think? What does all this evidence spell, Judge? Witnesses, bodies—what do you want? You want him to come after you? Would you give us an arrest warrant then?"

The judge's dagger eyes pierced Tony. "Get out of my office. Now, or I'll hold you in contempt!"

"We're not in court, Judge!"

The judge snatched up the phone. "I'm calling security."

"No need," Tony said, jerking the door open. "I get the picture."

Larry covered his face. This was going from bad to worse. "We need this warrant," he said, in a voice he hoped would appease. "There are children in danger, your honor. Every minute counts. Brandon knows we're bearing down on him, and he's going to get desperate. Please let us know the minute you decide to issue the warrant."

"You'll hear from me."

Larry followed Tony out, and Tony slammed the door behind them.

"Good going," Larry said. "That ought to change his mood."

"He's either senile or dirty," Tony said. "He doesn't want us to arrest Brandon, and there's a reason. We're going to the prosecutor's office right now. We'll get the warrant from him."

"Whoa—we can't just go over Wyatt's head without talking to the captain," Larry said.

"Fine. Then let's do it."

An hour later, they sat in Captain Sam Richter's office at the police station, watching him pace, clearly disturbed, as he processed the facts they had given him. "Did he say why the evidence wasn't sufficient?" he asked. "Did he tell you what he would need to give you the warrant?"

"No," Tony said. "He's not interested in helping us on this, Captain. If we handed him videotapes of Brandon beating and maiming the kids, the man would still have to take it under advisement. Something stinks."

"Yeah, I'd say so. But I don't like making enemies of our judges. There's got to be another way."

"What, then?" Tony asked. "We need to get this guy locked up tonight!"

Sam sank into his chair and leaned back, staring at the ceiling. "But if we go to the prosecutor, and it turns out that Judge Wyatt has just taken a conservative turn and isn't really doing anything wrong, we'll have made an enemy out of the person who's supposed to be our number-one ally in this game."

"He's a judge because he's supposed to have good judgment," Larry pointed out. "If he's lost that judgment, for whatever reason, then he needs to be removed from the bench."

Sam opened a drawer and dug around, then came up with a roll of antacids. He broke the roll of tablets in half and put four into his mouth. As he chewed, he leaned forward on his desk, studying both men. "Here's what I want you to do. I want you to follow Judge Wyatt tonight. Just tail him and see what he does. If he's dirty, maybe you'll get evidence of that. Tomorrow, if he still hasn't issued the warrant, you can go to the prosecutor's office— I'll even go with you—and we'll try to get the warrant from them."

"What about Brandon?" Larry asked. "Captain, he's a killer, and there are people that he needs dead."

"You follow him, Larry. Watch every move he makes. Don't lose him for a second. In fact, we might be able to set up a stakeout in that hardware store across the street from the home."

Larry shot Tony a frustrated look. "Captain, that may not be good enough."

"It'll have to be," Sam said. "I'm not willing to bring a judge down until I know for sure that I have an excellent reason. It sounds like somebody tipped Brandon off about the article, right after you showed it to Judge Wyatt. Maybe it was the judge."

"I'd bet my life on it," Tony said.

They went back to their car, then just sat there for a moment before Tony started the ignition. "How do you do it, Larry? How do you stay calm when the top of your head is about to blow off? This whole Christianity thing is new to me, I know, but I don't think I'll ever get to the point where I don't want to throw a man like Judge Wyatt against the wall and beat some sense into him."

"It's not a sin to be angry, Tony. Christ got angry."

"It wouldn't be so bad if I could trust that the work we do out here, on the streets, is going to count for something, that it was a partnership. We nab the bad guys, and the judges and courts put them away. Now the courts won't even let me nab the bad guys."

"What do you think Brandon's next move will be?"

"Whatever he wants," Tony said, throwing up his hands. "He can blow up the police station, for all Judge Wyatt cares. Get an automatic weapon and mow down every kid in his home. You think Wyatt would give us a warrant then?"

"He'd take it under advisement."

Tony's face reddened as he jabbed the key into the ignition and cranked the old car. "Sometimes I think I need to find another job."

"You couldn't leave this, even if you wanted to."

"Don't count on it. It sounds better and better every day."

He headed out into traffic. "You can take this car tonight. I'll use my car to follow Judge Bozo around."

"Take your cell phone so we can stay in touch."

"Nick and Beth are gonna keel over and die when they find out that we can't get that scumbag today. Not to mention Jimmy."

"We'll just have to do the next best thing."

"What's that?"

"Make sure no one else gets hurt before we can get him behind bars."

CHAPTER FORTY-THREE

St. Clair beach was busy this time of year, but Jake found a parking space. Jimmy got out before Jake could say anything and headed for the long pier shooting out into the Gulf.

The wind blustered through the boy's hair, making him look small and vulnerable. Jake followed him down the pier.

When they got to the end, Jimmy leaned over the rail and looked out toward the horizon. Jake sat down on a bench next to where Jimmy stood and looked up at him. "Want to talk now?"

"No."

"Then will you listen?"

Jimmy ignored him.

"Jimmy, I know how you feel."

"No, you don't."

"Yes, I do. There was a time when I pretty much despised my mother, too. And I was embarrassed by her, and I never wanted to see her again."

Jimmy gave him a reluctant glance. "What did she do to you?"

He sighed. "It wasn't so much what she did. It was more what she didn't do. She wasn't exactly June Cleaver."

"Who?"

He regrouped and tried to find a more modern reference point. "She wasn't a storybook mom. She had a lot of problems. She caused me a lot of problems. And while I was growing up, I remember always thinking that the minute I was old enough, I'd be out of there and never look back."

"I didn't have to wait that long."

"No, you didn't." He looked up at the kid. "What did she do, Jimmy? Did she hurt you in some way?"

"Hurt me? No. She didn't pay enough attention to hurt me. Unless you call leaving us without food for three days hurting us. She was so strung out on dope that she didn't know where she was half the time."

"Pretty messed up, huh?"

"Yeah."

"So when you went to the home, I guess it seemed like an improvement."

He sighed. "I didn't have so much responsibility."

"How old were you?"

"Seven."

Jake thought it over. He almost couldn't blame the kid for hating his mother. No seven-year-old should have responsibility for his home, himself, and his four-year-old sister.

"What about when you realized the home wasn't what it seemed to be?"

"It was okay," he said. "As long as I did what Bill said, I didn't worry too much. He took care of us. And he never touched Lisa. I knew I could take whatever heat there was to take, if they'd just leave her alone. While I was there, they did. Now, everything's all messed up. I don't know where we're gonna live, I don't know if Lisa's all right—and if they give us back to . . ." His voice trailed off. He didn't seem to know how to refer to Tracy.

Jake understood. "Mother" didn't seem to apply, and neither did "Mom." "Jimmy, I want you to understand that when Nick went looking for your mom, it wasn't to reunite you, necessarily. He just wanted to see if she was still in bad shape. He wanted to see if there was any hope there."

"Well, there's not."

"Maybe not. Not in human terms, anyway."

"What's that supposed to mean?"

"It means that when we think something's impossible, or someone's impossible to change, God sometimes comes along and does something really awesome, and the next thing you know, you've got a bona fide human being there with morals and a heart and a conscience."

"You talking about your mother?"

Jake smiled. "No. I'm talking about myself, kiddo."

Jimmy leaned his shoulder into the rail and looked at Jake, grudgingly interested.

"Have you ever heard the term 'morally bankrupt'?" Jake asked.

Jimmy shrugged.

"It's a term used to describe a person who doesn't have any morals. Someone who lives for today, and only cares about the pleasures of the moment. Someone who doesn't care who he hurts or what he has to do to get what he wants." He stood up next to the boy and leaned on the rail, looking out over the ocean. "That's what I was, Jimmy. I may not have been a junkie, and I may not have had a couple of kids to neglect, but I was morally bankrupt. And God taught me a few things."

"I don't know if I believe in God," Jimmy said matter-of-factly. "But if he was real, what did he teach you?"

"He taught me that I was no better than your mom, or my mom, or any other morally bankrupt person out there. Some of us wear it prettier than others, some of us are masters at hiding it, but the bottom line is that sin is sin. We've all got it. And until we trust in someone bigger than ourselves, it'll do every one of us in. Me, my mom, your mom, you, Lisa—"

"We're already done in," Jimmy said.

"No, you're not. Because God can turn things around. He turned things around for me, and made a new person out of the sorry slug I was. He can do that for your mom. He could even do it for you."

"You calling me a sorry slug?"

"No. But I'm telling you that it doesn't matter that you didn't have a father to bring you up and take care of and protect you. I didn't, either. It doesn't matter that your only other parent failed you. It doesn't matter that the adults in your life, for the most part, have been morally bankrupt and even abusive. What matters is that there's someone more important than them, someone who has a lot more authority over you than they do, someone who loves you more than you can even love yourself—even more than you love Lisa."

The little boy considered that as the wind ruffled his hair. "Well, you can believe that if you want to. I'm not gonna make fun of you. I just don't believe it."

"That's fine, kiddo. I'm no preacher, and I'm not trying to shove a sermon down your throat. But take it from me, one homeless, fatherless guy to another: God is taking care of you, whether you believe in him or not."

"I don't want him to take care of me. I'll be all right. I want him to take care of Lisa."

"Her, too. If I'm lyin', I'm dyin'. God loves you both."

"We'll see," Jimmy said.

Jake smiled and messed up his hair. "Yeah, we'll see. What do you say we go back to my place and chill for a while? See what Lynda's found out."

He sighed. "Whatever."

"Okay. Come on." He started walking back up the pier, and Jimmy followed behind him a few paces. After a moment, he caught up. "Jake, why'd you say 'one homeless guy to another'? You have a home."

"Not really. It isn't mine. See, when I was where you are, homeless and broke, feeling like I didn't have a single soul to love me, with no idea where I would live, God sent Lynda to help me. And she did, man. I've been living in her garage apartment ever since. But it's not really mine, and even though I'm paying rent now, I still feel like I'm mooching."

"When you marry her, you won't be a freeloader anymore."

The choice of words both stung and amused Jake. "I guess not. Listen, I've been thinking. If she says yes, I'm gonna need a best man. You think you might be up for the job?"

Jimmy's eyes widened. "Really? Me?"

"Yeah, you."

"Well, I guess so."

"Good. But I may be jumping the gun. Maybe I need to wait until the bride says yes before I start planning the wedding, huh?"

By the time they got to the car, Jimmy's mood had lifted, and he was a kid again.

B eth didn't know if it was sheer boredom or genuine concern that made her decide to slip out of her room to visit Tracy Westin. Without asking permission of the nurses, she pulled on the robe she had borrowed from Lynda and walked weakly to the elevators.

It was only one floor up. Fortunately, Tracy's room wasn't far from the elevators, so the walk wasn't long.

Tracy was sitting upright in her bed, still weak, and still connected to an IV and a monitor.

Beth knocked lightly on the door and went in.

Tracy looked up. Her eyes were red, wet, and swollen, and it was clear that she'd been crying. Something about that fragility touched Beth.

"Hi," she said. "I'm Beth Wright. Do you remember when I was here yesterday, with Nick?"

Tracy nodded, her expression holding more than a little suspicion.

Beth looked down at her robe. "As you can see, I'm a patient here, too. I had a little accident, but I'm okay."

She was babbling, she thought, and so far the woman hadn't said a word to her. She wished she hadn't come. Tracy wiped the wetness from her face, and Beth wondered how to comfort her. "Want to talk about it?" she asked.

Tracy shook her head.

"Okay." Beth pulled up a chair and gingerly sank into it. "You look better. You have more color in your face." She realized, kicking herself, that that might only be because she was crying. Didn't everyone's face turn red when they cried? She looked down at her hands. "Look, I know you don't know me from Adam. And you probably don't feel like spilling your guts to a complete stranger. I don't blame you. So if you want me to, I'll just go back to my room." She started to get back up.

"What kind of accident?" The woman's question startled her, and she turned back around.

"What?"

"What kind of accident did you have?"

"Oh. I was kind of in an explosion. Somebody sent me a package bomb, and I made the mistake of opening it."

Tracy's face twisted. "Really?"

"Yeah, really. Pretty awful, huh? You think I look bad, you should see my house."

Tracy drew in a deep cleansing breath, and wiped her face. "No wonder there was blood on Nick's shirt."

"You saw him?" she asked.

Tracy nodded slightly, and tears filled her eyes again. "He brought Jimmy."

Beth stepped closer. "He brought *Jimmy?* He didn't tell me he was going to do that. He came by a little while ago, but I was sleeping, so he just left a note."

"Apparently it was . . . spur of the moment. It turned out to be a . . . really bad idea."

"Why?"

Tracy's face twisted again as she relived the scene. "My kid took one look at me and took off running. I told you, he hates me. He has every right."

"I'm sorry." But Beth didn't know if she was sorrier for Tracy or Jimmy.

"Yeah, me too. Too late."

Beth stood there awkwardly, watching her cry for a moment before it occurred to her to hand her a tissue. "I wondered why they didn't bring Lisa," Tracy said, wiping her nose. "Is she dead?"

"Dead?" Beth asked, surprised by the question. "No, she's not dead. She's just . . . she's still at the children's home."

"Does she hate me, too? I was hoping . . . that she was too little . . . when she left . . ."

"I don't know," Beth whispered. "I've never met Lisa. Just Jimmy."

"Ohhh," Tracy moaned on a weak breath. "Why didn't I just die when I had the chance?"

"Maybe it wasn't your time."

"Why not?" she asked. "I've seen it all. I've done it all. I'm just so tired."

"There's lots more, Tracy. And just because Jimmy doesn't want to see you now doesn't mean there won't be a chance later. And speaking of chances, Tracy, you've got another one yourself—to pull your life back together."

"Yeah, right." She looked Beth over. "Easy for you to say. You have people you can trust. You probably have a job, money—and you don't have a monkey riding your back, so hard that no matter how you fight him, he's still there, reminding you, threatening you, pulling you . . ."

"Addictions can be overcome, Tracy. Think about it—it's been weeks since you've had any drugs. You could walk out of here and never touch the stuff again. Nick found you for a reason. Someone up there was looking out for you."

"Why now? He never has before."

"Maybe he was, but you just didn't notice."

"Yeah, right." She looked up at the ceiling. "If there's a God in heaven, he wouldn't waste his time on somebody like me."

Beth understood that sentiment. She had uttered it herself. "Nick wasted his time on you. Do you think God isn't at least as compassionate as Nick?"

"I don't know," she whispered.

"He is, Tracy."

"I abandoned my kids. I was a lousy mother. I shouldn't have even been allowed to have kids."

The old bitterness from childhood reared its head in Beth's soul, and she tried to argue. "Don't say that."

But Tracy had more to say, and she sobbed out the bitter words. "You want to know what I was thinking that last time I left them alone? I knew they were there without any food or anyone to watch them. But all I kept thinking was that I needed a fix. That was the most important thing. And I did whatever I needed to do to get one." She shook her head and covered her eyes. "I don't even think I was that upset when I got home and found them gone. I was too high by then, and I didn't want to come down. Somebody told me a few days later that the state had taken them, but I never did anything about it. I let them take my kids, and the truth is, I didn't even care."

Tears stung Beth's eyes, and she wondered if her own mother had had the same attitude. Had anyone cried when she'd been taken from her home? Had anyone felt any remorse? Did it change anyone's life, one way or another?

"So don't tell me about God loving me," Tracy went on. "If God loved me, he would have let me die before Nick found me. Then it would all be over, and I wouldn't have to deal with all this."

Beth tried to harden herself, so she wouldn't fall apart. "I'll see that Jimmy isn't brought back up here. Then you won't have to deal with him."

"No, that's not what I mean!" Tracy cried. "I *want* to see him. It just hurts . . . The past . . ."

The past did hurt. Beth knew that more than anyone. And it was hard having compassion for a woman who had left her children to be cared for by an indifferent and impersonal bureaucracy, to be turned over to a thief and child abuser.

"Tracy, you can change if you want. But you have to want to. Nobody can force you."

"I *do* want to. I just don't know if I'm strong enough."

Beth sat there for a long moment, wishing she had some strength to give her. But she didn't think she could spare any. Her throat tightened until she felt as if she were choking. She had to get out of here. She had to go somewhere where the memories didn't rush up to smother her. She had to get away from Tracy Westin. "I've got to go."

Tracy accepted that without a response.

When Beth reached the door, she turned back. "Maybe I'll come back by tomorrow. See how you're doing." But she had no intention of doing that, and she suspected that Tracy knew it.

CHAPTER FORTY-FIVE

Lynda was home when Jimmy and Jake pulled up. She came outside to meet them, looking a little apprehensive, and Jimmy realized that Nick must have filled her in about the fiasco at the hospital. He hoped they all felt real bad about it.

He got out of the car. "Has Bill been arrested yet? Can they get Lisa out?"

Lynda shot a look to Jake. "Uh—no, Jimmy. Not yet."

Jake stiffened. "Why not?"

She sighed. "Judge Wyatt is still giving them a hard time. He's taken the matter under advisement."

"You're kidding me!" Jake said.

"What does that mean?" Jimmy asked.

Lynda didn't want to say it, but she bent down to get even with his face and tried to find the words. "It means that it may be tomorrow before they're able to arrest Bill."

"Oh, man!" Jimmy cried, backing away as his face darkened. "No way! *No way!* They can't wait."

"Larry and Tony are tailing him tonight, Jimmy. They'll make sure he doesn't do anything. They'll know where he is at all times."

"But they can't see into the home!" he shouted. *"If he beats Lisa, they won't know!"* He was crying now, and he hated himself for it.

Lynda reached out to hug him, but he shook her off. "I told you! I told all of you!" He ran into the house and back to his room.

He threw himself on the bed and cried into the pillow, cursing Bill Brandon, cursing the police, cursing his mother, cursing

Lynda and Jake. His little sister's safety depended on them, and they were stupid, all of them.

He had to talk to her. He had to call Lisa and make sure she was all right. Wiping his face, he sat up on the bed and tried to calm himself so that he could talk clearly. He reached for the phone and started to dial the number, then thought better of it. He'd tried that before.

The computer. He hadn't checked to see if he had any messages from her or Brad.

He heard Jake and Lynda in the kitchen, and he went into the bathroom and blew his nose, splashed water on his face, and dried it off. He went into the living room, and they both saw him through the door into the kitchen.

"Jimmy? You want to talk now?"

"No," Jimmy said. "Can I play on your computer?"

The question seemed to surprise them, but he knew it was partial relief he saw in their faces. They thought he'd be playing games or something and were glad for the distraction. "Sure, Jimmy. That's fine."

He went to the computer and turned it on, navigated his way to the network, registered himself as a guest user, and signed on. In moments, the computer told him he had mail.

Lisa had gotten his message!

He clicked "read incoming mail," and found Brad's screen name posted at the top.

He opened the letter, and read as the color drained slowly from his face.

Lisa's hurt real bad from the beating Bill gave her. Jimmy, you need to come get her before he kills her. I'll leave Stella's window unlocked so you can get in. Please hurry!

Jimmy stared at the words, his heartbeat slamming against his chest. Then he sat back and closed his eyes in horror, trying to think. He'd known this would happen. He'd tried to tell them all, and they hadn't listened, because they didn't know Bill Brandon. He couldn't depend on them. He had to do something. He had to do something *now*.

His heart pounded so hard that he almost couldn't think. He had to get Lisa out of there. But he needed a weapon.

Beth's gun. He knew just where she kept it.

He navigated his way on the network to a game that had sound effects, and started it running. The sound would make them think he was still in there.

Then, leaving the computer on, he went to the back of the house. He knew that one of the bedrooms had an outside door. Quietly, he unlocked it and slipped out.

The backyard was fenced, but he climbed it and leaped down. Night had fallen, and no one was around to see him. Lynda's closest neighbors lived on the other side of the cluster of trees up the street. He ran through the woods until he came out on the street that ran parallel to Lynda's.

He was home free. All he had to do was figure out how to get to Beth's house to get the gun, and then get to the children's home from there without being caught. Then he had to figure out how to get Lisa out. He didn't know how he would do it, but whatever he did, it would be better than what all these grown-ups were doing.

CHAPTER FORTY-SIX

When Nick got to Beth's hospital room, she was standing at her window, peering out. For a moment, he didn't knock, just stood at the door without letting her know he was there. She must be doing well, he thought with a rush of relief, to be standing and walking without help. This morning, after the explosion, he had wondered if she'd even live to see another day.

He knocked lightly on the wall, and she turned around.

"Hi," he said.

"Hi." She had more color in her face than she'd had earlier, but the light was still gone from her eyes.

"Are you okay?"

"Yeah. They said they would probably let me go home as soon as the doctor came by one last time."

"Really?"

"Yeah. The thing is, I don't *have* a home."

"That's just temporary. You can rebuild."

She turned halfway back to the window and gazed out again. "What do you think of me now, Nick?"

He came further into the room and joined her at the window. "What do you mean?"

"Now that you know I'm a criminal." She couldn't look at him as she uttered the words.

"You're not a criminal. You're a hero."

She breathed a mirthless laugh. "Yeah, right."

"You are. If it weren't for you, no one would have ever figured out what Bill Brandon was doing with those kids."

"You would have. You already had a feeling."

"Feelings don't change things. They don't give you evidence. You came up with that."

"I *am* the evidence."

"That's not your fault."

She sat down on the edge of her bed, and Nick grabbed a chair and pulled it up to her bedside. Straddling it, he got close to her. "Beth, you can't blame yourself. You're a good person, no matter what Bill Brandon spent years trying to make you believe."

She didn't want to face him, didn't want to meet his eyes, but she forced herself to. "I'm not really a good person," she said. "I went up there to visit Tracy today, and I've got to tell you, Nick. I have a hard time with her."

Nick waited, then prompted her. "Tell me."

Beth sighed. She got up and went to the window, putting her back to him. "She brings back a lot of memories, Nick. A lot of really bad ones."

"Your mother?" he asked.

She closed her eyes.

"You know, I'd really like to hear about her," he said softly. "I want to know everything about you."

"My mother was like Tracy," she said, "only she wasn't a junkie. She was an alcoholic. My father got disgusted and left her—and me, too. I guess the Invisible Daughter wasn't important enough to take along. Eventually, the state took me away from her and put me in Bill Brandon's home."

He was quiet for a moment, then asked, "Have you heard from your mother since then?"

She gazed out the window for a moment, one side of her face cast in shadow, the other side in light. "She died a couple of years ago. Those distant relatives who were nowhere to be found when the state took me into custody managed to get in touch with me to tell me about the funeral arrangements. I didn't go."

Nick looked down at his hands. As many kids as he'd taken out of homes himself, as many as he'd seen neglected or abused by their parents, he would never have guessed that Beth had been one of them.

"All my life I kept thinking that something would happen, that she'd sober up and remember she had a child and come back and get me. She'd be this wonderful, perfect mom. But she never did. And then one day she was dead."

Nick got up from the chair and came to stand behind her. He touched her shoulder and leaned his forehead on the crown of her head. "Beth, I'm so sorry."

She swallowed back the emotion in her throat. "It wasn't that hard. It wasn't hard at all. I hardly knew the woman, and what I did know of her, I hated." When she turned around to face him, her eyes were blazing with tears. "I know we're not supposed to hate, Nick. I know that with all my heart, and I've asked God to help me with it. But I can't help it, I still hate. And the worst part is that the person I hate is dead, and there's nothing I could ever do to change it."

"You can forgive a dead woman, Beth."

She shook her head. "I don't think I can. Maybe after I've read through the whole Bible and learned all the things that I'm supposed to learn, maybe then I'll have the strength to forgive my mother. But right now, it doesn't seem possible. She doesn't deserve forgiveness."

"Probably not," he agreed. "But you do. You deserve to be able to let it go. Sometimes forgiveness does more for us than it does for the ones we forgive. Besides, God told us to forgive."

She shook free of him and walked across the room again, picked up a water glass from the bed table, turned it over in her hand, then set it back down hard. "You don't know anything about it, Nick. You've never been thrown away like a piece of trash. You've never been dumped into an orphanage under someone who's going to turn you into a thief for his own selfish gain."

"No, you're right. I never have."

"That's the thing with Tracy. Her life—her attitude—it reminds me so much of my mother's."

"She had some bad breaks, Beth. Maybe it's not too late for her."

"Bad breaks?" she asked with an angry laugh. "She *chose* to abandon her children. She got herself hooked on drugs. She was a junkie, and probably a prostitute, and you're telling me that she just had some bad breaks?"

"You don't know what her life was like, Beth."

"I know what *my* life has been like, Nick. I know that if everybody turned to drugs because of a horrible past, then I'd be the worst junkie in town."

"You're right. You have more strength. More character. You've risen above your past. There's something about you, Beth, that some people just don't have. It's what's so attractive about you."

She looked as if she didn't know how to respond to such a compliment. Nick sighed and rubbed his eyes. "But God's grace covers people like Tracy, too. When I found her, she was lying there helpless, almost dead. I don't know why God put it in my head to go look for her that day, of all days, but I did, and if I hadn't, she'd be dead now. That means that God loves her, for some reason that you and I may not be able to fathom. And she has the same opportunity for heaven that we have."

"That's absurd," she said. "God doesn't send junkies and child abusers to heaven. Tracy Westin has never done anything for God or anyone else. Even if she were to repent now and turn into Mother Theresa for the rest of her life, all the junk in her life up until now would still outweigh any good she could do. Even God's grace couldn't balance all that out."

"But that's the great thing about grace. It doesn't have anything to do with a balance sheet," he said with a smile. "How do you think that thief on the cross came out when God looked at his balance sheet?"

Beth tried to think. "I don't know. I still say he hadn't done that much wrong."

"He was *crucified*, Beth. Whatever he did wrong was bad enough to get him executed. The Bible calls him a thief."

She was getting confused. "But God wouldn't take someone like Tracy—or even me, for that matter—and give us the same reward he gives someone like you or Lynda! You've done good things all your life, Nick. You've probably never really done anything displeasing to God."

"Don't bet on it," Nick said. "In God's eyes, there's no real difference between your life and mine. The only thing either of us has ever done that would win us admission to heaven is to believe in and trust in Christ."

Her face paled again, and she sank down into the chair. "That's not enough. Not for someone like me. It wouldn't be fair to people like you."

He knelt in front of her, his eyes riveting into hers. "Yes, it is." He grabbed the Gideon's Bible off her bed table and flipped through the pages. "Here," he said. "Matthew 20:1." He read to her the parable of the landowner who paid the same wages to those hired at the end of the day as he paid those who had worked all day. Those who had worked all day complained.

Nick read, "'"I want to give the man who was hired last the same as I gave you. Don't I have the right to do what I want with my own money? Or are you envious because I am generous?" So the last will be first and the first will be last.'"

He handed her the Bible so that she could see it for herself.

Tears came to her eyes. "But what about redemption? I'm not stupid, Nick. There's a price for the secrets I've kept all these years."

"Christ redeemed you when he gave his life for you, Beth."

She just couldn't buy it. Not the Messiah, dying for her, leaving her blameless. It was too unbelievable. "I'm not sure I agree with your theology, Nick."

"All right," he said. "Just promise me you'll think about it. Pray about it, too."

"I will." She took in a deep, shaky breath. "Faith is a hard thing for me, Nick. Sometimes I feel like I've got holes punched in me. If I walk carefully, I can keep everything in, but if the slightest thing shakes me, it all comes pouring out. All the putrid, ugly things about me that I don't want anyone to see."

"Well, we'll see what we can do about patching up those holes."

CHAPTER FORTY-SEVEN

arkness seemed inviting to Tracy Westin. She watched lethargically out her window as the sun went down and twilight overwhelmed the sky. It would be night soon. But she needed more darkness than this; she needed enough to hide in.

She looked around her cold, sterile hospital room. It was better than anything she'd had in a long time, but she hated it. She didn't belong here. She didn't belong anywhere. Her life was hopeless, futile, and she didn't know where she had gone wrong.

Liar, she told herself. That was just one of the myths she'd been clinging to for years. She knew where she'd gone wrong— she'd gone wrong the first time she'd taken crack. It wasn't as if she hadn't known better. She had just wanted to be a part of things. She had wanted to fit in, to be a part of that group of people she admired who seemed so glamorous and exciting.

She'd never forget her first experience with the drug. It had been a high like she'd never experienced, yet afterwards she'd felt so low, so hungry for more, that it had changed her thinking. While she was pregnant, she had managed to stay off it, though she had occasionally smoked marijuana. She had told herself that she would clean up her act as soon as the baby was born. But it hadn't happened either time.

For years, she had blamed Jimmy and Lisa's fathers, the men who had wooed, then abandoned her when she'd needed them most. For years, she had told herself that she wasn't really to blame; she was just a victim, after all. But right now she didn't feel much like a victim. She felt like a monster who had ruined two young lives for no good reason. And that was hard to live with. So hard, in fact, that she really didn't want to live at all.

She was angry that Nick had found her lying in her room. If he'd just left her alone, she'd be at peace now. Or would she?

Was there really an afterlife? Was there a god cruel enough to prolong what she wanted so desperately to end? Would she pay the price for the sins she'd committed during her unhappy life? No, she told herself. If there was a god, he couldn't be that cruel.

Desperate enough to gamble that death meant an end to her existence and peace at last, she tore the IV needles out of her hands, peeled off the monitors glued to her chest, and threw down the oxygen mask that was making it so much easier for her to breathe. She didn't need this. She didn't need life. She didn't need another moment of it.

She pulled herself to the edge of the bed, sitting, trying to balance. If she got on the elevator and went straight up, would there be a window at the top from which she could hurl herself? It would be so easy. Just one step, and there would be an end to it all. And she couldn't get in anyone's way again, and she couldn't hurt anyone else, least of all herself. It would be the greatest act of kindness she had ever done for herself.

She touched the floor with her bare feet and tried to stand. Her legs wobbled beneath her, and she remembered how weak she had been when Nick had found her. She had thought she'd been getting stronger during these days in the hospital, but she knew now she was mistaken. She took a step, reached out to hold onto the bed table, then another step. She began to sweat and grow dizzy. How would she ever make it all the way to the elevator?

Finally, she backed up to the bed and sat again. She was too weak to kill herself, she thought bitterly. Wasn't that the way it always went? Finally had the courage, and now she didn't have the strength.

She wilted into tears and pulled her wobbly, bony knees up to her chest and hugged them tightly. She was sickened by her own frailty.

"What are you doing?" came the voice at the doorway. It was a stern nurse, and Tracy didn't have the energy to argue. "What do you mean taking that IV out of your hand? Girl, get that mask back on your face and get back under those covers!"

Tracy did as she was told. She didn't want to talk. She just closed her eyes, wishing to shut out the reality around her. The voices. The guilt. The demands.

She lay still as the woman reinserted the IV. It hurt—but that was fair. It was comfort that she couldn't endure. Never comfort.

"Where were you going, honey?" the nurse asked.

Tracy still couldn't talk, and as the woman put the mask back over her face, she felt sleep pulling her under. But not far enough.

CHAPTER FORTY-EIGHT

I t was already six-thirty, and Judge Wyatt hadn't yet left the courthouse. Tony sat at the wheel of his car, tapping his fingers impatiently.

The telephone on his seat rang, and he picked it up. "Hello?"

"Tony, it's me." Larry sounded excited.

"You got anything?"

Larry, who had been staking out the children's home from the hardware store across the street, began to chuckle. "He just came out and headed to a storehouse at the back of the campus. He opened the door, and voila! Inside sits a green van. I'm in my car; as soon as he hits the street, I'll be on his tail."

"Up to no good?" Tony asked.

"Definitely no good."

"Any kids with him?"

"No," he said. "He's alone."

The door to the side of the courthouse opened, and a cluster of people spilled out. At the back of the group, he saw Judge Wyatt walking regally, carrying his briefcase. He wondered if the brief-case contained the evidence they had given him, and if he indeed planned to "take it under advisement."

"Well, guess what. Our boy just came out, too. Call me if Brandon does anything."

"Yeah, you do the same," Larry said.

Tony clicked off the telephone and cranked his engine, waiting inconspicuously as the judge got into his Lexus and backed out. Tony waited until two or three cars got between them, then pulled out and followed the judge out into the downtown traffic. He had looked up the judge's home address, so he knew his likely route home—but that wasn't the direction that Wyatt headed. Curious, Tony followed at a distance, keeping a mental record of their exact route.

The judge slowed as they came to a gas station with a convenience store attached. Tony braked as the Lexus pulled into the parking lot next to a pay phone. He didn't follow, only pulled to the side of the road far enough away that the judge wouldn't spot him, and watched as Wyatt got out of his car and stood at the pay phone.

Who was he calling? Tony wondered. There was a cellular antenna on Wyatt's car, so Tony knew the judge had a car phone. The only reason he would have for calling from a pay phone was that he didn't want any record of the phone call—or didn't want it traced. Tony grabbed his phone, punched out the number of the police station, and asked for one of the cops that he knew would be around this time of day. "Hey, Mac, I need you to do me a favor. Find out the phone number for a pay phone on the corner of Lems Boulevard and Stone Street, and see if you can get a record of the last few numbers called from that phone. There's a call taking place right now; I want to know who's on the other end of the line."

"Okay, Tony, I'll try."

"Call me back on my cell phone. I'm keeping my radio off so my cover isn't blown."

He hung up as Judge Wyatt finished the call and jumped back into his car. When the judge pulled back onto the street, Tony let a couple of other cars get between them before he began to follow.

He still wasn't heading home, and he wasn't going back to the courthouse. Tony recorded every turn; the route had gotten too complicated to remember, so he scribbled the information without looking on a piece of paper on the seat next to him.

The phone rang, and he clicked it on. "Yeah?"

"Tony, I got the number of the latest phone call from that phone. It was a cellular phone number. 555–4257. It's registered to the St. Clair Children's Home."

Tony's heart tripped. "Are you serious?"

515

"That's right."

He watched the judge make another turn, and he followed. "Then my hunch seems to be right on the mark. Thanks, Mac."

The Lexus turned down a road that looked as if it was rarely traveled. Tony waited until the judge had rounded a curve before he turned in behind him. The road curved like an S, cutting through a dense forest. Tony passed an abandoned warehouse here and an old, dilapidated structure there. He started to get suspicious—was this some kind of trap? Had the judge spotted him?

No, not likely. Whatever Wyatt was doing, it had nothing to do with Tony. But Tony suspected that it had everything to do with Bill Brandon.

As he slowly rounded the final curve, a big warehouse came into view. Adrenaline pulsed through Tony, and he pulled off the road and into a cluster of bushes where he wouldn't be seen. He got out and pushed through the brush until he had a clear view of the warehouse.

"Bingo," he muttered. "Just what we've been looking for!"

Tony peered through his binoculars and read the sign on the building. He wrote down the name Winrite, Inc., along with the address, and waited for the judge to come back out.

He would look up the owner of the building when he got back to the station to determine what kind of business operated from here. A light went on in one of the rooms. After a few minutes, the light went out, and the judge reappeared in the doorway, locked up, and got back into his Lexus.

Tony got back in his car but kept his engine off as the judge pulled out of the parking lot and back onto the street.

Again, the judge headed away from home, and Tony found his heart beating faster as he tailed him. His gut told him something was going on. The judge was going to lead him someplace that he didn't want anyone to see.

The Lexus turned onto a street that took them near the underside of a bridge on the outskirts of town. It was hard to stay close enough to the Lexus without losing him and still not be seen, but Tony was good at this; he'd done it often enough.

When the judge pulled his car over near the bridge, Tony pulled his car off the road behind a grove of trees. After a minute or two, he saw another car approaching. It pulled alongside the Lexus and idled there a moment.

The phone rang again.

"Yeah?"

"It's me," Larry said. "Looks like Brandon's meeting with somebody. It's a light-colored Lexus."

"A Lexus?" Tony's heart pounded.

"That's right."

"Larry, I've been following the Lexus."

"You *what?* Who is it?"

"One guess."

There was a brief silence, then: "Bingo."

"Looks like we figured out why we can't get our warrant," Tony said.

"You were right all along, buddy."

"Wish I could hear what they're saying."

"I'll tell you what they're saying. Judge Wyatt's filling him in on the gory details of our meeting this afternoon. And Brandon's trying to figure out a way to get out of this whole mess. More buildings to burn down. More people to try to kill."

"No," Tony said. "Just one. Beth Wright."

"Don't forget the kid."

"Jimmy's safe. He's with Jake and Lynda."

"Called the hospital lately to see if Beth's all right?"

"I called earlier. She's getting out tonight as soon as the doctor makes his rounds."

"So where's she going?" Larry asked.

"Not sure yet, but I'll find out."

"Do that," Larry said. "I'd feel better if we had somebody watching her."

"We're low on manpower, buddy. With us watching these two, I don't know who's going to do it."

"Somebody'll have to," Larry said. "I'll take care of it."

CHAPTER FORTY-NINE

L ynda and Jake had talked through everything—the injustice of the judge's delays in issuing a warrant for Bill Brandon, the difficulty of Jimmy's reaction to his mother, the feelings of rejection that reaction must have caused in Tracy, their worry for Lisa, still in Brandon's clutches . . .

But they would solve nothing sitting at Lynda's kitchen table, so after a while Lynda went into the living room to check on Jimmy. Although the noise from the computer game had been consistent for the past hour, Jimmy wasn't sitting there. Shrugging, Lynda walked on past the living room, down the hall, and to the bedroom where he had been staying. There was no sign of him.

"Jimmy," she called. "Jimmy!"

When she got no answer, she went to the back door and looked out into the yard. He wasn't there. "Jake!"

Jake came from the kitchen. "What is it?"

"Jimmy's gone!"

"I thought he was playing on the computer."

"He's not." Growing alarm sent her running from one room to another, searching for the boy and calling for him at the top of her lungs, but there was no answer.

"Where could he be?" she asked Jake.

"I don't know. You don't think—"

"He's run away." Lynda headed for the telephone. "We have to call Larry and Tony."

Jake got to the phone first and punched out the number of the St. Clair Police Department. Larry and Tony were out, he was told, so he left a message and hung up. He didn't want to report the runaway, not yet, not until he'd consulted with Larry and Tony, and even Nick, on how to proceed. So far, Jimmy hadn't been officially reported missing. Reporting it now to people who didn't know the case might do more harm than good; if Jimmy were found, he'd probably be taken back to SCCH.

"I'm calling Nick," he said. "Then I'll call Beth. Maybe he went there, to the hospital."

"Do you think he may have gone to see his mother?" she asked.

"Doubtful," he said, "judging from the way he reacted today. On the other hand, sometimes our first reactions aren't what we really mean. Maybe he did go back to finally confront her."

"Why didn't he just ask us to take him? He knew we would."

"He was pretty upset," Jake said. "I guess we underestimated how much."

"But he seemed content in there playing on the computer."

"It was a ruse," Jake said. "He was just trying to distract us so we wouldn't see him when he ran away."

Lynda paced across the floor, running her fingers through her hair. "We should have kept an eye on him. We should have been watching him."

"We thought he was safe, Lynda. Who would have thought he'd leave here, knowing that Bill Brandon is still out there?"

"That's no excuse!"

Sighing, Jake dialed the number for Nick's house, but there was no answer, so he quickly dialed the hospital and connected with Beth's room.

"Hello?"

"Beth, thank goodness you're still there. I thought you may have checked out by now."

"No, I'm still waiting for the doctor."

"Beth, Jimmy's missing."

"What?"

"He's run away. He's gone."

"Weren't you watching him?"

"We thought he was playing on the computer. We were just in the next room. We're thinking maybe he went there to see you, or maybe even his mother."

Beth paused for a moment, thinking. "All right, I'll be on the lookout for him. But aren't you going to call the police?"

"We put a call in to Larry and Tony, but we're reluctant to report this to anyone else."

"Do it anyway!" she said. "Bill Brandon is out there, Jake. If he gets his hands on Jimmy, we'll never see him alive again!"

"But Brandon may have a police scanner. If he hears about the disappearance, he may find Jimmy before we do."

"Call anyway. *Please*, Jake. Maybe the police can find him."

In the hospital room, Beth hung up the phone and turned back to Nick. "He's gone."

"Where did he go?"

"They think he may be coming here. Maybe to see me, or you—maybe even Tracy."

"No way," Nick said. "Not after his reaction today. He wouldn't come to see Tracy."

"But, Nick," Beth said, "what if he thought it over and decided he does want to see her after all?"

Nick shrugged. "Well, maybe we'd better go warn her," he said.

"Yeah, maybe."

They told the nurse where they'd be in case the doctor came, then headed to the elevator. They got off on the floor above Beth's and walked quickly to Tracy's room. Tracy's eyes were swollen and red, and she looked as dismal as she'd looked when Beth had left her earlier.

"Tracy?"

She looked up, but her expression was lifeless.

"Tracy, we need to talk to you."

"About what?"

"About Jimmy."

She closed her eyes. "There's nothing you can say to me about Jimmy."

"Yes, there is. He's disappeared."

"What?" Her eyes came open fully, and she sat partially up.

"Tracy, I want you to listen to me, and I want you to listen carefully," Nick said. "Jimmy's been in trouble. The reason I came looking for you is that he and Lisa were in a children's home and Jimmy was being used in a crime ring. We're about to have the operator of the home arrested, but meanwhile, Jimmy's been hiding with us."

"And you let him run away?" Tracy asked. "How could you do that?"

"He's smart," Nick said. "He duped the people who were watching him by setting up a distraction, and he slipped out of the house without anyone realizing it."

"Well, is anyone looking for him?"

"Yes. But Tracy, we wanted to tell you, in case he comes here."

"Here? Why would he come here?" Tears spilled over her lashes, and she smeared them across her face. "I can't think of a reason in the world he would come to me."

"You're his mother."

"I'm *not* his mother!" she shouted. "He doesn't have a mother!"

Beth moved closer to the bed. "Tracy, you *are* his mother, whether you like it or not. Whether *he* likes it or not."

Tracy fell back on her pillows. "What if something happens to him?"

"We'll find him," Beth said. "They'll find him. He couldn't have gotten far on foot."

Tracy looked skeptical. "Like you said, he's a smart kid. He was smart when he was seven years old. He can go anywhere he wants to go."

"Not if people are looking for him," Beth said. "But Tracy, if he comes here, you have to tell us, okay? You have to call this number." She wrote down Larry and Tony's number at the station and set it on the bed table. "Do you hear me? You have to call."

"What if he doesn't want me to?"

"Do it anyway. He's in danger. The man who runs the home isn't in jail yet. If he finds Jimmy before we do, he may kill him."

"Oh, terrific," Tracy said. "So my son went from a bad situation with me to a worse one with some guy who could kill him, is that what you're saying?"

Nick leaned over her bed and touched Tracy's hand. "Tracy, look at me."

Tracy looked up at him with wet eyes that looked too big for her face.

"Tracy, there's a purpose in all this, whether you believe it or not."

"I *don't* believe it," Tracy said.

Beth felt her cheeks growing hot, and she tightened her lips. "Well, you'd better believe it, because maybe that purpose is to save and protect your son."

Tracy shook her head as if to rid it of the cobwebs. "What about Lisa? Is she in danger, too?"

"We're trying to get her out of the home," Nick said, "but we have to wait until the guy's arrested."

She closed her eyes, taking in the horror of it all. "What have I done to my kids?" she whispered.

More tears ran down the sides of her face, and Beth sat there staring at her for a long moment, feeling the pain that she didn't want to feel, because she didn't want to empathize with this woman who had abandoned her children. She wanted to hate her like she hated her own mother, but something about Tracy's pain touched her, and she leaned over the bed and touched the woman's hand.

"Tracy, it's not too late."

"What isn't?"

"It's not too late to become somebody to your kids. It's never too late until you're dead." Her voice cracked on the last word. "Take it from a kid who's been there."

Tracy brought both forearms up to cover her face. "I don't want to do this!" she cried. "I don't want to be here. I don't want to see my kids. I don't want to face them, and they sure don't want to face me!"

"If Jimmy comes, we'll help you," Beth said.

"And what if he doesn't?" Tracy cried. "What if he gets into more trouble? What if someone grabs him? What if—"

"Shhh," Nick cut in, trying to calm her. "Jimmy's a tough kid. He'll be all right."

"*What if he isn't?*" she screamed.

The silence in the wake of her question lay heavy over the room. "He will," Nick said finally. "Take my word for it. We'll find him within the hour."

"What if he went back to that orphanage?" she demanded.

"He would never go back there," Beth said. "He knows how dangerous that would be."

Tracy's sobs were deep, wrenching, soul-rending. "Are you sure I didn't die?"

Nick's own eyes were filling with tears. "What do you mean, Tracy?"

"When you found me lying there on that mattress, are you sure I wasn't already dead?"

"I'm sure," he said, glancing uneasily at Beth. "You're very much alive. Why would you ask a thing like that?"

"Because," Tracy choked out, "this feels like some kind of hell."

CHAPTER FIFTY

I t was getting darker. Jimmy knew that he couldn't hitchhike, since police were probably already out looking for him. For all he knew, his face could be on the screen of every television in St. Clair by now.

So he ran, as fast and as hard as he could, cutting through yards and plowing through woods, trying to get to Beth's house. His body was covered with sweat, and his shirt stuck to him, but he was glad that he had these running shoes. Bill hadn't skimped on shoes for the kids who "worked" for him. They had to be black, and they had to be quiet—for quick getaways.

His navigational skills were pretty good, just as his computer skills were, and he tried to remember where Bill had taken him the night he'd dropped him off at Beth's house. He had turned here, and passed that railroad crossing, then turned again . . .

By the time Jimmy found the long road that connected to Beth's dirt road, two hours had passed since he'd left Lynda's, and it was growing dark. He cut through the woods and hit the dirt road leading up to her house. He slowed to a walk as he headed up the dirt road, trying to catch his breath.

Because there were no streetlights on Beth's little dirt road, Jimmy was on the driveway before he saw that the house wasn't there anymore.

He squinted through the darkness at the gutted structure where he had hidden for so long, where he'd met the first adult who'd really cared about him in a long time, where he'd gotten to know the little puppy. He had known about the explosion, of course, but he had imagined it like one of those cartoon explosions, where one corner of a room gets soot on the walls, but nothing else is hurt. The condition of the house now stunned him, and he leaned back against a tree and slid down to the ground, almost dizzy with the reality of how close Beth had come to death.

And with that chilling thought came another: Bill had probably expected Jimmy to be at Beth's house, too. Had the bomb been as much for him as for Beth?

He felt that familiar pain in his stomach at the thought that his sister could have been killed delivering the bomb or setting the newspaper building on fire. He grew nauseous at the thought of her beaten up and awaiting rescue. He had to hurry.

But first he needed the gun.

There was nothing left of her living room. If the gun had been there, it was ruined now. Then again, she might have taken it with her in the car when she'd tried to go to St. Petersburg the day of the explosion, knowing that Bill was after her.

But where was the car?

He tried to think. It wasn't at Lynda's. It could be at Nick's. Or someone could have taken it to the hospital for her . . .

Yes. The hospital. It wasn't far from here. It shouldn't take long to get there.

He jogged back to the main road again, then cut through the trees skirting the street, hidden by the trees as well as the darkness.

Forty-five minutes later, drenched with sweat and panting, he reached the hospital. He went from one row to another, ducking between cars, until he spotted Beth's car. He closed his eyes and tried to concentrate on the gun being there as he approached it, as if wishing could make it so. Please be there . . . please be there . . .

The car was locked.

He looked toward the front doors of the hospital. Would anyone recognize him if he went in? He had no choice. Sliding his hands into his jeans pockets, the same black ones he'd been wearing since Beth had found him, he ambled up to the doors and slipped into the lobby. There was a coat rack in the corner of the room, so he checked to see if anyone was looking, then went over and grabbed a coat hanger. He shoved it into the front of his jeans, then pulled his T-shirt out to hang over it.

Quickly, he headed back out to Beth's car. Just as Bill had taught him, he stretched the coat hanger into the shape he needed, then maneuvered it between the rubber and the top of the window. In seconds, he had hooked the hanger onto the lock and popped it open.

When he opened the door, the light came on, making him feel vulnerable and exposed. He closed the door quickly, encasing himself in darkness.

He felt around on the seat. No gun. He bent and felt under it. Nothing.

Then he saw the glove compartment, and he punched the button and slowly pulled it open.

The gun lay there on its side, filling him with bittersweet relief.

His hands trembled as he took it. Quickly, he pulled his tee shirt up again. He stuck the barrel into his pants, as he'd seen it done on television, then tucked his shirt back over it.

He was ready. He could face a standoff with Bill Brandon now. He could rescue his sister, and maybe some of the others. He was ready to do whatever he had to do. And if he had to go to jail—whether for burglary or for murder—to see Lisa freed from Bill's bondage, then it would be worth it.

He got back out of the car and started walking in the direction of SCCH. His courage rose with every step, until finally he was running again. He knew the way to the home from here. And those who were looking for him would never even think to look there.

CHAPTER FIFTY-ONE

The party that Bill Brandon had insisted on having at the home was a first. He had never had one before—though occasionally local churches had given them Christmas parties—but this afternoon, he'd told the children that he was throwing a birthday party to celebrate all of the birthdays that occurred throughout the year. Everyone would be the guest of honor. He had let Lisa out of the back room for the occasion. Though Stella had dressed her up in her newest dress, she was pale and drawn. Weak from the fear of further punishment, she sat in a corner as the festivities unfolded around her.

This was some kind of trick, she thought wearily. He had called the television stations, and cameras went around the room, filming the happy faces of the children as they ate cake or tore into their presents—rag dolls for the girls and plastic race cars for the boys. It was as if he was trying to make the world think that they always did this, that he cared about the children, that he wanted them to be happy. She wondered what the reporters and cameramen would think if they knew where she'd been for the last day and a half, or if they could see the injuries under Brad's clothes. He, too, sat very still against the wall, pale and quiet, as if the effort of speaking might cause too much pain.

She got up, holding her rag doll by one arm, and went to the cluster of boys talking near Brad. She wasn't welcome among them, she knew, especially since Jimmy wasn't here anymore, but she wanted to hear what they were saying.

"I heard Stella say he was expecting someone."

"Someone like who?"

"Somebody from HRS, or cops, maybe. Probably what he warned us of the other day, after Jimmy got busted."

The faces in the circle changed, and Lisa couldn't hold her silence anymore. "Are they gonna arrest us? Did we get caught?"

"Shhhh," Brad ordered. "Are you crazy? Somebody could hear you."

"I told you she was too little to keep a secret."

"I am not too little," she returned. "I have kept the secret. But I don't want to go to jail."

"That's where Jimmy is," Kevin said.

"He is not! They don't have computers in jail!"

"Lisa, shut up!" Brad warned.

"Well, they don't!"

"What's that got to do with anything?" Kevin asked.

"Because Jimmy e-mailed me—"

Brad grabbed her wrist and jerked her to shut her up, when the other boys' eyes widened to the size of quarters. "You heard from him?"

"I'm not saying nothing," Brad said. "And neither is she. Are you, Lisa?" She didn't answer. "I can just tell you that Jimmy's not in jail."

"Well, what if he snitched on us? What if that's why the cops are coming?"

"It might be why," Brad said, looking back over the festive children and the cameras still going. "But I don't think so."

The door opened, and Bill came in, all smiles and laughter. He tried to act as if he genuinely loved all of the children in the home, bending over them and hugging them, wishing them happy birthday for the sake of the cameras.

"Why would Bill want cameras here if the cops are coming?"

"Maybe to show the world that he's really a nice guy, and that we're all happy kids who love it here, so that whatever Jimmy told them won't seem true," Keith said. "I wonder if he told them about my leg."

"He should have," Lisa whispered.

Brad hugged himself around the ribs that were probably broken. "I don't really care what he told them. I don't even care what happens to me. I just want them to get Bill. And I hope he tries to escape and they shoot him, just bad enough for him to hurt and see what it feels like. Then I hope he dies."

The other children only gazed at him, caught up in the terrors they wished on their keeper.

CHAPTER FIFTY-TWO

W eird," Larry told Tony via cell phone. Tony had followed the judge home and was now watching the house. Larry had set up his equipment on the second floor of the hardware store across the street, a vantage point from which he could see most of the buildings on the campus of SCCH. "Brandon just made it back to the home, and it looks like there's a party going on here. Television vans, music . . . I can see into the game room through a window, and I see balloons and streamers. Not exactly what I would have expected from a man who's desperate and knows we're coming after him."

"Sure it is. It's brilliant PR," Tony said. "He's trying to make the press think he's a wonderful guy. Get them all psyched up, so that when they get the real story, they won't believe it. Either that, or he can use it in court. 'Well, to be perfectly honest, Judge, I was just minding my own business giving a party for my beloved children, when the gestapo cops broke the doors down and arrested me in front of all of them. I only hope they're not traumatized for life.'"

"He knows we can't touch him tonight. Not until Judge Wyatt gives us the warrant, and you and I both know he won't do it."

"Well, I've been thinking. What if we went to the judge and told him what we know?"

"Like blackmail, Tony?"

"More like cutting a deal. We tell him that we saw him talking to Brandon, then he gives us that warrant, hoping we'll forget what we saw."

"No way," Larry said. "He's going down with Brandon. No deals."

Tony got quiet for a moment, thinking. "Then call the captain at home," he said. "Tell him about Wyatt's meeting with Brandon. Then try to get him to go to the prosecutor for two warrants tonight—for both of them."

"All right," Larry said. "But I don't want to leave for a while yet. I want to see how this party pans out. It could get interesting."

"At least the kids are safe while the cameras are there."

"Yeah. It's after they leave that I'm worried about. Any word on Jimmy?"

"Not yet. Lynda and Jake are basket cases. They've been out looking for him since he left."

"I hope that kid's all right," Larry said. "I just wonder what he's got up his sleeve."

"I'm just hoping he left of his own free will, and didn't get abducted without anyone knowing it."

"Well, we know Brandon and Wyatt didn't get him. I'd say he's just out there hiding somewhere, trying to figure out who he can trust."

"Let's hope it's not the wrong person."

CHAPTER FIFTY-THREE

Larry's car was the first thing Jimmy saw when he approached the children's home from the woods behind the hardware store. Larry must be in there, watching Bill. The fact that they'd put so much effort into watching him—yet couldn't arrest him—only reinforced the idea that Bill would get off scot-free. Nothing ever happened to Bill Brandon.

Jimmy stayed back in the shadows of the trees, trying to figure out how to get close to the cottages without Larry seeing him. He peered through the trees at the activity building. Something was going on at the home. It looked like a party. And television vans were outside.

He crossed the street a block down the road, then stole through the woods, staying in the shadows so Larry wouldn't see him. He came up on the other side of the building, out of Larry's sight, and peered through the window of the activities building. He saw Stella being interviewed by a local reporter, and across the room, Bill and some of the other employees of SCCH were also talking to reporters, smiling, laughing, gesturing at the balloons, the crepe paper, the happy children.

But not all the children were happy. Jimmy saw his sister Lisa sitting alone, holding a Raggedy Ann doll that she didn't seem interested in. She didn't look good. Near her, Brad sat hugging himself with a pallid, pained expression. Some of the guys around Brad whispered among themselves.

Jimmy turned from the window and looked across the lawn toward the cottages. The lights were all turned off. Maybe if he went in now and hid in the cottage where Lisa stayed, he could get her out tonight before anyone realized he was around. Brad had said he'd leave Stella's window open. He hoped he hadn't forgotten.

Stealing through the trees, he came up on the back door of Cottage B. He went to Stella's room and tried the window. It slid open easily. Quietly, he climbed in, shut the window behind him, and headed farther into the house. A strange mixture of sensations overwhelmed him as he walked through the building he had lived in for so long—homesickness and fear, familiarity and terror. Had any of this been worth it? Maybe everyone would have been better off if he had just found a way to get out of that attic and back to Bill . . .

No, that wasn't right. Eventually, Bill would have used Lisa in his little schemes, anyway. Eventually, Jimmy would not have been able to protect her. Eventually, Bill would have gone too far and killed one of the children. Eventually, they would have been caught. No, he had done the right thing. And what he was about to do was even more right—he had to save Lisa from Bill Brandon.

He went into the bedroom where he and Brad and Keith had slept, along with five other boys, in the bunk beds lined against the walls. Going to the bed that used to be his, he looked under it for the box of his belongings. They were gone; now another boy's shoes were there. Had Bill already replaced him? A sinking feeling began to pull him under. The feeling surprised him. He didn't live here anymore—didn't want to. But he didn't want to be forgotten, either.

He went to Lisa's room. He found his box hidden under her bed, and felt relieved that his sister had protected his things. *She* hadn't forgotten him.

He sat down on her bed, feeling so helpless, so dismal, so confused.

"It's not fair," he whispered to the darkness. "It's just not fair." He had done little to deserve all of this: the risks, the danger, the sadness. And Lisa had done even less. He closed his eyes and wished he had been able to protect her from the past few days. She was tiny, helpless—just the way Bill liked them.

Jimmy hoped he was getting to her in time. He knew she would expect him to rescue her, to make all the evil go away, to set everything right. She had always thought he was some kind of superkid, and he hadn't minded it. She'd looked up to him like he was her father. But he wasn't—and didn't have any more idea of how a father acted than she did.

He thought of the few men he knew that he admired. He admired Nick—the way he had gotten Beth out of the fire after her explosion and taken care of her. Nick had rescued Jimmy's mother, too—although part of Jimmy wished she had died. But then Nick was also the one who had placed him and Lisa in this home.

Tears came to Jimmy's eyes, and he wiped them away. Maybe Nick wasn't the one he wanted to be like. Maybe someone else. Someone like . . .

Jake Stevens. The name came to him with a warmth that burned in his heart. Jake was someone he could look up to. What would Jake do in this situation? How would he get Lisa out?

Lynda had told him how Jake had saved her from some murderer while he was still in his wheelchair. Even that hadn't stopped Jake. And Jimmy didn't plan to let anything stop him, either.

He heard car doors closing outside, and he peered through the window. The television crews were loading up, and Bill was standing outside with them, giving one last interview before they packed their equipment and disappeared. The children were still inside the rec room, and Jimmy guessed that Bill had them all doing cleanup detail before they could return to the cottages.

Just in case someone came back early, he slipped into the closet. He sat down in the corner and closed the door in front of him. It was stifling in there. There was no ventilation, and the hot Florida air was sweltering there where the air conditioner failed to blow. He reached into the waist of his jeans and felt for the pistol. It was there. If he needed it, he would use it. He wouldn't hesitate.

Across the street, Larry watched inconspicuously as the party broke up. Bill seemed to be trying to delay the television crew's departure. It was his last-ditch effort to appear to be a pillar of the community. He wanted to make friends with these people who, tomorrow, would have to condemn him on the news. He was running scared, Larry thought with satisfaction. He only wished he could walk up there right now, while the cameras were rolling, and slap some cuffs on the man's wrists. He wished he could expose him as a murderer, thief, and child abuser, and drag him away in front of all the children. Now *that* would be a party they could appreciate.

He picked up the phone and dialed Tony's car. Tony picked up. "Yeah?"

"The party's breaking up," Larry said. "Camera crews are going home. Has the judge moved?"

"Not an inch. He's tucked safely into his house. Doesn't look like he's going anywhere else tonight."

"Don't take your eyes off him, anyway," Larry said.

"I won't. I'm still trying to track the captain down. Call me if anything happens."

J ake pulled his old car into the driveway at Lynda's house, hoping to see Jimmy sitting beside the door, waiting to be let in. They hadn't found him, and their only hope now was that he had decided to come back home.

"He's not here," Lynda said, defeated.

"Maybe he came in through a back door or something. It's possible. He went out one."

Lynda's dull expression didn't change. "He couldn't trust us anymore. I can't believe we let this happen."

"We didn't *let* anything happen, Lynda," Jake said. "It just did. It couldn't be helped."

In the house, Lynda searched every room, hoping, praying that he was there, sitting in the dark, brooding. But he wasn't. "Where could he be?" she asked, fighting tears. "Oh, Jake, he could be in real trouble."

She saw the glow from the computer screen still on in the darkened living room, and went in to shut it off. "If he had just said something—" She realized the computer was still on-line, so she moved the mouse to exit the game. "We could have taken him ourselves, helped him if he needed it . . ."

When the game window closed, the mail window was still on the screen, and she started to close it, too—then froze when she saw the letter on the screen, from someone with the screen name Drab11. "Jake—Jake, this is e-mail! Jimmy's been communicating with someone from the home."

Jake rushed over and read the letter signed "Brad." "You're right. And he didn't like what he heard."

"I don't think we have to wonder where anymore, do you?"

"No, I sure don't. Come on, let's go. Maybe we can stop him before he does something stupid."

"Wait. First we have to call Larry and Tony. Maybe they can get to him before we can." Lynda ran to the phone and punched out the number to Tony's car.

"Yeah?" Tony answered.

"Tony, this is Lynda," she blurted. "We've figured out where Jimmy is."

"Where?"

"He's gone back to SCCH to get Lisa out."

"No. He wouldn't do that."

"He's doing it. I'm telling you, that's where we're going to find him. We're headed over there."

"No way. Let us take care of it, Lynda."

"You said yourself that you aren't authorized to do anything! Tony, there's a child's life at stake here. Somebody has to do something besides sitting around watching!"

"Lynda, we know what's at stake! If you get in the way of what we're doing, I'll gladly arrest you myself. Now stay out of the way!"

Lynda's face reddened. "I'm a lawyer, Tony. You just try and arrest me! I'll drag you into court for false arrest, police brutality, and anything else I can come up with!"

"Go ahead," Tony said, undaunted. "I'll arrest you anyway. It would keep you out of the way tonight while we're trying to get to Bill Brandon. After that, you can do anything you want to me."

Lynda grew quiet, and she covered her eyes with a trembling hand. "So help me, Tony, if anything happens to that kid . . ."

"Let us do our job, Lynda. That's the best way to make sure nothing will."

CHAPTER FIFTY-FIVE

I t was at least an hour before the children began coming back into the cottage. Jimmy heard their voices as they approached the bedroom. The girls who shared a room with Lisa were laughing and talking about their rag dolls, as if they'd been given some precious gift they'd never forget. He couldn't hear Lisa's voice.

He heard the sounds of them getting ready for bed, then Stella's voice barking out orders. He waited until the light went out and everyone had quieted down, then opened the door slightly so that he could see where everyone was. There was Lisa, lying in her bed on her side, still awake, staring dismally into the dark. Her rag doll had been discarded on the floor beside her bed, but she clutched her old teddy bear tightly.

Why had they gotten presents tonight? What was Bill up to?

He felt for the gun again, and it gave him courage to wait. He sat there for what seemed an eternity, hoping the others would go to sleep. But it didn't matter if they didn't. He had the gun, and that gave him power. He could take Lisa anywhere he wanted to, as long as he had the gun.

When silence had prevailed for a half hour or more, he opened the door ever so slightly. It creaked, but no one moved.

He crawled out on his hands and knees, staying down in case anyone's eyes were still open. But they all seemed to be asleep, which surprised him. In his room, which was an older group, that didn't happen. They often argued long after lights out, or they were up getting ready to do some dirty deed of Bill's.

He crawled to Lisa's bed, then got to his feet and bent over her. He shook her shoulder, and her eyes came open with a flash of fear, making him wonder if she'd expected Bill.

He held his finger to his mouth, hushing her, but she couldn't help the gasp that escaped. "*Jimmy!*"

He put his hand over her mouth, but it was too late—a little girl named Jill opened her eyes and sat up. "What are you doing here?" she whispered in surprise.

"Shhh." He waved frantically for her to be quiet. "Come on, Lisa," he whispered. "Come with me."

"Can I come, too?" Jill asked.

"You don't want to go where we're going," Jimmy said.

"I might."

"Just *hush*. I came to get my sister, that's all. And if you tell—" He pulled his shirt up, showing the gun.

She caught her breath and lay back down quickly. "I won't tell."

Lisa shrank back onto her pillow, horrified. "Jimmy, where'd you get that?" she whispered.

He shook his head and put his fingers over her lips. "Come on, we've got to get out of here."

She got up and ran to the shelves where all of their clothes were piled in little cubbyholes. She pulled out a pair of shorts and slipped on her shoes. "Wait," she whispered. "I've got to get the box."

"Leave it," he said. "It doesn't matter. We can't carry it."

"Yes, we can," she said. "We have to. It has pictures of our mama. I don't want to forget what she looks like."

She ran to the closet and pulled out a black backpack—which Jimmy recognized immediately as the kind that Bill issued to all the kids who worked under him. His heart sank. So Bill had gotten to her, too. She stuffed the contents of the box into the backpack, along with her teddy bear, and slipped it onto her small shoulders. "I'm ready," she whispered with a smile. "I knew you'd come to get me, but he told us you were in jail."

"He's the one who's going to jail," Jimmy said. "Not me."

"But we've all broken laws," she said. "He said if we get caught—"

"He lied," Jimmy said. "He's a liar and a murderer and a thief and you can't believe a word he says. Especially all that Bible stuff."

"He said the sins of the brother are visited on the sister. Jimmy, what does that mean?"

"It means that if I see him face-to-face, I might just use this gun on him." He went to the window and tried to open it. It wouldn't budge.

"It's nailed shut," Jill whispered. "Bill did it yesterday."

He breathed out a ragged sigh. "Okay, then we'll have to go up the hall." He turned with a menacing look toward Jill, who still followed them with her eyes, though she lay quietly. "Jill, if you make one sound or tell anyone Lisa's gone before morning, so help me, I'll come back here and get revenge. Got it?"

"Okay," she whispered. "Bye, Lisa. Are you coming back?"

Lisa looked at her brother, and he shook his head no. The little girl's face changed to an expression of deep sadness, and she lay back down. "Are you sure I can't come?"

"Yes," Jimmy said. "Not right now. Maybe later."

He took Lisa's hand and tiptoed with her up the hall, desperately silent. He heard Stella moving around in her own room, so he knew that he couldn't go back out the same way he had come in. They were going to have to sneak through the den. He could only hope that no one was there. But he'd been trained in walking through people's homes while they slept and not getting caught. They cut through the dark kitchen, heading for the den, when the sound of the front door startled him. He heard Stella dash from her room into the den to meet her guest.

"I think that was a success, don't you?" It was Bill's voice, and Jimmy almost panicked. He motioned frantically for Lisa to head back to her room, and he followed.

"Absolutely. You've got them eating out of your hand," Stella said.

"Let's just hope they keep eating out of it," he said. "Judge Wyatt is fighting hard, but they may find a way to go over his head by tomorrow. It might be time for me to get out of town."

"And what about me?" Stella asked. "I'll be implicated, too. We all will."

"Just say you didn't know what was going on. That you weren't actually involved."

"But according to the paper, they know that it was a little girl who delivered the package bomb to the post office—and that she was seen with a woman in a pickup truck."

"That was me!" Lisa whispered. She and Jimmy were standing in the doorway to her room now, trying to listen. Jimmy put his hand over her mouth to silence her.

"They can't prove that woman was you," Bill told Stella.

"Bill, I'm not taking the heat for attempted murder. You know I didn't know what was in that package—"

"You knew it wasn't a box of chocolates."

"What about Jimmy?" she demanded. "He's still out there somewhere, telling his story."

Jimmy moved his hand from Lisa's face, and they both listened hard.

"Don't worry about Jimmy," Bill said. "He's not going to be a factor."

"Bill, you'll never get to him without getting caught."

"I won't have to," he said. "He'll come to us, before we know it. Maybe even tonight."

Lisa's eyes rounded with terror. Bill was *expecting* Jimmy!

But Jimmy only stared into space, trying to figure out how Bill had known he was coming—and how he and Lisa would get past him now.

CHAPTER FIFTY-SIX

L arry's phone rang, and he snatched it up.

"We've got a problem," Tony said before Larry could speak.

"What?"

"Lynda and Jake think Jimmy's headed over there."

"Here? To the home?"

"That's what they said. Seen any evidence of it?"

"No," Larry said. "Why in the world would he come here?"

"Apparently, he got a desperate e-mail note from some kid there to come get Lisa out before Bill killed her."

Larry's hand slid down his face. "Tell me you're kidding."

"No, and Jimmy must have taken off to rescue her."

"But he's a kid! He can't take on Bill Brandon by himself."

"Well, let's hope Jake and Lynda are wrong. But just in case, keep your eyes peeled and let me know if you see anything."

CHAPTER FIFTY-SEVEN

By now, all of the girls in Lisa's room had awakened. They all looked at Jimmy as he and Lisa turned and came back into the room. "Don't anybody say a word," he whispered. He pulled out his gun again, just for good measure, and waved it in the air. "I'm not afraid to use this."

All the girls lay back down, their eyes wide as they watched to see what he was going to do next. Then Jimmy noticed that their eyes darted suddenly toward the door behind him.

"*Jimmy?*"

Jimmy swung around to see his friends Brad and Kevin standing in the doorway.

"What are you doing here?" Brad whispered harshly.

"Shut up!" Jimmy mouthed. "Bill's out there."

"I know he is," he said. "He came to get us. He wants Lisa, too."

"No," Jimmy said through his teeth. "He's not taking her." He stepped closer to the boys, keeping his voice as low as he could. "Cover for her. Distract him until we get out of here."

"I want to go, too," Brad returned. "Take me with you."

"No! Just Lisa. That's all I can handle."

"But you *gotta* take me, too," Brad whispered, starting to cry, something Jimmy had never seen him do before. "Bill's got it in for me lately. If you don't take me, you're gonna have to come visit me in the graveyard."

"No!" Jimmy cried. He reached out to push the boy away, but Brad winced and doubled over in pain.

Only then did Jimmy notice that Brad was wearing a long-sleeved shirt and jeans, rather than the shorts and T-shirt he usually wore in the summer. He remembered that he had done that, despite the heat, to cover bruises after Bill's beatings. "What happened?" he asked.

"Bill beat him up because of the e-mail," Lisa said.

A sense of dread washed over Jimmy. "What e-mail?"

"The one we sent you."

Jimmy's face went cold as the blood drained from it. "Bill found it?"

"Yeah, and was he mad."

The little girls were all sitting up now, and Lisa was on the edge of her bed, not sure what to do next.

Jimmy touched Brad's shoulder. "I'm sorry I shoved you, man. No wonder you wanted to leave so bad."

Brad wiped the tears off his face.

"The e-mails," he said. "You were the one who told me to hurry because Lisa had been beaten, weren't you? You're the one who left Stella's window unlocked?"

"No, man. That's not what I wrote. Bill must have sent that."

Jimmy felt such rage that his head threatened to burst. "It was a trap." His face grew hot and mottled, and he pulled the gun out of his pocket. "He knows I'm here. He set this whole thing up. Even left the window open for me."

One of the little girls buried her face in her pillow and began to cry, and the others sat huddled on their beds, eyes wide with fear.

"What's gonna happen?" Lisa asked.

"I'm gonna get you out of here, that's what," Jimmy told her. "All we have to do is get out the door. There's a cop across the street. As soon as he sees us, we'll be home free."

"Is that so?" The deep voice startled them all, and Jimmy turned and saw Bill standing in the doorway, leaning indolently against the frame. "Hello, Jimmy. Long time, no see. I've been expecting you."

With shaky hands, Jimmy raised the gun and pointed it at Bill. "All I want is my sister. Let us go, and nobody'll get hurt."

Bill laughed. "You don't know how to use a gun, Jimmy. And even if you did, you wouldn't."

"Watch me," Jimmy said through his teeth.

Bill started walking toward him, his hand outstretched. "Give me the gun, Jimmy, and then we'll go to my office and talk this thing out, man-to-man."

"Yeah? Like you talked to Brad?"

"Brad knows he deserved what he got. Don't you, Brad?"

"Yes, sir."

Bill got too close, and Jimmy shouted, "Don't take another step or I'll shoot!"

Bill laughed again. "Go ahead, Jimmy. You're not even holding the gun right."

Jimmy trembled as his finger tried to close over the trigger. It didn't budge. He squeezed harder. It was locked, and he didn't have a clue how to release it.

"Just give it to me," Bill said calmly. "I'm not mad at you, Jimmy. In fact, I've missed you. Things haven't been the same around here without you."

"Yeah? Is that why you've already put somebody else in my bed?" It was a stupid, irrational thing to say, and Jimmy knew it.

Bill shook his head. "Your bed is still empty. I put another kid's shoes there in case of an inspection. I didn't want them to know you were gone. I was afraid they'd come after you, lock you up. I was just protecting you." He leaned over, still reaching for the gun. "Jimmy, give me that thing."

"No." Jimmy backed away, and Brad backed with him.

"You have to cock it," Brad mumbled. Suddenly Bill's hand came down across Brad's face, knocking him down. The little girls screamed, and the others came running from down the hall to crowd around the door. Bill jerked Brad up off the floor and flung him back against the wall, and his fist came back to deliver another blow.

Jimmy cocked the gun and fired it.

B eth was watching Nick load her things onto a cart so that he could roll them out of the hospital when Lynda and Jake came in.

"Did you find him?" Beth asked the moment she saw them.

Nick swung around. "Is he all right?"

"No, we didn't find him, but we think we know where he is," Lynda said.

"Where?"

"We think he went back to the home to try to get Lisa out."

"No!" Nick cried.

"Apparently, he did." Lynda quickly recounted the story of the e-mail.

"Well, we've got to get over there!" Beth said.

"No, Tony and Larry are working on it. They made us promise to stay away."

"But we *can't* stay away. What if they mess things up?"

"They won't. We just have to have faith. Tony's been trying to track down the prosecutor to get a warrant. As soon as he gets it, we can go in there and get Jimmy and Lisa out. Until then, Beth, you can come back to my house. Your things are there from the other night, anyway. You can stay until your house is rebuilt."

A few minutes later, as Nick started the engine of Beth's car in the hospital parking lot, she looked uneasily at the shadows around them. "It's getting down to the wire," she said.

"Yeah, it's getting pretty hairy."

"He's going to kill somebody tonight," she said. "Might be Jimmy. Might be me." Beth closed her eyes. "What in the world have I started?"

"You didn't start it. Bill Brandon did."

"But I could have let it go. And the worst those kids ever would have been guilty of was robbing people's houses and businesses. They might have been beaten a time or two, but they wouldn't have been killed."

"Stop it. You're believing the lie that you did the wrong thing. You did the *right* thing, Beth."

He pulled out of the parking space and shifted into drive. They drove slowly past a van, and she jumped as she noticed someone standing on the other side of it. *Just a hospital visitor,* she realized with relief—but it could just as easily have been Bill, or one of his cohorts. He could ambush her at any second, and he wouldn't hesitate if he got the chance.

She was trembling now, and she reached into her glove compartment to get her gun.

"Oh, no."

"What?"

"My gun. It was here, but it's gone. Somebody's taken it."

"But the doors were locked. It didn't look broken into."

"Jimmy," she said. "Bill taught us how to break into cars as well as buildings. Sometimes there were valuable things in cars. Laptop computers, stereos, cellular phones, money—guns. Jimmy knew I had the gun. He came after it. He was here."

Nick braked and sat there for a moment, staring at her. Then he drove to the other side of the parking lot, where Lynda and Jake were standing and talking near Nick's car, which Jake had agreed to drive home for him. Nick rolled his window down.

"Jimmy was here," Nick told them. "And he's got Beth's gun."

When Nick rushed through Tracy's hospital room door, panting and sweating as if he'd run all the way up, she knew that something was wrong.

"I started to leave, but I thought you should know," he said. "We figured out where Jimmy is. We think he went back to the home to rescue Lisa."

She sat up abruptly and jerked the oxygen mask off her face. "Somebody's got to stop him."

"That's what we plan to do," he said. "I just thought you should know. He could still come here, if we're wrong, and if he does, you have to call us, okay?" When she'd promised, he nodded and ran out.

It took Tracy less than a minute to get the IV out of her hand and pull off the other monitors and cords. She got to her feet and wobbled to the window. Down in the illuminated parking lot, three cars caravanned out—probably Nick and his friends. What if they couldn't stop him?

She stood there for a moment, feeling totally helpless, completely alone, realizing just how badly she had failed her children so many years ago. But she hadn't been herself then. She hadn't understood what was happening. She hadn't cared.

She cared now.

In the closet of her room, she found the dirty clothes she had worn into the hospital. They were filthy, but they were all she had, so holding the counter to steady herself, she pulled them on.

When she'd dressed, she sat abruptly on the edge of her bed because she was so dizzy. It didn't matter. She was determined to get out of here. She had to find her son and her daughter and save them if she could. Maybe then she could redeem herself with them. Maybe for once in their young lives, they could believe that their mother cared about them.

How she would get there she had no idea, but she made her way to the elevator, punched the button, then flopped against the corner and waited for it to hit the first floor, feeling as if she would pass out at any moment. Her lungs felt as if a great weight sat on them, keeping her from breathing, but she pressed on. When the doors opened, she stumbled off and walked out into the parking lot.

Where would she go? How would she get there?

She looked around at the hundreds of cars lining the parking lot and wished one of them was hers. She did have one, sitting out in front of her apartment, though all but one seat was torn out and it had a rusted fender and was missing a door. If she could just get to it, she could drive it. The engine was one of the few things that still worked.

She saw two people walking out to their car, and she made her way toward them. "Excuse me," she said, then had a fit of coughing, which caught their attention. She struggled to catch her breath, supporting herself against the fender of a car.

"Are you all right?" the elderly lady asked her.

"Yes. I've just got a cold," she said, breathless. "Listen, I have a flat tire, and I really need to get home. Could you give me a ride?"

The woman set a maternal hand on Tracy's forehead. "Honey, you're burning up! Have you seen a doctor?"

"Yes, just now. I'm fine, really. I just have asthma—probably the stress of the flat tire brought it on. I have to get home. I don't live that far, I don't think."

"Certainly we can give you a ride," the man said.

"I don't have any money."

"We don't need any," he said. "Come on, dear. Let's get you out of this night air."

She tried to look stronger than she was as she sat in the backseat, but they kept looking over their shoulders with concern. They were nice people. Grandparent types. She wished Jimmy and Lisa could have people like them in their lives.

She gave them directions until they came to her corner, and she started to get out.

"Thank you very much."

The old man reached back across the seat to stop her. "Miss, are you sure you want me to let you off here? It doesn't look very safe."

"It's better than it looks," she said. "Bye now."

She closed the door and headed for her apartment steps.

The couple sat in their car, watching her. She knew they wouldn't leave until she had gone in. But she had no intention of trying to climb those stairs. Instead, she just stepped into the shadows and stood still until, apparently assuming she was safe inside a downstairs apartment, they pulled away.

She made her way slowly and with great effort down the block to where her car was parked on the road. The key was where she had left it, hidden between the vinyl and foam rubber of the torn visor. She pulled it out and jabbed it into her ignition. It coughed, then died. She tried again; finally, on the third try, it caught.

She sat behind the wheel, trying to wait out the dizziness. *Jesus, help me. My children need me. Let me act like a mother just once in this pathetic life of mine.*

The vertigo seemed to clear, and she pulled the car forward, trying to remember where the children's home was located.

CHAPTER SIXTY

The gunshot still rang in the air, and everyone froze. Jimmy had shot at the floor, but now he raised the gun toward Bill. "I told you I could do it," he said in a high-pitched voice that sounded as if it came from someone else. "Next time my aim is gonna be better." He looked down at the boy lying on the floor of the girls' room, half-propped against the wall where Bill had dropped him. "Are you all right, Brad?"

Brad stumbled to his feet, holding his ribs with one hand and his face with the other. "You gotta take me with you, Jimmy," he pleaded. "Please!"

Visibly shaken by the gunshot, Bill pointed at Jimmy with one hand and with the other gestured around the room at everyone else. "Everybody out," he said quietly, his voice trembling slightly. "Now!"

The ones clustered in the doorway scattered, and the girls in the room slid off their bunks and ran crying into the hall. Lisa stayed in her room hunkered behind her brother, and Brad stood next to Jimmy, facing Bill.

Jimmy kept the gun trained on the man who had exploited and abused him.

"You know, Jimmy, you may think I'm some terrible person," Bill said, trying to speak in gentle, soothing tones, "but that's only because they've brainwashed you, wherever you've been. Probably Beth Wright has been working her evil on you. But there's something you should know about Beth, Jimmy. That's not even her real name. She's really Beth Sullivan, and she killed my sister. But her wickedness will catch up with her. The Good Book even describes her in detail. It says, 'She has haughty eyes, a lying tongue, hands that shed innocent blood, a heart that devises wicked schemes, feet that are quick to rush into evil. She is a false witness who pours out lies and stirs up dissension among brothers.' She's like that, Jimmy, and the Lord finds those things detestable. But he knows my heart, and so do you. I forgive you for straying, Jimmy, because you're young and easily influenced. But in your heart, you know I've always thought of you as a son. My son."

Jimmy's cheeks mottled red, and he kept the gun aimed. Bill took a step toward him, but he backed up.

"Jimmy, if you do this, every child here will be farmed out to foster homes. Some of those homes are bad, Jimmy. Really bad. And those of you who have committed crimes will be locked up until you're so old that you'll never have kids of your own, or families. There won't be any hope for any of you. You kids are spoiled by all the nice things here, but you won't have that there. You and Lisa will be split up, for sure—since they don't jail men and women together—and you may never see her again."

"No!" Lisa cried. "Jimmy, is that true?"

Jimmy held his breath for a moment. "I don't know."

"But Jimmy! I thought we were gonna be together! I thought you said—"

"Listen to her, Jimmy," Bill cut in. "Do you want to hear your sister's screams as they drag her away from you? Do you want to wonder every night whose care she's in—and just what they're doing to her?"

Jimmy swallowed. He was getting confused. The thought of Lisa being placed in some foster home—or worse, a juvenile detention center or jail—where he didn't know who would be taking care of her, made him sick. Sure, Beth and the others had assured him that he and the other kids wouldn't go to jail, but he couldn't really trust what they'd said. They'd been wrong about other things. Still—"At least she won't be raised a thief or an arsonist or a bomb smuggler," Jimmy said. "Or even a murderer!"

"You've been watching too much television, Jimmy. You have a very loose grasp on reality."

"Like Beth?" he asked through lips stretched thin. "You almost killed her! And you did kill her dog. Dodger never did anything to you."

"It was just a warning, son," Bill said. "It wasn't meant to hurt anyone. I just wanted to put a scare into her to keep her from telling those lies." He bent over, his face too close to Jimmy's. "Jimmy, listen to me. All this time you were gone, I didn't report it, because I didn't want you to have to go to jail. Now you can just come back and pick up like you never left. No one will know. We'll just go on like we were . . ."

Bill's voice was mesmerizing, and Jimmy wanted so much to believe that he meant the things he said. Suddenly all that was familiar about Jimmy's life at the home began to call out to him—spending time with Brad and Kevin, his own bed, being able to watch over Lisa and protect her . . .

He lowered the gun slightly . . .

Bill lunged for him and wrestled the gun from his hand as Lisa screamed. He flung Jimmy to the floor, then turned the gun on them and laughed. Jimmy, Lisa, and Brad shrank back.

"I'm going to call a news conference tomorrow," he said, "and I'm going to tell the world that you three were responsible for the murder of my sister, the arson at the paper, and a hundred other crimes that haven't been solved. I'm going to tell them that you had a twenty-one-year-old cohort named Beth Wright who drove you, and every night you sneaked out to wreak havoc on the town. They'll have you locked in a cage in no time." He laughed cruelly, then regarded them tauntingly for a moment. "Or maybe I'll just decide to kill you first and dump your remains off a bridge somewhere. They'd never find you, not until the sharks had gotten their fill."

Lisa pressed herself into the corner of her room, trying to get smaller and farther away from the man who looked so natural with a gun. Brad stood next to her, a defeated, desperate look on his bruised face. Jimmy got up and stood in front of them both. "You'll have to kill me to get to them."

"I can do that." Bill backed to the doorway of the room and called out to Stella. She waddled into view, looking a little frightened herself.

"Go to the shed and get my Buick out," he said. "I'm gonna take these kids for a ride. After I get the stuff in the warehouse shipped and collect what's due me, then I'm going on a long vacation."

Stella dashed out, and they heard the door close behind her.

No one spoke until the car pulled up to the front door of the house and Stella came back in. "It's there, Bill. Just one thing before you go. What about us?"

"What about you? You're on your own. I'm getting out of here."

CHAPTER SIXTY-ONE

I'm exhausted," Beth said, getting slowly to her feet. She looked around Lynda's living room at Lynda, Jake, and Nick, who looked back at her with sympathy and understanding. "I need to lie down for a while."

"We'll wake you up the minute we get any word from Tony," Lynda said, with a weary smile.

Beth nodded and plodded down the hallway, apparently barely able to put one foot in front of the other. But as soon as she got into the guest room, her eyes brightened and her movements became quick and sure. She slipped out the back door of the guest room onto the patio and stole around the house to her car.

She prayed, as she started the car and pulled out of the driveway, that the others wouldn't hear her; she breathed a sigh of relief as no one followed. Then she headed for the children's home, determined to do something to keep Jimmy from getting killed. Even with a gun, she knew the boy was no match for Bill Brandon. Neither was she. But she might at least be able to distract Bill long enough for Jimmy and his sister to escape.

Her bandaged chest hurt as she drove to the home as fast as she could, knowing that Nick or Lynda or Jake might discover at any time that she was gone and come after her. She took every shortcut she knew to cover the short distance to the compound where she had grown up. After she pulled up to the front of the compound, she sat for a moment, letting the car idle with the headlights off as she stared up into the buildings where all those children slept at night, trying to forget the heartache and terror of their pasts—even though the present might be worse. Tears came to her eyes, and she covered her face with her hands. She hadn't seen Bill face-to-face since she'd walked out of the home on her eighteenth birthday. Just seeing him now would bring back a flood of despair and resentment and hatred. In truth, she might not come out of this alive. Bill wanted her dead, and wouldn't be likely to just sit back and watch her walk out.

She wished she had her gun. She couldn't go in there to face her enemy unarmed, not if she expected to help Jimmy.

She scanned the cottages. She wasn't even sure which one to try. And what would she do? Break in? Knock? What would she say when she came face-to-face with Bill? Was she really as tough as she thought, or would she melt in fear, as she had done as a child, the moment Bill's angry eyes had turned on her?

Hatred so real and vibrant that it seemed to have a life of its own welled inside her, and she suddenly realized that she didn't need a weapon. Her hatred of Bill Brandon was enough. It would propel her, drive her, protect her . . .

She wilted. That was a lie. Hatred wasn't going to get her anything. There had to be another way.

The words of an old favorite passage of Scripture came back to her, and she chanted them in a whisper. *The Lord is my shepherd, I shall not be in want. He makes me lie down in green pastures, he leads me beside quiet waters, he restores my soul.*

Her soul didn't feel restored yet, but that was her fault. There was a price that had to be paid, a sacrifice that must be offered . . .

He guides me in paths of righteousness for his name's sake.

She didn't feel righteous, either, but she wasn't finished trying.

Even though I walk through the valley of the shadow of death, I will fear no evil, for you are with me; your rod and your staff, they comfort me.

This was the valley of the shadow of death—it always had been for her. Now she tried to imagine walking into this valley with that rod and staff as her only weapons—and found confidence that they would be enough.

Armed with new courage, she got out of the car and slammed the door, not even caring if Bill heard her. She *wanted* him to see her, wanted him to forget whatever he was doing and come out to confront her. That might give Jimmy a window of opportunity to escape with Lisa.

As she entered the compound, she saw a cluster of crying children standing in front of one of the cottages, huddled together. The Buick that had tried to run her off the road days ago was parked in front of the door with the driver's door open. Across the compound, she saw Stella hurrying into a shed. The big woman backed a van out of it, and sped through the yard and away.

Beth approached the kids. "What's going on?" she asked.

"Bill's gonna kill them!" one of the children cried. "We heard a gunshot, but Bill's still in there yelling. He must have shot Jimmy or Lisa or Brad!"

Beth thought she might faint, but she forced herself through it. "Are there any other adults on the campus?"

"There were, but they all left!"

"Go over to the rec room," she ordered. "Get down on the floor and don't come out until I tell you. Do you hear me?"

She watched as they fled to the building across the campus.

Taking a deep breath, she tested the knob, then opened it. "Your rod and your staff, they comfort me," she muttered under her breath as she stepped inside.

She heard voices in the back room. Taking a deep breath, she held it for a moment, marshaling her courage and steadiness of mind. This was it. Then she yelled: "Bill Brandon!"

The voices stopped. "That's right," she called. "It's me. Beth Sullivan. You wanted me dead. Well, now's your chance."

CHAPTER SIXTY-TWO

The moment he had heard the gunshot, Larry had called Tony, explaining even as he pounded down the stairs and out the door what he'd heard. As he rushed across the street and toward the home, he said, "What the—Tony, you're not going to believe this."

"What!" Tony prompted.

"Beth. She's heading onto the compound—too far away for me to stop. Her car's out front here. Looks like she's heading for a group of children."

"What's she thinking of? If Brandon finds her, he'll kill her—he's already tried it twice."

"I'm right behind her," Larry said into the cell phone. "Send me some backups."

He tucked the phone into his belt pouch as the children fled to the rec room. As he rounded the corner, he could see Beth heading into the cottage where a Buick was parked out front. He pulled his gun out of his shoulder holster. Praying under his breath, he ran in a crouch the remaining distance to the cottage, went to the window, and looked through. Bill stood with a pistol pointed at three children—Jimmy and two others. The little girl had to be Lisa. The gunshot he'd heard hadn't wounded any of these people, apparently.

He heard Beth call out. Bill swung around . . .

CHAPTER SIXTY-THREE

Bill stepped slowly into the hallway, grinning at Beth. Then he motioned with the gun in his hand—her own gun, Beth realized—and Jimmy and two other children stepped out into the hallway with him, huddled together. Beth choked back her fear. "Let them go, Bill," she said. "Let it be just you and me, face-to-face."

He chuckled. "Well, well. Been a long time, darlin'. How are you?"

"Better than you expected," she said. "I'm just fine."

"Well, it was nice of you to drop in tonight. You missed the party, though. It was a good one. Made me some friends, I'll wager. You can never have too many friends in the media."

"Let them go, Bill," she said again. "You don't need them."

"Oh, I need them, all right," he said, slowly herding the children down the hallway toward her. "And as much as I'd like to finish the job I started a couple of days ago, I need you. I'm not stupid. I know the cops have been trying to get a warrant. I know that as soon as they do, they'll be out here to arrest me. But I won't be here. And neither will you. We're gonna be taking a little trip. I'll take all of you along for insurance."

"Just me," she said. "Let them go and take me."

"Let them go?" He threw his head back and laughed. "Beth, Beth, you know better than that." He was almost within arm's reach now. Could she grab the gun? No, too dangerous. If it went off and hit one of the kids . . .

"There are too many of us," she said. "We'll be too conspicuous. If it's just me . . ."

"Just you and me, Beth? Think about it. They'd shoot us as soon as look at us. You're nothing but trash, and you don't have family that'll sue them later. They'd be safe taking risks with a hostage like you. But with these cute little kids, they wouldn't dare take a chance, or they'd have the whole country coming down on them the minute they pulled the trigger. No, the kids are my ticket out of here."

"Where will you go?" she asked through her teeth. "Somewhere to ruin more lives? Are you going to keep killing everybody who gets in your way?"

"I might," he said with a grin. He grabbed her hair by the roots, and swung her back toward the door. "But right now, I need to keep you alive." He scowled at the three children huddled together. "Come on, kids. Into the car. All of you."

Jimmy held his sister close to him; tears ran down both their cheeks. "Beth, I'm sorry. I shouldn't have taken your gun. Now he's got it and—"

"It's okay, Jimmy," she said, her face reddening with pain as he jerked her by her hair. "Just do what he says."

Bill kept the gun trained on them as the children climbed into the backseat of the car. He shoved Beth into the passenger seat and said, "Scoot over. You'll do the driving."

He was just about to climb in after her when a voice cut through the night: "*Freeze!*"

Bill froze, then slowly turned to see Larry with his gun trained on him.

"Drop the gun and get down on the ground!"

Bill leaned down slowly, the gun still in his hand. His arm swung out, apparently to toss the gun, but instead he raised the pistol and pulled the trigger.

The children screamed as Larry dropped to the ground.

Bill dove into the car. "Let's go!" he told Beth. "Turn that key and get us out of here! Move!"

"You killed him!" she cried as she cranked the car and pulled across the lawn. "You killed him!"

"Yeah, and you're next! Now shut up!"

The children tried to muffle their sobs of horror as Beth tore down the dark street.

"Where are we going?" she asked.

"We're just gonna drive," he said. "Until I get far enough away that I don't need you anymore."

"And then what?"

"Then I'll find a bridge to throw you over. Every last one of you."

CHAPTER SIXTY-FOUR

Tracy was nearly to the children's home when she was overcome with dizziness. She pulled the car to the side of the road and tried to gather what little strength she had left. She was almost there. She had to make it.

Just when her head seemed a little clearer, a coughing fit hit her. It was getting harder to breathe. Her lungs felt heavy and full of fluid, as if they didn't have room for anything as mundane as oxygen.

She was still struggling to catch her breath when she saw a car race across the children's home lawn and shoot the curb onto the street.

The car sped toward her, and as it passed under a streetlight she saw Jimmy sitting in the backseat with a little girl next to him.

A little girl! Was it Lisa? Tracy sucked a huge gulp of air, despite the pain. Her kids were in danger. She was their mother; it was her job to stop him. Ignoring her weakness, she shoved her car into a tight U-turn, tires squealing, and followed the other car until she'd caught up with it. Then, stepping on her accelerator, she pulled up beside them and tried to pass.

The other car began to zigzag, to keep her from staying on the road next to it. But she wouldn't give up. Tears streamed down her face as she urged the old rattletrap ahead and, finally, almost through sheer force of will, she inched ahead of them. *This was it*, she told herself. Her last chance to do something for her children. Something important. Something that mattered. It was her last chance to show her children she loved them.

She cranked the wheel as hard as she could, throwing her car into a power turn, spinning out of control just a few feet in front of the other car.

Tracy felt the impact of the collision almost immediately, heard the crunching metal. She only hoped Jimmy and Lisa were wearing their seatbelts. Her car had none, nothing to hold her in, and the last thing she was aware of before she lost consciousness was the sensation of being thrown out of the car into the night air.

CHAPTER SIXTY-FIVE

Th>here was a moment of shocked silence just after the two mangled cars ground to a halt. Then the inside of the Buick erupted in frightened screams. But the loudest was Jimmy's—because he had seen, behind the wheel of the rusty old car that had passed them and then pulled spinning in front of them, the face of his mother.

With no regard for Bill or any further danger, Jimmy bolted from the Buick and ran to the other car, which now lay on its side. But there was no one in that car. He looked up then, frantic—and saw his mother, several yards ahead, lying motionless on the concrete like a discarded rag doll. "Mom!" he yelled through his tears. "Mom!" He fell down beside her, wailing at the sight of the blood oozing from her nose and mouth.

But she opened her eyes slowly and looked up at him. "Run!" she whispered. "Take your sister and run!"

Jimmy was crying so hard he could barely speak. "Why did you do it?" he asked. "Why?"

"Because I . . . love you," she whispered. "Run, Jimmy! Please run . . ." Her voice trailed off, and Jimmy watched her eyes go dead and empty.

He wanted to stay with her, but her words echoed in his mind: *Take your sister and run.* He looked back toward the car. Lisa and Brad had gotten out, too. Bill had hit his head, and was holding it with one hand as he tried to crank the car with the other. Jimmy couldn't see Beth.

Jimmy ran to his sister and took her hand. "Come on, Brad," he whispered. "Let's hide in the woods."

He pulled Lisa after him, and Brad followed in a painful, stumbling run. Then he heard a yell. Looking back over his shoulder, Jimmy felt a surge of panic as he saw Bill throw open the car door and leap out. But with Bill's first step toward them, Beth dove from the car, landing on Bill's back, and wrestled him to the ground.

"Come on!" Jimmy urged, and pulled Lisa toward the safety of the trees.

It only took Bill a moment to regain his equilibrium, throw Beth off of him, and get the upper hand, but by then, the children were gone.

He grabbed her by the throat and lifted her to her feet. "Back in the car," he said through gritted teeth.

He threw her in on the driver's side, then pushed her across to the passenger seat. She gasped in pain as she moved, and he saw blood seeping onto her blouse from some wound he couldn't see on her chest. He jumped in beside her, cranked the car, and it started. He'd noticed some significant damage to the front of the car, but it looked driveable.

"Are you just going to leave her on the road?" Beth screamed.

"Shut up!" he shouted, bringing his fist hard across her jaw. "Don't say another word or it'll be the last thing you'll say!"

Furious, he drove around the wrecked car and the body lying in the street, and flew as fast as he could out of the area.

CHAPTER SIXTY-SIX

J immy urged Lisa and Brad through the woods at a run, trying to make it to the road on the other side where they might find help. Maybe a police car would come by, and they could flag it down.

Not long ago, Jimmy realized suddenly, a policeman would have been the last person he would have turned to when he was in trouble. For that matter, he wouldn't have trusted any other adults, either. But since then, he'd learned something: Adults weren't all bad. Beth had come here tonight, despite her fears of Bill, for the sole purpose of rescuing the children. And then there was his mother. A lump rose in his throat again, and he swallowed it down.

He still didn't understand why she had done it. She had already proven she didn't care about them. She had let the state take them and dump them somewhere. Why come back now, sick and weak, and risk her life to stop Bill from taking them away?

It didn't make sense. But it changed things, somehow.

"Why are you crying?" Lisa asked him breathlessly as they fought the vines and bushes in their way. "Aren't you happy we got away?"

Jimmy wiped his face. "Yeah, I'm happy. I was just thinking about the cop and that lady in the street." He couldn't tell her the lady had been her mother. Not yet. Maybe someday.

Brad was panting and wheezing, and Jimmy wondered if he was going to make it through the woods. He needed to get Brad to a hospital; they couldn't just hide someplace. Somehow, he needed to find help. Besides, they had to get help for Beth. They were the only ones who knew that Bill had taken her.

And he had to get help for all those children back at the home, who wouldn't know what to do or what was going to happen to them next.

The trees thinned, and suddenly they came to the road. Not far away was a gas station with a convenience store attached. Jimmy reached into his pocket for the change that Jake had let him keep when they'd gone for a Coke earlier. He fished out a quarter. "Come on, let's go call for help."

"Who are we gonna call?" Lisa asked.

He thought about it for a moment. "Jake," he said. "We'll call Jake."

Lynda answered on the first ring. "Lynda Barrett," she said.

"Lynda, it's me. Jimmy."

"Jimmy! Where are you? We've been worried sick—"

Jimmy cleared the emotion from his throat and tried to speak clearly. "I need to speak to Jake," he said.

"Oh . . . okay." Lynda gave the phone to Jake.

"Jimmy, are you all right?" he asked.

"I'm okay," he said. "But Bill's got Beth."

"What do you mean he's got Beth? Beth's here," Jake said. "She's asleep in the guest room."

"No. She came here. Bill's got her in a car, and he's taking her away. I think he's gonna kill her! Jake, you've got to stop him!"

"Jimmy, where are you?"

Jimmy was crying again. He stopped and wiped his eyes. "At the gas station about a mile from the home. I think it's called Quik Stop. It's on—" He checked the street signs near the phone booth. "The corner of Jefferson and Third Street."

"Jimmy, we're coming after you. You stay there. We'll be there in ten minutes."

"No! Don't worry about us! Lisa and Brad and me will be okay. You gotta worry about Beth. He'll kill her. And there's something else."

"Yeah? What?"

"My . . . my . . ." Jimmy lowered his voice to keep Brad or Lisa from hearing.

"What? I can't hear you."

"My m—" He choked on the word, then tried again. "Tracy. She needs an ambulance. And so does that cop—Larry, I think it was. He was shot."

"Shot? Are you sure?"

"Hurry, Jake! They may not be dead yet."

"But Tracy's in the hospital, Jimmy. You're confused—"

"No!" he shouted. "She came here, too. We'd still be in the car with Bill if she hadn't. But first he shot Larry, and then he ran over her, and she's lying in the road . . ." His voice broke off, and he couldn't go on.

"Jimmy, stay right where you are. We'll be there in ten minutes."

Jake drove faster than he'd ever driven in his life. In the passenger seat, Lynda was on the cellular phone, trying to locate Tony or Nick. She heard sirens, but they were coming from the opposite direction.

She found Nick in his office. "Nick, it's Lynda."

"Hi. I've been working on what to do with all the children. It's not going to be easy, but I think—"

"Nick, listen to me," Lynda said. "Jimmy just called."

"Oh, that's great! You've found him?"

"Yes. He went to the home, and something went wrong. We're headed to get him. He says that Bill's got Beth."

She heard something crash on Nick's end. "He can't. She's at your house! She was asleep—"

"No, she snuck out to go to the home to rescue the children. But apparently it backfired, and he's got her now."

"Oh, no."

"Nick, you've got to—" Her voice stopped as Jake slammed on the brakes and skidded to a halt. Lynda dropped the phone and looked through the windshield.

The headlights shone on something in the road, and Jake whispered, "Oh, God, please don't let this be."

"Tracy," Lynda whispered.

T he police radio report of an officer down at the St. Clair Children's Home stunned Tony, but before he could call in to ask for details, his cellular phone rang. He grabbed it as he turned a corner on two wheels, on his way to SCCH. "Larry?" he asked.

"No, Tony, it's Lynda!" She was choked and could hardly speak. "I'm sitting on Tenth about a mile from the children's home. Tracy Westin is lying in the middle of the road—she was thrown from her car. I checked her pulse, but there isn't one—she's dead, Tony. Bill Brandon ran her down. And Jimmy said he shot Larry!"

Tony went cold. "Larry?"

"Yeah. I don't have details, but I hear sirens. They may have gotten to him by now, but they're coming from the other direction and they don't know about Tracy. Jake's gone to get Jimmy. Apparently Bill had him, but Jimmy escaped. Bill's still got Beth, though! Jimmy said he's in the Buick. Tony, he's holding her hostage!"

Tony's heart lurched. He longed to check on Larry, but he knew that Beth's safety had to come first. "Lynda, I'm on my way."

It took only a few minutes to put an all-points bulletin out on the Buick, and soon roadblocks had been set up on the outskirts of town, and the policemen in other parts of the county were alerted. Additional ambulances and squad cars were dispatched to the children's home. As soon as the prosecutor had been informed of the circumstances, officers were sent to check out the warehouse. When they tallied over a hundred thousand dollars' worth of stolen goods, the prosecutor issued warrants for the arrest of Judge Wyatt, Sheila Axelrod, and her husband—in whose names the warehouse was listed—and all of the employees of the children's home, who had fled.

At the home, Nick paced the lawn in front of the cottages as they loaded Larry into an ambulance. He was still alive, thank God; Nick had no idea how badly he was injured. All he knew was that Beth was in danger of the same fate. In a few moments, when he saw Tony's car barreling into the parking lot, he bolted toward him.

Tony got out of the car and met him halfway. "How's Larry?"

"Alive," Nick said. "But unconscious. He's lost a lot of blood. It doesn't look good."

Tony fought the panicked rage and the furious despair threatening to smother him, and looked toward the ambulance, on its way off the property with its lights flashing. He was halfway back to his car, intending to follow it, when a cop shouted, "They've spotted Brandon's car! It's heading up Highway 18 toward St. Pete. There's a high-speed chase underway." Tony hopped behind the wheel and cranked the engine, knowing there was nothing more he could do for Larry, but maybe he could help save Beth.

"He's going to kill her!" Nick shouted. "Please, Tony, let me come with you."

"Who'll take care of placing these children for the night?"

"My colleagues," Nick answered. "I've already called in every social worker in the county. They're on their way. They can handle it."

"Nick, listen—we just learned that Sheila Axelrod is involved. She's probably being arrested as we speak. That leaves you. You're the only one who can take care of these kids right now. We're counting on you."

"*Sheila?*" he asked, then backed away, trying to sort it all out. He shook the information from his head and decided he could only deal with one thing at a time. "But what about Beth?"

"We'll take care of Beth. That's our job."

Nick kicked at some invisible wall in the air. "How could she do this? How could she confront him? She's *terrified* of him—and she *knew* he would kill her!"

"She did it for the kids," Tony said. "And right now she would want you to think of the kids, too."

Nick hesitated. "All right," he said. "I'll stay. But call me the minute you hear anything!"

CHAPTER SIXTY-EIGHT

In the Buick, Bill cursed as the flashing lights grew closer behind him. He turned off onto a little country road, then slammed his accelerator to the floor, flying around corners and curves. But the police stayed close behind him.

He kept one arm clamped around Beth's neck, with the cold barrel of the gun pressed against her cheek. Beth sat as still as she could, frightened that the slightest provocation might cause him to pull the trigger. He had nothing to lose. Nothing except his hostage.

As he drove, she prayed. Prayed that he wouldn't lose the police. Prayed that they would manage to set up a roadblock ahead of him. Prayed that she would find an opportunity to escape. Tears streamed down her face, born of all the confusing emotions whirling through her heart.

"You've sure caused a lot of trouble," Bill said through his teeth, clamping his arm tighter. "Unbelievable."

Beth tried to lift her head enough to see the squad cars in the rearview mirror, but Bill let go of the wheel, grabbed a handful of hair, and jerked her head back against the seat. "Be still," he said. "I didn't tell you to move. I'm not ready to kill you yet."

Only then did he notice the tears running down her face. "I've never seen you cry, Beth, darlin'," he mocked, his eyes back on the twisting road again. "Tears become you."

She stiffened her lips, determined not to shed another tear in front of him.

"Funny how scared you are now," he said. "You weren't scared at all when you were coming after me with both barrels for that newspaper of yours, hiding Jimmy from me, putting the police on my tail, turning HRS against me. But you know what? It didn't matter. I have friends in high places. Nothing you did could have gotten me. Even now, I'll probably get out of this scot-free."

"If they don't kill you first," she muttered.

"They *can't* kill me," he said. "They won't even aim a gun at me as long as I've got this one pointed at your head. You're my ticket out of here."

She didn't respond. And as the road emerged from the woodland and led them through a complex of industrial buildings, she watched his eyes dart, searching for something. "We're gonna find us a building," he said, glancing at the rearview mirror to gauge the distance between himself and the nearest cop behind them. "If I drive up to the front door, we'll have just enough time to get inside before they catch up."

"And then what?"

"Then I can negotiate."

"For what?"

"For a plane. I'm leaving the country, and you're coming with me."

"I'm not going anywhere."

"Yes, you are," he chuckled. "If I have to drag your dead body with me, you're going. Like I said, you're my ticket, and I'm not letting you go."

He swerved into a gravel parking lot in front of a building with light coming through the windows. Through the glass, they could see a man heading for the front window, probably alerted by the sirens. Bill skidded to a stop in front of the door. Grabbing Beth's hair, he pulled her behind him as he bolted from the car and, putting his shoulder to the door, broke through into the building.

The man who'd been working there backed into a stack of boxes, knocking them over. "What the—"

"Get out!" Bill screamed. "Get out or I'll kill you!"

The man stumbled to the door and ran out into the night. By now the parking lot was filling with police cars—skidding in the gravel, sirens blaring, their doors flying open as the officers leaped out to crouch next to the cars, guns drawn.

Bill threw Beth down on the floor behind a desk, reached to the wall behind him to turn off all the lights in the room, and grabbed the phone.

Wincing in pain, Beth looked down. The front of her shirt was spotted with blood where her wound was bleeding through the bandages. She tried to push back the pain and concentrate, instead, on finding some means of escape.

"Now we wait for them to call," he said. "Should be just a matter of minutes."

Beth jumped when the telephone rang almost on cue. He picked it up confidently, wiping sweat out of his eyes with the back of his gun hand. "One wrong move and she's dead," he said.

"What do you want, Brandon?" Beth could hear the voice from the phone's ear piece.

"A plane," Bill said. "I want a plane to take me to Cozumel."

"We're not going to get you a plane, Brandon."

"Then you'd better start calling her next of kin." He chuckled and glanced down at her. "Not that she has any."

"If you let her go, we'll talk about a plane."

Bill laughed. "You think I'm stupid? She's the only reason you haven't killed me yet. I'm not letting her go."

Bill hung up, sat down, and tried to catch his breath. Beth leaned back against a file cabinet. He kept the gun leveled at her, just inches from her face. Desperately, her eyes searched the darkened room, lit only by the flashing lights coming through the windows. This appeared to be a small accounting office. She looked for a knife, a letter opener, anything she could use as a weapon if she needed one. She saw nothing.

Bill got down onto the floor next to her and dragged her face close to his. His breath smelled stale, and she turned her face. "You know, Beth, I always liked you. Sure will be a shame when I have to kill you."

She glared back into his eyes. "Go ahead, Bill. Kill me." But she knew he wouldn't. Not yet.

Bill chuckled. "In good time, darlin'. In good time. How do you feel about being buried in Cozumel? 'Course, we could work out a burial at sea, if you'd prefer that. I could rent a boat and take you out over the Caribbean."

The phone rang again, and he jerked it up. "You got the plane?"

"This is Tony Danks," Beth heard the voice say. "I'm a detective with the St. Clair Police Department. I'm on my way over, and I think we can work something out."

"A plane is all I want worked out," Bill said. "I want a plane to get me out of the country. You have one hour, and then I'm gonna kill her."

"The minute you pull the trigger, we'll be on you like fleas on a mutt. I'd think twice before I tried that," Tony said.

"Get me the plane," Bill said, "and nobody else has to die."

Tony punched "end" on his cell phone, then punched in the number of the hospital emergency room. Concentrating on high-speed, one-handed steering down this curving road through the woods, he asked the nurse about Larry's condition. He was put on hold for what seemed an eternity, and finally, the nurse came back on the line and told him that they weren't allowed to give out any information until Larry's family was contacted. Tony slammed the phone down on the seat next to him and kept driving. Was Larry dead? Was that why they couldn't give him any information? He breathed a prayer that it wasn't so, rubbed the mist stinging his eyes, and pushed his car even faster.

Moments later, he skidded into the parking lot of the building where Bill was holding Beth. He grabbed his cell phone, made a quick call to the airport, then called the children's home and asked for Jake, who was still waiting there with Lynda and all the children.

"Jake, I need a favor," he shouted into the phone. "We've found Brandon. He's holed up in a building, holding Beth hostage. He wants a plane and a pilot. We're running out of time, Jake. We've got a plane, but we need a pilot. Do you have your license back yet?"

"You bet I do," Jake said.

"All right, get to the airport as fast as you can. We're trying to come up with a plan."

Suddenly Tony heard Nick's voice on the line. "Tony, where's Beth?"

"He's holding her hostage, Nick. He's demanding a plane."

"Don't let him take her out of the country!" Nick cried. "You've got to stop him!"

"We're going to."

"I'm coming over there right now," Nick said.

Tony thought about that for a second. "The other social workers are there to take care of the kids?"

"They are."

"All right. If you promise to stay out of the way and not do anything stupid, I'll give you the address."

CHAPTER SIXTY-NINE

L ess than fifteen minutes later, Nick found himself crouching with Tony behind the squad cars in front of the building where Bill held Beth. Beside him, Tony dialed the number of the phone inside.

"We got you a plane," Tony said when Brandon answered. "And a pilot. How do you want to be transported to the airport?"

Bill hesitated. "My car," he said.

"You know we're not gonna let you drive off without an escort."

"Fine," Bill said. "Escort me. But once I hit the airport tarmac you stay back. I'm getting on that plane and out of here, and if anybody tries to stop me, Beth will be history."

Nick held his breath as the building's front door opened and Bill Brandon stepped out with an arm around Beth's neck. He opened the car's passenger door and climbed in, pulling her with him, then slid across to the steering wheel. He was obviously trying to keep Beth between him and the police, so that they wouldn't be able to get a clear shot at him without endangering Beth, too.

Nick watched as Bill's car started and pulled out on the street. The police jumped into their cars and Nick into his, following at the end of the procession.

"Lord, you've got to save her," he said as he drove. "I don't know why you brought her into my life, but I haven't felt like this about a woman in a long time, maybe never." His voice cracked as he drove at breakneck speed behind the procession of police cars, with a killer at the front of the caravan who seemed to be in control of it all.

When they reached the airport, the squad cars stayed back as Bill headed for the waiting plane. Nick stopped his car back beyond the fence and got out, standing with the cops to watch.

Bill pulled Beth out of the car and dragged her toward the plane. The only way into the plane was to climb up onto the wing and go in from there, but to do that, Bill had to let Beth go for a moment. Nick watched, holding his breath, as he lifted her up onto the wing, then quickly followed her before she could balk and run.

Nick let out a heavy, disappointed breath as the plane began to taxi out toward the runway.

"What now?" Nick asked Tony.

"Pray," Tony said. "Pray hard."

I n the plane, Jake tried to stay calm as Bill panted on the seat behind him, still holding Beth in a wrenching grip with one hand and pressing the barrel of the gun to her temple with the other. Jake didn't know whether she had noticed that he was the one flying the plane. When Bill had searched him after getting on, he thought Beth may have realized it was him. "Come on! Get moving," Bill said, "before they pull something."

"St. Clair Unicom," Jake said into the microphone. "Cessna 3–0–2–2 Delta requesting takeoff."

There was a crackling on the other end. "Cessna 3–0–2–2 Delta, go ahead. All's clear. Runway 3."

It was the same runway where Jake and Lynda had crashed, but he had overcome the fear of crashing months ago. Still, he had never flown at gunpoint before, and he'd never had a man like Bill Brandon in his plane. He glanced back at the couple entangled on the seat behind him. "Cozumel, huh? Nice place. I've been there."

"Shut up and fly the plane," Bill said. "And turn the light on back here. I don't want any surprises."

Jake cut on the dim light over their seats. Instantly, the light cast a reflection of the two onto the windshield in front of Jake, offering him a clear view of the backseat. He taxied the rest of the way to the runway, straightened the plane, and increased power to the engine. Beth wasn't fighting, and Bill had relaxed his hold on the gun. From the expression on his face and the way he was sweating, Jake had the feeling that Bill Brandon didn't like to fly.

The accelerating plane approached the end of the runway and lifted off, and Bill's face seemed to grow paler. His hold on Beth was looser now, and he seemed distracted—as though airsickness was assaulting him now.

Jake met Beth's eyes in the glass, hoping she was thinking what he was thinking. With a little help from Jake, Beth might be able to knock the gun out of his hand.

He thought of that first trip with Lynda, when he'd played the hotdogger and dipped and zigzagged all over the sky like a Thunderbird. Even Lynda, a seasoned pilot, had gone pale at that. A good dip might just push Bill over the edge.

Jake took a deep breath, braced himself—then shoved the control yoke forward, making the plane drop, them quickly pulled it back up.

Bill fell backward against the seat, but Beth was ready. With a quick swing, she knocked the gun from his hand. "You sniveling piece of trash!" he shouted, bringing his backhand across her face as he dove for the gun. She slid to the floor on her knees, and just before he grabbed the pistol, she reached it herself. His grip on her wrist made her drop it, but she managed to knock it with her elbow, sending it sliding under the seat.

"Jake, help!" she screamed as Bill hit the floor, grabbing her hair and banging her head into the floor, while he groped under the seat for the gun.

Jake couldn't abandon the controls and felt helpless as he tried to find something that could be used as a weapon. "Get the gun, Beth. You have to get the gun!" He looked back and saw the blood seeping through the side of her shirt around the edges of the bandage on her chest. Still, she lurched under the seat, reaching, stretching . . .

Jake pulled the plane up, made a steep climb, then dove suddenly, making Bill slide toward the front of the plane. "*Now*, Beth!" Jake shouted.

Twisting her body sideways, Beth dropped onto her stomach and pushed further under the seat until, at last, with a desperate, painful lunge, she reached the gun. Sliding backwards out from under the seat, she put her back to the plane's side wall and pushed with her feet until she was as near upright as she could get in the small plane. She pointed the gun at Bill's forehead.

"I got it, Jake!" she shouted.

Jake glanced back at her. Blood was dripping down her temple where Bill had slammed her head into the floor, and more blood soaked through her shirt. Her eyes were venomous as she aimed the gun at the man who had tormented her for most of her life. Her hands trembled as she clutched the pistol in a life-or-death grip.

"Don't shoot, Beth," Jake said. "I'm turning around."

"I won't shoot," she said. "Not until we're on the ground."

There were strings of wet hair plastered to Bill's forehead, and beads of sweat rolling down his face. He looked up at her. "Come on, Beth. You couldn't pull that trigger. You know I didn't raise you to be a killer."

She cocked the hammer and through her teeth said, "You raised me to do what has to be done."

"Beth, don't do it! You may shoot the plane," Jake said. "I don't want to crash again!"

"He'll finagle a way out of this," she said in a dull voice. "He could go free, get off without even a fine. They're all in it with him."

"All who?" Bill asked.

"All your friends. They're all making a mint off what you're doing to those kids. You'll keep on doing it. You'll find a way. Unless I kill you. And I can do that. All I have to do is wait until we touch down, then pull this trigger and watch your whole world end. Then it'll all be over."

"Let him go to jail, Beth," Jake said. "Let him see what it feels like to be locked up in a place he can't leave. Let him see what it feels like to live the way he made you live, Beth."

"It's different," she said. "He's not a child. There's no way to show him how much worse it is for a little, innocent kid who can't defend himself."

"Then let God teach him that, Beth."

Bill latched onto that idea. Breathless and beginning to shake, he said, "That's right, Beth. If I've made mistakes, if I've hurt anyone, the Creator will deal with me. 'Vengeance is mine, saith the Lord.' It's not yours, Beth."

"Don't you dare quote Scripture to me!" she screamed. "I've heard enough of your filthy distortions and your twisted paraphrases. Maybe God will get his vengeance on all those kids through me. Maybe he wants a bullet in your head for defiling his Word."

"Don't believe it!" Jake shouted. "That's twisted thinking, Beth!"

"That's right, Beth, darlin'. You don't want to pull that trigger."

The plane touched down with a bump, and Jake slowed the plane to a stop.

Bill was looking up at her, as though he knew she would never shoot. Her finger trembled over the trigger. She thought of all the ways she'd tried to purify her life, the score sheet she'd been keeping. But all of that meant nothing if she could still contemplate murder for revenge. If she could still hate, after all she'd learned about God, maybe she didn't have it in her to be a child of God. That reality filled her with choking despair, and for a split second, she thought of turning the gun on herself.

But something stopped her. Some still, soothing voice from the center of her soul: *You don't have it in you, but I have it in me.*

She had a quick, fleeting memory of the discussion she and Nick had had about the thief on the cross, and the grace that God had extended to him. For the first time, it made sense.

Beth's law-keeping was worthless. Her good works were empty. It was only through Christ's power that she could have any righteousness at all.

Nick was right.

She moved her finger from the trigger, keeping the gun pointed at Bill Brandon. Murder—even if some would consider it justified—would only destroy it all.

"Radio in and tell them I've got him. Tell them to come get him."

In moments, police had surrounded the plane. Nick jogged up just as they helped Bill Brandon, handcuffed, down from the plane's wing and led him away.

As soon as Beth stepped down from the wing, Nick caught her in a crushing hug. "Are you all right? You're bleeding."

"Not much," she said. "I popped a few stitches, but I'm all right."

"Don't be such a tough guy," he said. "I know you're in pain." He wrapped his arms tighter around her, and in a moment, he felt her body quaking with tears. She stood on her toes and wrapped her arms so tightly around his neck that he felt tears burning his own eyes. She was sobbing now, sobbing out her heart and her soul, sobbing in a way he'd never seen her do before.

Somehow, he didn't have to ask what she was crying for. He knew she was crying for the children in that home who had robbed all night and then studied all day, those children who had been deprived of their ability to trust, those children who would carry the guilt of what they'd done all their lives. He knew she was crying for herself, for the child she had been, the child who'd had no one to protect her from evils such as Bill Brandon. He knew she was crying for a lifetime of loneliness, a lifetime of wishing she could belong somewhere.

And he vowed that, if it was the last thing he ever did, he would give her that place to belong.

He lifted her and began to carry her back, and she kept her face buried against his neck. "Where are you taking me?" she asked him.

"Back to the hospital," he said. "So they can make sure you're all right."

"I don't want to spend the night at the hospital," she said. "I don't want to be alone."

"I have no intention of leaving you alone. I'm going to sit with you all night long."

"Why?" she asked.

"Because I don't think I could tear myself away from you if I wanted to," he whispered.

CHAPTER SEVENTY-ONE

Tony burst through the ER doors and bolted to the desk. Someone was talking to the receptionist, but he couldn't wait. "My partner was brought in here with a gunshot—Larry Millsaps!"

The receptionist shot him an annoyed look. "I'll be with you in a moment, sir."

"No, I have to know now! Is he dead or alive?"

"He's alive," she said. "Now if you'll wait . . ."

Tony sank back in relief, feeling as if he could finally breathe. "Alive? You're sure?"

"Yes, I'm sure."

"I have to see him, then." He started toward the double swinging doors leading to the examining rooms, and the woman stood up.

"Sir, I'm sorry, but you aren't supposed to go in there." When he kept walking, she picked up the phone. "I'll call security!"

Breathing a weary sigh, he turned around and flashed his badge at her. "I'm a police officer, and my partner was shot tonight. I'm going in there, and if security would like to try and stop me, they're welcome to."

She sat back down, and he pushed through the doors.

He went from room to room, looking for Larry, hoping that he wouldn't find him comatose or on the verge of death. His heart pounded as he rounded the corner in the hall, looking into every room—

"Tony?"

He swung around and saw Melissa Millsaps, Larry's wife, looking pale and fatigued, standing in a doorway across the hall.

"Melissa!" he said, stepping toward her. "How is he?"

She nodded without speaking, and led him into Larry's room.

Larry lay on a gurney, his left shoulder bandaged and his arm in a sling.

"It just missed his heart," she said as tears came to her eyes—tears that didn't look as if they were the first she had cried tonight. "Angels were watching over him."

"Then he's . . . gonna be all right?"

Larry opened his eyes, and looked up at his partner. "'Course I'm gonna be all right. Takes more than a bullet to stop Larry Millsaps."

Tony began to laugh with such relief that tears filled his own eyes. Larry reached up to take his hand, and Tony grabbed it and squeezed it hard. "Thought I'd lost you there, buddy."

Melissa went to the other side of the table and stroked his forehead gently. "Me, too," she said.

Larry looked up at Tony, his eyes heavy. Tony knew they had probably given him something strong for the pain. "You get Brandon?"

"Locked up tight," Tony said. "Right where he's gonna be for a long time. Him and Sheila Axelrod and the good Judge Wyatt."

Larry grinned. "What about the kids? And Beth?"

"When you're feeling better, I'll tell you about how everything happened. But Beth's fine. They're still processing the kids, though," Tony said. "But they'll be all right. Nick's looking out for them."

Larry closed his eyes and smiled, and Melissa leaned over him and pressed a soft kiss on his eyelid. He reached up with his good arm and held her face against his. "Sorry I scared you," he whispered to his wife.

"It's okay," she said. "I've given you a few scares, too. You owed me one."

Tony told Larry to get some rest, then went back out into the hall. Emotion overwhelmed him as he realized how close he had come to losing his best friend. And how close Melissa had come to losing her husband.

He felt a sudden urge to talk to Sharon, the woman who had meant so much to him for the past several months. He wanted to hold her and tell her that he loved her, to ask her if they had a future together, to take care of her and her children. There was so much ugliness out there, so much horror—and Tony just didn't want to stand alone anymore in a world like that. He went through the emergency room doors, picking up purpose with every step.

He got into his car and sat there for a moment, looking up at the sky as he had done months earlier, when he had opened his heart to Jesus Christ. Tony knew that he wasn't really alone now—his Lord knew all of the weariness in Tony's soul, all the wounds in his heart—and all the reasons that this man who never committed, wanted to commit now.

Tony began to smile as he cranked his car and headed to Sharon's house.

CHAPTER SEVENTY-TWO

Beth slept better than she'd ever slept that night, knowing that Bill was in jail, along with all of those who'd worked with him, including Judge Wyatt, Sheila Axelrod, and a number of others whose names and fingerprints they'd gotten from examining the warehouse.

When she woke the next morning, still in the hospital, Nick was sitting beside her bed, where he'd been when she'd fallen asleep last night. He looked sleepy as he smiled at her. "Hi."

"Hi," she said. "You really did stay all night, huh?"

"Right here in this chair." He handed her the newspaper. "Thought you might want to see this."

"What?"

"The *St. Petersburg Times.* Phil did it. He got them to print your article this morning, along with several sidebars about last night, and the arson at the paper, and the bomb in your house, and even Tracy Westin."

She sat up slowly in bed and read her headline. "I don't believe it. I had given up."

"Whatever Brandon and Judge Wyatt may have planned for squirming their way out of this, it isn't likely to work now—not with all this publicity. I think the media will dive into this story today. Maybe even the national networks. Better get ready to be a hero."

"I'm no hero," she said. "I'll never shake the stigma of being one of Bill's kids." She sighed. "What about Jimmy and the rest of them? Will they be punished?"

"Nope," he told her. "There's a quote right here by the prosecutor. 'We have no plans to prosecute any of the children who participated in these crimes, nor any of those who participated as children and are now adults.' All he wants is for you to be witnesses in the trial."

She closed her eyes in relief, whispering, "Then they aren't presuming we're all guilty until we're proven innocent?"

"Not at all," he said. "You're altogether innocent."

"Not altogether," she whispered. "But I believe in the power of Christ's forgiveness now."

"Wanna talk about it?" he asked.

She swallowed and tried to sort through her feelings. An image of Tracy, weak and sick, trying to stop the car that was carrying off her children, offering her life in exhange for theirs, overwhelmed her. No matter what Tracy had done in the past, in the end, she had loved her children enough to die for them.

Beth closed her eyes as tears streamed down her face. "I can't quit thinking of Tracy," she whispered. "What she did—I think that's the kind of love you tried to tell me about. The kind that could ransom those little kids."

"That's right," Nick said, stroking her forehead. "The same kind of love that could ransom a woman with a painful past."

She breathed in a shaky sob. "And no score sheet can ever outshine that kind of love, can it?"

Nick shook his head, and she saw the tears in his eyes. She covered her face as her tears fell harder, as her soul swelled within her.

"Oh, Jesus, I believe you," she prayed aloud through her tears. "Ransom me. Not just from Bill, but from myself. From all the lies I've believed. From all the pain I've hardened myself to . . ."

Nick held her hand tightly as she prayed, encouraging her prayer with words of his own.

When she opened her eyes, she was smiling, but the tears continued nonetheless. Nick was crying, too. For a moment, they just looked at each other and laughed through their tears. When Nick took in a deep, cleansing breath and began to wipe her tears, her smile faded. "I just thought of something," she said. "You remember how I compared Tracy to my own mother?"

"Yeah," Nick said.

"Well, I wonder—would she have done what Tracy did? I mean, if Tracy had the capacity for that kind of love in her, maybe, in the end, my mother could have cared, too. If she'd been put to the test—who knows?"

"God knows," Nick said. "That's why you're thinking of it right now. Maybe God can help you forgive her."

A light of realization dawned behind Beth's eyes. "Yeah, I think I can," she whispered in wonder. "I think, if God can forgive me for all that I've done—yeah, I can forgive my mom."

Nick pulled her up into his arms and held her as tightly as he could without hurting her. For the first time in her life, she belonged. Right here, in his arms. Together, they cried and clung together until there were no more tears, and laughter joined their hearts.

When he let her go, she reached out and touched his stubbled jaw. "I guess you'll be getting Sheila Axelrod's job, huh?"

He looked thoughtful. "I've had a lot of time to think tonight—about my job, about all these problems we've seen, about how hard it's going to be to place those kids. And I think I've come to a decision."

"What?"

"I want to apply to take over the home. I want to give those kids a chance to see what God's grace is like. I want to bring them to him—to the real Lord, not some perverted version like Bill had. I want to be a father to all those kids."

Her heart burst. "Oh, Nick, you'd be wonderful at it, and you have such a heart for them."

"I'd need helpers," he said. "I was thinking about that nice couple, the Millers, who wanted so badly to be in the foster parent program. Maybe they could be cottage parents, and I can think of other retired couples who'd be good, too. And I thought that, well—maybe you could help."

"I'm too young to be a cottage mother."

"You're not too young to be my wife."

She stared at him for a long moment, stricken with disbelief. He took her hand, kissed it, and set her palm against his jaw. "What do you think, Beth? Would you make me the happiest man in the world and be my wife? Have my children? Let me be your family, and then we can be the family for all those kids."

Beth threw her arms around his neck, too choked up to answer. Somehow, Nick was pretty sure that she was going to say yes.

CHAPTER SEVENTY-THREE

wo weeks later, Lynda bought Lisa a new bathing suit and got special permission to take her and Jimmy out to the beach that morning. But Jimmy and Jake were cooking something up, and they were late arriving.

"What do you think those two boys are doing?" she asked the little girl.

"I don't know," Lisa said. "Can we build a castle while we wait?"

"Of course we can. Come on. Let's go down to the water."

"But we'll get wet."

"It doesn't matter. A little water never hurt anybody." Lynda got down on her knees just out of reach of the waves, and began helping the child pile the sand into a castle.

"When I grow up," Lisa said with a self-conscious smile, "I want to live in a castle."

Lynda laughed. "I thought that, too, when I was a little girl. And when I grew up, I got something just as good as a castle. But you know what? It didn't make me happy."

The little girl hung on every word. "What made you happy?" she asked.

"People," she said. "People I love. People who love me."

"I have people who love me," Lisa said. "Jimmy loves me. And my mom."

Lynda's smile slowly faded. "Do you remember your mom, Lisa?"

She shook her head and looked across the water. The breeze blew her hair back from her face. "Not really," she said. "But

Jimmy's been telling me about her. He told me how much she loved us."

"She did," Lynda agreed.

"She died, though." Her wistful eyes focused on the half-formed castle, and she started patting the sand again. "Do you love Jake?"

Lynda grinned. "Very much."

They heard a plane overhead, and Lisa looked up as Lynda dug up more sand.

"Look, Lynda! What does it say?"

Lynda looked up. It was a skywriting plane, and it was writing something across the sky. Lisa stood up and waved, jumping up and down. "It looks like . . . M-a-r-r-y . . . Marry . . . me . . ." Lisa read. "L-y-n—"

Lynda got to her feet and shaded her eyes as she stared up in disbelief. "Marry me, Lynda." She caught her breath. "It's Jake, Lisa! He's asking me to marry him! What should I say?"

Lisa began to dance and wave her arms with delight. "Tell him yes! Hurry!"

The cellular phone in Lynda's beach bag rang, and she pulled it out and, with a big grin, answered, "Yes, I'll marry you!"

Jake laughed out loud. "Will you, really?"

"Of course I will! Now get down here so I can kiss you!"

CHAPTER SEVENTY-FOUR

That night, after they had taken Jimmy and Lisa back to the home—which Nick was already running on a temporary basis until the state approved him to take it over permanently—Lynda and Jake sat out on the swing in her backyard, moving slowly back and forth.

"There's something I want to talk to you about," Jake said. "Something important."

"More important than marriage?" she asked, smiling down at the ring sparkling on her finger.

"Not really. But maybe *as* important."

"What?"

"It's about children."

"I want them," Lynda said. "Lots of them. And I hope they look just like you."

He laughed. "I'd rather they look like you. But I was thinking of a head start, kind of. I was thinking of adoption."

Her eyes caught his grin, and she sat up straight and cocked her head to look at him. "Jake, you're not thinking what I think you're thinking, are you? Because I've thought it myself, only I didn't think you'd think—"

"Jimmy and Lisa," he said.

"Yes!" she shouted. "Yes! We can be the best parents anybody ever had, and—"

"Let's call Nick," he said. "I don't want to waste any time!"

CHAPTER SEVENTY-FIVE

Six Months Later

T he plane Jake had named *Trinity* circled the airfield, to the cheers of the dozens of children—most of them residents of the St. Clair Children's Home—then descended for a landing on the long dirt runway. Nick and Beth watched from a crowd of children as Jake Stevens rolled the plane to a stop, and Lynda Barrett Stevens turned back to the crowd with her bullhorn.

"All right, guys! Who hasn't been up yet?"

"Me, Mommy! I wanna go!" Lisa jumped up and down in front of her, waving her arm in front of her face so she wouldn't be missed.

"You can go anytime!" Jimmy said. "Let Dad take *them*, Lisa!"

"But I wanna go too! I wanna see their faces!"

Lynda laughed and hugged the child that had brought so much joy to the home she and Jake were making together. "All right, sweetie. You're in the next group."

Melissa and Larry Millsaps counted off the next group of kids Jake would take up for a flight, then herded them over to the wing, where Tony Danks and his fiancée, Sharon Robinson, stood waiting to pull them up and help them into the plane.

The children roared and cheered as Jake turned the plane around and taxied back up the airstrip.

Nick slid his arm around his wife and pulled her close. "They're loving this," he said.

Beth laughed and ran her fingers through her hair. She had let it grow out some and had returned it to its natural color. "Yeah, it was a good idea. And you know he's not just showing them the clouds. He's got a captive audience up there to tell them all about Jesus."

"The way things have been going at the home, they might just tell *him* about Jesus. You're a great influence for them, Beth. You never let an opportunity go by—"

"When they lie down, and when they rise up. I wish someone had explained it all to me earlier. Then I would have known that I was loved. That I wasn't just some throwaway kid that nobody wanted."

"Not one of these kids feels like a throwaway," Nick said. "They're happy, aren't they?"

"Yeah, I think they are. Bill Brandon's brainwashing goes deep, but Christ's grace is deeper."

"Way deeper," Nick said. He leaned over and kissed his wife, then pulled her into a crushing hug as the plane circled over their heads, and the burgers sizzled on the grills, and the children laughed and squealed and ran across the grass.

And the joy they all felt was a divine gift that couldn't be doused or destroyed by men, because God had chosen to bestow it on them like a beautiful package under a Christmas tree—

Or a marriage that blossomed brighter with each passing day—

Or an eternity without threat or malice.

Miracles, they were, all shining and bright beneath the warm rays of God's smile.

AFTERWORD

Recently, I was sitting in the Green Room at CBN Headquarters in Virginia Beach, waiting to go on *The 700 Club*, when God taught me one of those lessons that he often teaches when we least expect it. The producer had just come in and told me that I'd be squeezed on at the end of the program, and that I might get six minutes.

My heart sank, because I wanted so much to give my whole testimony about how God had convicted me to leave my career in the secular market and write Christian fiction only. There were so many miracles God had performed in my life, so many things I wanted the *700 Club* viewers to know about. But there was no way I could tell them all of it in six minutes.

The guest coordinator of the show and the executive producer were in the Green Room with me, and when the producer who had delivered the startling news retreated, I looked at the other two and confessed that I was nervous. That was an understatement. The truth was that I was in a state of sheer panic.

Without batting an eye, Jackie, the guest coordinator, began praying for me. She asked God to remind me that he had brought me here for a reason, and that he wasn't going to forsake me now. Immediately afterward, the two were called away, and I was left in the room alone.

Instantly, I began to pray again. I asked God not to let Terry Meeuwsen, the interviewer, waste time with fluffy talk about writing and publishing, but that the Lord would give her the exact questions that would move the story forward rapidly enough that I could get out the most important parts of my testimony. I asked him to give me peace about going out there under such time constraints, as well as a clear head so that my thoughts and my words would flow smoothly. And I prayed for the hearts of those viewers who needed to hear what God had done for me.

Peace fell over me, and when the producer came for me, I was calm. Terry asked pertinent and intelligent questions that jumped the story forward when it needed to jump forward, and I was able to get my testimony out. The interesting thing is that some parts of the story which I might have left out, God saw fit to leave in. Terry's questions prompted me to answer them.

What was the lesson I learned that day? I learned that when we do anything by our own strength, we have the potential of failing. But when we empty ourselves of our own intentions, our own plans, our own goals, God will fill us up with his Holy Spirit. When we're directed by the Creator of the universe, how can we fail?

God gives us everything we need. Christian friends, teachers, churches, pastors, the Bible . . . But if we just use those things to get us to some end—whether it be a successful interview or salvation itself—they're nothing more than tools. Without the Father to guide us, the Christ to motivate us, and the Holy Spirit to empower us, we have the potential to fail.

But thanks be to God, through Jesus Christ our Lord, that "he who began a good work in you will carry it on to completion until the day of Christ Jesus" (Philippians 1:6). And thanks to our Father for giving us not just the tools, but the reason and the power to go along with them. And thanks to him, especially, for giving us the outcome—success, always, pure and divine, the way he designed it.

ABOUT THE AUTHOR

Terri Blackstock is an award-winning novelist who has written for several major publishers including HarperCollins, Dell, Harlequin, and Silhouette. Published under two pseudonyms, her books have sold over 5 million copies worldwide.

With her success in secular publishing at its peak, Blackstock had what she calls "a spiritual awakening." A Christian since the age of fourteen, she realized she had not been using her gift as God intended. It was at that point that she recommitted her life to Christ, gave up her secular career, and made the decision to write only books that would point her readers to him.

"I wanted to be able to tell the truth in my stories," she said, "and not just be politically correct. It doesn't matter how many readers I have if I can't tell them what I know about the roots of their problems and the solutions that have literally saved my own life."

Her books are about flawed Christians in crisis and God's provisions for their mistakes and wrong choices. She claims to be extremely qualified to write such books, since she's had years of personal experience.

A native of nowhere, since she was raised in the Air Force, Blackstock makes Mississippi her home. She and her husband are the parents of three children—a blended family which she considers one more of God's provisions.

TERRI BLACKSTOCK

#1 bestselling suspense author

TRUE LIGHT

a RESTORATION Novel

Be sure to read this sample chapter from Terri Blackstock's novel *True Light*

ONE

THE BUCK FELL WITH THE FIRST SHOT, and Zach Emory couldn't help being impressed with himself. From his deer stand, it looked like an eight- or ten-pointer. If the weather stayed cold, he'd be able to make it last for several weeks' worth of meals.

He climbed down from his deer stand and pulled up the collar of his jacket. It was so cold his ears were numb, and his fingers had begun to ache. But it was worth it. Even in the pre-outage days, Zach had spent many mornings sitting in a deer stand freezing to death, just for sport. Now it was a matter of survival.

He jogged toward the animal that lay dead twenty yards away. His brother Gary would be crazy with envy. They had a competition going, and Gary was two up on him. Zach hoped Gary had heard the gunshot and would come to help him move the deer. It would take both of them to lift it into their rickshaw.

He bent over the buck. Ten points. And a perfect shot right through the heart. His dad would finally be proud, and if he was lucky, his mother would drag herself out of bed to get a look.

He heard footsteps behind him and turned to see a man emerging from the trees, walking toward him. Zach squinted, trying to place him. He'd seen him before, but he couldn't remember where.

"Did I score or what?" he asked as the man came closer. "He's a ten-pointer. Got him in one shot, right through the ticker!"

The man didn't look like he'd come to celebrate. He stopped about thirty feet away ... and raised his rifle.

Was he going to shoot? Zach's hands came up, as if that would stop him.

The gun fired—its impact propelling Zach backward, bouncing him onto the dirt.

TWO

THE BUILDING SMELLED OF MOTOR OIL AND GREASE
—A scent Deni Branning associated with progress. A symphony
of roaring engines brought a smile to her face as she rolled her bike
inside. Oh, for the days of noise pollution and hurry—of bumper-
to-bumper traffic, honking horns, blaring radios, and twenty-four-
hour TV.

All over the large warehouse, mechanics and engineers with
black-stained fingers worked at converting engines. The building
had been purchased by the feds a few months ago, when they insti-
tuted the draft. Instead of drafting soldiers, the government had
conscripted all of those with experience as mechanics. Later,
they'd added others to the conscription list: electricians, scientists,
and engineers. Many of them were allowed to live at home and
work in the local conversion plants, but others had been sent
across the country to serve where they were needed.

Pushing down the kickstand on her bike, she reached into her
bag for her notepad and looked around for someone in charge. She
saw Ned Emory, from her neighborhood, standing nearby with a
clipboard, instructing a group of mechanics with a disassembled
engine laid out in front of them. She headed toward him.

"Excuse me," she yelled over the noise. "Mr. Emory?"

He turned. "Yeah?"

She could see that he didn't recognize her, even though his
son Zach had been close friends with her brother for years. "Deni
Branning. Jeff's sister?"

Recognition dawned in his eyes. She reached out to shake
hands with him, but he showed her his greasy hands. "Better not
shake. What brings you here?"

"I'm writing an article about your work here. Do you have
time for an interview?"

As if he hadn't heard her, he turned back to the men, barked
out some orders that she couldn't hear, and started walking away.

Glancing back over his shoulder, he said, "I heard the newspaper is back up and running. They hired you, did they?"

She caught up to him and tried to match his steps. "That's right. *The Crockett Times*. They liked what I'd been doing on the message boards around town. This'll be the cover story for next week's issue."

He didn't seem impressed, so she pulled out her big guns. "You guys are like rock stars. Everybody wants to know what you're up to."

Pride pulled at the corners of his mouth, and she knew she'd struck a chord. "Sure, I can give you a few minutes. What do you want to know?"

He started up a staircase, and she blew out her frustration as she followed him. "Is there someplace we can sit down?"

"I don't have time to sit down." He reached the top of the stairs and headed across the concrete floor to an area where a dozen mopeds sat in various stages of completion. "Hey, Stark! I need at least four of these done by the end of the day. Get Bennett over here to help you."

Deni's gaze swept over the bikes. "Wow. How can I get one of those?"

"You can't. They're not for the private sector." He was walking again, but she hung back, unable to tear herself away from the coveted mopeds. She stepped toward one and touched the seat.

He turned back and gave her an impatient look. "Do you want to do the interview or not?"

She shook off her longing and forced herself to focus. "Of course."

He led her past a table filled with generators, and again, her longing kicked in. "Do those work?"

"They do after we harden them against the Pulses."

Her heart quickened. If they were making hardened generators here, it wouldn't be long until they actually had electricity. Could there really be lightbulbs at the end of the tunnel?

"When will those be available for the public?" she asked, catching up to him again.

"Our illustrious supernova will burn out before we can finish supplying the hospitals. They're priority number one for the generators right now. Without robotics, assembly lines—electricity, for that matter—we have to do everything by hand, one at a time. And even if we could produce enough for the public, there's one missing ingredient."

"Gasoline," she said.

"You got it." He reached a series of offices with glass walls, overlooking the work on the floor below them. "We can't get enough gas without operating tanker trucks, and once we get it here, we don't have electricity to work the pumps."

She was well aware of the chain of problems. "But aren't you guys all about creating work-arounds?"

"Right now we're just trying to help critical services operate. Like I said, the star will likely burn out before we get caught up with that. Then we'll shift our objectives from sustaining to rebuilding." He headed into one of the offices, dropped his clipboard on his desk, and motioned for her to take a seat.

As Deni sat down, something outside the glass caught Ned's eye, and Deni turned to follow his gaze. Someone was running up the stairs.

Ned frowned as his son Gary came running toward his door. "Dad, Zach's been shot!"

"What?"

Deni caught her breath and got to her feet.

"We were hunting at the Jenkins's place. I heard some gunshots and ... when I found him .?.?."

"Is he dead?" Ned blurted out.

"I don't think so. I got help and somebody went to get an ambulance. They're taking him to University Hospital."

Ned grabbed his son's shoulders. "What condition was he in when they took him?"

Gary trembled as he raked his hands through his hair. "There was blood all over his shirt ... front and back."

Deni's heart stopped. Her brother's best friend.?.?.

Ned raced out of the office and hurried down the stairs, Gary on his heels. Deni followed them as far as the top of the stairs, then waited there as they hurried through the building. All the engines went quiet, and everyone stared as Ned ran to a beat-up Buick. "The keys!" he shouted. "Where are the keys?"

Someone tossed them to him, and he got in and started the engine. Gary jumped in beside him. Two guys pulled up the garage door and the Buick rumbled out.

Deni muttered a prayer for Zach as they drove off—and then a thought struck her. Jeff, Deni's brother, sometimes hunted with Zach. Could they have been together? What if he'd been hurt too?

She had to get to the scene of the shooting. She ran downstairs, grabbed her bike, and pedaled out behind them.

THREE

"ZACH? ZACH, CAN YOU HEAR ME?"

Zach tried to open his eyes, but they were glued shut. Something was shaking and bumping him—and with each jolt, pain exploded through him.

"Zach, we're getting you to the hospital, okay, buddy? Stay with me."

Was he in an ambulance? How long had it been since he'd been in a running car? Weeks? Months? Years? His brain couldn't find the answer.

He tried to breathe, but something was crushing his chest. Drowning . . . choking . . . gurgling.

Something sliced through his throat. "We're gonna help you breathe, buddy. Hang on, we're almost there."

He couldn't breathe. Gagging. Smothering. Gasping.

The ambulance jerked to a stop, people all around him yelling, probing, pushing.

As they rolled him into the building, Zach knew he was dying.

FOUR

THE MEETING HAD BEEN DRAGGING ON FOR HOURS. Doug Branning shifted in his seat and wished they would take a break, so the attendees could dash outside to the Porta-Johns lined up around the Birmingham Jefferson Convention Complex. For weeks, he'd looked forward to the symposium of economic leaders in the area. His success as a stockbroker had gotten him an invitation, and he hoped to hear about when the banks would open and what the plan would be for infusing money into the economy.

Because the big complex was without electricity, chairs had been set up in the multileveled lobby of the big building, so they could take advantage of the light from the windows. He'd sat riveted for most of the day as financial leaders argued that opening the banks would have a destructive effect on the economy. Others countered that opening them would help. Doug wasn't sure which side of the fence he landed on, professionally. But as a victim of this disaster, he wanted his cash.

The government leaders who'd come in for the symposium and who had been conducting meetings like this in several major cities, were here to gather advice from local leaders and update them on the state of the economy. So far, all Doug had done today was listen.

"The banking systems lacked sufficient records of their account balances to open the banks a few months ago," Edward Freelord, Federal Reserve Chairman, said, his voice carrying over the crowd. "When the computers crashed, most of the banks had only a few current hard copies, and those have had to be reproduced by hand. Local banks now have the information they need for their local account holders, so it is feasible for them to open. We're considering instructing them to give account holders no more than 2 percent per month of their balance, to avoid a run on the banks."

They'd already established that the law would prohibit foreclosures on property during the Pulses, since no one was able to make payments right now, and the banks would not be allowed to loan money except to those involved in rebuilding the infrastructure and helping the government function.

Several of the audience members weighed in on Freelord's idea, offering pros and cons that Doug was sure the leaders had already considered. But Doug's mind was busy calculating the scenario's direct benefit to his family. He'd had about 15,000 dollars in his checking account at the time of the outage, and another 30,000 dollars in savings. His stocks and bonds and other investments totaled over a million dollars, but those were worthless right now.

He jotted the figures in the margin of his legal pad. With the government's suggested plan, his family would be entitled to 900 dollars a month. With the new rock-bottom prices, they would be in great shape.

Once again, the world would be separated into the haves and have-nots, and his family would rise to the top. It wouldn't help his friends in the Sandwood Place Apartments, most of whom hadn't had any money even before the outage. But maybe it would help them indirectly, as money spent in the economy trickled down to make their lives better.

Would it? That was a pipe dream, he feared. But he'd deal with it later.

Someone tapped on his shoulder, and he glanced up to see Jeff, his sixteen-year-old, standing over him. "What are you doing here?" Doug asked in a whisper.

"Sorry, Dad." Jeff looked upset, and Doug knew something was wrong. "I have to talk to you."

Doug got up and followed Jeff back up the aisle, to the front door. They stepped out into the cold. "What is it?"

"Dad, Zach Emory was shot this morning!"

"What? How?"

Jeff told him the little he knew.

"You weren't with him?"

"No, I was helping Mom set up at the swap meet. They said he was really bad, that he lost a lot of blood. Some people who were there when the ambulance came weren't even sure he was alive." His chin trembled, and he settled his misting eyes on Doug.

"Dad, I want to go see if he's all right, but Mom told me to come by and get you first."

"Of course," Doug said, glancing through the glass back up at the podium.

"You don't have to leave," Jeff said. "I can go by myself. It's just that Mom thinks I'm a kid who can't be alone in the city."

"I can leave now. Don't worry about it."

"But what if you miss something important? Like when they're opening the banks?"

Doug shook his head. "This is just a fact-finding mission. They haven't made any decisions yet."

They headed to the bike rack and unchained their bicycles. Getting onto his bike and pumping out into the street, Doug couldn't imagine what Zach's parents were going through. He looked over at Jeff as they rode. The boy's gaze was fixed on the road, but Doug could see the pain behind his eyes. Zach was one of Jeff's closest friends.

He prayed as they rode, but his prayers were selfish. As much as he wanted Zach to be alive when they got to the hospital, he wanted even more to protect his son from the pain of sudden and unjustified loss.

Only God could control that now.

Last Light

Terri Blackstock,
#1 Bestselling Suspense Author

Today, the world as you know it will end. No need to turn off the lights.

Your car suddenly stalls and won't restart. You can't call for help because your cell phone is dead.

Everyone around you is having the same problem ... and it's just the tip of the iceberg. Your city is in a blackout. Communication is cut off. Hospital equipment won't operate. And airplanes are falling from the sky.

Is it a terrorist attack ... or something far worse?

In the face of a crisis that sweeps an entire high-tech planet back to the age before electricity, your family faces a choice. Will you hoard your possessions to survive — or trust God to provide as you offer your resources and your hearts to others?

Yesterday's world is gone. Now all you've got is your family and community. You stand or fall together. Like never before, you must rely on each other.

But one of you is a killer.

#1 bestselling suspense author Terri Blackstock weaves a masterful what-if novel in which global catastrophe reveals the darkness in human hearts — and lights the way to restoration for a self-centered world. *Last Light* is the first book in an exciting new series.

Softcover: 0-310-25767-0
Audio CD, Unabridged: 0-310-26880-X

Night Light

Terri Blackstock, #1 Bestselling Suspense Author

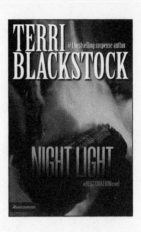

In the face of a crisis that sweeps an entire high-tech planet back to the age before electricity, the Brannings face a choice. Will they hoard their possessions to survive — or trust God to provide as they offer their resources to others?

#1 bestselling suspense author Terri Blackstock weaves a masterful what-if series in which global catastrophe reveals the darkness in human hearts — and lights the way to restoration for a selfcentered world.

An era unlike any in modern civilization is descending, one without lights, electronics, running water, or automobiles. As a global blackout lengthens into months, the neighbors of Oak Hollow grapple with a chilling realization: the power may never return.

Survival has become a lifestyle. When two young thieves break into the Brannings' home and clean out the food in their pantry, Jeff Branning tracks them to a filthy apartment and discovers a family of children living alone, stealing to stay alive. Where is their mother? The search for answers uncovers a trail of desperation and murder ... and for the Brannings, a powerful new purpose that can transform their entire community — and above all, themselves.

Softcover: 0-310-25768-9
Audio CD, Unabridged: 0-310-26921-0

Pick up a copy today at your favorite bookstore!

More great books from
Terri Blackstock

Sun Coast Chronicles

Softcover 0-310-20015-6

Softcover 0-310-20016-4

Softcover 0-310-20708-8

Softcover 0-310-20018-0

Pick up a copy today at your favorite bookstore!

ZONDERVAN®
.com

Cape Refuge Series

This bestselling series follows the lives of the people of the small seaside community of Cape Refuge, as two sisters struggle to continue the ministry their parents began—helping the troubled souls who come to Hanover House for solace.

Cape Refuge
Softcover: 0-310-23592-8

Southern Storm
Softcover: 0-310-23593-6

River's Edge
Softcover: 0-310-23594-4

Breaker's Reef
Softcover: 0-310-23595-2

Pick up a copy today at your favorite bookstore!

ZONDERVAN®
.com

Three ways to keep up on your favorite
Zondervan books and authors

Sign up for our *Fiction E-Newsletter*. Every month you'll receive sample excerpts from our books, sneak peeks at upcoming books, and chances to win free books autographed by the author.

You can also sign up for our *Breakfast Club*. Every morning in your email, you'll receive a five-minute snippet from a fiction or nonfiction book. A new book will be featured each week, and by the end of the week you will have sampled two to three chapters of the book.

Zondervan *Author Tracker* is the best way to be notified whenever your favorite Zondervan authors write new books, go on tour, or want to tell you about what's happening in their lives.

Visit *www.zondervan.com* and sign up today!